Shadow Woman

Shadow Woman

THOMAS PERRY

RANDOM HOUSE NEW YORK

Copyright © 1997 by Thomas Perry

All rights reserved under International and Pan-American Copyright Conventions. Published in the United States by Random House, Inc., New York, and simultaneously in Canada by Random House of Canada Limited, Toronto.

ISBN 0-679-45302-4

Random House website address: http://www.randomhouse.com/
Printed in the United States of America on acid-free paper
24689753
First Edition

Book design by Bernard Klein

For my mother
  my sister
  my wife
  my daughters

Any person, whether old or young, male or female, might become possessed of an evil spirit, and be transformed into a witch. A person thus possessed could assume, at pleasure, the form of any animal, bird or reptile, and having executed his nefarious purpose, could resume his original form, or, if necessary to escape pursuit, could transmute himself into an inanimate object.

Lewis Henry Morgan, *League of the Iroquois*, 1851

Shadow Woman

Pete Hatcher pushed through the warm, dry night air that was trapped between the tall hotels and casinos, feeling the stored heat from the sun still rising from the concrete to his ankles. He had tightened his back muscles to keep his spine straight and his shoulders back, but it felt like a pose, so he tried to lose his self-consciousness and slouch a little. It was hard to do anything for so many days without ruminating on the way it must look, what they must think about it. He had tried to look formidable and alert, as though he would be hard to kill. The idea was worse than childish. It was the reaction of an animal trying to convince a predator that he wasn't weak enough to take down just yet.

The part of Las Vegas that he loved was the Strip, with the exaggerated shapes of its giant buildings lit up in candy colors that burned against the blue-black desert sky, but being downtown like this was different. The carnival neons and incandescents glared from all sides and bounced off asphalt and concrete, then washed across the faces of the people walking with him as a dead yellow-gray that cast deep shadows in their wrinkles and sunken eyes.

He followed a couple who seemed to sense it. Each eyed the other and the woman became uncomfortably aware that the ghastly light that had skinned the life from her beloved's cheek must have done the same to her own. She bravely forced a smile that only gave her face deeper hollows and the bared teeth of a skull. The pair reached the roofed-over mall, retreated to the nearest glass door, and escaped into the soft blue of a bar lit with the twinkle of tiny star-white bulbs. When they had taken a few steps into the cool, machine-made air, Pete saw them both give a little shrug-and-shudder to be sure none of the leftover street magic was clinging to them.

Hatcher followed them through the bar into the big casino, then skirted the margin of the gaming floor, ignoring the din of the bells on the slots and the rattle of coins in the collection pans that bounced off the walls above his head to excite the customers. He moved deeper, staying far from the blackjack tables and crap tables, where bright overhead lights shone on the green felt and turned the dealers' starched white shirts into semaphores. He stepped to the little window in the wall a few feet apart from the cashiers' cages.

He said to the middle-aged woman behind the glass, "There was supposed to be a ticket for the midnight show left for me."

"Your name, sir?" He had somehow assumed she would know his face, but her expression was only attentive.

"Pete Hatcher."

Hatcher took the ticket and read the seat number while he was still in the light, then handed it to the girl in the fishnet tights and frock coat at the door and let her lead him into the show. Hatcher never looked back to see whether the two men were still following. They were.

The round walls of the room were lined with big plush booths in three tiers, and the space in front of the stage crowded with rows of long, narrow tables arranged like the spokes of a wheel so nobody in the cheap stackable chairs along them could see better than anybody else.

The woman he had been told to call Jane was already seated in the dark booth when he got there. She was thin, with gleaming black hair braided behind her head, a long, graceful neck, and bare shoulders that showed no trace of a line in the tan and made him want to believe that she was in the habit of sunbathing naked. He felt an unexpected, tearing pain when he looked at her, so he glanced at the stage. This was what he was about to lose—not the money or the fancy office or the clean, hot desert air. It was the women, ones like her. They weren't ever from here, but this was where Pete had always found them. It was as though they were the winners of some quiet beauty contest, judged not by a bunch of potbellied Chamber of Commerce types but by the women themselves, before they were even women. They seemed to take one look in the mirror and know that the creature looking back at them didn't belong in Biloxi or Minneapolis.

The woman said, "Pete?"

"Yes?"

"Kiss me." He turned in surprise and she was offering him her cheek in that strange way the best of them did, so he could press his lips against that incredibly smooth place just in front of her ear and smell the fragrance of her hair. He lingered there for a moment to whisper, "I thought we were blending in. You mean beautiful is the worst you can do?"

She ignored the question, drew back to end the kiss, and said, "Good enough. Dates want you to kiss them; hookers don't. If the management thinks I'm in business, they'll have their own people watching me. Did you know you're not alone?"

"I haven't been alone in two weeks," he said. "My phones are bugged, my apartment, even my car. When I'm asleep they switch on a camera with an infrared lens that's above the smoke detector in my ceiling."

"That's a very good sign," said the woman. "If the bugs and cameras had disappeared, that would be a very bad sign. It would mean they expected that pretty soon the police would be taking a close look at everything you used to own."

"It's not the sort of sign that makes me want to rush out and buy next year's calendar."

"Don't worry about what didn't happen," said the woman. "Worry about what you have to make happen."

"What?"

"The instant that the box opens—"

"What box?"

"Just listen. When the box opens, you get out and walk—do not run—to the exit door that's facing you. Go outside, get into the black Ford that's parked in the reserved space at the end of the lot. Drive north on Route 15. It will take you to St. George, Utah. That's about all the time I can buy you. You'll still be an hour from Cedar City. Don't stop to pee or something, just keep driving. There's a small airport in Cedar City, and your ticket is reserved at the Southwest Airlines desk under the name David Keller. From now on, that's you. The papers I promised you are in the wallet under the seat of the car.

There's a suitcase in the trunk. You'll just make your flight, and you'll be in Denver before daylight."

"What about the other stuff?"

"Everything you'll need at first is in the suitcase. The diplomas, honorable discharge, bank books, and so on are in your new apartment."

"And?"

"And what?"

"That gets me out, but what about you? They've seen you with me. They'll have nobody to take it out on but you."

Her eyes settled on him in puzzled curiosity, studied his face for a moment as though they had found something rare and unfamiliar there, then drifted toward the stage. "I'm good at this, and you couldn't help me anyway. Don't think about me. Think about what you have to do."

"Anything else you haven't told me?"

"Volumes," she said. "I like to spend more time with my runners before I set them free, but you don't have it to spare. All you really need to know is that if you never make a mistake you'll live forever. Right now, just concentrate on tonight. If you live through this, you'll catch on."

"What if they've got somebody waiting at the back door for me?"

She placed her long, thin fingers on his hand, and her voice went soft and low, like a mother talking to her child. "Then hit him fast, and hurt him as badly as you can. He won't have the stomach for a one-on-one fight for keeps. It takes much more courage to spend two weeks pretending you don't know you're in trouble than it does to join a pack stalking a lone man. I've been watching you, and I've been watching them. You can do this."

He sighed, but his lungs had taken in so little air it came out in a shallow puff. "I sure hope you're right. I assume you took your fee out of the money when you took it to Denver?"

She shook her head. "It doesn't work that way. A year from now, maybe two, you'll think about the way your life is. And you'll remember how you felt tonight. And then you'll send me a present."

He raised his eyebrows. "How do you know that?"

"I don't. But over the years I've gotten a lot of presents."

As the house lights dimmed, Pete raised his eyes to see where tonight's shadows were. He found them in the tier above, seated in a booth where they could catch a glimpse of him in profile whenever they wished. He leaned back, hiding his face from them, but the woman gently leaned on his back and pushed him forward as she whispered in his ear, "Let them see you. Keep your face where they can see it."

A small projectile spitting sparks like a comet streaked over their heads. It exploded at center stage in a loud bang and a billow of lighter-fluid flame six feet high, followed by a fog of dry-ice smoke that quickly spread from curtain to curtain and drifted over the footlights into the audience.

A bright spotlight beam appeared and frantically swept across the wall of smoke, trying to penetrate it and find some solid object. In a moment a few wisps seemed to congeal and resolve themselves into the shape of an old, bent, wizened woman in bulky rags, leaning on a cane. She hobbled forward out of the fog haltingly, then seemed to notice the audience for the first time. Pete looked at the people around him. They were hushed with surprise, as though they had forgotten that they had bought tickets and sat here sipping watered drinks waiting for this.

The old woman glared at them, then gave a low unearthly cackle and lifted the cane into the air. As it reached the height of her shoulder it shortened and narrowed, and as it went over her head it was clearly a wand.

She tapped herself on the top of the head and the rags instantly incinerated in a flash of sparks and smoke. The spotlight fought its way through the smoke and found in her place a young, shapely woman who stood erect and wore a sparkling gold spandex skin that seemed little brighter than her mane of honey-blond hair. The deep, resonant voice of the announcer shouted, "Ladies and gentlemen . . . Miranda!" and then was drowned in music and applause.

Pete leaned to the side and said, "She's got my attention. I hope she's got theirs."

The woman beside him watched his eyes. "If she doesn't yet, she will. She used to strip."

Miranda paced the empty, dim stage like a cat, doing the impossible for the willfully gullible, receptive crowd. First she reached into the air and began plucking things out of it: white doves that couldn't have been hidden in her brief costume and flew out over the audience, then returned to a perch at the back of the stage; a single rose that she tossed over her shoulder onto the floor; then, one after another, four rabbits. It was as though she were completing the compulsory round of a conjurers' competition, executing a sampling of the standard tricks.

Only slowly did it occur to the audience that something strange and unplanned was happening. The rose she had thrown behind her was changing. It grew longer and longer, then arched upward a little. Then it began to writhe and slither. Miranda produced a magician's top hat, put it on her head, then took it off and held it before her stomach. The rabbits, one by one, ran toward her, leapt into the hat, and disappeared inside it. She collapsed the hat and flicked it offstage like a Frisbee.

The audience was distracted. The rabbit trick was a bit out of the ordinary, but the audience was captured by that rose. It was now seven or eight feet long. The petals had fallen off, and now it arched its back, slowly raising its head behind Miranda, and spread its hood. It was a king cobra, its green-black skin looking oily in the lights. As she took her bow, it coiled to strike. Miranda seemed to sense something was bothering her audience. She frowned at them, then reached up into the dark air again, produced a pearl-handled revolver, pivoted gracefully, and shot the serpent through the eye. It jerked spasmodically, then fell. A wind passed across the stage, swirling the smoke in little eddies. The snake crumbled into dry flakes that blew away, leaving only a new, fresh rose in its place. Miranda squeezed the pistol in her hands until it became a ball the color of mercury, threw it into the air, and watched it explode.

While Miranda took another bow, Jane studied the audience, trying to detect anyone watching the two shadows for a signal. After a moment she was satisfied that they had come alone. A company like Pleasure, Inc., could afford as many as they wanted, but they wouldn't put more than two on Pete Hatcher. Pete wasn't crazy enough to attack even that many. She leaned close to him and whispered, "Your time is here. Take one last look at it, and then never come back. This part of your life is already over."

He turned to look at her face, but it was veiled in darkness again. The music grew loud and frantic, and the audience murmured and then drew in its breath as Miranda took a little run and jumped off the eight-foot stage onto the floor. She danced up the aisle, glanced at a man sitting at one of the tables, reached into his ear, and extracted a pair of satin and lace panties. The man grinned appreciatively, but the woman beside him looked, then bared her teeth in something that wasn't a smile. Her left hand moved furtively along her haunch.

The audience gasped its religious conviction that the hand was quicker than the eye, and as Miranda danced along the tables, their approval drowned out all but the beat of Miranda's music.

As she drew near Pete Hatcher, he turned his eyes away from her toward Jane. She said, "Good luck, Pete," and Miranda's surprisingly strong, sinuous fingers wrapped themselves around his forearm. Pete looked up into Miranda's face as he rose to his feet, but when she was this close he saw nothing soft or reassuring there. Her unnaturally perfect teeth were set in the performer's clench, so she could be nervous or winded without showing it, and between the black eyeliner and the blue-gold eyeshadow, the eyes themselves had that mad, manic stare that they all had, not seeing him at all because she was living in her mind a minute or two ahead of everyone else. Her mask of makeup was not the color of a human being, and it reflected light in tiny metallic sparkles that were not what mortals were made of.

Pete let her lead him by the hand down the aisle to the stage, and he let the polite applause that acknowledged he was a good sport carry him to the steps until it was overwhelmed by the audience's celebration that Miranda had returned to the stage. While the spotlight had followed Miranda to Pete's booth, unseen hands had been busy up here. There was a couch placed at center stage. Miranda led him like a woman leading her lover. She spoke to him only in a hard, professional tone as they went. "I'll walk you through this. For now, just lie there. Don't move, don't touch. Got it?"

"Yes," he said. He lay on the couch and discovered that it was hard, a board with a layer of cloth over it. The audience roared again, and he could tell it was because Miranda, facing away from them, had snaked a hand up behind her back and unsnapped the top of her outfit. Her hands went to the waist of her tights and made a first, tantalizing tug. She stepped closer to Hatcher, placed a knee on the couch, and everything happened at once. At the front of the stage there was a flash and a big puff of smoke. For a second Hatcher could see streams of smoke piped upward at the footlights, and then he saw nothing. He felt an abrupt jerk as the silky material under him separated, yanked toward both sides of the stage by unseen wires. He felt the dislocation of air as Miranda flailed around in the dark a few feet from him, but he saw nothing.

The light came on, and the first sight was Miranda, this time wearing a Victorian-looking black corset with garters and black stockings and holding a long silver stiletto. She said, "Mug for them," so he looked her over uneasily. When Miranda had timed the laugh, she stepped closer. "Good. Now stand up and look at the couch."

He got up and stared down at it. The couch was now an ornate lacquer-and-silver box about four feet long. She opened the top and said, "Climb in. When it's closed, bring your knees up to your chest."

He wasn't surprised to see the box. Jane had mentioned the box. Pete took one look out at the audience. He could see Jane sitting alone in the booth, now illuminated by the bright houselights, and fifty feet behind her and to her right, the two shadows. One was the guy he had seen outside his window after dark on Tuesday. He had the melancholy, tired look of a cop who had been on his feet too much. The other was short, stocky, and bullnecked like an Irish middleweight, with a round, reddish squint-eyed face.

As he stepped into the box he gazed past them at the ridiculous baroque lounge, its oversized booths with scrollwork molded from sawdust and glue and painted purple, then fitted with cushions of foam rubber upholstered with shiny fabric. He loved all of it, being part of it. He loved to see the women looking at it: the ones from the Midwest who wore crisp pastel dresses you could never quite see through and took the long way out of Caesar's to look in the windows of the shops at yellow diamond necklaces and solid silver samovars and sable coats, not because they wanted them but because they were placed there to be seen, just like celebrities. He loved the dealers in their little pressed man-outfits and bow ties and shiny shoes, and the tall dancers in costumes that made them hard and gleaming like human jewels, and the women from the dry plains who tiptoed out to the pool with hotel towels wrapped around their hips because they were having second thoughts about their new bathing suits—maybe not even how much skin they showed, so much as what owning a suit like that might mean about them. Hatcher lay down in the box, let her slam the lid on him, and waited.

Jane watched Miranda work through her variation of the ancient conjurer's tricks. Miranda whirled the box around on its casters, watched the mechanical feet at the end of the box kick and wiggle while she sliced the box in half, then wiggle again when she separated the two boxes. Finally, she flung open the lids of the two boxes, and there was nobody inside at all. She closed the boxes, whirled them around a bit, then had two burly assistants in turbans lift one on top of the other. She opened the single door, and out stepped Pete Hatcher. He bowed, shyly received a kiss from Miranda, and walked toward the steps.

As he reached the floor of the lounge, the lights swept back to Miranda. She was climbing into the box herself. The two assistants turned the box around a few times, tapped it with Miranda's discarded wand, and a big flame shot upward. All the while, the silhouette of the good sport she had drafted from the audience could be seen making his way in the darkened room to Jane's booth.

He sat down and said in Miranda's voice, "He's on his way, Jane."

"Thanks, Miranda," said Jane. "It's a great show."

On stage, the two befuddled assistants opened the box. Out stepped a man who looked very much like Pete Hatcher. The spotlights quickly searched the room. When they found Pete Hatcher's booth, the figure of Pete Hatcher leapt to its feet, threw off the coat and wig, stepped out of the pants, and became Miranda. She milked the applause, curtsying and throwing kisses, then ran back to the stage. She tore a curtain from the back of the stage to reveal what looked like Pete Hatcher lying stiff and seemingly asleep, floating three feet off the ground. She covered him with the curtain, levitated him a few feet higher, where he would be out of her way, and went on with her act. Jane looked at her watch.

Miranda proceeded to keep the audience confused and agitated with her smoke and mirrors and costume changes. From time to time she would bring up other members of the audience to shill for her, and when they had done their parts, she would cover them with cloths and levitate them too, until after two hours there were six men and women floating above the stage. As Miranda was taking her final bow, she suddenly seemed to remember something. She turned, looked up at the six bodies floating in the air, and hurried toward them. She stepped to the first, snatched the cloth away, and revealed that there was nothing at all under it. She pointed to a table at her feet, and the woman who was supposed to be floating smiled at the audience and waved happily. One by one, Miranda snatched the cloths out of the air and revealed each of her volunteers, sitting in their seats watching the show. When she pointed at Jane's booth, the man sitting beside Jane gave a graceful little bow that ended in an outstretched arm lifted toward Miranda in a gesture that began in appreciation and ended in surprise.

The audience's eyes shot to the stage in time to see another flash and puff of smoke, and Miranda was gone. Only the pile of cloths lay where she had stood a moment before. The smoke grew in volume and thickness, and slowly, the pile of rags stirred and began to rise. The hydraulic platform under the stage pushed Miranda upward, and as she rose through the cloths, they hung from her like thick draped clothing. She was, once again, the old, bent crone who had begun the show. She limped to the edge of the stage where she had left her wand, tapped it once on her palm, and it grew into the walking stick. She winked slyly at the audience and slowly walked through the smoke and disappeared.

The doors opened at the rear of the lounge and the audience filed out with the lights still low, Miranda's eerie music still in their ears and wisps of theatrical smoke still in the air. Jane and her companion made their way toward the door with the others, deep in the gratified, chattering crowd. Before they stepped into the light of the casino, Jane said, "Thanks," and the man, one of Miranda's assistants, stepped to the side and was gone.

Jane walked purposefully across the casino alone, under the enormous crystal chandeliers, where she could be certain the two shadows would see her. She went into the lobby and stopped at the front desk to pick up her room key.

She made her way back across the casino and up into the bar that overlooked the long rows of green felt tables. She sat down at a table for two and waited. In the mirror above the bar she could see Pete's two shadows. The tall one was wandering around looking over the heads of the gamblers to see where Pete Hatcher could have gone. The second man was behind Jane and to her left, just at the perimeter of the bar, where he could slip away if he needed to.

She waited a few minutes for the barmaid to show up, then ordered a martini and a scotch and water, and watched the barmaid throw down two napkins, one in front of the empty chair, then head for the bar to get the drinks. The sight of two drinks on the tray coming back to the table seemed to make all the difference to Pete Hatcher's shadows. They were reassured, almost as though they were watching Pete. They might not know where Hatcher was right at this moment—the men's room, somewhere in the labyrinth of slot machines, where they had not looked for him—but they knew where he was going to be in a few minutes. The few minutes accumulated into a half hour, then forty-five minutes. The small shadow left to see if Pete Hatcher's car was still in the lot and came back to report to his friend that it was, but they weren't feeling confident anymore. Something was wrong, and they weren't yet sure what it was.

She glanced at her watch. Katie . . . she corrected herself: Miranda . . . had promised to transport Pete Hatcher out the stage door near the start of her act, so the show had given him a full two hours to make the Utah border. Jane's little pantomime of being stood up had bought him the third hour to get to Cedar City. His plane would be loading passengers just about now. It was time for Jane to start making herself disappear.

She left a twenty-dollar chip on the table and stepped out of the bar. The two men hesitated for a second, then followed. They had to give her plenty of room and try not to look interested. Jane walked toward the elevators, and she knew they had no choice but to follow. If they lost her, they had nothing. She took the elevator to the fifteenth floor, went into her room, kicked off her shoes, and called the garage. "This is Miss Seymour in Room 1592. I'd like my car right away, please." As she listened to the parking attendant's answer she was already stepping out of her gown.

She heard the doorknob rattle a little. She looked at the door, but it didn't budge. She could see the shadows of feet under the door. Jane kicked the dress under the bed, slipped on her slacks, pulled the sweater over her head, then heard a sudden thud. She looked at the door. The double-edged blade of a knife had pierced through the thin oak veneer of the hollow door beside the lock. She froze. An unseen hand worked the blade around a little and withdrew it. There was another dull thud, and the blade punched through again.

She snatched her purse, quickly slipped out through the curtains to the balcony, and quietly slid the door shut. She had misjudged them. They should not have been willing to take a chance like this yet. Maybe she had been too eager to get Pete out of sight and she had missed some sign, forgotten to ask some question. There was no way to fix it now, no time to think. She had to get out.

She had nothing with her. This was not the hotel where she had been sleeping. It was just the room she had rented to disappear from. In a few seconds those two would have the door open. She looked around her at the balconies of the other rooms. They were narrow and far apart, and even if she somehow managed to reach one of them without falling, she would only be in the next room. She leaned out as far as she could and looked down. On the floor below her there was a balcony just like hers, but it had to be twelve feet down.

Jane saw a thin wedge of light fan into her room as they opened the door as far as the chain would allow. She unclasped the leather strap of her purse, clasped it around the bottom of the vertical railing support closest to the wall of the building, tossed her purse to the balcony below, stepped over the railing, and lowered herself into the empty air. She was trembling with fear and awe at what she had done as she dangled there, six feet above the railing of the fourteenth-floor balcony. She wanted to drop but found her hands would not obey the command to open. It looked as though she would fall, scrape the outside of the balcony, and plummet two hundred feet to the pavement.

She bent at the hip and began a gentle swing. The first sweep brought her out away from the balcony and tipped her down a little so she had to look directly through all that empty night air at the tiny figures on the lighted concrete below. After a sickening pause at the end of the arc, she began to swing forward. When she judged that the balcony was under her, she let go.

She dropped and hit the concrete balcony hard, slid a little, and bumped the railing so it gave a low vibrating sound like a tuning fork.

She turned and saw that the sliding door into this room was closed. As she stood and reached for the handle, she knew that, whatever else happened, she was not going to put herself outside the railing again. She tugged on the door and it wouldn't budge. She lay on her back, covered her face with her purse, and kicked out at the glass with both feet.

The glass gave a loud crack, but it didn't break inward. She went to her knees, lifted a long jagged shard out, set it beside her, then used her purse to push a bigger one inward. She crawled inside, hurried across the empty room, burst out into the hallway, ran to the elevator, and punched the button. But as she glanced upward she saw that the number lit up was fifteen. The elevator was coming down from above.

She turned and ran for the sign that said EXIT, slipped inside the door to the stairwell, and waited. The bell rang, the elevator doors parted, and she saw that nobody was inside. She ran for the elevator and got past the doors just as the big man emerged from the stairwell and dashed toward her.

She rode the elevator down to the garage level. When the bell rang she took a step toward the opening doors, but then the space was filled with a blur of moving flesh and gray fabric as the shorter man with the pink swine face charged inside the elevator. He slapped the button and used his body to block the opening while the doors slid together again, trapping her inside with him.

Jane predicted his half-formed strategy, because the small space made it inevitable. He had enclosed her in a tiny compartment, so he would sweep her into a corner before she could do much flailing and use the strength of his upper body to keep her there and stifle the screams. She put up both hands in a weak defense, half cringing before the blow, half supplication that it wouldn't come. The man lunged toward her.

Jane's right hand jabbed out, more to stagger him than to do harm, but he was moving faster than she had expected. Her knuckles glanced off the bridge of his nose and into his left eye. His hands went up, too late, and Jane rocked back against the wall to deliver the kick to his knee that she had planned from the beginning. She felt the knee break; he dropped to the floor, gasping in pain.

She sidestepped past him and hit the OPEN DOOR button. As the doors slid open his hand shot out to grasp her ankle. His grip was so strong it hurt, tightening like the jaws of an animal as he pulled her toward him. She said quietly, "Think. If you drag me back in there alone with you and your broken leg, are things going to get better for you, or worse?"

She felt the hand slowly, reluctantly release its grip. The door closed, she stepped away, and hurried toward the valet loitering beside her rented car. She was already chattering. "It's here already? Gee, you guys are really fast. I'm sorry it took me so long. Thanks a lot."

She slipped a ten-dollar bill into the hand of the valet, threw her car into gear, and drove out along Bonanza Road and into the darkness to the west.

2

J ane drove out of the desert into Los Angeles while the morning traffic was still moving and the glaring sunlight was on the back
of her car instead of in her eyes. The car was rented on a MasterCard
that said she was Wendy Aguilar, so if someone in Las Vegas had seen
the license number, then asking the right questions would lead the
chasers to a fictitious woman who had disappeared in Los Angeles.

She never used her own name, never started off in the direction of
her final destination, never missed a chance to mislead, but never bet
her life on any plan she had made in advance. What had kept Jane
alive during a dozen years as a guide was not mechanical precautions
but unremitting watchfulness. She lived by scrutinizing the fluid events
and configurations around her—momentary gatherings of people,
minor financial transactions, crowded travel routes—for opportunities
to deceive.

As she drove the rented car up Century Boulevard to return it to
the agency, she spotted a convenient place to acquire a small extra
measure of safety. She turned off the street beneath the tall white sign
that towered above the car wash and stopped at the entrance to the

tunnel lined with spraying nozzles and whirling brushes. She slipped out of the car and let the two men loitering nearby climb into the front and rear seats, steer it forward until the conveyor track caught the front wheel, then ride it through the tunnel to wipe the prints off every window and piece of chrome and vacuum the inner surfaces to pick up hairs and threads. Even if these men overlooked some trace of her and the clean-up crew at the rental lot missed it too, the process put two more people with their own clothes and hair and prints into the car. She used her ten minutes away from the car to stand in the shelter of the cashier's kiosk and watch the street to satisfy herself that no other car was idling nearby to wait for her.

When the men had finished, she pulled forward to the full-serve gas pump to have the tank filled, so any prints on the gas door or cap would belong to still another man. She drove the car around several blocks to dry it, crossed her own trail after a few minutes, and returned to the lot where she had rented it two weeks ago.

She took the shuttle van to the airport with six other people. It was always crowded in the morning at LAX because anybody who wanted to be on the East Coast by the end of the business day had to be in the air by eight. The shuttle van stopped at the loading zone, so she was only in the open for five quick steps, surrounded by men and women who were in as much of a hurry as she was. She had nothing but the canvas carry-on bag she had kept in her trunk.

Jane shopped for a flight on the television monitors on the wall as she walked. This time she decided that American Airlines Flight 653 to Chicago was the right one. From there she could go anywhere without much delay. Until a few years ago she would have paid cash for the ticket, because that gave her the option of making up a name. Now they checked identification on every flight. She rummaged in her purse and selected Terry Rosenberg's driver's license and credit card, because the name was common enough and wasn't definitely female. Years ago, when she had just begun as a guide and had seen these trips as a series of brief adventures rather than an accumulating succession of risks, she had sometimes made up names like those of heroines in romance novels. Dahlia Van Sturtevant had been one, as had Melinda-Gail La Doucette. Over the years she had slowly, painfully refined the whimsy out of her routines. A name like Terry Rosenberg might actually send a tracker off in the wrong direction: Destiny Vaucluse was a taunt.

She went through the metal detectors and walked to one of the more distant ladies' rooms because they were less heavily frequented than the ones near the entrances and because nobody she met after the security check was likely to be carrying anything that would make killing her a neat, quiet task.

Jane had no reason to believe that the men who had been watching Pete Hatcher in Las Vegas represented any danger to her. Even if they had seen her rental car and had the license number, it would take them a day or two to learn that she had returned it near the L.A. airport. They had seen the Miraculous Miranda make Hatcher disappear, but they had also seen her make him reappear, and they had followed him out of the show into the casino. If their employers were grounded firmly enough in reality to know that there was no such thing as a coincidence—that nobody vanished from the stage and the world the same night without planning—it would get them very little.

Miranda was a Las Vegas headliner because she was a spectacular performer. She was a headliner at Bogliarese's Inside Straight because Vincent Bogliarese Jr. waited for her in her elaborate dressing suite after each midnight show for a frolic while she was still in makeup, sweaty and excited from her triumph. There was a rumor that they were married, but Jane didn't know if it was true, and it didn't matter. As long as Vincent was nearby, Miranda was not a woman that anyone but an old friend could safely approach to ask even an easy question.

Jane washed off her makeup in front of the sink, dressed in a pair of blue jeans and a black silk blouse with a print of bright chrysanthemums, put on a pair of sneakers, threw her old clothes in the trash, and covered them with a newspaper she found on the counter. She let her long black hair hang loose and brushed it out, then put on fresh makeup and a pair of sunglasses. She inspected herself in the mirror, decided she looked as different from the woman who had been in Las Vegas as she needed to, and went out.

She bought breakfast and waited for her flight in the cafeteria, because fewer people could pass close by and look at her face here than in the waiting area. Every move Jane made while she was working was calculated to shift the odds a little more into her favor. Taking Pete Hatcher out of the world from a standing start had presented special problems and forced her to accept special risks.

Usually the ones she took out of trouble could be taken more quietly. A woman with bruises would show up at a shelter in the middle of a big city a thousand miles away and talk to a counselor. After an hour or two of listening to options and remedies that had already been tried and gotten her more bruises, she would tell the counselor that what she really wanted was magic—to simply have it all end and start again as somebody else. The counselor would pick up the telephone, and maybe the woman would notice that the counselor's other hand was busy erasing her name from the sign-in list.

The ones who were children usually arrived at Jane's door in the night, holding the hand of some adult who didn't think of herself as a hero, who maybe hadn't even run the inventory of statutory punishments for what she was doing but already knew that the punishment for doing nothing was worse.

The usual victims were the helpless, and they were almost invisible to begin with. The authorities who had not seen their agony were no better at noticing their absence. Their names were simply added to the enormous list of people all over the country who were missing, and after they had left Jane's hands those names were no longer theirs. The petty criminals—the adults who had burned up one life by an accretion of small mistakes and infractions—were almost as easy. They often came to her at a time when they, at least, believed they were in no immediate danger. That meant they had no friends, no plans, and no temptations to keep their minds off the emptiness they had created for themselves.

Pete Hatcher had been the other kind. He was already trapped, and she had to get him out while their eyes were on him. He had been a successful middle manager in a town where the locals were all in the same business and engaged in ferocious competition to dominate it. Once he had come under suspicion at Pleasure, Inc., there had been little that could happen to dispel it.

When he asked why he was being isolated and kept out of meetings, they decided he must have been waiting anxiously for signs that his disloyalty had been discovered. When he mentioned the possibility that it was time to find a new job, they thought he had been conspiring with a competitor who had already prepared a safe haven for him. When he offered to resign with no job in sight, they figured he must not need one—had probably found a way to skim casino proceeds or helped an accomplice fix a game. It was when he did nothing that their worst fears were aroused. They suspected he was staying in place because he had made a deal with some federal agency and had been bullied into collecting evidence for them. They had watched him for weeks, waiting to find out which it was so they could clean it up after they killed him.

Casinos were like a lot of businesses. A tenth of what went on was disguised by showmanship, and the rest was invisible. Part of what wasn't easy to see were their gigantic security departments. They had people to guard and transport the vast sums of cash that appeared each day, other people to watch the dealers, cashiers, and croupiers to be sure that the nimblest fingers in the world never palmed anything, others to investigate possible high rollers, still others to find them if they didn't pay. They had more to simply protect the casino itself—people who watched for undesirable visitors who had come to prey on the guests and quickly, quietly hustled them away before they disturbed the unreal tranquility of the gambling palace. It had always struck Jane as ironic that probably the safest place in the country for a woman traveling alone was inside any of the big Las Vegas hotels.

In a way, the security was what had saved Pete Hatcher. Without that enveloping but unobtrusive protection, a woman named Paula might not have felt comfortable enough to go there by herself, and certainly wouldn't have dared get friendly with a gambler like him. A year later, when he was in trouble and trying to think of places to stay that his bosses wouldn't know about, he had remembered Paula's number and she had remembered Jane's.

Jane heard her flight announced over the loudspeaker, picked up her canvas bag, and walked toward the gate. She held herself with her spine straight and looked directly ahead, never allowing her eyes to focus on those of the other travelers, never turning away to give them permission to study her. She walked quickly, joined the line after it had begun to move efficiently but was long enough to include a lot of other people who would be more interesting for a bored observer to stare at than she was, and disappeared into the loading tunnel.

As soon as the plane was in the air, Jane pushed her seat back as far as it would go and closed her eyes. She had been anxious for two nights, trying to work out a path for Pete Hatcher that wouldn't lead him in front of a gun muzzle, then spent the third running. She knew she could sleep only fitfully now, because she had not dreamed in four nights and her mind was holding a jumbled backlog of jarring impressions that would plague her sleep. But lying with her eyes closed prevented other passengers from trying to talk to her, and that was another of her precautions. The road home was where the worst of the traps were, because she had already given dangerous people a reason to want her. That was when they would be making their best attempts to track her or place friends of theirs in her path.

Jane got off the plane in Chicago and found another, under the name Tracy Morgan, that took her to Rochester, New York. In the airport store she bought a packet of pipe tobacco, then drove a few miles southeast of the airport to Mendon.

Jane parked her car along the road above the bend of Honeoye Creek and walked to the quiet little park at Mendon Ponds. She sat where she always sat when she came here, at a picnic table with a surface scarred with carved initials, took out her manicure kit, and trimmed and buffed her nails.

The two little lakes were glassy and greenish. The tall, thick trees along the bank away from the road grew out of the water from submerged roots and protected the ponds from the tiniest breeze. The only ripples came from long-legged water bugs that skittered across the surface now and then.

Three hundred feet away, up the grassy bank, a mother with very white legs and feet sat in the shade of a sunhat and big dark glasses, watching her two little golden-haired children digging with plastic shovels in the muck. If the mother wasn't careful, they might actually find something, Jane thought. The People had lived here once. That black mud made it easy to grow corn, beans, and squash with a digging stick, and the weeds came right up with a tug.

The village was called Dayodehokto, a phrase that meant "a bend in a creek," so the rows of longhouses had probably been close to the stream on the far side of the trees, but the cultivated fields had stretched for a couple of miles in all directions. A Dutchman who came through here in the 1670s counted 120 longhouses with twelve or thirteen fires in a line down the center of each one. On opposite sides of each fire were a pair of compartments, where two adult women slept with their husbands—when the men were home—and their children. After allowing for the usual exaggeration, Jane guessed the village would have contained nearly three thousand people on June 23, 1687, when this quiet little spot had its moment of importance in global politics.

For twenty years, Louis XIV, the Sun King, had been ordering successive governors of New France to exterminate the five Iroquois nations, but particularly the Senecas, who lived the farthest west and were most disruptive to the fur trade with the Indians of the western Great Lakes.

He had received no satisfaction in the past, but this time he had found himself a soldier. The Marquis de Denonville efficiently assembled the total military force of New France—probably a thousand soldiers, traders, and trappers. The Sun King sent him two thousand French regular troops, half the number he had requested, along with a regal apology about being strapped for cash. Denonville gathered six hundred allies from the Indians of the west—Miamis, Illinois,

Potawatomis, Hurons, Ottawas. They all met at Fort Niagara, where the river emptied into Lake Ontario, traveled in four hundred boats and canoes to Irondequoit Bay, and marched south along the trail to this village.

The army was confident that the people they were attacking were almost all women and children. Seneca men were out in the forests for most of the year, hunting or raiding distant tribes. The Senecas had no reason to expect an attack, because they had been assured that Louis XIV and their ally the English king James II were friends at the moment.

On the first day, the French expedition made good progress down the trail toward this spot. They marched with half the Canadian woodsmen and Indians in front, then the French army, and then a rear guard of Indians and woodsmen. On the second day they reached the edge of the cornfields but found them strangely deserted. At this time of year, the Month of Strawberries, the corn was still unripe and needed constant tending. The fields should have been full of women, chattering as they weeded and turned the soil. The marquis conceded that his tactic of surprise had failed, but he was sure the mission might still succeed if his men were quick enough. The French force ran toward the village in their eagerness to cut down the fleeing women and children before they could vanish into the forest.

The front of the column passed within a few yards of something they were not expecting—a group of Seneca warriors lying on their bellies in the brush. The Senecas waited until the vanguard had moved on, then tore into the center of the column, where the French soldiers were, first firing their rifles and then falling on the soldiers with tomahawks and war clubs. The French fell into disorder, firing at trees, bushes, or their Indian allies and then scattering along the trail in both directions. The Senecas killed over a hundred and then disappeared into the forest again.

It took the marquis the rest of the day to rally and reassemble his men, then force them to set up a secure camp for the night. In the morning he cautiously advanced into the village of Dayodehokto and discovered that the ambush had been a delaying tactic. The longhouses were already in ashes. The only living things left were two old men who had stayed to exercise the privilege of dying while defying their enemies. They were obligingly cut into pieces and boiled to make soup for the French allies.

It took Denonville's army six days to burn all of the cornfields here and the fifty thousand bushels of dried corn that had been stored. When that had been accomplished, the marquis, less optimistic now, marched on to two more deserted villages, then returned to Montreal to contemplate what a lot of trouble he had gone to just to cook up two old men.

The Senecas and the rest of the five Iroquois nations retaliated by making New France from Mackinac to Quebec a very dangerous place for a couple of years. They attacked Frontenac and Montreal, killing hundreds and carrying off hundreds more. French traders traveling in the far north disappeared. It would be a hundred years before the villages in Seneca country would be raided again. The next time it would be the Americans, and again the women would lead their children into the forest in time to escape the scheduled extermination, leaving the enemy to be satisfied with burning cornfields.

Jane gathered her nail clippings, smiled and nodded at the woman and her children, and walked along the perimeter of the pond into the trees until she came to Honeoye Creek. The area around the ponds was a favorite picnic spot for people from Rochester, and not one in a thousand knew anyone had ever lived here. It had become one of the secret places.

Jane took out the package of tobacco she had bought in the airport. "Jo-Ge-Oh, it's me," she whispered. "Jane Whitefield." She sprinkled a pile of brown shreds on the flat bank where the Little People would be sure to find it. "Thanks for the break in Las Vegas. Pete Hatcher is gone now." There was no such thing as a prayer of supplication in the old religion, only ways of giving thanks.

She scattered the crescent fingernail clippings along the muddy bank. "This ought to keep the possums and raccoons away while you light up." The Little People had a terrible tobacco addiction, and they prized human fingernails because the scent kept away the animals that were bothersome to anyone that short.

Since she was a child, Jane had particularly admired the Jo-Ge-Oh, because they took the hunted, the wounded, and the defeated and hid them from their enemies. Time was different for the Jo-Ge-Oh, so the person they helped would simply vanish and then emerge from the forest thinking he had been with them for a day, but find it was now many years later, after all his enemies were dead and buried.

Jane liked to visit the Little People in places where Senecas had once needed to fade into the forest. The three hundred years that had passed on Honeoye Creek might not make much difference to the Little People. It might be a few days to them. And here was a Seneca woman, not changed much from the last one they'd seen on this spot, coming to bring them the customary present, as women like her had been doing for thousands of years.

The bus labored up Delaware Avenue out of Buffalo, building its momentum slowly after each stop, then coasting to the next one, until Jane saw her corner. She stood up, and the driver pulled over to let her out under a streetlamp. She walked along the uneven sidewalks across the south end of Deganawida in the dark, her canvas bag over her shoulder, her feet feeling without effort the places where the concrete slabs were pushed up by the big old trees, as Jane had learned to do when she was little.

She walked along Erie Street, unconsciously noting what was going on behind the lighted panes of glass without staring at them. She probably knew the occupants of every third house in the little city. Her parents had known more of them, and her grandparents still more, because they could have told her who was related to whom for generations back.

Jane felt so good about having these sidewalks under her feet, so glad to breathe the air in a place that made sense to her, that she allowed herself to think about what it would be like never to leave again. For the first time in two weeks, when her mind was drawn to Carey McKinnon she did not goad it away from him. He was going to ask her again if she would marry him. That would be in six months, and that was not much time to get ready. It occurred to her that if she had been someone else, getting ready would probably have meant worrying about trivia: dresses and china patterns. But what Jane Whitefield was going to have to worry about was how to make the bride invisible.

Jane let her eyes settle on her house as soon as she had turned onto her block. There were no lights, no curtains that had been moved since she had left, no cars parked on the block that she had not seen before. The reading lamp near the corner window in Jake Reinert's house next door was on, and she took a couple of steps along the sidewalk in front of his house until she could see a slice of light under the blind of the porch window. She saw the book on his lap and his thick, pink, callused right hand tilting it up a little as he read, to keep the lower segment of his bifocals on it.

He and her father had been raised side by side in these two old houses on this quiet street, and by now he seemed to be able to sense subtle changes in the atmosphere—a footfall on the porch next door would bring him to the window. She had even seen him stop what he was doing to stare if he heard the engine of a car going by that he didn't recognize. She had her house wired with a very good burglar alarm, but she had met people who made a living fooling better ones than that. She went to her car in the garage and took her house key out of the lining of the rear seat, then walked back to her front door, unlocked it, and slipped inside quickly to punch her alarm code into the glowing keypad before it could go off.

She stood in the doorway and studied the signs. The air in the house was stale, so no window had been broken. Before she had left the house she had vacuumed the carpet, leaving a pattern and the pile pushed upward. The carpet had no indentations from heavy feet. She walked to the table beside the couch and lifted the telephone off the cradle. The dial tone was clear and distinct, so nobody had disconnected the phone line to isolate the alarm system. She was home.

She set the telephone back on its cradle as the bell rang, vibrating her fingertips. "Hello," she said into it.

"Hi, it's me." His voice had a smile in it, as though his throat were tight. "Welcome home."

"Hi, Carey," she said. She blocked the little laugh of pleasure that almost escaped. Then she wondered why she had to and remembered that she didn't have to anymore. She was home, and this was Carey. "How did you arrange this?"

"I don't know what you're talking about."

"You're so full of—"

"Wait," said Carey. "I'm getting a psychic image. Take about five minutes to unpack that black bag you've got over your shoulder, take a shower—and I wouldn't mention anything so indelicate if I weren't a board-certified physician—but I sense you have to pee. Then the archetypal little black dress. And matching underwear: you might get into an accident, and the gang in the emergency room is very critical. Nothing too flashy, but not the jeans-and-sneakers ensemble you've got on now."

"Jake saw me come home and called you."

"Old people are so prompt. I guess it's because their dance cards aren't quite as full as they once were. You didn't eat dinner on the plane, did you?"

"I wasn't on a plane."

"The broomstick, then. Whatever."

"I haven't eaten. But what brings on this sudden manic outpouring? Did a rich hypochondriac move into town while I was gone?"

"No," said Carey. "But I'm hungry, and I keep seeing these 'Lost Dog' posters near the hospital cafeteria."

"Suspicion is a sign of a devious mind," she said. "I mean a big sign, not like all the other signs."

"I knew I could develop a quality that would appeal to you. So get ready. I'm on my way."

"I'll be listening for the sirens."

She dressed in a few minutes and left her front door open while she walked up on Jake's porch and rang the bell.

He opened it and smiled at her. "Hello, Janie. I'll bet you came for your mail." He stepped backward to let her in and pointed to the pile of mail in the shoebox on the coffee table.

She lifted the shoebox, shook it beside her ear, and listened. "Six bills." She shook it again. "Only three checks, all small." She frowned. "And my subscription is about to run out."

His sharp old blue eyes focused on her. "You're dressed like a girl for once," he said. "To what do we owe this honor?"

"You called him, so don't pretend you didn't. And it'll be on your conscience if I'm sweet-talked into doing anything."

"None too soon, either," said Jake. "If you're going to have anything to live down, you'd better get started on it."

She looked at him slyly. "Tell me something. When did he ask you to call him?"

"Some time ago. And I won't apologize. Judging from that getup, the attention isn't unwelcome."

"How long ago?"

"I guess it was the day after you left. He came over here with that look they get when they're telling you that whatever they're going to do to you might be a little uncomfortable. I was sorely relieved when I found out it was something that was none of my business, so I jumped at it with enthusiasm."

"I thought you weren't going to apologize."

"I'm explaining." They both heard Carey's car pull up in front of her house.

"I accept your explanation." She turned toward the open door. "But don't let it clear your conscience, because you didn't apologize."

He sat down in his chair and picked up his book. "Tell him he owes me a favor. I know you won't admit *you* do. And close that door. There's a draft on my hind legs."

Carey was standing beside the passenger door when Jane stepped out onto the porch. She held up her hand, hurried to her own door, tossed the mail on the couch, set the alarm, and locked the door, all the time thinking about the first glimpse of him. He was wearing a dark gray suit that must be new, and it was one she might have picked for him. His long legs and arms seemed comfortable in it, somehow, and the fabric along the lapels looked so soft and smooth her fingertips wanted to touch it. The color made the thin sandy hair that never seemed to stay where he thought he was supposed to put it look almost golden under the streetlamp.

As she came down the steps she gave him a little smile. "You're not trying to impress me, are you?"

"Not me." He opened the door for her. "The only reason I'm bringing you along is I'm trying to make the car look good. I'm trying to sell it, and I notice they always use young women in the commercials."

"No flies on you," she said. "You're what Jake calls a 'go-ahead young man.' "

He drove slowly and carefully up the street. She liked that. It was something that only people who had been raised in places like Deganawida seemed to have the sensitivity to do. If people had to look up from what they were doing to see if someone was running over the kids or grandma they didn't forget whose car it was, or who was in it. Whoever it was forfeited part of his claim to being solid and respectable. In Deganawida that respectability meant that people would strain to put a benevolent interpretation on anything they saw, and a third party who asked prying questions would be enveloped in a fog of laudatory generalities that applied to everyone and no one.

As Carey drove along River Road to the south he said, "I missed you."

"I missed you too," said Jane. She looked out across the half mile of moving river at Grand Island. When she and Jake's girls were children there were still lots of places over there where they could walk across a swampy field and fight their way through impenetrable thickets to streams full of perch and sunfish. The lights of the Holiday Inn across the water were in the spot where there used to be pilings from the old ferryboat landing and a vast empty field of dry weeds like hay. Sometimes they would search the pebbly shore with sticks and find big, heavy pieces of rust-encrusted iron that did not suggest any known use but had probably come from old-time lumber boats.

Carey drove east out of Buffalo on Main Street into the open suburbs, until they came to a sprawling restaurant built around a coach stop from the early 1800s, along the road that was laid over the Seneca trail. There were big stone fireplaces where resin-soaked pine logs flared and crackled, fed a steady stream of fresh oxygen by the air-conditioning. The walls were lined with buggy whips and harnesses and Currier & Ives prints, and when the food came, the roast beef was served with Yorkshire pudding.

They sat at a table beside the front window. Jane smiled as she surveyed the dining room. "I forgot this place existed."

"Me too," he said. "I picked it because it's a good place to talk."

"You picked it because it reminds you of your house." Jane had seen an old Holland Land Company map that Ellicott, the company agent, had used for the sale of Seneca land in 1801. Clearly marked in its place was "McKinnon house." "What do you want to talk about—horses?"

Carey was quiet and serious. "Last time, you told me about your trip. Are you going to tell me this time?"

"I think I did what I wanted to do." Her eyes scanned the empty tables around her to be sure none of the waiters had drifted too near. "But it wasn't smooth."

"You mean somebody's looking for you?"

"Maybe, but not hard, and not for long. It had nothing to do with me." She scanned the restaurant again, and when her eyes returned to him, she smiled. "Sounds brave, doesn't it?"

"I'm awed, as usual," he said.

"Don't be. Twenty-four hours ago I was as scared as anybody alive. I could almost taste the strawberries."

He cocked his head. "What strawberries?"

She looked down and shook her head. "It's just an old expression." She paused. "Really old. It means you came so close that you could already taste the wild strawberries that grow by the path to the other world."

He looked down too, and then up again to fix his eyes on hers. "Want to tell me what brought that on?"

"I made a mistake—took a chance to buy some extra time for my rabbit. I ended up in a high place, looking down, the way you do in a bad dream." She patted his hand. "Since I didn't fall, I guess you could say nothing actually happened. What did you do while I was gone?"

"Surgery every morning at seven except Friday. Office visits from one to five. Hospital rounds five to seven."

"And then?"

"I thought about how to talk to you. You're not that easy. You have a long history of standing up and walking around whenever anybody says anything, so I decided to take you to a restaurant."

"Big talk, huh? Serious stuff?"

"Yes. You told me what happened on your trip in December. You said that I should think about what I'd heard. If I asked you again after I'd thought about it, you would say yes."

Jane said, "No, I told you I loved you. I told you that if you asked me again after one year, I would say yes. And if you do, I will."

Carey's long, strong fingers moved up his forehead and pushed back the shock of hair that had begun to creep down. "I'm a very quick thinker. I've been thinking about it for six months. No. Let me start again," he said. "You and I have known each other for almost fourteen years. We were sophomores that night at Uris Library when Sally introduced us."

"Right," she said. "You were doing sickening drawings of invertebrates. Compound eyes and mandibles."

"So whatever fundamental judgments we needed to make about each other have been made. That was what this was about, wasn't it? You told me something that I hadn't known about you. You wanted to be sure I didn't assume I could ignore it and then start mulling it over after it was too late."

"That's part of it," she said. "We have to be friends, because we are. We don't have to get married. That brings on a whole new set of rules and agreements that are very rigid and binding, and nobody should do it who has any doubts."

"Are we still talking about the same thing?"

"I'm not talking about one thing," she said. "I'm talking about everything at once, because that's what marriage is. You take all of the complexity of your life—Who is this person? Do I approve? Where do I want to live? Who are my relatives? What time do I get up? What do I wear? What work do I do?—and compress all of it into just one question: Do I get married or not? That was why I picked a year."

"You made your decision in a day."

"I'm very introspective, and I spend a lot of time alone."

He shook his head and chuckled sadly. "I want it on the record that I haven't seen any other women since we talked about this."

"Come on, Carey," she said. "You're so dour and businesslike. It's not like you. This is about being alive and happy. We're old buddies. We know way too much about each other to start making speeches. I'm glad to hear you're not molesting the nurses . . . anymore. But that's just my possessiveness. I'm not checking compliance with an agreement."

"You started it. In December."

"I had no choice," she said. "That was disclosure."

"It seems to be what's standing in the way now."

She sighed. "You are a person who spends his life taking patients who are probably going to die and fixing them up. It's an obsession. It's what you have instead of a religion. I told you because not telling you would have made everything else a lie. I had just come home from a trip where I had killed some people. I am, technically and legally, a murderer. That's not a small thing. It puts you in danger too—again, technically and legally. But also philosophically. Emotionally. I did something that is against everything you believe and everything you know."

"How do you feel about it now?" He lowered his voice. "Are you sorry? Afraid? Proud?"

Her eyes turned on him in a glare, then turned away again. "It's something to be avoided."

"Do better than that."

"It was the most horrible experience of my life. If the same circumstances came up tomorrow—no, right now, tonight—I know I would do it again. It would be much harder because I would know what it was going to look like. It also taught me some other things I had avoided knowing."

"Like what?"

"All these years I was telling myself that what I was doing was unambiguous. I was taking people who were in the worst kind of trouble and making them disappear. That made sense. Whoever was in danger of dying didn't, so nobody did. But I should have admitted to myself that one day I wasn't going to run fast enough, or I would take a wrong turn. Until it happened I didn't realize that what I was doing wasn't just saving people. I was choosing a side. There aren't any good guys in a fight to the death. So now I know, and you know."

"Yes," said Carey. "I know. I've thought about it every day for six months. My reaction is another surprise. I find it doesn't matter to me. It's another life, another time—like a war. What does matter is this: Is it over? Do you plan to stop making people disappear?"

"Done," said Jane.

"What?"

"I mean, Okay. I'll stop doing what I've been doing."

"It's that easy?"

"Answering quickly doesn't mean it's easy. It just means I didn't wait until now to decide. When I said I would marry you, that was part of the bargain." Jane shrugged. "I was a guide because it was the right thing for me to do in that time and place. If you're waiting for me to apologize for it, you'll wait forever. It's just not something you do if you're somebody's wife."

The waiter brought the check on its little silver tray and Carey set a credit card on top of it, then went through the ceremony of adding the tip and signing it. The waiters and busboys were all very solicitous and friendly, because Carey and Jane were the only patrons who had not left, and they meant to sweep away all obstacles to their swift departure so the shift would end.

The car was waiting at the door. As soon as they were inside and the car was in motion, Carey said, "I love you. I've done all the thinking I need to do. I want you to marry me now, not six months from now." He stopped at the edge of the highway and looked at her, but there was no answer.

"Drive for a while," she said. He turned left and went east, out into the country. She sat in silence and looked out the window at the dark landscape. There were woods now, and farmhouses.

"Are you thinking about it?" he asked.

"I'm thinking," she said. "I'm thinking about how to tell you everything that's in my mind." She drew in a breath and seemed to try to begin, then let the breath out. "There!" she said. "Pull over up there by that orchard."

"Where?"

"Beside the fence."

The car slowed, and then the tires ground on gravel, and the car stopped. "Oh, even better," she said. "Pull into that drive up there."

"What are we doing?"

"Just do it." She cajoled, "I want to show you something. I promise you'll like it."

He slowly drove the car through the opening in the fence and up a dirt road into the orchard. The road was pink with blooms that had spilled from the apple trees on both sides. He bumped along deeper into the orchard as Jane stared eagerly out the windshield. "Okay, stop," she said, opened the door, and stepped out.

She walked to the far edge of the orchard and sidestepped a few paces down a little slope, then stopped. She slipped off her shoes and walked down the hill a short distance, paused at the edge of a thick patch of ankle-high wild plants with round, serrated leaves that covered the lower slope, then turned and looked up at Carey McKinnon. "Come down," she said. "I knew I could find some."

He cautiously stepped toward her, looking down to be sure of his footing. When he looked up she was bent over, fiddling with something under the hem of her skirt. Then she pulled off her stockings and handed them to him. "Put these in your pocket for me, will you?" She walked barefoot among the thick, soft plants, then bent over and ran her hands into them, touching here and there in the dark.

Carey stepped closer and she held out her hand. In the palm were a dozen little round shapes no bigger than a half inch across. "What's that?"

"Dessert," she said. "Wild strawberries."

She popped one onto her tongue and squeezed it against the roof of her mouth, then chewed it. "They're perfect." She held out her hand again and poured the little strawberries into Carey's palm.

He tasted one and smiled. "They're good. Soft, sweet." But she was already bent over, running her hands quickly among the fuzzy leaves of the little plants.

Carey knelt on the weeds with her and picked strawberries until they had a double handful. Carey gave them to her and then spread his new coat in the weeds and they sat on it, feeling the warm June air and the intense darkness of the new moon and eating strawberries.

They turned to each other and kissed, then slowly and gradually the kisses grew longer and deeper and they leaned back to lie on the coat, the tall weeds now sheltering them on both sides like a nest. Carey's hand began to move along her body—breast, waist, hip—and the clothes Jane had chosen didn't need to be tugged up and pulled down tonight. In the darkness they seemed to melt away, and she hoped, knew he had asked her to wear them with this moment in mind. Or maybe his asking and her compliance and this moment were part of the same event, one long act of asking and complying, her wanting him to ask, even turn his eyes in some direction so she could offer before he even formed the desire. The kisses were long and hungry now, and the hands—the long, gentle fingers and the wide, smooth palms moving everywhere, touching and outlining her shape in the darkness, the skin feeling itself traced and caressed so she could see herself with her eyes closed, the smaller, graceful shape and the curves she had somehow forgotten were her until now, when he saw them, touched them, pulled her against him. The embrace defined them both, his body all tense, hard muscles, the skin tickly with hair, but the boundary between them gone.

There was only the smell of the strawberries and the taste of them on her tongue, the warm, dark motionless air that might never change at all, and this heartbeat and this indrawn breath. But there was time because the feelings were growing, moving down to her belly and thighs, too many breaths until it grew into a longing, an ache, and he knew it. Then she was relieved, so much better, happy, actually happy, out of time now entirely, because if this feeling went on forever it would not be enough, but it went on, and she heard her own breaths coming quicker, and her voice coming out with them, and it was going to go on until she was obliterated, burned up like a moth flying into a blast furnace. And in this moment of wanting and having, that seemed just fine to her . . . better, best. And then time came back because this could not go on, was about to pass, not gasping for breath, but filled with it, and then so light and cool, shivering almost and the word *delicious* coming into her mind and passing away again because contentment was too lazy and pleased to hold on to it.

They lay naked on the hillside in the little space of flattened weeds, smelling the strawberries again. She opened her eyes to extend the depth of her gaze far up into the night sky.

For the first time in ages, she heard his voice. "Were the strawberries what you wanted to show me?"

"Sort of," she laughed. "It's kind of a multidimensional experience. In the old days, they used to court in strawberry patches."

"I'll bet it wasn't quite the same."

"I'll bet it was," she said. "See, they would slip out of their longhouses at night and meet in a place like this."

"I mean they didn't make love."

"Of course they did." She laughed. "That was what they were doing out here in the middle of the night. Maybe right here."

"I can see why strawberries grow on the way to heaven." He ran his hand along her hip, smoothing it gently. "Ripe and sweet and perfect and rare."

She sat up and looked at him with a tiny hint of a wish. "Just the opposite. The reason they were so precious was that they weren't rare at all. They grew from one end of Iroquois country to the other. No matter what, they came up every May and ripened every June. They were easy—always there, always as many as you wanted, and always just as good as the first one you ever put on your tongue."

He sat up and looked at her closely, his eyes blue-gray and shining. "That was what you wanted me to know."

"You're getting better," she said. "You have a shot at 'Most Improved Naked Man.' "

"I'd like to think I was already smart enough to appreciate you, and never let myself forget how special you are, even after a few years of getting our strawberries in supermarkets like other people." His hand moved gently from her shoulder down her side to her hip, thigh, knee, shin, foot. "But I'm glad you took me on the field trip."

"Me too."

He said quietly, "It's not like you to waste all this wisdom on the first naked man you meet in a strawberry patch. To make it worthwhile, you'd almost have to marry me."

"Yes," she said. "I will."

The boardroom for Pleasure, Inc., overlooked the Polynesian water slide. Somebody had once joked that the architect's plans had been folded and the contractor hadn't noticed. It sounded true because mistakes in Las Vegas were not little slip-ups that made a few chips fall between the floorboards. They were hideous, gargantuan blunders, like building a billion-dollar casino on ground that was a foot lower than the adjacent square mile of parking lots, so the whole place got inundated with water in a flash flood every five years. But the location of the Pleasure Island boardroom had been no mistake; it had been a suggestion from Calvin Seaver, vice president for security.

Seaver stepped from the elevator and stared out through the double layer of one-way glass at the beautiful waterfall and the rocks and the lush tropical plants and flowers. He saw a pair of boys—he guessed eight and ten years old from the memory of his own boys—and then the father, a guy in his late thirties with a little baby fat around his middle and a U.S.N. anchor tattoo that showed he wasn't troubled with neck pains from holding up his brain. They stood on the platform ten feet from Seaver, waiting for something. He guessed it was Mom. And there she was. Not bad. A trace of cellulite in the haunches and sag in the tits, but nothing for her to worry about. She plunked down at the top of the slide with them, and all four went slipping down, around, under the waterfall, and out of sight. Good for them.

Seaver was trained to feel a presumptive hostility, watching the guests for some sign that they were going to cause a need for his services, but the reason he was the best was that he could tell the sheep from the goats. These were sheep. They wouldn't know how to cause trouble, because it wasn't in their nature. During their stay they would never know that he was watching over them, protecting them while they played and while they slept, making sure that nothing disturbed the artificial tranquility around them.

Those four were evidence that things were going beautifully. They would stay maybe five days. Mom and Dad would get a taste of canned glamour and carefully controlled risk. The boys would spend some time in the virtual-reality arcades, getting the feel of paying money to get excitement, and ensure Pleasure, Inc., of repeat business for the next fifty years. The family would pay Pleasure, Inc., more than they spent on this year's taxes to their home state, and then they'd be gone.

The goats were different—card counters and con men and short-change artists and call girls and pickpockets—always trying to fade in among the sheep, but restless. He knew half of them by sight, but he didn't need to. He could detect it in their eyes the first time he saw them. They were hungry. He had sensed something too eager in Pete Hatcher's eyes early on, but he had misinterpreted it. His mistake was in accepting the bosses' assurances that all Hatcher was after was pussy.

He glanced at his watch and moved on down the hallway. Seaver was probably the only one who could see this part of the complex clearly when he looked at it. The elevators and the long, narrow hallway gave his people plenty of time and means to isolate anyone who had some business that wasn't on the board's agenda. The double panes of one-way glass kept anyone from amplifying the vibrations to pick up a conversation or using any sort of photography. Being next to the water slide ensured that nobody who wasn't wearing a bathing suit could get close, and anybody scanning with a directional microphone from a distance would pick up the waterfall and eighty customers talking about nothing.

It wasn't the sort of security that an underground room would have, but it had worked well enough so far. What he was worried about these days was some kind of futuristic emergency—some loser driving a car bomb through the front entrance, or some Japanese cult releasing nerve gas in the climate-control system. He had consultants working on countermeasures, but so far nothing they had brought him was good enough to bring to the big guys. All the plans involved lots of rebuilding to make space for some strategy they could not guarantee would work.

The big guys were never reluctant to spend money on remodeling. What they hated was having to shut anything down while they did it. But Seaver believed in outside consultants, and he was confident that they would solve these problems, one by one. Security was a matter of batting down specific threats. Nothing worked all of the time for all purposes.

He opened the door to the boardroom, stepped inside onto the thick carpet, and quietly took a seat at the enormous rosewood table. The door closed silently behind him. The automatic closer had been Seaver's idea too. The time when people were going in and out was a gaping breach in the room's integrity. Anyone who managed to defeat the other obstacles could learn a lot by picking up a few seconds here and there and studying what he had heard.

This time there was no meeting of the Management Team. The only ones in the room were the big guys themselves, Bobby Salateri, Max Foley, and Peter Buckley. They met this way more often than people would think, to talk without the twenty upper-level functionaries who ran housekeeping or finance or public relations or security.

Peter Buckley first deigned to notice Seaver. "Morning, Cal."

"Peter," said Seaver. Then he added, "Bobby, Max," as the others saw him. Then he waited. They took their time, and it was a compliment to him.

"Having water misters all over the place is okay this year. It's okay next year," said Salateri. "How does it look ten years from now? I mean politically?"

"It's not exactly all over the place," said Foley. "It's just on the golf courses. The sun shelters are already plumbed. It's just a matter of installing these little fixtures around the roof. That's thirty-six misters. They'll make the players feel cool and comfortable."

"Yeah, I know," said Salateri. "It's nothing, really. But every single time some TV station does a report on wasting water I see footage of misters over some hot dog stand."

"The estimate says the trees around the shelters will catch some of the water and the shade will keep the mist from evaporating as fast. If there's ever rationing, it's just that much more water grandfathered in."

"That's a point I hadn't thought of," said Salateri. "I can buy it on that basis. How about you, Peter?"

"Sure," said Buckley. "If things really get stupid, we've got something we can give away: Pleasure Island shuts down misters to save water."

"I'll have them go ahead," said Foley. He turned to Seaver. "Little problem last night, huh, Cal?"

"Yes," said Seaver. "I wish I had some excuse. I don't."

"So where does that leave us now?" asked Buckley.

"Hatcher wasn't on any flight leaving McCarran, or a train. A bus is too haphazard for him. He undoubtedly drove out. If he had the sense to keep driving, he could be in Chicago by now." He reached into his breast pocket. "My resignation is ready, if you want it."

"Stick it in your ear," said Salateri. "This isn't the fucking army, where you get to resign your commission and hand in your sword and go write your memoirs. We've got a parasite that could eat us alive. We need you more than we did yesterday."

"Thank you," said Seaver. It was the only thing Salateri had ever said to him that could have been a compliment.

"How did he lose your people?" asked Foley. "Maybe that's the place to start."

"He met a woman at the Inside Straight for the midnight lounge show. The Miraculous Miranda picked him out of the audience, made him disappear a couple of times, and brought him back. The last time, she didn't. He probably slipped out the stage door. My men got suckered. They followed the woman and a decoy out of the show, then lost the decoy too. The woman was a pro. She got them to watch her for an hour, then split them up and cornered one of them in the elevator. She left him with a broken leg, a broken nose, and some damage to his eye."

"A professional what?" asked Salateri. "Boxer?"

"I don't know what term she uses on her business cards," said Seaver. "But I don't think Hatcher could have set this up for himself. I don't know what part in this Miranda played—maybe just picking him out of the crowd was enough, and magicians will sometimes do that as a favor if you send a waiter backstage and ask. Maybe—"

"It doesn't matter," interrupted Buckley. "I'm not about to start grilling Miranda, and I hope you're not."

"Only if you asked me to," said Seaver. "If she knows anything, there's no reason for her to tell me, and no way I can make her. If the woman is a pro, then Miranda probably doesn't know much."

Salateri shrugged and made a face of distaste. "I'll see if I can talk to Vincent." He sat quietly for a moment, then noticed the others staring at him. "Why not? You think if Vincent Bogliarese wanted to do us harm he'd do it this way—have his girlfriend sneak the guy off in a puff of smoke? Get real. He'd send eight hundred guys in shiny suits to pull our guts out and set fire to them." He added, to no one in particular, "I say that, of course, with the greatest respect, and in confidence. The man is a friend of mine. I'm not saying he'll find out anything for us, but it won't hurt to ask."

Max Foley looked at Seaver. "It looks to me as though we really have to handle this ourselves, Cal. This screw-up is yours, but the underlying problem isn't. It's ours, the three of us. We picked out Hatcher, we misjudged him, and we trusted him with a lot of things we shouldn't have."

"That's right," said Buckley.

Salateri nodded sadly. "He was smart, easy to be around, he be-haved like a man. Now we're in trouble, and we don't even know what kind."

"We can guess," said Foley. "No matter what he thinks he's going to do now, at some point he's going to end up in the hands of the F.B.I." He added, "Unless he doesn't."

Buckley leaned back in his big chair. "Do we have anybody on our payroll who can take care of this kind of problem?"

"No," said Seaver. "We've been very careful not to hire anyone like that full-time. They're not the sort of people you want to have around year in and year out. Other employees figure out what they're there for, and so on."

The three men sat in a row and looked at him. "You've been in the security business for a long time," said Foley.

"And a cop before that," added Salateri.

Foley continued. "Yes. You must know someone who would be able to do it. I mean a full-service specialist, who can find him and handle the rest."

"There's someone I can probably get," said Seaver. This was going to be the delicate part. He wasn't sure they knew what this in-volved. "I'll need a lot of cash. Maybe a hundred thousand to start, and more later."

"Cash?" said Buckley. "Well, hell, Cal. Cash is what we do. Go downstairs and give this to Eddie." He rapidly scribbled a note and handed it to Seaver, who glanced at it: "Give Seaver whatever he wants. P.B." Buckley folded his hands across his belly. "Who is this guy?"

"It's a Mickey-and-Minnie team. I'll talk to them today."

"Just don't bring them here," said Salateri. "I don't want to meet anybody like that."

"And if you're going to hire them, don't call them from here, either," said Foley. "A year from now I don't want some prosecutor going down the hotel phone bills and finding their number."

Seaver nodded. "Of course. I'll be flying to Los Angeles to talk to them in person. There are just a couple of things I should tell you. They'll give me a price, but expenses will be on top of that."

"This goes without saying," said Buckley. "What else?"

"Once they leave their house, it's done. I won't be able to call them off. They'll keep at it as long as it takes, and they won't check in with me or be any place I can reach them. If we find out tomorrow that Pete Hatcher was the most loyal employee the world has ever seen, it'll be too late. He'll already be dead."

"I guess this is the time to ask." Buckley looked at his two partners. "Are we all sure we aren't going to change our minds?"

"I'll chance it," said Foley.

They both looked at Salateri. He knitted his brows and held up both hands. "You know it would be too bad if we were just being paranoid. I mean, an innocent guy suddenly has his bosses decide he's the enemy, and then they get him tossed in a Dumpster somewhere. But he already knows we had him watched, and he knows we were considering getting rid of him. If he was our friend, he's not anymore. What good would he be to us now?"

Linda Thompson sat in her bedroom and rubbed the creamy mask onto the perfect white skin of her cheeks and forehead, staring into the lighted mirror. This one was blue, and it left three small round holes for her eyes and mouth. The white towel wrapped around her blond hair above her blue face made her look ghostly in the intense glow of the makeup light. She walked to the bed and lay down to wait. The blinds were closed, but the window behind them open, so they clacked back and forth in the dry, hot southern California breeze. She opened her robe and let the air blow across her naked body while it dried the facial mask. She had already covered herself with lotion, and the air made her skin tingle.

Linda was beautiful. She had never been anywhere since she was nine when somebody had not mentioned it, or looked at her in a way that made mentioning it seem like saying it twice. She knew it was the kind of beauty that was startling, because it seemed to take up space of its own. It was the initial premise of every transaction she had with other people. They didn't seem to understand that it wasn't a gift. It was a torment, because it was perfection, and maintaining perfection was a lot of work. Linda hated work.

It was only eleven in the morning and she had already done five point five miles on the stationary bike, worked for an hour on the exercise machines, and done a half hour in the pool. She knew she would have felt less bereft now if she could have had four fried eggs and a half pound of bacon, which was what Earl had eaten in front of her before he had gone out to work the dogs. Linda had not eaten since the cracker and asparagus last night, and Earl had thrown that nauseating mess into a pan in front of her and set off a racket of sizzling and popping and smelly grease. When she had said she didn't want any he had given that crooked smirk and eaten all of it himself. Wolfed it down, was the expression, and it was made for Earl.

He was tall and lean with big knuckles and a jaw that showed what he was: ten generations of white trash in assorted depressing hollows out of God's line of vision in the South, and probably the ten generations before that being the same thing in England, all twenty generations of them screwing with people only one or two branches over on the family tree, so they were all completely devoid of common consideration and never gained an ounce.

The air seemed to tear itself apart with a sound that wasn't quite a bark but a scream. She sprang from the bed amid low growls and the howl of the hound as it turned to defend itself. Linda didn't have the patience to run down the hallway to the living room, into the dining room, and out the door, so she raised the blinds, sat on the windowsill, swung her legs out, and jumped to the grass. She sprinted toward the kennel, muttering to herself, "He's absolutely retarded."

When she reached the high chain-link fence she could already see the bloodhound backed into the corner trying to keep the Rottweilers away from his hamstrings. His left ear had been chewed, and there was blood dripping from his muzzle.

Earl was standing in the corner of the pen, absently rubbing the bristle of his unshaven chin as he watched the big, heavy black dogs hurl themselves at the hound.

Linda spoke loudly enough for him to hear. "Call them off, Earl."

He turned slowly and looked at her, but she didn't wait. She barked, "*Halt! Aufhören mit!*" The two Rottweilers stopped and backed up until they were beside the fence.

"Oh, it's you," said Earl. "The face didn't ring a bell." She traced his line of vision and found herself looking down. She hastily closed the robe and tied it.

"What are you doing?" she asked wearily.

"Trying to see how two of them work when they've got something cornered."

"They bite the hell out of it until it bleeds to death. What more could you possibly find out?"

"I wasn't sure. That's why I did it. Now I know."

"And?"

"It might come in handy some time. I think I could beat two of them. Don't know anybody else who could."

"So what are you going to do with this thousand-dollar purebred bloodhound you brought home a week ago? You can't enter it in a show now that it's all chewed up. You can't even put it out to stud."

Earl glanced at the dog cowering in the corner of the exercise yard, not daring to move. He shrugged. "Science."

Linda walked into the house and opened the cupboard beside the sink. She pulled out the Heckler & Koch .45 A.C.P., pressed the button at the rear of the trigger guard to release the magazine, and checked it. She had to be sure Earl hadn't left it unloaded the last time he had pissed her off. No, there was a full load of ten Federal Hydra-Shok hollow-points. She slipped the big pistol inside her robe, clamped it there with her left arm, and stepped out the door.

When she reached the kennel, he had already let the bloodhound out of the pen into the run, and he was busily giving the Rottweilers chunks of red steak. She walked beside the fence of the long, narrow track to the spot where the bloodhound was lying on its belly trying to lick some of the gashes in its chest, but not really able to. She flicked off the safety, pushed the muzzle of the pistol through the links of the fence, aimed at the dog's round, bony cranium, and blew it apart.

The report of the big pistol brought Earl around the kennel into the exercise run. He looked at her blue face with the staring eyeholes, but he didn't speak.

She answered him anyway. "Any vet who got a look at him would have called the police."

He said, "You going to bury that?"

She had already started back across the lawn. Her blue mask had hardened, and now it burned against her skin as she whirled and snapped, "You know goddamned well I'm not."

Linda walked back into the kitchen, released the magazine, and left the pistol on the counter for Earl to clean. She knew if she cleaned it, he would clean it again. In her bathroom, she gently washed the mask off and patiently, thoroughly rubbed moisturizer from the tiny jar onto her face with her fingertips, staring into the mirror over the sink.

That was Earl. She had no doubt that he had figured out how to kill two Rottweilers attacking him at once. But the part that made him Earl Bliss was that if he hadn't been sure, then tomorrow or the next day she would, likely as not, find him out there in the pen with a Ka-Bar knife doing it. He was a severe annoyance between jobs. He could not rest.

She knew that this afternoon he would be out in the Angeles National Forest sighting in the new rifle for the fourth time. It was a British Arctic Warfare suppressed military sniper rifle with an olive-drab stainless-steel barrel and a Schmidt & Bender 50-millimeter scope. Everything about it was adjustable, from the pull and travel of the trigger to the recoil absorption of the butt plate, so Earl would spend days and days adjusting them. The plain A.W. military-issue model started at over three thousand dollars, but the suppressed model with the silencer was highly illegal and had probably set him back five times that, because he had never told her what the Mexican cop had asked for it. Earl always needed the latest and fanciest piece of equipment, and then he had to take it completely apart and put it back together to see exactly how it worked.

That combination of constant self-improvement and morbid curiosity was what she would have extracted as the most horrible part of Earl, but she could not even hold that thought firmly, because it was also the best part of him. And cutting things away from him wasn't possible. Earl had no surface, like other people: he was the same all the way through, like a chunk of steel. All you could do was move your head to look at the same qualities from different angles. That was how she had come to love and hate him at the same time.

He looked at everything the same—dismantling gadgets, testing the dogs to see how they worked, or her. Every time he heard or read or saw something that could be done to a woman's body, he would do it to her, watching with an expression between detached curiosity and, maybe she just hoped, fascination, to see how it affected her: to see how she worked. The result didn't seem to matter to him in any emotional way. It didn't matter if he had her panting like a bitch in heat, crawling to him and begging for more, or sent her whimpering into her room to lock the door for three days. He didn't take care to repeat the good things to make her happy, or avoid things that would remind her of something that had hurt her. He just wanted to see how she worked.

She had let him put her in a dark mood, and now she began to construct a fantasy about him. He would come in from burying the bloodhound. He would go to the sink in the kitchen to wash his hands. She would come in behind him while his hands were engaged and wet. She would put her left hand on his shoulder softly to show him she didn't give the dog issue undue importance, then use it to tousle his hair while she freed her right to reach into her robe.

But he was Earl, so it would take him a half second to realize from the feel of her fingers or the sound of her breathing that something was up. She knew she would not be able to say anything or he would hear the tension in her voice. She would use that half second to tighten her fingers on his hair, jerk his head back, and bring the fillet knife across his throat. She had been composing these little plays about him since she was in high school, when she first went to work filing and running errands at his detective agency, and as she had known it would, this one began to change.

He would sense her excitement instantly and give that little snort of a laugh as his right hand shot up like a striking snake to catch her left. The knife was still hidden under her robe, held there by the tie-belt on the outside, and she was afraid it would fall out, so she turned away and leaned her hip against the edge of the green marble surface of the island in the middle of the kitchen to keep it there.

The move gave him an idea, so he reached around her and pulled the belt of the robe so it opened, and put his big hand between her shoulder blades. He pushed her forward and she felt the shock of the cold, hard marble, first on her breasts, and then her belly, and the hard corner of the marble against her pelvis. She had no choice but to wriggle farther onto the marble to keep the fillet knife flat under her belly so it wouldn't slice her open or clatter to the floor, only that brought her buttocks up and parted her legs, and she had to hold herself absolutely rigid to keep from moving against the blade. And he—

The ring of the telephone beside her bed was like something breaking. She snatched the receiver off the hook and punched the button that was lit. She was too annoyed to see which number it was, so she said, "Linda Thompson."

"Hello, Linda." She recognized the voice, and her anger began to turn into hope. "Can you and Earl meet me someplace for lunch?"

A job, she thought. Thank God.

Linda sat beside Earl in the front seat and watched each shopper pull into the big parking lot, drive up and down a couple of aisles, coast between two diagonal slashes of white paint, then go through the ritual of checking the whole car: the mirrors to be sure the car's ass wasn't hanging out far enough to get clipped, the passenger seat to collect purses or glasses or hide a bag they bought in the last mall from the smash-and-grab crowd, then the lock buttons. The excruciating sameness of it was getting on her nerves. People were as predictable as gophers. You knew the next three things they were going to do before they did.

The car smelled like dogs, that nauseating dog-food smell they exuded from every pore. Earl had used the car instead of the truck again. She decided not to say anything, because it would spoil the next hour.

Earl was brilliant in his own way. Raising and training attack dogs was a great sideline for a detective agency that didn't do much business. In a city the size of Los Angeles you could pick up any breed you wanted from the pound for the price of the shots, which was up to sixty bucks now. Some of them had papers. You trained the dog to sit, heel, shit outdoors, and maul people, and you could sell it for fifteen thousand.

But Linda was ready to work now, and that was Earl's fault too. He had trained her practically from childhood to his rhythms. He was only really alive when he was hunting. Between times he only played at it and got more and more irritable.

Seaver was precisely on time, as she had known he would be. He was one of those guys who seemed to see himself as though he were still in the military. For the ones like him, that wasn't some kind of interruption in his existence but his initiation into manhood. She saw him pull the rental car between the diagonal lines, but he didn't behave like the others. He was out and walking as soon as the keys were out of the ignition. He still carried himself straight, only now there was a little gray at the sides of his short hair. The aviator sunglasses he used to wear had been replaced with plain black frames, but the gray summer suit with the bright white shirt still had that animal-in-clothes look because it was cut too snugly and the collar was too tight, the way the army had taught him to dress.

He got into the back seat and Earl drove off. "Hello, Cal," said Linda. "You're looking good."

"You too," said Seaver. She knew that he had thought of a compliment, but he had pressed his tongue against the back of his teeth because he had known better than to say it in front of Earl.

"Let's go to Ivy at the Shore," said Seaver. "We can talk business while we're on the freeway, and then eat in peace."

"When's your plane out?" asked Earl.

"Four o'clock," said Seaver. "If I'm back in my car by three, I'll make it. If not, I'll take another flight."

As Earl accelerated down the ramp onto the San Diego Freeway Seaver stared at the bottom of the first overpass. Some time soon it was going to be a bad idea to transact this kind of business on a freeway. Already the California Department of Transportation had tried placing cameras on the overpasses so when there was a traffic jam they could see what had caused it. And lately thieves had put machines on the bridges to capture cellular phone numbers and codes they could program into clones. He opened his coat, took out a thick manila envelope, and handed it over the seat to Linda. "In there is all the information I have about a target I want found and taken out."

Earl glanced at the unopened envelope. "What is all that?"

"Photographs, a surveillance videotape, two audiotapes—one on the phone, one live—his employment history. I thought I could save you some time."

Earl smiled. "He must be important."

Seaver felt a distaste for the tactics of bluff and barter. "The price is going to be three hundred thousand for him. We'll cover legitimate expenses."

"Hear that, Earl?" said Linda. "No illegitimate expenses this time."

"I mean," said Seaver, "that I'm not the client. I just picked you for the job. If it's too outrageous, the client is capable of getting rid of me and hiring somebody else to deal with you."

"I hear you," said Earl. "Why is this guy worth that much? Does he have something I have to bring back, or what?"

"No," said Seaver. "He's got information in his head. He can't hand it off or sell it, because nobody else can testify to what he saw. He'll have to be alive to do it."

Linda smiled at Seaver and he thought about what a strange creature she was. She had what used to be called cupid's bow lips, big, liquid green eyes. The smile would have been merely beautiful if it had been prompted by something else, but death seemed to excite her, and when her pulse went up the eyes got more green and there was a delicate flush in the pure white complexion. Her face was hypnotic, and the need to keep looking at it was like an itch. "Smell something, Earl? A Green Beret, right? No, I know. C.I.A. Forced retirement." She turned the eyes away, toward Earl, and the blond hair hid them like a curtain.

When she took the light of that face away from him, the frustration made Seaver involuntarily suck in a breath through his teeth. He quickly dispelled any hint that he had been thinking about anything but business by blowing the breath out through his lips in a contemptuous huff.

"The price is high because the client doesn't ever want to think about him again. I hire you, and you handle it. The end," said Seaver. "I don't think he'll put up any resistance. But I have no idea where he is. When he disappeared, he had professional help, so he's probably got reasonably good cover in place."

"How long ago?" asked Earl.

"Day before yesterday, about midnight, he drove out of Las Vegas. We don't know anything about the car."

"So the trail's cold. What about the professional help?"

"We don't have much on that, either. It was a woman, mid-twenties to thirty, tall, dark hair, probably brown eyes, but there are two versions. Very fit."

Linda laughed aloud, her voice somewhere between a taunt and a seduction. " 'Very fit.' " She imitated a man's voice the way a child would have: "Have I ever told you you're very fit? I want to look deep into your probably-brown eyes."

"She beat the shit out of one of my security men," said Seaver. "But even he said she was pretty. He didn't volunteer it, because it wasn't what he remembered most about her, but he didn't deny it."

"She sounds interesting," said Earl.

"Oh, now I'm getting jealous," said Linda. The lips came together like a kiss in a studied pout that Seaver knew should have been repellent but made him wish that Earl were dead. She brightened again. "Got her on tape, or any fingerprints? She might be the way to find him."

"Sorry."

"She would have been the one to leave the car for him," said Linda. Her voice was wheedling now. "She was there before he left Las Vegas, and she must have stayed somewhere."

"I know," said Seaver. "I've had my men watching surveillance tapes for twenty-four hours, and she hasn't turned up. The first time anybody saw her was the night she took off."

Earl Bliss swung onto the Santa Monica Freeway and watched his rearview mirror. Nobody in a car behind them seemed to change his mind and follow. The others said nothing while he pretended to be considering the offer. After a decent interval he said, "We'll get started on it after lunch."

It was after dark. Linda could hear him out in the kennel, giving the dogs their dinner. She had already heard him call Lenny on the phone and tell him they were leaving and to pack up and move in at seven in the morning. Linda walked through the house to make sure everything was as it should be. Windows had to be closed, valuables hidden away, checks written for the bills. She took the Heckler & Koch .45 out of the cabinet by the kitchen sink and the Para-Ordnance P-14s from the bedrooms, the den, and the garage and locked them in the gun cabinet behind her closet. Lenny would just stumble onto one of them and blow a hole in something. If he had some kind of trouble while they were gone, he would be more likely to survive it with the gun he always brought with him. Anyway, with a couple of the dogs running the perimeter he'd be safe enough. Nobody cared enough about Lenny to kill him.

Earl always left most of the packing to Linda, because she was the woman. She supposed that meant she was too fastidious to put dirty clothes in by mistake.

She heard his heavy feet on the walk outside, then heard them clomping into the hallway. She called, "You want to take these Colts, right?"

He came in and looked at the pistols she had taken out of the gun cabinet and set on her dresser. They were Colt Model 1911A1s, the most common handgun in the United States, and probably the world. Colt had made them since 1925, over a million of them during World War II alone, and other manufacturers at least that many. The government had kept issuing them for forty years after that, and every army and police force in the Western world had carried some copy with minor variations. The sheer age meant the cops had lost track of most of them long ago, and ballistics identification was a fantasy. Seven .45 rounds were plenty if you didn't plan to have anybody shooting back, and the bulk of the gun was only a problem on the way. You could drop it after it was fired.

Earl said, "These will do fine."

She could tell by the look on Earl's face that it was time for the ritual to begin, so she started. "I'm worried." She had to be the one who said the first words, because he liked it that way.

"There's a lot to worry about," he said. "This is a big job, and it won't be easy."

"I could tell as soon as Seaver started talking," she fretted. "He didn't want to look in my eyes. You spent the afternoon on the computer. Didn't you find anything?"

He pursed his lips and shook his head. "Seaver didn't miss much. No criminal record. No marriages, no out-of-town property. The only car he owned is the one that's still there. I found court records for probate when his old man died. He inherited a few bucks, and there were no other close relatives mentioned in the will."

Linda frowned. "Not much for us there. It will be hard."

"But this is one we've got to win," he said. "The money is good. If we do this one, it will get better on the next one."

"If we blow it, Seaver's bosses will send somebody to look for us." She knitted her brows. "He as good as said that, didn't he?"

"It's a Las Vegas hotel. It's got to be Mafia."

"Got to be," she agreed. "We do it right and we get lots of jobs and lots of money. We fail—don't find him, or try, and botch it—and they're not going to leave us alone."

"It's an important job. More important than anything we've ever done. Life or death."

It was working, and Linda could feel it. Already her breaths were quick and shallow, and her stomach had little quivers in it. The adrenaline was pumping into her veins. She could see Earl's eyes were beginning to get that narrow long-distance gaze. She searched for a way to turn up the pitch, and found it. "We're starting out dead, really. Because they already have us—know who we are, where we live. They'll kill us unless we get him."

That seemed to work for Earl. "He's got our life. We're dead until we get him. We have to find him to take it back."

Earl's anger transported Linda. Her energy was beginning to crackle out in little bolts of rage. "And who the hell is he to do that? He knew he was going to die—deserved to die—but he decided it wasn't going to be him. It was going to be somebody else."

"He knew what he was doing," said Earl. "He knew there would be somebody who had to come along and clean up the mess he left. Somebody like us would be put in his place, in a deep hole, and have to dig their way out of it." His throat was choked with anger.

"Oh, he's not worried about us," she muttered. "He's someplace laughing at us. Both of them are. That woman who got him out of Vegas. They think they're smarter than anybody who would need the money bad enough to come for them."

Earl stood up and began to pace. "Not just smarter. Better than us. Like even if we did luck onto him it wouldn't matter, because he'd beat us."

Linda's pulse was fast, hard, and strong now. She was transfixed with hatred and fear. Her jaw was clenched and her long fingernails were jabbing into the palms of her hands, leaving little red crescents. She could see the veins standing out in Earl's neck. He was moving again, too full of energy to keep still. He was picking things up and tossing them into his suitcase. He seemed to see what a mess he was making of it, so he went and gathered the two Colts from the dresser and headed for the door. He stopped in the doorway and said, "Just be sure you're ready by six."

J ane sat on the couch and stared around her at the baseboards in the living room. There were nicks that her father had patched with the best synthetic wood mixtures they had sold at the time, then painted over, but she knew where they were twenty years later. The one by the kitchen door was from the new refrigerator he had bought as a surprise for her mother, which was still on the other side of the door running right now. Jane remembered seeing the man pushing the two-wheel hand truck it was strapped to miscalculate and nick the doorway. The man who was supposed to be guiding him saw it, spit on his finger, and rubbed the spot, trying to believe it was just a dirt mark but feeling the groove.

The imperfections in the surfaces were events. Her great-grandfather had built most of the house himself, and her grandfather and father had painted and varnished it, and her grandmother and her mother had rubbed every square inch of it clean a thousand times, so if she put her hand here, or here, she was touching their hands.

She said aloud, "I got married yesterday," as a test, and it failed. The words didn't sound convincing, because they didn't have behind them the resonance of wonder. All of the people who would have come rushing in from the kitchen and the dining room, making noise and smiling—or maybe looking worried—were just memories now. Birth, marriage, death. That was all they put on tombstones, and that seemed to be about all anyone wanted to know unless you were pretty remarkable. Jane Whitefield had spent the past twelve years straining every nerve to keep from being remarkable, because attracting attention was dangerous. It seemed she had succeeded, and now she would have to succeed some more, because she had Carey.

Jane turned her attention to the pile of mail that Jake had left for her, setting the bills beside her and the advertisements on the floor for the wastebasket. She came to a stiff white envelope with no return address. Probably it was another wedding card. It would have the usual flowered bower with bells, and beneath it would be the archetypal stiff little people, one in white and the other in black. There was no way anybody could be expected to obtain one that was remotely evocative of a marriage between actual human beings. For some reason there was no market for such a thing. But this mail was old. It had come while she was in Las Vegas, and she had forgotten about it in the rush and excitement of getting married. This couldn't be a wedding card.

She tore it open and saw that it was a plain white folded sheet. Printed in ballpoint pen was "You told me I would be thinking of you just about now. So here's a present. Chris." Inside was a cashier's check with the purchaser listed as Christine McRea. The stub attached to it said "Repayment of Principal." Jane glanced at the machine printing on the check: one hundred thousand and 00/100 dollars.

Christine McRea had come a long way since the night when she had knocked on the door of this house. Her name had been Rebecca Solomon then, and she had made the mistake of assuming that when a judge said the names of people serving on a jury were confidential, that meant an enterprising reporter wouldn't be able to find hers and print it later. When Jane had met her, she had already used all the money she had saved on her secretary's salary just to get as far as Cleveland, and had hitched a ride the rest of the way with a pair of itinerant heavy-equipment operators who had begun to hint at things she could do to repay their kindness.

Jane tore up the note, slipped the check into the pile of bills, and got up off the couch, determined to accomplish something before Carey got here. She would need the address book in her office for the thank-you notes. A few of the people Carey had invited were reachable only through his secretary's computer, but almost everybody else was in her old book. She had known him for so long that their friends were nearly all shared. Most of Jane's relatives lived on the roads along Tonawanda Creek—Sandy Hill Road, Sky Road, a few on Judge Road. She could have sent all of those notes in care of the reservation, but the older ladies would not have approved. She set the floppy old leather book by the door and went upstairs.

She took a few favorite outfits and laid them carefully on the bed, then heard the front door open and close. "Carey?" she called. "I'm upstairs."

Jake's voice called, "Are you decent?"

Jane laughed. "No, Jake. But I'm married now, so I can be as indecent as I want."

"I mean am I invited up?"

"If you can make it up the stairs."

Jake came along the hallway toward her room. "It was a near thing, but I rested frequently and phoned my doctor for advice on the landing. Where is that quack, anyway?"

"He'll be here in a few minutes. He's helping me move a few things, so I thought we'd need both cars. Now that I look at it, I don't think we will."

"I wanted to tell you that I had a good time at the wedding."

"That's because your daughters came. Thanks for giving me away, though, Jake. There was never a man who looked as relieved to get rid of anybody as you did. Everybody make it to the airport on time?"

"Oh, yeah," said Jake. "The kids will make it to their final exams and the husbands will be at work Monday morning to keep my girls wearing the latest fashions and a bit too broad in the beam to fit them. The reception reminded me of when your parents got married. All the food and everything, a lot of the same faces, too, but of course we're all a bit the worse for wear."

Jane selected some of her shoes and set them in a cardboard box. "Last night wasn't really a reception. It was another wedding. In the old days you just asked the two clan mothers if it was okay, and then everybody had a feast."

"I wish your parents could have seen it. God, I remember your mother in her white gown. She was probably the most beautiful woman I ever saw, close up. You're a pleasant-looking female citizen from a thousand yards out on a cloudy evening. But she could knock a rooster off a full henhouse with a veil over her face. She could have been an actress."

"She was an actress," said Jane. "She made herself up."

Jake was silent for a moment. Little Janie had gotten those arctic-blue eyes from her mother, but that penchant for saying the unexpected, like dumping a bushel of apples in your lap to show you what the bottom ones looked like, that came from Henry Whitefield without any dilution. He backed away from that part of it. "She was a wonderful woman."

He had never figured out how much Jane could have known about her mother's past. She had somehow found herself at the age of nineteen in New York City without visible means of support. No, that was exactly the wrong term. Spectacular, sure-fire means of support were still visible on her, well into her forties. Jake had never heard anything specific about how she had spent the years from one to nineteen, or even what part of the country she had started in. Maybe that was the deepest secret of all, and maybe his wife, Margaret, had heard all of that from her too, and found it too ordinary to repeat to her husband.

But she had spent the next few years downstate in the company of a succession of men who were accustomed to having their pictures taken twice—head-on and in profile. Maybe she had not made a choice. Women had a way of dancing with the man who asked, and a lot of the natural-selection business that determined who was first in line, or even who considered himself worthy, got settled among the men themselves.

Jane smiled. "She was a very smart woman. She had figured out that your life is pretty much what you decide it is. She picked the right person to be and spent the rest of her life being that person as hard as she could."

It was true. Whatever had happened to Jane's mother in the first years of her life, it had taught her something she never forgot. Whatever decisions she needed to make were all behind her before Jake had met her. Henry had a wife and Jane had a mother who could have come out of the television shows of the time—house neat and clean, something hot bubbling on the stove, and her looking fresh and crisp and reassuring.

Jake watched her daughter bustling around in the same house, and he unexpectedly had a vision of the future. It wasn't a vision he could take credit for. It was more like a prophecy that he had merely overheard. She was busy inventing Mrs. Carey McKinnon, the way her mother had invented Mrs. Henry Whitefield. He guessed the perfect wife wouldn't act the same these days as she had thirty years ago.

On that score alone, he expected that watching Jane over the next year or two would provide a supplement to his education. And Jane wasn't the same woman as her mother. Henry had made sure she got raised in the old Seneca way, where you didn't waste much breath telling kids what to do, so their self-reliance didn't get stifled. God knew the Whitefields had gotten a whopping return on that investment.

And Janie had a different order of determination entirely. She had consciously chosen to do something with the first part of her life that was more than heroic, because if you saved somebody's life once, that was bravery. When you did it a hundred times, that was pure stubbornness. If she had now chosen to be somebody else, the perfect wife, then letting your feet get in her path on her way to it would be a good way to lose a foot. This new person, this Jane McKinnon, was not going to be somebody you faced down eye-to-eye.

He heard the sound of Carey McKinnon's tread on the front porch and looked down at him through Jane's window. Henry would have been pleased. Jake could see Carey's head beginning to shine through the thin, sandy hair, so he was no kid anymore. Jake hoped he had enough sense by now to understand the nature of the gift he had been given, but he supposed he probably didn't. It often seemed to Jake that wisdom had settled on his own head like a wreath from heaven some time around age sixty, after it was too late to do him much good and was more of an irritation than a pleasure. He said, "Well, I've got to move on, or the damned dandelions will get a foothold on my lawn again and I'll spend the whole summer on my knees digging them out with a knife."

"Good. I thought you were just hanging around to get free medical advice."

"Not me. I want mine duly recorded in an office in front of witnesses so I can sue for malpractice. See you, Mrs. McKinnon."

"See you, Jake."

Jake met Carey carrying boxes up the stairs. "Take good care of her," said Jake. "I'll tell you why at your fiftieth anniversary, if you're not senile by then."

"Better write it down, Jake. Don Herbick keeps calling me from his mortuary to ask about your health. I say, 'Not yet, Don. But keep the motor tuned up.' "

"I suspected you probably worked closely with an undertaker, Dr. McKinnon. But I won't desert you now that you've got a wife to support."

"It's always good to have your unqualified endorsement, Jake. I could hardly ask for anybody more unqualified."

"It's a pleasure to serve." He walked out and closed the door.

Carey set the empty boxes on the floor and put his arm around Jane. "He's right about you. When I walked in, I could hardly believe it. You actually married me."

She smiled, craned her neck, and leaned back against his chest to give him a gentle kiss. "I'm glad to know that you're not here about a refund. But don't assume everything Jake has to say about me would make you happy. He's got no excuse left for illusions about women." She stepped away from him, picked up the dresses on hangers from the bed, and slipped the hooks over his hand. "To business. Take these down and hang them on the pole I've got across the back seat. Do not toss, crumple, or otherwise render them unsuitable for wear. Then report for further orders."

He walked off down the hall and clomped down the stairs. She looked around and began to pull things out of her dresser drawers and put them into boxes. Carey came back and stood in the doorway. "It just occurred to me," he said. "What are you going to do with this house? Sell it?"

She paused and looked at him. Why did she have to be the sort of person who already had calculated everything and made the decisions? "Come sit with me," she said.

They sat together on the bed. "This is one of the conversations we should have had before. I'm through being a guide. I will never take another fugitive and slip him to a new place with a new identity. But for a while, this house is going to be a problem. I can't place an ad in the paper announcing that I'm going out of business. It's more than a little likely that one or two people are going to arrive here in the next year or two expecting to find that kind of help. I know that ahead of time, and I'm prepared to accept the way I'll feel if I find out one of them tried on his own and didn't make it."

"How can you?"

"That's not going to be an issue between us. It's like what the insurance companies call a pre-existing condition. My problem."

"So you're going to keep it here, empty?"

"If we sell it, then maybe—no, probably—one night the new owners are going to be sitting downstairs watching television, and somebody is going to arrive and tell them things I don't want them to hear. Or even worse, one of the chasers will have followed him here. This isn't theoretical. It happened once."

"It's going to be a hard place to unload. I suppose you don't want the phone company reassigning your number either."

"I can afford to keep paying the bills. In a few years there will be fewer people who remember the address. The ones who do will know that it's not the solution to anybody's problem anymore. Then we'll cancel the phone, sell the house, and use the money for a trip around the world or something."

He laughed. "Don't be ridiculous. I'm not going to use up your money. We should have had that conversation before, too. I will support my wife. Keep whatever money you have safe, in case of an emergency."

"You're wrong," she said. "This is the emergency, tonight. Things are happening fast that will get set in cement, so we have to do all of them right. We take each other on, unconditionally. What I used to do has put you in jeopardy: not much jeopardy, but some enterprising F.B.I. agent could still stumble on somebody I helped, and you could wake up one morning to the smell of tear gas and the sight of men in bulletproof vests and baseball caps knocking down the door with a battering ram. There are also some very slimy people out there who still want to find some victim they didn't get to torment enough, and would be very happy to step over your body for the privilege of asking me questions." She paused to let the two unpleasant possibilities settle in his imagination. Then she smiled. "However. I did make a lot of money at it. You'd better share the rewards, because you've already taken on the risks."

He shrugged. "We can use it to buy a lot of life insurance."

She laughed and kissed him. "I'm serious. About once a month or so, you'll see a lot of mail from my two business managers. One is Stewart Hoffstedder. He's fictitious, basically just a mail drop in New York I use to pay bills for imaginary people, so you don't want to know about any of that. The other one is named Michael Mesnick, and he's real. He's a former I.R.S. agent. If you ever fall into the morass of my finances, call him or his assistant, Kim Henmi, and they'll straighten it out. Do not say anything about how ill-gotten my gains are. They think I'm a career consultant who spends too much money on travel and not enough on pensions."

He gave her a hug and stood up. "I'll try to remember." But she was still sitting on the bed. "That's it, right?"

She sat quietly for a moment. "Here is the rest of it. I don't think I want to have to say this twice, because it's a little . . . embarrassing. What I intend to do with the rest of my life is be your wife. I'm not reserving anything, holding anything back. This is the only life I expect to have, so I'm not willing to let it go wrong by little increments because I wasn't paying attention. I will always be available to you, at any hour of the day or night. If you want to talk, I'll talk. If you don't want to talk, that probably means you should try even harder to talk. I'll be listening."

Carey sat on the bed hard, as though his legs had given way. "The sweet old-fashioned girl? Jane Whitefield?"

"Jane McKinnon. Older than old-fashioned," she said. "Primal, actually." He hugged her again, but as he smiled at her, he saw she wasn't smiling. "The only thing I won't do for you is play dumb."

The supple, gentle touch of his arm around her seemed to stiffen, and after a second the arm dropped away. "I hope this is because you're getting everything out of the way at once—housecleaning day."

"It is."

"Then I guess I don't have any grounds to feel insulted. So I'll just say that I love you. I married you. If I had any reason to imagine I couldn't live up to the agreement, I would have to be insane. I don't expect to ever give you any reason to feel . . . insecure. Okay?"

She gave him a peck on the cheek. "Thanks. I'm sorry to bring that up again. Maybe we just know too much about each other. You're a very attractive man, Carey. And you're getting better instead of worse. You like women, and we all sense it, and so we all nuzzle up to you. And you're also a very successful doctor in a provincial town. Everybody likes to be around men like you. None of that is going to change just because you're married. What I'm saying isn't 'Watch your step because I'm onto you.' I'm saying, I know you like women a whole lot. And I like you a whole lot. You're used to variety and excitement and . . . whatever. I understand it. So here I am. I'm not everybody in the world, but I'm going to try to be everything to you. Just ask. No, you don't even have to ask, because I'm saying yes now, for all time."

"The strawberries," said Carey.

She threw her arms around his neck and squeezed him hard, rocking him back and forth. "I'm so glad. You don't know how relieved I am."

"About what?"

"You're nowhere near as dumb as you look. It's just the cheap haircut, after all."

Earl Bliss had once taken a locksmith course during the dead time while he was waiting for his next job to find him. Everybody in his graduating class had been a deep-bottom loser, with no serious hope of finding work fixing locks, but every one of them had learned to handle a pick and a tension wrench. Earl had gotten a great deal of use out of his set, and tonight he held them in his teeth until he and Linda reached the row of mailboxes in the lobby of Pete Hatcher's apartment building. He quickly slipped behind Linda while she watched the hallway, then set the tension wrench in the lock, pulled the pick out of his teeth, and opened the little door that said #6 HATCHER.

He handed the mail to Linda and walked on toward Hatcher's apartment door. Linda had always loved Las Vegas hotels, but the idea that the people who dealt cards and waited on her actually lived in Las Vegas had always depressed her. It reminded her of the summer when she was seven and her mother had gotten two days of work in a bikini movie. Linda had been allowed to believe that she was being permitted a rare glimpse at glamour. She knew now that her mother just had not had a place to leave her while school was out.

Linda had been dragged along and had watched a whole group of them waiting in line for a turn to climb into a dusty trailer on the hot, black road above the beach and wriggle into swimsuits handed out off a rack, all of them women like her mother—pretty, but at twenty-five already looking worn and a little bovine.

They were just supposed to play volleyball behind two men who got into a fistfight, but they knew even less about volleyball than the two men did about fighting, so as the sun rose higher and began to sear eyeballs and heat the sand enough to burn their feet, they got breathless and fell and bumped into one another, a couple of them crying. And then—she never was told how her mother had managed it—they had gone to live with Dwayne.

She recognized him as one of the men who had been up at the trailer that day. He was in charge of something or other—could it possibly have been lighting, on a beach? She remembered the long, dull, hot days of the summer living in that apartment on Winnetka Avenue, the doors of the apartments all open on the blindingly bright, lying promise of the empty pool, trying to catch a breeze that could never come because the building itself blocked it from entering the courtyard. Her mother had thrown Dwayne out in a rage one day and had to be reminded the apartment was in his name.

Linda followed Earl and watched him open the door lock with as little effort as he had needed with the mailbox. When she joined him he was already blocking off the bathroom window with towels and duct tape to keep the light from shining through it.

When Earl had finished, she closed the bathroom door, turned on the light, and took out the mail. They sat on the rim of the bathtub together and opened it. Before she even got to the bills, she could see they had something. It was a thick monthly bank statement with a stack of canceled checks inside. She curbed her eagerness and handed it to Earl, then opened the bills, one by one. There was the power bill, which was worth nothing. There was the phone bill, which was worth a lot because it would have the numbers he had called and the cities. There was a bill for rent on this apartment. When she saw the envelope with the Visa logo on it she felt hopeful, but then she saw it wasn't a bill at all but an offer for a new card. Earl stuffed the mail into Linda's purse and stood up.

They put on the latex medical gloves and began to search the apartment. She could tell that Hatcher had not been given much time to prepare before he left. There were objects here that were worth money and could have been sold or pawned—gold cufflinks and rings, even a good watch with a couple of small diamonds on the dial.

But the same objects told her that somebody had given him a lesson or two about disappearing. Distinctive jewelry was as good as a scar or bright red hair. There were a couple of empty frames on the mantel, but not one photograph was left anywhere.

Earl came and shone his Maglite into the fireplace and carefully examined a pile of ashes. Whatever had been burned in there, it wasn't done for heat in Las Vegas in June. Linda could see that Earl wasn't going to be able to tell what it had been, so she left the room.

She found Hatcher's bedroom and systematically worked her way through it. From his pillow and the sheets under it, she gathered a dozen hairs and put them in a plastic bag. In the bathroom she made a list of all of the brand names she could find—toothpaste, shaving cream, razors, soap, shampoo, hairbrushes. She took the razors in case there was blood from a nick and gathered more hair from the brushes. They were more likely than the others to have been pulled out with the follicles. She searched hard for prescription bottles, so she could find the names of the doctors and pharmacies, but found none, so she moved to the kitchen.

She studied his eating habits. He didn't own anything even mildly interesting—a crêpe pan or a wok or a can of jalapeños or a jar of saffron. She dutifully noted the brand names in the cupboards and refrigerator, but they were all just the ones advertised on national television, and he had kept little food in the house. He probably had worked late at night and eaten in the hotel restaurants. She lingered at the refrigerator, opening bottles and unwrapping packages of food in the freezer because amateurs sometimes left valuables there, and he had left in a hurry.

Linda returned to the living room and found Earl busy unzipping each cushion from the couch to check inside the cover. The couch itself had been tipped over so Earl could look up among the springs. He had also tipped over the coffee table, chairs, and lamps. Earl heard her enter and said, "You get started on the bookcase."

Pete Hatcher had not been much of a reader. Linda wrote down the title, the author, and a description of each book, removed it from the shelf, looked behind it, held it up, and flipped through the pages with her thumb to see if anything fell out or had been taped inside, but found nothing.

At three in the morning Earl began to tip the furniture back onto the depressions in the rug where they had stood before, so Linda went from room to room making sure she had left no signs of her presence.

It was after five when they reached their motel. As soon as they were in the room Linda lay down on the bed and closed her eyes, but

Earl was restless. After ten minutes, the sound of him shifting in the squeaky chair by the table and scribbling things on paper made her open her eyes. "Aren't you tired?"

"Nope," said Earl. "I'll sleep later."

"What are you doing?"

"I'm trying to get a picture of how to do this." He frowned and let his eyebrows bounce up once for emphasis. Linda hated that.

"How's it going?"

"According to Seaver, he had lots of friends. He was one of those guys who had everything. Everybody loved Pete Hatcher. Especially women." The contempt and envy in Earl's voice made Linda feel almost sorry for him. "He may have changed his name, but that isn't going to change. He's not the sort that's going to be lying low for long. He'll need company. He'll be out shaking hands and telling lies about himself." He looked at Linda and she seemed to remind him of something. "He'll be looking for women. According to Seaver, he's a regular old snatch-hound."

"That doesn't exactly limit his movements," said Linda. "Sex he can find anyplace. It would be better if there was one woman he couldn't live without. Her we could find."

"No sense thinking about what we don't have. What we do have has got to be enough to get us there." He consulted his notes. "He used a pro to get out of here. She had him drive out in a car instead of getting on a plane in Las Vegas. It wasn't a rented car, because then he'd turn it in wherever he ends up. So she bought it for him. If she's any good at all, she wouldn't let him stay in Nevada, right? It's too small."

"Right."

"So he's out of state, with the car. He's got to do something with it. If he sells it, keeps it, or abandons it, then it gets new plates and the old plates get returned to the Nevada D.M.V. There are only a million, two hundred thousand people in the whole state. How many cars? About half that many. How many of them are going to have their plates turned in this month?"

"I have no idea, do you?"

"No, but not many."

"What if it's in her name?"

"If it was, it won't be. He has to insure it in the new state, be able to get pulled over and ticketed without getting hauled in."

"He'll need a license to do any of that."

"If she didn't get him anything else, she got him a new license and birth certificate and Social Security card. Those I can't start with.

But the new car registration I can probably get at the end of the month."

"Suppose he just drove it to an airport outside of Las Vegas? That's what I'd do."

"Yeah," said Earl. "We'll have to cover that possibility too. It's not going to be simple. This woman is a problem. She didn't let him make a lot of mistakes. There's nothing easy left: no personal letters, no pictures, not even any old credit card bills. Oh, that reminds me. Where's the bank statement we got? He just might have written a check to his new name."

"In my purse."

He snatched her purse off the doorknob where she had hung it, pulled out the statement, and opened it. He quickly shuffled through the checks, then sighed. "Jesus Christ," he muttered, then slapped the checks down on the table.

"What's wrong?"

"He had a balance of sixty-two thousand bucks. He wrote a check for sixty to 'Cash.' You want to know who took it and gave him the sixty in cash?"

"No bank I ever heard of would. . . . Oh, don't tell me."

"Yep. Pleasure Island Casino. The stupid bastards had him under surveillance, and they let him walk up to a cashier and write a check for his fuck-you money."

"That's got to be his idea," said Linda. "I'm sure he's seen them do it for gamblers. But he wrote it for less than his balance, so he doesn't have the bank and the police looking for him too. That's her."

Earl shrugged. "Her again. Yeah." He stared into space for a few seconds. Slowly, his jaw began to work, the knotted muscles grinding his teeth together. "Let's think about her. She sees, probably before he does, that his time is coming. They've watched him enough so if they were just going to fire him, he'd be gone already. She knows they're not going to take their eyes off him while he's alive unless she makes them. She tells him how to do a quick housecleaning. She gets him a car, and some papers. She arranges to meet him in the one place in Las Vegas where there aren't a million lights. She gets him out." Earl's face assumed a look of puzzlement. "But then she doesn't go too, she hangs in to buy him time."

Linda sighed. "This isn't getting me anywhere. So she bought him time."

Earl's irritated look froze her. "You're not thinking. You know any pros who are going to hang around to get in a fight in an elevator if the client's already driving out with a big head start?"

"No women, anyway."

"No men either. The pay doesn't go up any for bruises. She must have thought he needed the extra minutes, and that means he wasn't safe until a particular time."

"It can't be anything but an airport," said Linda. "He wasn't going to be invisible until the plane was in the air."

"How much time did she need to buy him?" Earl leafed through the piles of tourist literature the maids had left on the coffee table. He found a number and dialed. "Yes. I'm interested in the midnight show, but I want to see another show, too. Is it one of those things where you have a bunch of warm-up acts? What time does the Miraculous Miranda actually get on stage?" He wrote something down. "Then when does the show end?" His pencil scribbled another note. "That's too bad. I may have to catch her act on another trip. Thanks." He hung up and studied his notes. "Okay. Miranda comes on right at twelve, first thing. She's on the stage for two hours."

"So what?"

Earl scowled. "So this woman figures Hatcher is going to have two hours to drive before the lights come on again and somebody sees he's not sitting next to her. He's driving to an airport, and she's planned on two hours. His plane has to leave pretty soon after he gets there, because she doesn't want him sitting in an airport when Seaver's people start looking for him. She wants him to arrive about the time the plane is boarding, so he can walk right in and disappear."

"Seaver said she bought him an hour after that."

"Right," said Earl. "She did it, but she couldn't know in advance that she could do it. How could this one woman think she could tie up those guys that long? No, she was counting on two hours, and whatever she got after that must have been insurance. Figure he drives sixty miles an hour, so there's no chance he'll lose twenty minutes getting a speeding ticket."

Linda stood up and pulled the map out of her suitcase. She measured 120 miles on a piece of dental floss, tied it to Earl's pencil, and ran it in a circle around Las Vegas. "Kingman, Arizona, on Route 93; Bullhead City, Arizona, on 95. Maybe Lake Havasu if he pushes it on Route 95 south. Baker, California, on 15 south. There's no airport for another hundred and twenty miles, so scratch 15 south. Nothing at all on 93 or 95 north, so scratch them. That leaves 93 or 95 south into Arizona or 15 north, into Utah. If it's 93, it's Kingman. If it's 95, it's Lake Havasu City. Both have airports."

"What about Utah?"

"No airport until Cedar City. About a hundred and eighty miles."

"Okay, scratch that too. We're down to two possibilities, then," said Earl. "He flew out of Kingman or Havasu City. Now what we've got to do is see what flights go out on a Tuesday night at those airports between two in the morning and, say, three. There can't be many."

"What if they go to Chicago and Dallas? Little airports usually just feed big ones."

"We'll just hope the other things we're doing give us a break, and tell us which one."

"What other things?"

He pawed through her purse and saw the apartment rental bill. "First thing is, put on some gloves and mail this in with some cash. I want to make sure his landlord doesn't evict him, in case we need to go back there."

"Okay. But where would he fly?"

"Put yourself in his place. This woman must have asked him what places he could go. He can't go to Atlantic City or Reno or some other place where they gamble. He's going to pick a place he knows a little about. A place he likes, right?"

"I would think so. The better he likes it, the longer he'll stay put, and the harder he'll be to find."

Earl clasped his hands behind his head and stared at the ceiling. "No close relatives, no permanent girlfriend, lots of friends, too many to narrow down . . ."

"Vacations?" asked Linda. "Business trips?"

"Maybe. If we can get a hotel charge on a credit report, we'll have a place to start."

Linda lay perfectly still. "I just thought of something. He knows he's in danger. He knows she got him out in the nick of time. He's never done this before, and he doesn't know if we're stuck in this motel or already staring at the back of his head, right?"

"That sounds right," said Earl. "But—"

"What's the first thing he's going to buy?"

"If he dumped his car at some airport, he'll buy another one."

"I'm not saying he won't do that," said Linda. "But what else do they always do? They buy a gun. If he flew out, he doesn't have one. If she set all this up in a couple of days, she probably wouldn't have time to get him one and leave it for him in the new town. Unless it's stolen, she'd still have the five-day waiting period."

Earl grinned and squeezed her so hard her neck hurt. "Whatever else he does, he'll do that. And that puts him on a list. It's a list we can get, because it's a public record. She'll probably tell him not to, but the minute he's on his own in a strange place, looking over his shoulder, he'll do it." He sat down and wrote more notes. "First, we've got to find out what airport he used, then what flight he took. Tomorrow I think we'll drive into Arizona and see if we can find a car with Nevada plates that got left in one of those two airports at two in the morning on Tuesday."

Linda Thompson pumped harder on the stationary bike, slowly adding speed, watching the digital readout on the little electronic podium in front of the handlebars. Thirty miles an hour, thirty-five, forty. She moved her legs faster, then pushed the thumb-lever forward to jump to a higher gear, and the speedometer told her she was going fifty. She gradually worked the gears back until the pedaling was almost effortless. She kept moving her legs for a long time to avoid getting knots in her muscles, but she had lost interest in the machine. Nobody went fifty on a bicycle. The scale was designed to give suckers a warm, cozy feeling.

She dismounted and looked out the glass wall of the exercise room. She was still alone. The gawkers were probably at their sales meetings. She went to the weight area, did a few more bench presses, a few more curls, then went to work on her latissimus dorsi, always using light weights and many repetitions to keep the muscles supple and avoid adding ugly body mass.

She had been eager to begin hunting, and it was frustrating to be stalled for days right at the start. Hatcher might have been dumb enough to ditch the car at the Kingman airport or the Havasu airport, but the woman had not been dumb enough to let him. Earl wasn't saying it yet, but none of the flights out of either airport fit the schedule. The woman wouldn't set it up so that Hatcher had to drive out of Las Vegas at midnight and wait in an airport until seven for a flight. That was the kind of thing they did later, when she and Earl were getting close, and they were scared and desperate. At the beginning they still had a choice, and the first moves were smooth and efficient.

She walked into the tiny changing area and came out the other door in her swimsuit, cap, and goggles. She ran her toes along the surface of the water and verified that it was cold. It was a pretty good trick to have a cold swimming pool in a place where it was over a hundred degrees in the shade. She slipped in and endured the shock, then began to swim slowly up and down, warming her body and letting the long, slow strokes stretch the muscles and clear her lungs. It was already nearly eleven, so she decided she would do only a half mile and get out. Hotels started to get busy around noon, even in places like Havasu, Arizona. She resented having to do everything in the morning each day. Linda was a night person.

When she had finished her swim, she slipped back into the dressing room, and in a few minutes she was walking back up the hallway of the hotel. She opened the door and found Earl sitting at the table, tapping the keys of the laptop computer. Then she saw that the bags were packed.

"What is it?" she asked. "What are you looking at?"

"Airline schedules." Earl grinned that strange grin he had. At times like this his face seemed more animal than human. "I think I figured out why none of the flights he could have gotten out of Arizona fit."

"Why not?" She set down her gym bag and waited. She was relieved that he had not made her bring that up. But he must have found something else. He actually looked happy.

"Listen carefully," said Earl. "He takes the car from the parking lot in Las Vegas. It's about midnight. He drives two hours south toward Kingman or Havasu, Arizona. What time is it?"

Linda shrugged. "Two o'clock. Nothing takes off for four or five hours, and then it's just local stuff."

"Right. Suppose he doesn't drive to Arizona. Suppose he drives north about a hundred and eighty miles at sixty miles an hour. He's at Cedar City, Utah. What time is it?"

"Three o'clock."

"Nope. Four o'clock. He's crossed from the Pacific time zone into Mountain."

Linda sat on the bed. "But Utah is in the same time zone as Arizona."

"Yeah, but Arizona doesn't do daylight savings time. That's why we didn't have to set the clocks forward when we got here." He looked at her intently. "Okay. He's driven three hours to Cedar City. It's four o'clock. What time is it in Las Vegas?"

Linda lay back on the bed and stared at the ceiling. "Three o'clock. She's just finishing up with Seaver's men."

Earl nodded. "We ruled out Cedar City because it was too far to reach before Seaver's men started looking. I would have ruled out his flight, too, because it left so late. She couldn't have hoped to buy him enough time to make it, so why would she bother to buy him any time at all? But it wasn't late. It was just the amount of time she was buying for him. It's Flight 493 to Denver, at four eighteen A.M."

Earl looked at her expectantly, but she opened her suitcase, took out a comb, and walked to the mirror.

"Aren't you interested?"

"Interested?" asked Linda. "Oh, sure."

"Then why aren't you happy?"

She sat down on the bed facing away from him to comb her hair so he couldn't see her. "I was thinking about them. Hatcher and that woman. It's such a simple trick, and I'll bet when they thought of it they were laughing at us."

J ane heard a noise in the dark outside. She sat up and listened. The noise came again. She crept to the wall beside the bedroom window and leaned slowly to the side to bring one eye to the edge of the curtain to see. The wind was blowing from the east, making the long, leg-thick limb of the old maple tree behind the house bob its heavy foliage up and down. When it moved, there was a creak. There it was again, a rubbing sound that came once, then was quiet, a sound an intruder would make while he slipped into the house.

She stepped back from the window and watched the soft, hot wind blow the curtain inward so a little glow of moonlight showed her the room. Sprawled on the other side of the bed was Carey, his eyes closed and his jaw slack in an almost-snore, a long silence and then, after it seemed too late, a soft, gentle indrawing of breath. She admitted to herself that she would probably wake up this way for a few more months. She had slept—happily fallen asleep—beside a few men over the years, and Carey was one of them. But now she was sleeping in Carey's bed in the house where Carey had been a baby, which was now her house too. She had been in another life too long, a place where noises that might be intruders didn't always turn out to be made by the wind. She sat on the bed and spent a minute staring at him. She let herself adore the big foot sticking out from under the sheet, the long, hard muscles of the arm. She leaned over to stare at his eyelids. She could see his eyes moving in little nervous twitches underneath, and she knew he was dreaming.

She resisted the urge to touch him. She was his wife now, and that was different. She was supposed to take responsibility for the fact that he had to be at the hospital at six if he was going into surgery at seven, not wake him up and ask him what he was dreaming. She slowly lowered herself beside him, then lay on her back, closed her eyes, and listened to the wind fluttering the leaves of the maple outside the window until they made no sound.

After a time, she sensed from the way that the trees around her kept revising their shapes until she got them right that she was in a dream. It was night, and low, thin clouds made the moon a small ball with a rainbow ring around it. She didn't like the dream, but when she tried to fathom why that was, she found she had already known the answer before she had wondered. It was because the place where she was standing was familiar. She had not moved. She was still on the ground where Carey's house was going to be built some day.

She felt uneasy as she looked toward the street, because she saw only a narrow gap in the trees. There was no use trying to walk and find her way home, because if the path was there, the road was not yet on top of it, and the forest still stretched like this from the ocean to the Mississippi, and from the tundra to the Gulf of Mexico.

Jane tried to fight the growing sensation that she was being watched. She tried to force herself to be rational. This might be the Old Time, but that didn't mean there were such things as witches. There were no witches. If there ever had been, they had disappeared from the earth before Jane had been born. But her own memory told her she was lying.

She had been in the courtroom in Atlanta when the judge had looked past little Max Curtin, who sat behind the table that came up nearly to his chin, not seeing his pale face and thin bird-bones showing he hadn't just fallen down a lot but had not even been given enough to eat. The judge could see no grounds to take him away from his cousin. But the cousin had heard the words, and turned around quickly to gaze at Max Curtin's face, and the cousin's eyes had glowed, not only in triumph, but because he was drinking in the sight of the terror and despair that showed in the little boy's face. The Grandfathers would have taken one look at the cousin and known he was a witch.

She could feel the Workers of Evil were out there, feel them turning their attention to her. She had been thinking about them, and they had heard her thoughts, and now they were looking up, their faces vacant but alert. They were somewhere in the forest, and they began to turn and move toward her. She could feel the emptiness that was in them begin to fill up with excitement, anticipation. They were concentrating on her now, thinking about how happy she had been, and how easily that could be taken away from her. And they were coming.

Jane caught herself worrying about Carey sleeping unprotected in his bed, and she felt a jab of alarm. She had to force herself to hide him in the back of her mind, where they would not find him. She turned her attention to the witches. As long as she concentrated on them, they would see only their own reflection in her mind. There had seemed to be dozens of them when she first had thought of them, all pricking up their ears to search the air for her. But now she saw that they had winnowed themselves down to just two. Because they stood for all witches, they had to be a man and a woman.

There were footprints on the path, so sooner or later it had to lead to a place where people lived. Jane set off and followed it, then worked up to a run. It was hard for Jane to run on the trail at night, and she was ashamed of how clumsy she had become. She had been lazy for the past three months, and she began to get winded after only a hundred yards. Her foot hit the edge of the path, where it was higher, and she tripped. She gave a little gasp of surprise, and she knew it had reached the man and the woman and told them she had been flushed from hiding.

Although they were far behind her, only now reaching the clearing where she had started, she had no trouble seeing them. The man burst through the bushes, breaking branches and trampling the brush at his feet. He saw the path. He hunched over and stared down to read it for fresh tracks. He leaned forward on his knuckles, and his heels came up like those of a runner at the starting blocks. He grinned with a horrible emotion that looked like appetite, and his grin changed him. His lips kept moving, curled upward, and his bared teeth seemed to grow. His heavy jaw thickened, and he sprouted hair along his back, and then his haunches and arms. His small, black eyes lost none of their intensity as he started to move along the path on four feet.

The woman was quiet. She seemed to materialize out of the forest without moving a leaf, as though her feet didn't quite touch the ground. She stood still for a few breaths, listening. Jane didn't let herself think about what the woman was sensing about that place, but it was why Jane was trying to draw her away from there. The woman didn't hurry. She watched the man lumbering away down the path, growing bigger and heavier, his claws now long and black and the fur thick and impenetrable. He was a wolf.

The woman smiled to herself and held her arms up, her long, graceful fingers fanned out, made longer by her pointed nails. She looked up at the moon glowing through the clouds, ringed with the faint colors of the spectrum, and as she did, she seemed to rise. Her fingers were impossibly long now, her neck was elongated to look up-ward, and her face in the moonlight was beautiful and ghostly. The bright, liquid eyes opened wider.

Jane could see the fingers were the shafts of feathers, and she watched the feathers spread along the woman's forearms and then all the way to her shoulders. The woman's skin glowed white and smooth and flawless, and she had a soft, shapely grace that made Jane not want to turn her attention away. The arms were definitely wings now. The woman's white neck seemed to curve, stretching up toward the moon, and Jane's heart beat faster—a swan! In the old stories, swans were never evil. As soon as Jane allowed herself to feel hope, it expanded in her chest and she almost cried with joy. The female ap-parition wasn't a witch at all. She was probably some powerful woman asleep somewhere, who was now entering Jane's dream to help her. Jane had acquired an ally, a sister.

But the woman's face had not stopped changing. The eyes kept growing bigger and brighter, and now they seemed to ignite, to burn with a light from inside that looked like fire. Suddenly the woman ducked forward in some wrenching physical reflex like a retch. Her shoulders shrugged, her neck shortened, the flesh of her feet shriveled and left only curved talons. She was no longer human. She gave the great wings a flap, and she soared into the dark sky. She was an owl.

Jane was stung with shock, and in a few seconds the hurt threat-ened to soften and degenerate into heavy-footed despair. She strained to run harder, staring at the darkness ahead to discern the deeper black of the trail ahead of her feet, the empty air between the trees that could show her the way.

Jane could hear the wolf behind her and to her right, his body lean and hard but heavy, crashing through the underbrush. He knew the path because he was a human, and he was cutting across the curves. Jane stepped off the path and ran to the right, into the cover of the forest. She had to go more slowly now, slipping through thick-ets, sliding down inclines and then straining to scramble up the next rise, tiring herself just to get to level ground again. At the bottom of a steep, rocky hill she found the beginning of a stream. She turned with it and trotted for a few hundred paces, splashing along the stony creekbed until she came abreast of a rocky ledge and pulled herself up onto it just because it was difficult and the wolf would expect her to avoid it. Then she shifted her course toward the path, and in another mile she came out onto it again. She knew she had fooled the wolf. Her feet seemed light, running on the clear, even ground.

Then she felt rather than heard the sound above her, not so much a sound as a displacement of air behind her neck. She took two more steps and then whirled and swung hard at the same time so it would be her fist that arrived first instead of her face. Her knuckle felt the soft, downy brush of the breast feathers but swept past, hitting nothing solid at all.

The owl rose high into the air and a high-pitched screech came from its throat, then echoed from the rocky glen Jane had just left. The owl circled above her and called again. Jane could hear the sound of the wolf's claws scraping the stones as it came up out of the gully, then heavy paws thumping the leafy ground, and the grunting breaths growing louder.

Jane turned again and ran. There was no concealment now, because the owl flew low under the canopy of trees, its wings flapping only to make the curves, sometimes a few feet behind and sometimes so close that Jane turned to strike out at it, but always screaming with that almost-human voice to tell the wolf where she was.

Jane ran with a sob in her voice, feeling the futility of it. An owl could see better than she could, and easily avoided her blows, and a wolf could run all night if it could smell its prey. As soon as she had thought of smelling, she imagined she smelled something pungent in the air. Was it something she had invented because she wanted it so much, or was it really smoke? It must be smoke. All she had to do was follow the smoke to the village, a clearing somewhere ahead where people slept in their longhouses and tended their crops and made love and sang. All she had to do was reach a circle of light. She ran beside the path, weaving in and out of the big trees so the owl couldn't swoop in behind her neck with its talons.

The owl seemed to sense that it didn't have much time. Maybe it smelled the smoke too, and maybe it had known where the village was. It stopped screeching and swooped upward.

Jane stepped back onto the path and sprinted, lengthening her strides and holding her head high to open the airway, pumping her arms and knees. She smelled the smoke more strongly now, and she knew she was close. She would dash for the nearest longhouse, duck under the bearskin flap that covered the door, dive through the little anteroom where the corn and beans and squash were stored, and roll into the little circle of light thrown off by the first cooking fire.

She could see a sharp off-turning in the trail ahead, and she knew this must be the path that led up to the village. She cut across a patch of low three-leafed plants she thought were strawberries, but as her ankles slashed through, her skin began to burn. It was poison ivy, but she didn't care. She dashed up the path, climbing higher and higher. She reached the little plateau on top and stopped.

There, in the clearing, was a strange, horrible sight. The wolf had begun to change back into a man, and he squatted on human legs beside a pile of green brush that he had half-ignited with his human hands. It was smoking heavily but giving off no light at all. The man stood and turned his wolf snout toward her. She could see the sharp yellow teeth and the eyes that gleamed like pale gold-green beads. "Hello, Jane," he said. "Smell the smoke?"

Jane heard something behind her. The owl alit and began to change back into a woman. "You're ours now."

"No."

"We're going to make you into a skin woman. He'll flay the skin off you carefully, and I'll sew it back together, and we'll hang you from that tree limb over there. The soft breeze will fill you up a little and there will be a sound like a quiet song coming from your mouth. People passing by on the trail will look up this path and see you. Maybe they'll just want to pass the time, and maybe they'll be alone and running, looking for a place to rest and someone to help them. But they'll stop. They'll step off the trail and up this little path alone."

Jane threw herself on the woman, digging her fingers into the throat with her left hand and drawing back her right for the first punch. She could feel the witch changing shapes under her hand, first the scales of a snake and enough of the neck free so the head could curl around and sink its fangs into her forearm, then the scales turning into thick fur and the body widening into a lynx, the jaws now chewing to get free of the hand.

Jane swung hard and woke to the light streaming through the white curtains onto the polished hardwood floor of the bedroom. She held her eyes open in the glare, her breaths coming fast and shallow, afraid that if she closed her lids the dream would still be there. She spun her head and saw Carey, then slowly began to calm down. She was wet, covered with sweat so her nightgown clung to her. She sat up and waited for the dizzy feeling to pass, then eased her weight off the bed. She looked at the clock radio on the nightstand. It was almost six. She walked down the hall quickly, turned on the shower in the guest bathroom, pulled the nightgown off over her head, and threw it on the floor. In a few minutes she would be clean and clear-minded, and Carey could awaken to hear her making his breakfast downstairs.

As she stepped into the shower, she tried to get over the dream. Since she was a child she had heard people clicking their tongues and saying that dreams of the Old Time had begun to come back. The pessimists said it happened only to Senecas who had begun to forget who they were and what they were supposed to do. They were paying the price for repressing their true inclinations. There were others who said the dreams were returning because the supernaturals had stayed on the land with the Senecas all this time and finally gotten used to the way things were now, just as the Senecas had. They recognized that the people had not changed in any way that mattered, and so they had begun to touch them more often in sleep.

Jane felt the terror and claustrophobia of the dream beginning to wash away with the hot water and mental exercise. There wasn't much mystery about it. She had been holding down a quiet tension since the night when she had agreed to marry Carey. She had done the little she could do to make herself unobtrusive. She had taken a new name and moved into a house that no runner and no chaser could know about. She was living as quiet a life as a woman could. She had even been careful to leave untouched all of the things that pertained to Jane Whitefield: the old house looked occupied, the telephone was connected, the mail carrier still came every day.

She had told Carey that she had kept the house as it was because she couldn't think of a way to keep her old life from popping in to alarm the new tenants. It had not been exactly a lie, but it was part of the truth. What she had not mentioned was that anyone—victim or persecutor—who was able to satisfy himself that she had moved out of that house, and not merely gone on a trip, might keep looking and find this one. The old house kept them one extra step away from here—not much protection, just something that might buy her the time to see them before they saw her.

The dream had been her subconscious mind protesting, reminding her that the few small obstacles she had placed to hide her own trail were pitiful. No matter how fervently Mrs. Carey McKinnon wanted to ignore it, Jane Whitefield could not forget that the trail behind her was full of wolves.

J ane parked her car in the gravel driveway in front of the small frame house under the big hemlock tree. When she got out she stepped into a little cloud of dust that settled on her shoes. A dog in the back yard began to bark, then dashed toward her with menacing yaps. It was a little black mongrel with brown eyebrows, the kind that she had seen running around yapping on the Tonawanda reservation since she was a child, so she knew what it would do before it did. It ran up until it was five feet away, then straightened its forelegs, skidded to a stop on the grass, and began to hop up and down, wagging its tail.

"Maggie," came a deep voice from the porch. "Come." The little dog trotted happily around Jane once, then scampered up the steps onto the porch and ran through the open screen door to alert the others in the Peterson house. "Hi, Janie," said the man. He stood up from his rocking chair so Jane could see him over the railing. He was very tall and had the square-chested, long-legged look that she remembered noting in his father when she had come here with her own father for visits in the old days.

"Hi, Billy," she called. "Is this a good time?"

"There is no bad time," he said as he put a sprig that had fallen from the hemlock into his book to mark the page, set it on the stack on the wicker table beside him, then folded his reading glasses into his shirt pocket.

He met Jane on the walk and let her hug him, then leaned his head down and turned his cheek to catch her kiss. "Married life agrees with you, Janie."

He said it in Seneca, so Jane answered in Seneca. "The old man wanted to come too, but I made him go to work so I could keep being a grand lady who wanders around doing nothing."

As they stepped up onto the porch, he saw her notice his books, and reverted to English. "Just some reading for my undergraduate course in the fall. Basic abnormal psychology."

"What we used to call Nuts and Sluts."

"That's the one," he said. "The department makes me take a turn every third year."

The little dog pushed through the screen door again with its nose, and then a woman nearly as tall as Billy with hair like Jane's came out from behind it holding three glasses of lemonade on a tray. "Hi, Janie," she said. "I thought you might like a cold drink."

Jane took a glass. "Thanks, Vi," she said, and they exchanged pecks on the cheek while Billy took the tray to keep the other glasses level.

Violet Peterson sat on the porch swing with Jane and smiled. Jane looked around her. "Did you sell the kids?"

Violet said, "They're in school, believe it or not. Veronica's taking a computer class every morning, and Delbert's doing art." She glanced at her watch. "I pick them up in an hour."

"So serious," said Jane.

"It's great," said Violet. "If I don't make them do something in the summer they run around in the woods like—"

"Like we did," said Jane.

"Exactly," said Violet. "Kids are wonderful, but anybody who says they don't drive you nuts is in a state of denial." Her lips pursed and she said slyly, "You'll see."

Jane sipped the cold lemonade and listened. The red-winged blackbirds at the edge of the marshland a hundred yards away were calling to each other.

Billy said, "You have something on your mind?"

"You must be a psychology professor," said Jane. "It's kind of a delicate problem. Delicate politically."

"Politically?"

"I came to see my friends Billy and Violet, but before I go, I want to do some lobbying with Sadagoyase."

She could feel the weight of ages as he stared at her. Sadagoyase meant Level Heavens. It was the name that had been given to the member of the Snipe clan who held that sachemship in each generation since the first Sadagoyase, one of the forty-nine who had sat at Onondaga with Hiawatha and Deganawida to establish the Iroquois League. Each of them for a thousand years had probably sat in front of the doorway of his wife's house on a day like today, with the blackbirds calling in the hot sunshine, and listened to a woman like her who had come to talk politics.

"Is this about the gambling?" asked Violet.

"Yes, I'm afraid it is," said Jane. "I'll bet you're both sick of it."

"Not at all," said Sadagoyase. "It's good that you came, because I've been meaning to give you a call about it."

"Me?" asked Jane. "I thought I was being clever sneaking around to the sachem of another clan. Why would you call a Wolf?"

"You said it was delicate politically. It's been voted down four times, but it keeps coming back up. I need to know what key people think, the ones who are educated and can sway public opinion."

"I don't know," she said. "Everything I see about it tells me to leave it alone and let other people decide. I'm not here to offer advice about the general issue. I just wanted to make one little point and skulk away."

"But I'm asking your advice."

"I'm not the one to ask. Whitefields haven't lived on the reservation in three or four generations."

"Being a Seneca isn't a matter of residence."

"I had a mother who started out Irish. A colleen, as they say. It sounds like the name of a dog that's not quite a collie, doesn't it?"

"Cornplanter had a father named O'Bail. Mary Jemison was a year out of Ireland when she was captured. She had thirty-nine grandchildren by Hiokatoo. You want to tell their great-great-grandchildren they're not Senecas? There's probably nobody within rifle shot of here who doesn't carry DNA from somebody who was adopted twenty generations back. It's a nonissue."

Jane sighed. "I would love it if the people could have a little dependable money coming in. There are already over a hundred Indian casinos all over the country, and I heard somebody refer to gambling as 'the return of the buffalo.' But I've got worries. If I say those worries out loud, people I love and respect are going to say things that hurt me."

"What will they say?"

"They'll remind me in that quiet, gentle way people around here have that I've never been poor. And I'll know that they could have said more."

"What could they say?"

"I'm one of them too. Maybe I would say it to myself. There I would be, this doctor's wife who lives in a house like a fortress in Amherst, driving Carey's BMW up to the dilapidated council building to tell them gambling money isn't good for the nation."

Sadagoyase raised his eyebrows. "Maybe living that life makes you objective. The traditionalists, the longhouse people, trust you because they know you're at least as conservative as they are. They're an important constituency."

"I'm an anomaly, and they know it," she said. "I'm a leftover Indian Rights radical from ten years ago. A lot of what I know comes from the Old People, but a lot doesn't. It comes from staring at old archives at Cornell and Rochester that were written by Europeans who studied us the way doctors study viruses. I'm not a radical now. I'm a spoiled rich woman who has a hobby."

"Good for you," said Sadagoyase. "I'm a professor teaching the theories of a dead man from Vienna. Now answer my question and I'll listen to whatever you came to tell me."

Jane shook her head and smiled sadly. "All right. Here goes. I'm not a spiritual believer in the Gaiiwio of Handsome Lake. I don't believe there's anything left after we're dead, at least not in broad daylight like this. But whatever happened when Handsome Lake got drunk and passed out in 1799, he woke up with some sense. I think there wouldn't be any such thing as a Seneca now if he hadn't."

"You want to be more specific?"

"Don't sell any land. Accept as much education as you can get, but keep up the ancient cycle of celebrations. Drinking liquor might be fine for whites, but for us it's poison. Don't abuse your wife and kids the way whites do. And—here it comes—don't gamble."

She glanced at her old friend, but Sadagoyase was waiting in silence. She said, "He didn't mean don't play the peach-pit game or bet on snow-snake matches. He was a warrior, brought up in the Old Time. He got his scalping knife wet at Devil's Hole. He was saying, 'These are the temptations that the modern world is sending our way. Watch out.' I think he was right."

"What about now?" he asked. "Is he still right?"

She took a deep breath and let it out slowly. "For hundreds of years the Five Nations kept the peace, managed a unified foreign policy with fifty or sixty other nations, and played the Dutch, English, and French off against one another. Now on half the reservations there are competing governments and splinter groups, and Iroquois burning their own buildings and taking shots at each other. And every time one side looks like it's losing, they call for intervention by the New York State Police or Quebec or Ontario Provincials, or the Canadian or American federal governments. They've always gotten it, and they always will."

"Are you worried about hard feelings or loss of sovereignty?"

"I don't think those are two issues. They're the same. I'm not saying all of that would happen at Tonawanda. But it would be especially stupid if any of it happened here. Everybody around here knows that in 1838, when the state was kidnapping chiefs to force them to sign the land treaty, not one single chief from Tonawanda let himself be caught. I hope people remember that the reason for that was that the chiefs were willing to risk their lives to disappear, and the people were willing to risk theirs to hide them. That's not just why we're still here. It's who we are."

"So what you're afraid of is just that I'll get dehorned?"

"Not you, Billy—Sadagoyase. Once gambling comes in, you've got to think of what else happens. New York State will want a vested financial interest the way they did with the Oneidas, and they'll have to police the gambling and everything around it."

"That boat sailed in 1821," said Sadagoyase. *"The State of New York versus Tommy Jimmy."*

He needed only to allude to the case because it was one of the legal precedents that had established the boundaries of the modern Seneca world. A witch named Koquatau had murdered a man at Buffalo Creek, and Tommy Jimmy had been appointed by the council to act as her executioner. He had followed her into Canada and, as soon as he had her back on Seneca land, had cut her throat. He had been defended at his trial by Red Jacket, one of the greatest orators of his time, and acquitted on the grounds that he was following Seneca law. After that, the state had asserted its jurisdiction.

"Same principle, different consequences," said Jane. "There's a big difference between having the cops investigate a crime every ten years and having dozens of them move in with you to protect the financial interests of the legislature and its cronies."

"What cronies?"

"Building hotels and casinos can't be done without money from outside. That means some big corporation with investors and boards of directors is going to have more to say about what goes on here than we are. It may have occurred to you that Senecas haven't had a lot of luck trusting either the state of New York or corporations in the past. This state has a perfect record. It has never, even in the most minimal way, lived up to any agreement that it has ever made. It has never even felt itself constrained by federal laws."

Jane could feel that she had talked herself into an agitated heat. She paused, let the passion cool for a moment, and said, "I guess I'm working up to what I wanted to say. I read in the paper that there are already offers from gambling companies on the table. One of them is an outfit called Pleasure, Inc."

"That's right."

"If the decision is that we're not in the gambling business, forget I ever told you this. If there is gambling, make sure no agreement includes Pleasure, Inc."

"Why not?"

"I met a man who used to work for them. They're criminals in the usual ways: skimming money from the casino, feeding illegitimate cash into the games and redeeming the chips with checks and credits to launder it, investing secret profits in illegal enterprises. They're capable of killing people when it suits them."

"How in the world did you meet anybody who knew that?"

"It's just one of those crazy things that happens if you travel a lot. You meet people you wouldn't otherwise."

"You should have paid the airline for an upgrade," said Sadagoyase. "Why would he tell you and not the police?"

"He was afraid of them, and he wasn't afraid of me. I just have that kind of face."

"But—" he began.

"No more questions. I won't answer them, and that will spoil this beautiful day. Use the information as you think best. If you think it will help in council, you can use my name. I can't tell you his." Jane stood up to leave.

"What will you do if gambling comes in?"

Jane gave a little shrug. "I'll give myself an extra fifteen minutes to drive out here in the traffic, and another fifteen to find a place to park."

"All Senecas would be entitled to a share of the profits. Would you take it?"

She shook her head. "No. That I couldn't do."

He watched as she bent down to kiss Violet, her long straight black hair swinging to touch his wife's; she came to him and did the same. Then she turned and walked to her car. As she passed under the big hemlock and the sunlight fell in bright dapples on her head and shoulders, he felt himself losing perspective. He could not help feeling he had just received an official visit from his grandmother's grand-mother.

It was nearly noon. The three men at the far end of the enormous conference table had begun to look bored. Calvin Seaver watched Stella Olson's eyes sweep down the page of her report to the summary. This was one of the reasons why Seaver was in awe of Stella. Some of the people in this room would have decided to hold the big guys' attention by tickling them with cheerful patter, or just droned on, insisting that if these three persisted in owning a casino, they would have to hear all about how it was run. Stella just said in her clipped, soothing voice, "Thirty-two hires, two terminations, eight on medical leave, four resignations, for a net gain of eighteen, which will cover all existing positions until the end of September." She sat down, closed her folder, and watched the three men attentively. Seaver saw Max Foley's eyes slip to one side, then the other, and come to some understanding with his partners. "Are the salary figures in the report?"

Seaver couldn't tell whether the three partners had decided to humiliate her because she had been the one to hire Pete Hatcher or to ask a polite question because Stella had earned the right to their attention, but he knew that probably Stella could tell which it was. She was a poker player, and she seemed to have a gift for reading faces. She came back at them without looking down at her papers.

"Salary and benefits on the eighteen new hires adds up to an additional $52,500 a month. Lower starting salaries on the fourteen replacements offsets $5,833 of it. So the extra cost is $46,667 for this month only. On September first we lost eight regulars who went back to college for additional work, and eight shifted from full to part time. We have three scheduled retirements. We'll make up the $46,667 on October fourteenth."

Peter Buckley smiled. "That's marvelous work, Stella." Even Salateri seemed to make an exception to his habit of never praising and gave her a reluctant nod. Seaver decided they must have given Stella a slow one over the plate. That way when she walloped it out of the park, the others would see how it was done.

Max Foley looked around expectantly. "Anybody have anything to talk about that's more urgent than lunch?" The men and women around the table looked like statues. "No? Then you know where we are."

All of the twenty managers stood up and began to glance at watches, gather papers, and file out. A few of them chatted affably, but Seaver knew it was all harmless banter. He knew because he had periodically tape-recorded the whispers and murmurs, amplified them, and listened to them to be sure nobody said anything once the soundproof door opened that constituted a violation of security.

As Seaver stood to join the queue, Buckley caught his eye and lazily gestured at a chair near the end of the table. Seaver set his papers on the table and pretended to put them in order until the others had gone, then walked over and sat down.

This was one of the times when the three partners looked like one entity, some Hindu deity with six arms and three faces. They all turned to watch Seaver, but Salateri was the face who spoke. "Cal," he said. "We're wondering what stage we've reached on the Pete Hatcher thing."

It was Seaver's impulse to say, "It's taken care of," but he knew that was not what the triumvirate had held him apart to hear. He pursed his lips thoughtfully, then said, "I made the arrangement I mentioned. I gave them one hundred for expenses. We agreed on an eventual price of three hundred, plus any overhead they incur beyond the hundred."

"And?" prompted Buckley.

"They haven't asked for the rest yet."

Foley frowned. "What does that mean?"

Seaver said, "They haven't finished yet."

Salateri shook his head in disgust but said nothing. To Seaver's surprise, it was Buckley who pursued it. "Doesn't that make you . . . a little uncomfortable?"

Seaver resisted the glib, easy answer. "It's not as quick as I had hoped," he conceded. "But I'm not concerned. I picked these people because I was confident that they would be able to find him and take care of it quietly, without the sorts of problems these matters can sometimes cause." He held his palms up. "I still think so. The delay just means that the professional who helped Hatcher disappear also helped him stay hidden for a while."

Foley snorted. "I think it's time to ask a few specific questions. Just who are these people?"

"Their names are Earl Bliss and Linda Thompson. They have a detective agency in Los Angeles."

"Why did you pick them?"

"They've done a few things for me and for acquaintances of mine, and they've always delivered. The choice of specialists isn't very good. They're the best of a bad lot."

Foley's brows knitted. "A bad lot?"

"As a rule, paragons of mental health don't do wet jobs. Usually the people available for that kind of work have felony records. They look like they've spent a lot of time lifting weights in some exercise yard and have lots of memorable tattoos. They've all learned that you can get out of just about any sentence if you've got something juicy to tell the authorities about somebody else, and they're all certain to be in trouble again. So they can be a problem that doesn't go away."

"What's different about the ones you hired?" asked Foley. "Are they paragons of mental health?"

"I can only guess, and I would guess not. But they don't seem to have problems that get in the way. And these people fit the Pete Hatcher problem."

"How?"

"They've done a lot of skip-tracing and bail-jump cases, so they're set up to find people quietly and without fuss. If they get noticed while they're looking, they can say they're on that kind of case, and show licenses to make it believable. There are two of them, and this kind of work is best done in pairs, which is why police officers work that way. If you have to, you can watch a building twenty-four hours a day, and it's very hard to slip behind someone who can look in two directions at once. And one of them is a woman. Two men together are probably a team of some kind, but two people of different sexes are just 'a couple.' "

Salateri seemed to be bursting, but he confined himself to a measured tone. "If they're so good, why is it taking them so long to find one guy? It's been almost four months."

Seaver sighed. "The Justice Department has seventy thousand people, and sometimes it takes them twenty years." He saw that this did not please the three men, and he regretted having let it slip out. "I don't mean to be flippant. But the problem isn't going out and finding the Pete Hatcher we knew. He has professional help. She's probably been doing everything for him. At some point he'll stop paying her, and he'll be on his own again. He'll float to the surface."

Max Foley blinked his eyes, took off his glasses, and set them on the table, then produced a white handkerchief and meticulously cleaned the tinted lenses. "How do I put this?" he asked himself. "The world is a complicated place, full of pieces that somehow fit together, and each one affects the others. Most people just don't know how."

Seaver could sense that what was coming was terribly important, and that he would need to catch every word and remember it. Then it seemed to him that they might be about to fire him. He waited anxiously.

Foley put on his glasses and his eyes widened to look at Seaver. "That's what we do—the three of us here. Together we know how the pieces fit. It can't be written down. It's too much for one person to keep in his head, so we each know one part completely, and some of the rest."

Buckley said, "We think we haven't explained our problem well enough to you."

Seaver began to wonder. There were worse things than being fired. Maybe he was about to hear a description of one of them. "Explained what—Pete Hatcher?"

Buckley nodded. His arm came up in one of his vague, limp gestures. "And so on."

Seaver could feel the danger. "All my life I've operated on orders," he said. "If I got the orders wrong, I apologize. Repeat them, and I'll do my best. But I don't need to know any more than I do."

"Who said you had a choice?" snapped Salateri.

Peter Buckley gave a deprecating smile and said, "You think we're going to tell you something that will make you a liability. That's perceptive, but I'm afraid there's nothing we could tell you that would make you more vulnerable than you already are." A moment went by.

"Now you're thinking that we're going to tell you something intended to give you a better appreciation for the importance of Pete Hatcher: what we win if we win, what we lose if we lose. If that happened we wouldn't be sorry, but that's not why you're here. We're hoping that if we tell you more, you'll think of new ways to help us."

"I'll try," said Seaver.

"You know we gave Pete Hatcher quite an education," said Foley. "We started him in personnel with Stella. Then we had him work customer service on the hotel side for a while. First the tennis shop, then he was a starter at the golf course. Then we shifted him to the casino side. He worked the floor as a runner for the pit bosses." He turned to his partners. "Help me here."

"Finance," said Buckley. "First purchasing, then accounts. Then I think it was entertainment."

"Right," said Salateri. "Ticket sales, then booking." He glared at Seaver. "I think that was when we sent him to you."

Seaver nodded.

"Then we started promoting him. He seemed to have potential," said Buckley. "He was young, not a genius, but not stupid. He didn't care how hard he had to work, he seemed to get by just fine. He had one rare and special gift. That was the way he got along with people. Everybody liked Pete Hatcher: grandmas, little kids, people from foreign countries who might interpret some normal gesture as an insult."

Salateri looked as though he were sucking on something sour. "We gave him a taste of everything. We trusted him with little things, then tried bigger things. He never let us down."

Buckley sighed wistfully. "We began to rely on him. That was where we got into trouble. Las Vegas is a special place. There's never been anything like it in the world. When the country goes into a recession, we do better. People flock here in the summer, when you can burn your hand on the roof of a car. Sometimes it seems as though the laws of economics don't apply here. But they do."

"This is a business like any other," said Foley. "If this company is going to survive, it has to diversify, expand, form alliances. Staying put means dying. We've presented Pleasure Island as a family attraction. We may have done ourselves incalculable good for the future, but in the meantime, it has cut the number of dollars we take in per customer. Kids don't spend much. All they use is the beds and the food, which we practically give away to attract business."

"We've looked into other areas," said Buckley.

Foley said, "One we've been studying is off-site gambling. The attraction is obvious. At some point, the number of people who can fly here and bring serious money to the tables will reach a peak. Other companies have already figured out that they can start casinos near big population centers—first in New Jersey, then on riverboats in the Midwest, then Indian reservations. Each casino somewhere else clogs one healthy artery and turns the flow from there into a trickle. So we looked into growing some new arteries."

"You're thinking of building more casinos? When?"

Foley shrugged. "This has been in the works for several years. After some study, we decided that the most promising idea was Indian reservations. We put fifteen reservations under scrutiny, and came up with one we want."

"Where is it?"

"Upstate New York. Draw a triangle from Rochester to Buffalo to Niagara Falls, and it's in the middle. It's less than two hundred miles from Cleveland and Toronto, less than four hundred from New York and Philadelphia, less than five hundred from Baltimore, Detroit, Hartford, Indianapolis. It sits just off the New York State Thruway. If you go by car from one of those cities to the other, you may very well have to go past it."

Seaver looked at the three men, keeping his expression empty. He had no way of knowing whether it was a good idea or madness.

Buckley seemed to read his mind. "You're thinking that we're not exactly diversifying. But we are. Think of a full-service world-class resort. Casinos and hotels, of course. That's our strength. Only this time they would be exclusive, on land only we had access to. But best of all, we could offer things that nobody else can do, anywhere."

"You could?"

"An Indian reservation is a peculiar place, in the law. They can already sell tax-free gas and cigarettes. Why not foreign cars? High-ticket jewelry? Designer clothes? Appliances? Besides the tariffs, the sales tax in New York is eight and a half percent."

"Are you saying that's legal?"

"It hasn't been tried yet. We think we could use the precedent of those companies that sell tickets to police benefits. As long as they give a cent to the police, they can keep ninety-nine for overhead and profit. We give a cent to the Indians and they still make millions a year. This could all be in the open. But what would not be in the open is even more intriguing. Indians have exclusive hunting and fishing rights on their land, with no external regulation. We could have live hunts with game we release: bag a rhino in Upstate New York. We could build a private port a few miles north, on Lake Ontario, connect it to the resort by rail, and offer cruises: package tours for Mom and the kids. For Dad, maybe a members-only junket with high-stakes games and even some exotic companionship. We could rotate girls in and out maybe once a week. The port would also give us access to the St. Lawrence Seaway into the Atlantic. We could take anything out, bring anything in." He looked sad. "It was all intriguing. Very intriguing."

Seaver shook his head. "I never heard a word about any of this. I'm amazed."

The three smiled. "The world is a complicated place," said Foley. "No one head can carry all of the pieces."

"What about Hatcher's? Is this what he knew?"

Salateri muttered something to himself that could have been a curse. "Hatcher knew nothing about this, because none of it has happened yet."

"There have been delays," said Foley. "The Indians have to accept the idea, and we haven't really approached them yet, just left our card, you might say. First we needed to do feasibility studies, find out what wasn't possible, then make it possible. The big delay has to do with the Indian Gaming Act. The federal law says that gambling is okay under conditions established by the state where the reservation is. Before we go handing money to a bunch of Indians we needed to be sure that we could get the state legislature's approval. And we had to make friends in Albany and Washington."

"How do you do that?"

Buckley smiled. "We'll have to learn about the Indians—keep them in the dark while we study them. Politicians, on the other hand, are a tribe whose customs we know."

"Hatcher handled the payouts," Salateri blurted.

Seaver frowned. "I thought he didn't know anything."

Salateri scowled defensively. "It was all indirect. We didn't want to see a videotape with a time and date in the corner and a shot of Hatcher counting out hundred-dollar bills to some New York politician in a hotel room. We set up a fund."

"What kind of fund—cash?"

Buckley said, "It was a corporation that received some of its money in cash. We had a lot of land—here, in San Francisco, in Los Angeles—which we sold to the corporation for an imaginary sum before we brought Pete in. We converted various plots to parking lots—put asphalt over them. Pete was in charge of taking the money we said came in, and paying it to people we said were investors or creditors. He paid it to other corporations, middlemen, girlfriends, relatives, some to bank accounts in the Cayman Islands."

"And Hatcher didn't know what he was doing?"

"Never," said Foley.

Salateri said, "He might have suspected that the money that started the corporation came fresh from the casino tables. There were a couple of times when he told us the numbers on the official slips were lower than the count that night. Max told him that it was because we needed a lot of cash in the vault in case somebody hit the million-dollar jackpot on the big slot. That way we could take publicity pictures of the guy up to his ass in hundreds. The money only gets reported when it's taken out of play."

"He bought that?"

"Maybe for a while, maybe never. He stopped asking. The worst he would have thought was that we were still skimming cash and mixing it in with the take on the parking lots." Salateri shook his head. "Can you imagine that, after all we did for him? He turned his back on us because we were taking money out of our own casino— our own money! I still can't believe it."

Buckley shrugged. "We should make it clear that the corporation with the parking lots and so on wasn't the problem. There was nothing wrong with it but where the money came from, and there's no way he could have traced it. I think he resented the fact that he was the one who signed the slips with a short count on them." He gave a puzzled little smile. "You see, that was enough to cost him his virginity."

Seaver stared at the floor for a moment, then looked up at the row of three faces. "So the problem is that he can say he's pretty sure that at one time, money was being diverted from the games and put into his own corporation. Then he paid it to a lot of people he didn't know? I'd say let him."

"Let him?" Foley looked troubled.

Seaver said, "When I was a cop, we needed evidence of a crime."

Peter Buckley looked at him kindly, sympathetically. "I'm afraid you're missing the problem. Pete Hatcher doesn't know anything. If he somehow strained his capacities and figured out the names of the people in New York State who ultimately received the money, he never heard of them. They're state legislators and bureaucrats and party functionaries in a distant place. People in their own state wouldn't know who they are. But the F.B.I. would. And if they heard the little that Pete Hatcher could be assumed to remember—say, four or five names, dates, and amounts—they could trace the money backward to the accounts Hatcher controlled, and then forward to find out where the rest went."

"But even if they did, the most they would be able to prove was that Pete gave money to politicians. Maybe that it came from here, but not who took it. If he signed for it, then he took it. And half the equation is missing. You have no interests in their state, and they aren't doing anything in return for the money." When he saw that the three men were looking at him without changing their expressions, he said, "You abandoned the project, right?"

"No," said Max Foley. "Unfortunately, it isn't right."

"Why not?"

Salateri's impatience made him look as though he were swelling up. "There are people in New York State who are already in the gambling business. They are big, scary people. In the twenties, if they didn't like you, they mixed a tub of cement and put your feet in it. Now, if they want cement, they make a phone call and five hundred cement trucks arrive, with fifty government building inspectors to certify they did it right."

"What have they got to do with this?"

Salateri's eyes narrowed. "You think we can go into their front yard and set up a business they've been in for a hundred years and expect them not to notice? They needed to be consulted, mollified."

Seaver was beginning to sense the gravity of the partners' predicament. "Did Hatcher pay them too?"

"He doesn't know that either," said Foley. "The Justice Department would take about thirty seconds to figure it out. And what Hatcher paid them wasn't to buy them out. It was to buy them in. Without their help we wouldn't have known which politicians could be paid off, how to approach them, where to put the money."

Seaver frowned and considered. "I know I'm being slow, but let me be sure I understand where we are—"

"For Christ's sake!" Salateri shouted. "Hatcher doesn't know he knows anything! But if the F.B.I., the New York State Police, the Nevada Gaming Commission, or the fucking dogcatcher hear a word of it, they'll know everything!"

"It seems to me that if we could somehow separate the issues—"

Salateri was white with rage. "What did they teach you in the police academy—how to shake down doughnut shops? We have one deal that connects a Las Vegas casino, half the politicians in New York, and the Mafia. In one deal! That blows the politicians, who might have to go get a job. And that blows seven or eight fat old grandpas, who have to spend their last few years locked up with friends and relatives. But not us. We're not going to jail with them. They're not going to let us make it up the courthouse steps to hear the charges."

Buckley looked at Seaver with gentle regret. "It seems to us that we can't pull out of this and tell them we managed our business badly. We can't let them get an inkling that anything is wrong. We're staying alive one day at a time by convincing them that we move slowly, cautiously, prudently."

"This is something they respect," said Salateri. "For five generations they've been nibbling away at the world like termites, until now you can't pull a board off a toolshed without finding them behind it. The problem is, the longer we bullshit them, the harder they're going to take it."

Seaver squinted down at the carpet.

Peter Buckley said, "You're thinking we should tell them the truth and ask them to find Hatcher for us."

"Well," said Seaver, "I was considering it."

"Very alert of you," said Buckley. "They could certainly do it."

"Sure," said Salateri. "They have people in every city in the country. He couldn't run to Europe, because they had that sewn up before Great-Grandpa got on the boat to come here. In South America, Southeast Asia, North Africa they have drug suppliers with armies to protect the crop. I never heard of them having anybody at the South Pole, but I wouldn't rule it out. They'd find him. But he doesn't know much, and we know a lot. Who's the biggest threat? And they don't have to hunt around and find us to end it."

There was a moment of silence to give Seaver's mind a chance to catch up, to understand. "What would you like me to do?"

Foley said, "We're thinking of hiring a second team. Maybe a third. Pay all of them. Whoever succeeds gets a bonus. How does that strike you?"

"It makes me nervous," said Seaver. "Earl and Linda are good. Most likely, by now they know where he is, or at least what region. If they find him and there are other people nosing around, they'll notice them. They'll have to assume those people can only be bodyguards for Hatcher, or police of some kind. They'll kill them. Or try to."

"So what?" asked Foley.

"Then it's not a clean hit where an anonymous newcomer came quietly and went quietly and nobody notices. It's a fight between professionals with lots of gunfire and unburied bodies and blood."

"And?"

"And, as Bobby pointed out, no matter where this happens, it's in the middle of some Mafia family's territory. They're going to want to know who these shooters were, who they worked for, who they were after. It would be hard to imagine them not turning up Hatcher.

If he's killed or wounded, he'll be identified. If he gets very lucky and escapes while our own shooters massacre each other, somebody will survive, and the local family will hear Hatcher's name."

Buckley stared at Seaver with interest. "Any ideas that would get around those problems?"

"Not offhand. I'll think about it."

"How about if we had somebody at least as good as Earl and Linda, somebody they know by sight, whose interest in Pete Hatcher won't require any explanation? Somebody they'll see as an ally?"

Seaver's collar tightened and he began to sweat. "I don't think they'd see it that way. I don't know where they are. There's no way to call them off, or warn them."

"But they wouldn't shoot you, would they? How could they expect to get paid the three hundred thousand if they killed their employer?"

"They couldn't, but—"

"Good," said Foley.

Seaver flailed hopelessly. "But what would happen here? Who would run security for the hotel? The casino?"

Salateri blew out a breath in a mirthless chuckle. "Your errand boy, Bennis, or somebody. Who cares? If you don't get Hatcher before he talks, we won't have a hotel and casino," he snapped. "There'll be a bunch of U.S. marshals in here running the place for the government, or a bunch of paisans running it for the ones we screwed in New York."

Buckley's voice became avuncular. "I think it's rightly your responsibility now, don't you?"

Seaver sat in the chair, helpless.

Foley scribbled on the pad at his elbow. "Give this to Eddie downstairs." He tore off the sheet and held it out.

Seaver glanced at the small note. "Give Seaver whatever he wants. M.F." Seaver stood up. He took a step, then paused and looked at the three men. He knew that there must be an answer, but he could not bring his mind to stop racing long enough to concentrate and find it.

"Good luck," said Buckley. His cheeks constricted to bring up the corners of his lips in a false smile, then went slack again.

"Don't let the door hit you on the ass on your way out," Salateri muttered.

T onight was a sort of birthday, because David Keller was three months old. He had spent the time cautiously, patiently finding out who that was. He had spent the previous thirty-three years acquiring a working knowledge of Pete Hatcher, and now most of that work had been wasted. Any quality that David Keller shared with Pete Hatcher would probably get him killed. That was the most distinctive characteristic that David Keller had been able to establish about himself, and it determined all of the others. David Keller was a suspicious, fearful person. He lived in a two-bedroom apartment on the fourth floor of an old brick building in downtown Denver that had no elevator and overlooked a triangle of grass that wasn't big enough to be called a park. It looked like a spot where the surveyors had not been able to make three roads intersect and had to leave a scrap.

In the evening, when David Keller cooked his simple dinner and washed the dishes at the small, scratched porcelain sink, he could look out the window, across the tops of trees, and see the side of a topless bar with a turntable contraption over the door that had a female mannequin dressed in a sequined outfit revolving around and around like a mechanical dervish. The apartment was small and dark, built at a time when lumber must have been cheap, because everything was old, varnished wood—a built-in sideboard in the dining room and cabinets in the living room and, everywhere, ten-inch baseboards.

David Keller lived in his little apartment like a man holding his breath under water. In the two conversations that Pete Hatcher had with Jane Whitefield he had memorized a few lessons that David Keller now followed mechanically. "Most people who don't make it get caught right away," she had said. "If you can put a break in the trail that lasts three months, they won't have much to work with, and there won't be as many people looking."

He had asked, "If I last for three months I'll be okay?" and she had shaken her head. "I'm just saying, if you're going to make a mistake, don't do it before then." Pete Hatcher had been the kind of person who had wanted to know all of the limits—where can I go and what can I do?—but David Keller was not.

David Keller carried the limits in his mind with a shuddering sense of awe that he should ever have considered going near them. It was lucky for him that he had somehow come to his senses before he had made some impulsive mistake.

Women had always taken up an enormous portion of Pete Hatcher's thoughts. He loved to look at them, to smell the scents that hung in the air close to their hair, to touch their smooth skin, to hear their soft, high voices. He savored the unconsciously graceful little movements they made with their hands. But Pete Hatcher had no philosophy. He had never set aside the time to sit by himself, wondering why things were the way they were. That never seemed to get anybody else anywhere, so how could he be so unrealistic as to think he, of all people, could figure it all out? He had simply known the obvious—that the standard, plain, no-frills human being was a man. There could be no purpose for women to be so radically different from men unless they were created to be enjoyed and cherished.

One afternoon nearly two months after David Keller had arrived in town he had gone to a supermarket on a Sunday afternoon. A pretty woman in her early thirties wearing a Denver Nuggets baseball cap with a long chestnut ponytail stuck out through the back walked past him, and their eyes met. A couple of times after that, when he went up an aisle, his eyes lingered on her again—on the black, skin-tight spandex bicycle shorts that the oversized sweatshirt didn't hang low enough to cover the way she pretended to think it did, because women bent at the waist to reach the lower shelves, instead of at the knees. Once, she had caught him appreciating her, and she gave a little smile of acknowledgment.

Suddenly, without warning, Pete Hatcher had struggled to come to life. The opening lines had begun to rise to his throat automatically: "Do you ride a bike?" he would say, just in case she didn't, and he had to talk about something else. "Riding in Denver traffic is taking your life in your hands. I guess I'm not as good as you are." She had been reading the label on a jar of wheat germ, so he could say, "I heard that stuff is good for you, but is there any way to get around the taste? What do you put it on?" There was nothing to saying the first words. It usually took him five or six syllables to see in the woman's eyes whether she was pleased that she had attracted him or startled that some creep had been drawn to her. He had never made a mistake after a whole sentence, because women were much more alert and aware of the people around them than men were. He knew that if he noticed a woman, she had noticed him first. She had already decided what she would do if he spoke.

He knew he had to push Pete Hatcher down, strangle him before he got David Keller into some kind of trouble. Then he met the woman again on the far aisle, which was lined with wine bottles. It was a bad place, because it was out of the way, almost private. He had to look at some labels and put a bottle in his cart to assert his right to be here.

But she came to him. She said happily, "I guess you don't like football either."

David Keller was startled. Football? Then he remembered. It was late summer, and preseason games must be on television already. He hadn't owned a television set in months, and what might be on it had slipped his mind. He smiled and shrugged. "I've been known to watch a game now and then, but it's such a beautiful day."

"Yeah, it's great, isn't it? I've been out riding my bike." Her voice was high and cute, and she moved in little explosions of excess energy that reminded him of the quick, abrupt dartings of a little bird. He was fascinated. He caught himself wanting to see her do things—any things, but he was already allowing his imagination to form preferences as to what they might be.

"Riding a bike?" he said. "Riding in the traffic around here is too much for me. I guess I'm not as good as you are. You're in better shape, too."

She gave him the hint of a smile. It said, "That already? Be patient." But her voice said, "It's not bad on Sundays. If you like off-road, you've got Bear Creek, Cherry Creek, Chatfield . . ." Her bright brown eyes narrowed. "You're new here, aren't you?"

He felt suddenly scared. "Yes."

"One more southern California refugee, right? Someplace hot and low altitude."

"Los Angeles." He lied with the best smile he could manage. She had instantly known he was a stranger and picked up the quarter of the country he had come from. What was wrong? What was he doing wrong?

She lifted her sweatshirt a few inches so she could reach the pen stuck in the waistband of the tight pants. The flash of white skin forced him to weather a flood of wishes. "Here," she said as she wrote something on her shopping list and tore it off. "If you need directions, just give me a call."

It was all right. She could hardly be less threatening. He took the paper. Above the phone number it said "Kathy." He smiled again and said, "Thanks, Kathy. I'm David . . . David Keller."

She raised an eyebrow. "You don't look like a David."

His heart stopped.

"Maybe a Mike . . . maybe a Jim."

He desperately reminded himself of all of the times when women had said things like this. She thought it was fun to nudge men off balance just a little. He smiled. "I'll give my mother a call and see what she can do."

"You might give it a try," she said. "I guess moms all want their babies to grow up to be Davids. Most of them grow up to be Buck or Ace or something." She was giving him a chance, buying him time to notice that he liked her and think of a way she could be with him that would preserve her self-respect.

It wasn't difficult for Pete Hatcher to think of an invitation. She would like to go pay for her groceries and meet him next door at the health-food place for one of those fruit drinks they made in blenders. She could even have been persuaded to meet him for another ride at one of those creek places she had mentioned and show him the bike route, if they went in different cars. Dinner would have made her feel at a disadvantage because it would mean she had picked up a man and made a date with him. But David Keller was not Pete Hatcher, could not afford to be.

"Well," he said, "I'd better get the rest of my stuff and get home. Thanks." He put the slip of paper in his pocket.

The disappointment hovered behind her bright smile, but she turned to look at the wine bottles on the shelf. "See you." She didn't push her cart away. Instead, she waited and let him move up the aisle away from her.

As he stood in the line at the check-out counter, he was filled with regret and sadness. But for the first time, that feeling was outweighed by something new. He was afraid of her. His disguise was transparent, his identity obviously false. He wanted to leave his shopping cart and slip out the door, hurry along the windowless side wall of the building, and disappear.

After that Sunday, David Keller always ate in his apartment, and when he needed supplies he walked to a small grocery store on Sixteenth Avenue after dark and paid cash for them, then carried the bag home in his left arm to keep the right one free to protect himself.

He had gone to a movie a mile away once, but he had been unable to get used to the sensation that people were looking at him. He knew, objectively, that they were. They might be wondering why a thirty-three-year-old man had nobody to go to the movies with, or they might only be looking at him because when the lights were still on in a theater there was nothing else to look at but a wall of white at the front of the room. But David Keller didn't want people looking at him, and he especially didn't want them wondering. When Pete Hatcher had walked into a room, people had lit up. He could still see them, hear their voices. "Hey, Pete. Have a seat." And he would see pleasure on their faces, and he would make a joke out of it. "What, you're so glad to see me, I owe you money, or something?" He had spent a good part of those thirty-three years learning about Pete Hatcher by seeing him through other people's eyes.

David Keller didn't exactly miss being Pete Hatcher. He had simply begun to realize that being Pete Hatcher had been easy. Being David Keller took a lot of thought, and there seemed to be no reward beyond waking up each morning and verifying that he was still alive. And because when he awoke he found himself still alone, he could regale himself with the strong likelihood that he would be alive to latch the windows and close the curtains that night.

He sat in his little dining room and stared past the gouged sideboard at the mirror above it. The glass had little black specks where the backing was showing through, but he could see himself well enough. He had gotten his hair cut short and lightened it, so he looked a little bit different from Pete Hatcher. The odd thing was that he didn't seem to look like anybody else, either. Some time in his childhood he had been given a game that consisted of a board with a pink oval and a collection of eyes, ears, noses, mouths, and hair. Usually, when he selected features, he could put them together and they would practically scream out what they were: a pirate, a Chinese mandarin, a cowboy. But once in a while, when he put the pieces together, nothing happened. It was simply an oval with two eyes, a nose, and a mouth. That was what he saw looking back at him in the mirror tonight: it was a face, but it didn't seem to belong to anybody.

He had lived for three months on a couple of conversations with a woman he didn't even know. "If you want to be invisible," she had said, "you have to do what other people do. Think average."

"What's average?"

"The average man your age makes about thirty-five thousand dollars a year." He had felt distress, wonder. Could that possibly be all? She had tried to mitigate it. "The good news is that he doesn't save any of it. But he's always doing something. Busy busy busy."

"Busy at what?"

"Watch people. Whenever they're out of their houses, they're engaged in some obvious activity. If you were a cop, you could stop every one of them and ask what they were doing, and they could all bore you silly with details. They're dropping clothes off at the cleaners, then stopping by the drugstore for dental floss, and then they're going to head home for dinner at the time when everybody else is too. An experienced cop wouldn't even have to ask them, because he can read it on them: the way they walk, the way their eyes are set. The people you have to worry about think like cops. Men between seventeen and seventy don't just hang out, sit on a park bench or something. If they're out in a park, they're jogging for their health or walking fast because they have someplace to go."

"Where do I live? What do I do?"

"You rent an apartment. It's in a large building, but not a building that's fancy enough so they do any checking before you move in. I've already found one and rented it for you. I used an identity that's old enough to stand up if it needs to. Nothing else is in your name. I'm your girlfriend. If anybody ever asks about me, we broke up and I moved out."

"What do I drive?"

"For now, nothing. I'll have to get you out quick, so I have no time to do it for you. Here's a short lesson. Leasing a car triggers an all-out credit search. Buying a new car on time does the same. But it's going to be tricky for you to write a check for the full price tomorrow or the next day, because it's what the people who have studied you think you'll do. So don't. What you want is to find a used car for sale by the owner: it's the only market where paying in cash is necessary, and it will keep you off a car company's customer list. Have a mechanic check it out. For most people that's just to see if it's any good. For you, it's also because he'll warn you if it's stolen. Register it and insure it under your new name. Car registrations are public records, and insurance companies sell lists of customers. There's no way to avoid that. Just don't do it right away."

"How long should I wait?"

"If you do it tomorrow, you'll be on a short list. The longer you wait, the longer the list."

"What else?"

"Don't do anything that brings you to the attention of the police, of course. If you see a fire or an accident or a politician, walk the other way. There could be news cameras. Don't vote, file any legal papers, serve on a jury, buy land, buy a gun, or get married, because those create public records."

He had heard the list, and none of those things had been anything he would have done anyway. At any rate, Pete Hatcher would not have done them. He looked at his face in the speckled mirror. The part of this that was beginning to weigh on him was that he had not had enough time to get used to the idea before he had done it. One day he had been Pete Hatcher, walking through the cavernous casino in his tailored summer-weight suit, and a few hours later he had been sitting here in this small, dark apartment in Denver.

She had asked him where he wanted to live, where he could live without being recognized. He had not been able to think of a place. She had rattled off a list of cities and when she had said Denver, he had said yes, just because it was a city where he had never lived, never been for more than an hour or two to change planes, and now even that was safe because it wasn't even the same airport. She had said Denver was okay, because it was only eight hundred miles from Las Vegas, and a person running for his life didn't usually stop that soon.

There were lots of things she had not told him, because there had been no time. She had not told him that David Keller would one day sit in this room and look at himself and find that he had not the slightest vision of a future—not just what to do, or what to expect, but what to want, who to be. And she had not told him that David Keller would be afraid.

It was late. Through the open kitchen window he could hear faint traces of the music from the bar floating up through the still, late-summer air, and cars hissing past it on Colfax. He closed the window and locked it, sat on the single bed in the small bedroom where he slept. He should have felt safe. She had chosen a fourth-floor apartment so he didn't need to worry about somebody climbing in the windows. It wasn't even in a male name, so it would be hard to trace him here. Pete Hatcher had left Las Vegas with over six hundred thousand dollars. He could live like this for ten or fifteen years without poking his head above the surface.

He took his shirt off and lay in the tiny, dark room, on the surface of the bed. He had found David Keller was not comfortable taking all his clothes off in a bed. There was something especially frightening about having them come for him while he was naked, so now he always kept his pants on and his shoes. He had forgotten something. He got up, walked into the kitchen, opened the drawer, and took out the butcher knife. He wrapped the blade in a dish towel and set it beside his left hand in the bed, so they wouldn't see it behind his thigh, and he wouldn't roll over on it. He rested his hand on the handle and lay back in the darkness, feeling the drops of sweat forming on his forehead in the airless room.

As he waited for sleep he thought of the woman in the supermarket. He wished, more fervently now than ever, that he could have responded to her differently when she had spoken. She had been in the market on a Sunday afternoon with nothing much to do, and she had liked him. She had not wanted to put him in danger. She had wanted somebody to play with—to ride bikes, like kids. He had thrown away her telephone number, but maybe he could still find her. He could buy a bicycle, go to one of the places she had mentioned, and just happen to meet her.

No, it was impossible. She would talk, and he would have to talk too—pay out to her an endless series of lies, like beads on a string. There was something too quick about her for that. She would remember what he said, see that bead sixty-seven wasn't the same as bead nineteen. Or she would tell people about him, even make him meet them, and then he would have two or three strings of lies going at once, then more. They would all get farther and farther out of control until he got himself tangled in lies. She would never be in this bed with him, lying with her soft chestnut hair on his chest. Not her, not anyone. The difference between being alive and being dead had all but vanished.

He awoke to the glare of the sun hitting the window above his head and throwing a square patch on the wall. He closed his eyes again and lay perfectly still. If they had come into the apartment while he was asleep, they would have gone straight to the bigger bedroom, and their muffled creaking and rustling would be what had awakened him. He listened for a long time, as he did every morning, at length satisfied himself that no sound had caused him to wake, and sat up. He sensed a change. The world was different this morning.

He went into the big bedroom, laid out some of his favorite clothes—the plain blue oxford shirt, the blue jeans between new and broken in—and stepped into the shower. This was the best part of the day. It always seemed to him that in the morning the universe was starting out clean and fresh. Anything could happen.

It wasn't until he was dressed and eating his breakfast under the open kitchen window that he recognized what was different. It was David Keller. He was through holding his breath.

He found the car after an hour of looking in the newspapers. He knew he couldn't buy something like a Mercedes. Even an Audi or a Saab was pushing his luck. It should be dull and American and cheap. The sliver of an ad said, "96 SL2, 4 door, air cond., automatic, PS. $12,000 OBO." He called the number and he could hear a baby crying in the background. The woman said, "You should probably come after dinner, when my husband is home. I can't answer any questions about it. I don't know a thing about cars."

He made his voice sound worried and disappointed. "Oh. That's too bad. I just got to town, so I've got nothing to drive, and I start work in a couple of days . . ." A little of Pete Hatcher seemed to come back to him. He could sense there was something bothering her. "Oh, I'm sorry. I'm being stupid. Your husband's not home so you don't want some stranger showing up. And of course, I don't want to buy a used car in the dark. So I guess I'm out of luck. . . . Hey, I have an idea. Is the car on the street?"

"No, but I could move it."

"Great. I'll just come by and take a look at it. If it's not what I want, I won't bother you."

"I guess that would be all right."

He took a cab to the house and stood beside the gray car for a time, peeked at the underside, cupped his hands to lean against the window to peer at the number on the odometer, wrote down the license number and serial number, examined the tires. He was running out of things to do when the door of the old duplex opened and a young woman came out on the porch carrying a one-year-old girl on her hip. She had a corkscrew strand of blond hair that kept coming down across her left eye. She had been watching him, as he had hoped, and decided he didn't look like a psychotic.

She said, "You the one who called about the car?"

"Yes," he said. "I'm sorry to come at such an inconvenient time." He smiled at the little girl. "Hi, cutie."

"That's okay," said the woman.

"Well, I'm interested." He looked back at the car. "Is there anything I need to know about the car? Any accidents?"

"No. My husband's dad bought it, drove it for a year, and died. He seemed to like it, and he took care of it. I'm not going to be working again for a while, so we'd just be paying insurance on it for nothing."

"I understand," said Keller.

"Would you like to drive it?"

Keller said apologetically, "If it's all right."

"I called my husband and he said it was okay." As she held out a set of keys, Keller sensed that she wasn't telling the truth.

He took the keys and said, "I'll be right back." Keller drove the car around the block and pulled up in front of the house. This wasn't exactly the way Jane had said to do it. It seemed better. The woman had seen him for a few minutes, could suspect him of nothing, and seemed too busy and housebound to talk to anybody about him. He got out of the car and walked to the porch. She came out and he held up the keys. "I'd like to buy it."

She brightened. "Well, wonderful." After a second she added, "My husband will be happy. It kind of reminds him of his dad."

"Do you know what time he'll be home? I'd like to get this done today." He showed her the envelope. "I brought the money."

"In cash?"

"I didn't want to have to wait for a check to clear. I'm not exactly an old customer of the local banks."

"We don't need to wait for him. Come on in."

Keller followed her into the house. She opened a drawer of the buffet, where she kept the dishes, and pulled out the pink slip. Keller handed her the envelope and watched her count the hundred-dollar bills. When she had finished, she leaned over the coffee table and signed the pink slip and handed it to him.

Keller glanced at the slip. It had been signed by Ronald Sedgely with the new owner as Maura Sedgely, and now she had signed it. The car was hers? There was no husband coming home tonight. Either Ronald Sedgely was her father, and she wasn't married, or she had gotten the car in a divorce from Ronald Sedgely. The discovery made him feel elated, filled with confidence.

He wasn't the only one. Everybody was lying. Everybody was hiding some vulnerability. Opening your face and telling people the truth about yourself wasn't normal. She was normal. She was a single mother trying to deal with a man who called on the telephone and might try to cheat her on a car deal, or might even be a maniac who would rape and kill her in front of her baby. Pretending there was some guy who had to approve the deal and knew all about cars, and just might pop in to protect her, that was the sensible thing to do. She was perfectly normal. He was normal.

Keller drove the car to the D.M.V. to register it, drove to an insurance office he had picked out in the telephone book to insure it, and found that neither was as difficult to do as he had feared. They wanted to know the answers to questions he had prepared for a month ago. Jane had assured him that his driver's license was genuine. It must have been true, because everybody's computer loved David Keller. He had no outstanding warrants, no problems of any kind, and not even any disturbing blank spaces. He had gotten a new license a year ago, after driving in New Jersey for twelve years.

As David Keller drove around town, he couldn't help feeling grateful that human beings were so simpleminded. All he had needed to do to break free of the depression that had been paralyzing him was to get out and drive around in a car on a summer day with his window rolled down. It was such a small improvement that it made him laugh.

It made him even happier when he looked at it in reverse. He had bought the right kind of car in the way Jane had said was the safest. He had bought it from the ideal seller, a woman who didn't even know his name. Maybe he had done it a little early for Jane's taste, but she had not known how invisible he had been for three months. He had made no mistakes at all. And the car made him feel safer.

He would park it somewhere away from his apartment. If they found the apartment, he could sneak down the fire escape, get in his car, and go. If they found the car, he would see them watching it before he went near it. He would hide some emergency supplies inside the car—money, maybe ten grand in a clever place. And what else would he need if they found him?

The clerk in the gun shop was a woman. She was short and gray-haired and probably had been pretty once, but her face looked as though she had spent some time squinting into the sun. When she walked around the counter and he saw that she was wearing a pistol in a holster on her hip, he thought at first that it was some kind of illusion. Then he noticed that everybody in the store was wearing one, even the stock boy with the broom.

She let him stare down through the glass case for a few minutes, then came up and stood beside him. "Anything I can show you?"

He shrugged. "I'm not sure. Yes, I guess so. I just don't know what."

She smiled like an aging dance-hall girl in a Western movie. "Let's narrow it down. You want to buy a handgun."

He smiled back at her. "That's right."

"Are you an old shooter?"

"No. I've never even fired one of these."

"What do you want it for? Target range or protection?"

"Protection. You know, burglars and so on."

She stared at him for a moment as though she were estimating his hat size. "Well, okay. You know, of course, that if somebody comes into your house, what he really doesn't want to see is one of these." She pointed to a short-barreled pump shotgun on the rack behind her.

"I suppose not," he said. "But I'd rather have something small."

She nodded. "And you've never fired a pistol. Are you mechanically inclined? Fix your own car?"

Keller shook his head. "Never."

She opened the case thoughtfully with a key on her belt, selected four pistols, and set them side by side. "There's this," she said. "It's a Beretta 92. A good, reliable nine-millimeter semi-automatic. A lot of police forces use it, and there's a similar model that the army uses. This is the kind of gun that you have to take apart to clean and oil, and put back together right. I don't recommend that for a novice."

"What do you recommend?"

She showed him a revolver with a short barrel. "This is a Ruger SP 101. It's a .38 Special and it's small and lightweight. It doesn't pop up and hit you in the face from the recoil when you fire it. It's easy to care for, and won't let you down." She leaned close to him and spoke from the side of her mouth. "It's the model we usually recommend for women who don't know anything about guns." She watched him for a reaction.

He smiled. "That sounds like just the thing. I'll take two."

"Really?"

"Is that a bad idea?"

"No," she said. "I'd be delighted to sell two." She pulled a set of forms from a tray behind the counter. "Fill these two out, and after the waiting period is up, you can come get your guns." She put away the row of pistols, then stopped, holding the one he had picked out. "As you know, it would be illegal for you to carry a concealed weapon. This is a model you have to be very careful with in that regard. It would be possible to put one of these in your coat pocket and go out without noticing it. Your friends wouldn't see the bulge. Of course, when you reached in and discovered your mistake, the compact size would be a great advantage because you could take it back home without embarrassment." She winked and locked the gun in the case.

Linda Thompson sat at the edge of her chair in the dark and watched the front door of Pete Hatcher's apartment building. She liked looking through the night-vision binoculars, liked the way everything showed up green and glowing. She even liked the fact that Earl had spent nearly nine hundred dollars on them. His aching need for the best toys and gadgets gave her a lever to keep him a little bit off balance. Any time he felt the urge to say something about what she spent, she had been able to point to a gizmo that cost twice as much. She was careful not to let Earl notice how much she liked looking through the binoculars. They made her feel as though she had the senses of some sleek, beautiful animal lying in wait in the jungle, its eyes bright and yellow, able to see its dim-sighted, clumsy, hoofed enemy stumbling through the underbrush toward her.

Tonight she could feel her heart beating in her chest, the blood carrying more oxygen to her fingers and toes than it had since they had arrived in Denver. The air was clear and thin here, and she had hated that until her body had adjusted to the altitude.

Linda was feeding on Pete Hatcher's fear and indecision. Five nights ago she had seen him walk down the street at about nine, and come back at nine thirty carrying a single big grocery bag back to his apartment. He had done the same thing three nights ago. Tonight, she knew he was thinking it was time to go get some more food. She was sure he wanted to get into his car and drive somewhere—to a giant supermarket in some other part of town, or to a good restaurant. He had not done it because he was afraid. He was afraid to go where there were bright lights and a lot of people, even though his craving for them was almost physical. Those moments in crowded public places must be precious to him because they felt like safety, but he seemed to know they were not good for him. People would see his face. His car represented the same kind of problem. He had probably bought it because it kept him from feeling helpless and trapped, but he sensed that he needed to keep away from it.

She saw him at the window of his apartment. He stood to the side in the darkened room and looked out, first at the little park, then up and down the street. She raised the magnification and studied his face. He was getting ready, and he was anxious. She saw him move away from the window. "I think he's coming down," she said.

She listened to Earl's voice behind her ear, but kept the binoculars trained on the front entrance of the apartment building. "Everything's ready," he said. "Don't worry." He was talking to her like one of his dogs, low and soft. She liked it. "Just keep him in sight. That's all you need to do."

She saw Hatcher stop inside the lighted entry and pretend to check his pants for his wallet and keys, just buying time while he studied the street outside for signs of danger. He would do one last thing, and she waited for it, holding her breath. He reached behind him and put his hand under his coat to tuck in his shirt. She had known he would tell her. He was carrying the gun, the cute Ruger SP 101 he had bought a week ago. He had bought it because he was afraid, and now that he had it, he was afraid of the gun. "He's got the gun in his belt in the small of his back, under his coat."

"Fine," said Earl.

"He's out. He's walking straight down the street toward the store."

"Time to go," said Earl.

Linda handed him the binoculars. While he was putting them in their case, he checked his watch. "It's nine twelve. Give him until nine twenty-two to get there and get busy shopping. Be there at nine twenty-seven."

"Right," she said, and went out the door without letting herself look at his eyes. Let him wonder.

As she drove along the dark street, she teased herself gently. It would have been much easier to sit comfortably in the darkness of the hotel room and watch through the night-vision binoculars while Earl popped him with the fancy British sniper rifle through the window. The silencer on that thing would have made the whole episode sound like a bird bumped against the glass and broke its neck. But Earl could never feel satisfied unless he made Linda get a taste of it too.

Earl couldn't just crudely cut him down with a rifle. Linda had to fool him first, make him into an accessory to his own death. He wasn't going to be a leaking corpse lying on a kitchen floor. He was going to be one of those guys who walked off toward the grocery store and simply never came back. If the police got called in a week or two, they wouldn't know whether to look for a corpse or a rent jumper.

David Keller walked out of the small grocery store trying to evaluate the odds. If he continued to walk to Danny's to buy his food, he could just go on buying a little bit at a time and paying cash. If he went to a big supermarket and bought everything he would need for a couple of weeks, he would decrease the frequency of his trips. That would decrease his vulnerability. But he would have to take the car, and he would be seen by more people, and flash more cash, and that would increase his vulnerability.

He hurried to cross the little blacktop parking lot in front of the store where he was lit up by neon beer logos in the window and the yellow sodium light over the tall Danny's Market sign. He moved quickly onto the sidewalk, where he could stay out of the light. Jane had not had time to explain everything to him, but she had told him he would do well enough if he just maintained the right attitude. He reached behind him to feel whether the revolver was riding up under his coat.

As he touched the lump he felt a small twinge of anxiety. She had implied that a gun was not a good idea. She had said, "You're out of Las Vegas, trying to live a new life in, say, Chicago. You see the same car outside your apartment for three nights in a row. On the fourth night, at midnight, you see the car pull up again. Two men get out. After a minute you hear a knock at your door. What do you do?"

"Do I have a gun?"

"Yes."

"I get it ready, hold it where they can't see it, and open the door to see who they are."

"Right hand or left?"

"Right."

"They're your new neighbors, young single guys who go out every night, a lot of fun. They noticed you watching them through the window, so they knew you were up and decided to ask you over for a drink. One of them holds out his right hand to shake. Or they're cops. The good guys. They're watching the neighborhood because somebody has been selling drugs. They came up to see who you are: maybe you're a witness, but maybe the reason they haven't caught the dealer is that there's a lookout, and it's you. At that hour they're going to ask if they can come in to talk to you. Or maybe you were right, and they're professional killers, come to get you. You have the gun in your right hand. You open the door with your left, so you're ready. They know who you are, but you don't know them. They won't hesitate. You will."

"What was the right answer?"

"What would you do if you didn't have a gun?"

He had shrugged. "I guess I'd figure out who they were without answering the door. You said it was after midnight."

"Good," she said. "Now you know the main thing about guns."

"I'm not sure I do."

"They make you act differently. And they're no good unless you're positive. You have to be so sure that you're willing to kill the two men at the door right away—not look closer, or ask them anything, just pull the trigger."

"If they come to my door, intending to kill me, shouldn't I do that?"

"That's up to you. What would you do after you killed them? There's been a lot of noise, and now there are two bodies bleeding in your doorway. Five quarts of blood each."

"Run, I suppose. Get away. I couldn't very well hang around to talk to the police."

"Good. What if you didn't kill them, just ran instead? Do you get anything from killing them first?"

"More time?"

"It's after midnight in an apartment building. You've fired at least two shots into a hallway. Your neighbors are up dialing 911. The response time on 'shots fired' calls in a big city averages around three minutes, and they usually redirect the helicopters at the same time."

He had said, "I give up. Forget the gun." Maybe he had known even as he said it that he had been lying. Now, while he walked down the dark, quiet street lined with big, dark houses that had been segmented into apartments, he felt a little better because of the gun.

He turned the corner and walked down the darker side street, carrying his grocery bag in his left arm. He saw the woman long before she saw him. She had the hood of her car open, and she was standing in front of it, leaning over and staring down into the engine with a little keychain flashlight.

Keller walked along the sidewalk until he was within twenty feet of the car. She reached out tentatively and touched something. It must have been hot, because she instantly drew back her hand, gave a little "Oooh!" and sucked her fingertips.

He could see her face in the dim glow of the little flashlight, and it looked so perfect that the air in front of him solidified and cut his speed by half. She had long, shiny blond hair that was pulled tight along the sides of her head and held back in an intricate braid, and skin that glowed. As she drew her fingers out of her mouth he saw long pointed nails that showed she had not spent much time staring into the engines of cars. She wore tight blue jeans and a jacket of some fabric that looked like canvas but couldn't have been, and the engine she was staring into belonged to a pearl-cream Lexus LS 400 that cost about sixty thousand dollars. She walked around to the trunk and opened it as Keller came abreast of the car. When the light came on and he could see her eyes welling with tears, he stopped.

Whatever anyone thought of women like her, none of them were in the business of ratting on fugitives. As it happened, David Keller liked women like her very much. He missed them. Instead of approaching and spooking her, he called to her from the sidewalk.

"I see you've got trouble. Can I call the auto club for you or something?"

She swung her head around, startled. She didn't seem to have remembered that she wasn't marooned alone on the surface of the moon. She studied him for a second, seemed to be noting that he had clean pants and a respectable sport coat on. But the fact that he was carrying a grocery bag seemed to make the difference. Jane had been on the money once again. If people could see that you were out on your own business, it was better than a pile of testimonials.

She smiled, and he could see the lush, ripe lips part to show perfect white teeth. She shrugged and held her shoulders in an embarrassed cringe. "My membership lapsed. I called them, and they ran me on the computer, and then I noticed my card was expired."

"I'm sorry," said Keller. He stepped a little closer to her car—not to her, but to the open hood. He would let her do the approaching. "I used to have one of these. They're usually pretty dependable . . ." The sentence died in his throat. He could not believe he had let that slip out. It wasn't like looking at a ten-year-old car and saying, "I used to have one." This one was new.

But he could see that the effect he had wanted to convey was the only one that she had caught. She was coming around the car to join him. She had snatched a clean red towel from the trunk, and she was wiping her hands with it. He said, "At this time of night, I'm afraid all the mechanics might be home teaching their sons to overcharge." He stared at the engine, pretending he knew what he was looking for. "How is it acting? Does it turn over?" He set his bag in front of the bumper.

She was right beside him now. He could smell the scent of her hair. Things must be going much better than he had imagined. She was much closer to him than was normal. They were almost touching. She leaned over the engine and pointed to a box bolted to the firewall that had colored wires plugged into it. "When I opened it, I could smell something burning over here."

He leaned in too, trying to see if the insulation on one of the wires was melted. He felt a light touch on the small of his back, and the hard, heavy weight of his pistol was gone.

Almost instantly, his head was pushed to the side. The pain was horrible, and it was coming from a heavy metal object pressed to his temple. He could feel the red cotton towel covering it, but he had no time to think.

She was speaking low, almost in a whisper. "Police officer. Come around to the back of the car." He hesitated, but she tugged his coat hard, and he tried to straighten so fast that he banged his head on the hood. When he reached the back he noticed that the light in the trunk had gone out.

"Get in," she ordered.

"Look," he said. "I can explain the gun. I was just trying to help you."

"You have the right to remain silent." She lifted the rag off her hand and he could see the gun now. It was big and square and ugly, with a muzzle that looked cavernous. "Get in the trunk, please. Anything you say can and will be used against you in a court of law."

Keller was dazed. His mouth was dry and he couldn't swallow. He was getting arrested by a Denver cop, a woman decoy. On an illegal weapons charge. They would find out who he was. There had to be a way out of this.

"You have a right to have an attorney present during questioning. If you cannot afford an attorney, the court will appoint one for you.

Have you heard and understood these rights?" Her thumb with the beautifully polished, tapered nail came up and cocked the hammer.

David Keller climbed into the trunk. Why did she have to put him in the trunk? Didn't they have a second car with regular cops who hauled you away when they caught you? Of course. She wasn't a decoy at all. She was off duty. She had just seen the gun at his back, plucked it away, and stuck hers in his face. The trunk slammed down on him and the world went black.

Linda stood behind the trunk of the car, squeezed her eyes closed, and smiled, smelling the thin, delicious night air. She had found the mark, taken his gun away from him, and locked him up, all by herself.

Part of the pleasure of it was that she was not alone. She had done it from start to finish with Earl watching her. He had seen her pretending to burn herself and sucking her fingers and crying just a little bit, just enough to seem soft and feminine and vulnerable. And he had seen her stand on her tiptoes to bend over the engine in these tight jeans, just arching her back a tiny bit, enough to make the mark ashamed of himself for thinking that way, and enough to give Earl something to think about too. For Earl, part of the experience was that it made him want to hurt the guy, to break bones and teeth for Linda.

Linda didn't really think much about the mark once she had him. He was necessary, but he wasn't really a player in the event. She was just using him to act out for Earl's eyes how desirable she was. The mark was a mirror for both of them. He let Linda see how beautiful she was through his eyes, because she never could quite look at herself the way men did, and so watching them look was the only way. And Earl could look at the way she affected this mark, and it made Earl feel more that way about her—as though he were seeing her for the first time too, and because he was feeling desire, he knew exactly what the other man was feeling, and that made him wild. The night was filled with invisible sparks of energy shooting back and forth around her. It was magic.

This was the part of their lives that she craved. She loved it when they were out in the night hunting together, thinking hard together about the mark and his habits and what he would do, and deciding what they would do to bag him like this. And now the hunt was right at its climax, with Earl out there in the dark concentrating all of his attention on her. In a minute he would emerge from the shadows to obliterate the mark and reclaim her. They would drive him up into the mountains and bury the body before dawn. She felt as though somebody had taken one of those electric-shock machines they had in hospitals and pressed the paddles to her chest to jump-start her heart.

She saw Earl appear from the alley behind the little market, walking along briskly. He was primed. She stepped to the front of the car and slammed the hood. That let her see the police car.

Then it was pulling up beside the Lexus. The cop was young, and she could see his lips were straight across his face with no smile, but she knew it was waiting to come, because the eyebrows had that wanting-to-be-concerned look that cops sometimes got. He stopped the car, got out, and left the door open so he could hear his radio. He didn't do the things they did when they were suspicious—put their nightsticks in their belts, say something into the radio. She could hear the nasal voice of a female dispatcher squawking out meaningless words and numbers, but he didn't answer. Instead, he stepped closer to Linda and said, "Having car trouble?"

"No," said Linda. When she smiled she could feel that she had actually induced a blush. Her cheeks were hot. "I thought I heard something in the engine, but it was just my imagination. Everything is fine."

He glanced at the car, then back at Linda. "Why don't you start it up, and I'll listen?"

Linda sensed that it was a devious way of being sure the car wasn't stolen without coming out and asking for her license and registration. She was glad he was so young and handsome, because the sight of him right after Hatcher would be sending hot flashes of jealousy up Earl's spine mixed with the alarm and the wonder at how desirable the bait really was. She smiled as prettily as she could for both of them and said, "Well, if you wouldn't mind . . . ," then obediently opened the driver's door and sat behind the wheel.

The shot was so loud that her legs kicked out and pushed her back against the seat. Blood and brain from the cop had spattered the windshield. She scrambled out of the car as though it were on fire.

Earl's strong hand clamped her arm. She danced at the end of his arm, tugging to get moving, but he tightened his grip. "He's still alive, right?"

At first she thought he meant the cop. "How could—" she began, then remembered. Hatcher was still in the trunk. She held her panic in check as she hurried to the trunk, unlocked it, and lifted the lid three inches. She stuck her big Colt into the dark space, then pulled the trigger four times before Earl grabbed her and slammed the trunk.

In the sudden silence she could hear the sirens too. More police were coming. Earl dragged her toward the alley, his grip so tight that she could feel the blood beginning to collect below it, so her fingers throbbed. His voice was a raspy whisper. "Don't ever fire blind into the trunk of a car when your ass is that close to it again, you dumb bitch. The gas tank is right under it."

She had forgotten about the gas tank. Imagining the bright orange explosion she had flirted with gave her a giddy feeling of luck, but even better, she detected that the strain in Earl's voice was genuine concern. He had just dusted a cop to reclaim her, and he really didn't want to lose her. She let him pull her along the alley, then lead her up the dark space beside the market and over to the next street. In another minute and a half they were on the pedestrian mall along Sixteenth Street, far from the sirens and far from the cops cruising around looking for a getaway car.

When he saw her turn her head to look at the display window of a boutique, Earl gave a sullen nod and followed her inside. Linda bought a silk summer dress that made her feel light and pretty, a little bit like a butterfly.

Pete Hatcher was crouching on his knees, shaking. He could tell that he must have lost some of his sight and hearing. He had seen the trunk begin to open. He had just found the safety latch inside the lid by touch and gotten the courage to release it when he had heard the keys in the lock and seen the crack of light appear.

He had been terrified that the cops would see his hand near the lock, so he had reflexively recoiled, scuttled back into the corner of the trunk behind the loose spare tire and curled up. He had seen the pistol appear in the opening, but he had never expected the gun to go off. The blast, the flash, and the shower of sparks made him bring his knees to his chest, clap his hands over his ears, and close his eyes.

She had fired again and again at the spot where he had first lay down when she locked him in—first where his head had been, then his belly, then halfway back up, to his chest, then his head again.

He heard nothing now, but his ears were still ringing, so he wasn't sure that there were no sounds. The woman had every right to think he was dead, so now she would drive the car somewhere. He waited for the sound of the engine, but it didn't come. He tried to figure out what he should do, but first he had to know why she had shot at him. No, that was wrong. Somebody was going to open the trunk again soon, expecting him to be dead. When they discovered that he wasn't, they would certainly correct the oversight. He could die that way, or he could try to run.

He pulled the safety latch behind the lock and cautiously pushed the trunk open a crack. He heard the sound of a police radio, then saw the police car. He closed his eyes and felt sweet relief. She couldn't kill him if the other cops had already arrived. That was probably why she had done such a hasty job of it—to finish it before they got here. He popped the lid up, then swung his leg over the rear bumper, misjudged the height of the trunk, and toppled over onto the street. He began to sit up, then lay back down again and stared along the underside of the car.

He could see the body of a policeman lying on the street at the front, almost under the radiator. There was a big hole in his forehead as though the skull had been punched outward, and blood draining down over his left eye into a pool. Hatcher's brain tried to take all that it knew and make sense of it. Did she imagine Hatcher had killed the policeman earlier, and then think she was executing him for it? What was he thinking? It was impossible. She had killed the policeman. She was no cop.

His breathing stopped. He had no idea how long he had been hearing the sirens. He was alone with the body of a murdered policeman. He had just bought two guns, and this woman had probably used one of them on a policeman. It might be lying around here someplace, and if it wasn't, the police certainly had a way to know he had owned two and had only one left.

Hatcher stood and backed away from the car, his head swiveling around, first to see if the madwoman was still nearby waiting to fire, then to see if any of the people in the houses had come out, then just to see where he was going. He walked to the front of the car and picked up his grocery bag. He turned, and then his feet were pounding on the sidewalk, carrying him away, the momentum building and building, his mouth open in a grimace so the air hissed in and out through his clenched teeth.

His mind burned through the mass of impressions into a bare, heightened clarity as he ran. There was no moment of indecision, no wavering among choices, because he had no choices. He knew the police would come toward this spot from three directions at once, because there were only three ways for a car to come. They would flood each end of the block and come up the alley. He took the fourth way, entering the lobby of an apartment building that looked a lot like his own, walking through it, down the first-floor hallway and out the back door, then beside the next one and across the street, where he entered the lobby of the next one, so he emerged on his own street a block from his apartment.

He walked into his entryway and climbed the stairs for the last time. He knew that the madwoman almost certainly believed he was dead. Even if she had any doubts and knew where he lived, she would have had a difficult time getting here before he had. He opened the apartment door, slipped inside, and locked it behind him.

He had no difficulty working out the order of tasks. He made the telephone call first. She wasn't home, but he left a message. Then he collected the cash from its hiding places in the apartment, packed his clothes quickly, and wiped his fingerprints off all the surfaces he usually touched. He took all of the food jars and bottles out of the refrigerator, put them into the sink, and ran water over them until he was sure they carried no fingerprints, then put them all into a big plastic trash bag with his groceries.

He went out, locked the door, wiped the doorknob, walked quietly down the hall, and carried his suitcase and his trash down the back staircase. He put his trash in the Dumpster. Then he walked around the corner to where his car was parked, set his suitcase in the trunk, and began to drive.

Earl and Linda sat in a cowboy bar in Golden, a half hour into the mountains west of Denver, and watched the eleven o'clock news on the television set on the wall above them. The newswoman was reporting "the senseless, execution-style killing of a young police officer."

Earl knitted his eyebrows. "Now, that's typical, isn't it? They haven't found out why it happened, so they say it was senseless. They read the words on the prompter, but they don't seem to know what they're saying."

Linda could see the newswoman standing about twenty yards away from the Lexus, and behind her the police crew was dusting it for prints. The car trunk was open. "The police are urging anyone who has information about the incident to contact them. They have no solid leads as to why anyone would have shot the officer. One theory I've heard is that even though the new Lexus sedan had not yet been reported missing, the officer might have seen something suspicious and pulled it over."

Linda held her breath, waiting for Earl to notice what had not been said. Finally she knew that he already had. He swallowed the last of the beer in his glass, set it on the table, and said, "Well, we'd better go see if we can figure out where he's gotten to now."

"I'm sorry, Earl," she said. She wanted to waste some time in the bar, where there were people, before she blithely stepped into the dark with Earl. He was perfectly capable of hiding his anger until they were somewhere along a deserted road. "I'm really sorry. I don't know how I could have—"

"I did it," he said. "I stopped you before you could do him right." He added, "I keep thinking, 'So she might have put a round into the gas tank. If we'd been back a few yards it wouldn't have been so bad.'" He pulled her up by the arm. "Better than this, anyway. This is a joke."

When they reached the neighborhood where Hatcher had been living as David Keller, they drove past the place where he had parked the used Saturn that evening. For an instant Linda felt the thrill of surprise and anticipation: the space was not empty. But when Earl drove closer she could see that the car in the space was a Thunderbird.

Earl left their car a block from the rear of Hatcher's building and they climbed the back stairs. Earl opened the lock effortlessly and they stepped inside, put on their gloves, and began the search. As soon as Linda opened the refrigerator, she knew what the rest of the small apartment would be like.

After fifteen minutes, Earl sat down on the couch. "He's getting better at this."

"He doesn't have as much stuff to worry about," said Linda. "She made him travel light."

"Let's see," muttered Earl. "He's in the trunk of the car. You put four shots in there. You would think with four rounds rattling around in there and bouncing off things, one of them would have clipped him, wouldn't you?"

"Yes. I did. But it didn't happen. There's no blood anyplace."

"He knows he's a lucky man, but he's scared to death. He hears us leave, he pops out and runs like hell—probably through back yards, or the police would have picked him up. He's too stupid to do the wrong thing and run across town. He comes right back here. What does he do?"

"It looks like he spent some time cleaning up."

"Right. He couldn't have done that for us. We know who he is already. He must think the cops are going to come here looking for him. What else did he do?"

"He took his car."

"That's last. What's first?"

"He packed his stuff. Probably some money, the other gun he bought."

Earl nodded. "He did that. Put yourself in his mind. You're scared. You're so scared you just ran home as fast as you could. You clean up, throw everything in a suitcase. You're about to go out the door and drive until you run out of gas. Where are you going to go?"

Linda's eyes narrowed, and she bit her lower lip, then released it to reveal a little smile. She looked across Earl at the telephone on the table. "Does it have a redial button?"

Earl opened his briefcase and found the little microcassette recorder. "Testing," he said. "You'd better work." He clicked two buttons. "Testing. You'd better work," it said. Earl pressed two more buttons, then looked at Linda. He lifted the receiver, clamped the tape recorder to the earpiece with one hand, pressed the redial button with the other, and recorded the series of quick musical tones.

Linda counted the tones. "Eleven numbers. Long distance. An area code and a number."

Earl hung up before the phone on the other end could ring. Then he played back the recording of eleven tones and handed the recorder to Linda. "Get the numbers." He stood up, took a penlight, and began to shine it on the surfaces of the furniture.

Linda lifted the receiver and said into the recorder, "One," then pressed the one button and recorded the tone. She said, "Two," pressed the two button, and recorded the tone. When she reached six, she hung up to avoid completing a call, then got the last four numbers on tape.

It took Linda another ten minutes to decipher the recorded tones of the woman's telephone number. "I think I have it. Should I test it?"

Earl said, "Give it a try."

Linda said aloud, "One. Area code seven one six," then dialed the rest of it. After four rings she heard a woman's voice. "Leave a message when you hear a beep." Linda hung up. "It's the woman. She has her answering machine on."

Earl took his penlight and opened David Keller's telephone book. "Seven one six. . . . That's New York . . . Buffalo, New York." He closed the book and looked at Linda. "Maybe this time we got lucky, not him, and not her. She's got her answering machine on. He called her no more than an hour or two ago. Maybe it's on because she's already talked to him and gone off to meet him. But it just could be that he got her machine too, and left a message."

Linda looked at the phone as though she could see down the wire to the other end. "Most machines will play back a message if you're away. Ours will do it if you push a two-digit code. Some use codes with three or four, but it might be worth a try."

"There are only a hundred possible combinations. And we aren't paying the phone bill."

It was two o'clock when Linda heard a change. "Leave a message when—" and the recording stopped. There was a click, and she could hear the answering machine rewinding, then another click. Linda held Earl's tape recorder beside the earpiece of the telephone.

"Jane? Jane? It's me. I'm in trouble. Somehow they found me. A woman tried to kill me tonight. I've got to get out. I'm going to head north, to Cheyenne. No, too close. Billings. I'll try to make it to Billings, Montana. I'll call again when I get there."

She was laughing with delight when she played the recording for Earl, but he was staring at the wall, and he wasn't smiling.

When it ended, he sat in silence for a moment, then glanced at his watch. "We'd better get going. I've got to put you on a plane, and then head up north."

"Put me on a plane?"

He spoke so gently that she was afraid of him. "He saw your face, honey. Having you around isn't going to do me any good in Billings."

"You're sending me home?"

"Home?" His grin came like a sudden snarl. "No. You've got to go do something about her."

"Jane? Jane? It's me. I'm in trouble. Somehow they found me. A woman tried to kill me tonight. I've got to get out. I'm going to head north, to Cheyenne. No, too close. Billings. I'll try to make it to Billings, Montana. I'll call again when I get there."

The shock in his voice made Jane's scalp prickle, and a hot, sick sweat began to materialize on the back of her neck. The machine's inhuman voice said, "End of messages," and clicked off. She pressed the button again and heard Hatcher's voice. "Jane? Jane?" She listened to the rest of it, each word of it giving her bits of information that Pete Hatcher probably didn't know.

He had made a mistake, but even after he had seen the executioner, he had no idea what he had done wrong. He had stayed hidden for three months, so it had nothing to do with the escape route. He must have done something as David Keller that they had expected Pete Hatcher to do. He had gotten himself on some list.

"I'm going to head north, to Cheyenne. No, too close." She felt something clutching her stomach. He had been sitting in his apartment in Denver all this time, gotten up a hundred mornings and gone to bed a hundred evenings, and it had never occurred to him to plan the best way to get out if they found him. It sounded as though he was running his finger up a road map while he was talking, looking for a route that sounded safe to his panicked brain.

She had told him to prepare contingency plans. After something happened, he wouldn't be able to think clearly, he would forget details, leave things behind that he needed. But had she told him? She tried to remember their two conversations. She thought she had told him. She had tried to instill in him an attitude. Other people could make decisions at the last moment, but a fugitive could not. He had to know in advance the places where he was willing to show his face, what he was willing to do, what he was going to say when somebody asked him a question.

Jane slowly felt the suspicion harden into a certainty. She had not taught Pete Hatcher how to stay alive. The excuses began to flood her consciousness. Getting him out of Las Vegas had not been a question of redirecting a running man. It had been like staging a prison break. He had been watched, followed, suspected by people who seemed to have no other duties. She had needed to slip him out between the guards from a standing start, and then spend most of her energy delaying the pursuit. But repeating the circumstances to herself accomplished nothing. Words were enough to apologize for her haste, but not enough to absolve her if Pete Hatcher died.

Now he was on his way to Billings, Montana, a city with a population of no more than eighty thousand, where finding his car would probably be no harder than driving around for an afternoon and looking for it. She knew about the car from his telephone message too. If he had to decide in the middle of the night between stopping in Cheyenne and going on up Interstate 25, then he was driving a car he owned.

She looked around her at her bedroom. It occurred to her that she had taken very little out of here when she had gotten married. It was as though she had subconsciously tried to leave Jane Whitefield behind, where she could cause no trouble. There were most of her clothes, hanging in the closet with dry cleaners' bags over them, and there was her old dresser.

She walked along the hall and down the staircase, then through the kitchen to the basement steps. She turned on the light and looked around. The house had been built in the days when they used stones for basements, the beams under a house were just rough-planed tree trunks, and the floorboards were held to them with square-headed spikes. She walked to the old set of shelves her great-grandmother had used to store her preserves—sweet peeled peaches and pears in sugary water, stewed tomatoes, applesauce, corn soup, and strawberries, all in big mason jars with rubber gaskets and glass tops with a steel-clamp contraption that held them tight. The fall canning had lasted through her grandmother's time. Only the old jars had survived her mother's.

Jane went to the oil furnace, moved the stepladder beside it, then disconnected a section of one of the heating ducts. This was a round one that was left over from the days when the house had been heated by an old coal furnace. It wasn't connected to anything anymore, but it ran from the now-empty site of the coal bin, turned upward, and connected to the floor under the kitchen, where there had once been a wide brass grate. She looked inside, found the box, and set it on the top step.

She separated James Weiss's papers from the others—his birth certificate, New York driver's license, his credit cards, his Social Security card, his college diploma, the life insurance policy he had bought six years ago. James Weiss was one of the most credible identities she had ever assembled—certainly among the best of the adult males.

James Weiss had no pedigree, but his credentials had a long and complicated history. His birth certificate was genuine. Years ago, a man Jane knew had gotten a job in a county courthouse in Pennsylvania, where he had quietly added fifty birth records. Jane had bought twenty of them. She had liked the idea so much that she had allowed two women who worked in county clerks' offices in Ohio and Illinois to repeat it. The woman in Ohio had offered to do it because she had known a little girl for whom Ohio had turned into a dangerous place and knew that Jane had been the one to make her disappear. The woman in Illinois had made the new people and sent their birth certificates to Jane as a present on the anniversary of her own disappearance from a tight spot in California.

James Weiss had been one of the Illinois woman's creations. Jane had gotten him a Social Security card and a driver's license by sending a young man who owed her a favor to apply for them. The college diploma was the product of another ruse she had invented at about the same time. She had searched alumni magazines until she found a James Weiss who had graduated from the University of California at Berkeley. She had run a credit check on him and gotten the information she needed to request a transcript and a duplicate of his diploma. Anyone who wished to could call and verify that they were genuine.

Jane had found an insurance company that did not require a physical exam for a life insurance policy under two hundred thousand dollars, so she had bought him one for a hundred thousand. She had kept building Weiss's identity in small ways over the years, just as she had a number of others.

For most of the people she had taken out of the world, Jane had bought false identities from professionals. But she had always been aware that professional forgers were not permanent fixtures on the landscape. Lewis Feng in Vancouver had been murdered. George Karanjian in New York had gotten too rich to take chances and retired.

Jane bought and used identities for herself by the dozen so she could travel unimpeded, then destroyed the ones that might have been compromised. But she also kept about fifteen that she had built on her own—some here at her house, some in safe-deposit boxes in banks in New York, Chicago, Los Angeles, and Toronto.

She selected six matched sets of papers for couples, added them to James Weiss, put the heating duct back together, and went upstairs to make her telephone calls. She called the airline first. The flight to Chicago would leave in two hours. Then she took a deep breath, let it out, and dialed her home number.

Carey answered. "Hello?"

"Hi, Carey," she said. "I want you to do something for me and not ask any questions until you get here."

"Get where?"

"Can you meet me at the house in Deganawida?"

He hesitated. "Well, sure. Do you want me to call somebody? Dress for dinner? Bring bail money?"

"Just come." She hung up. She wished she had laughed when he had mentioned bail money. It should have been funny. If she had been the wife she wanted to be, it would have been. She went downstairs to find the small brown suitcase she had left in the little office that had been her mother's sewing room. Then she checked the latches on the first-floor windows, changed the light bulbs of the two lamps that were on timers, and hurried upstairs.

She was packing the suitcase when Carey came into the bedroom. He looked at the suitcase, then looked at Jane. He said, "I hope you called because you needed me to help you carry a few things home."

Jane smiled a sad little smile. "There's something I want you to hear." She stepped to the answering machine, pressed the button, and watched Carey's face while Pete Hatcher's voice came on, scared, dazed, and breathless. "Jane? Jane?" When Carey had heard the message and there was the clatter of the telephone receiver being hurriedly set back in its cradle, she pressed the other button to erase the message, then stepped close to him. She touched his arm and it felt hard and stiff, but when she tugged it, he sat on the bed with her.

He said, "I can't believe this is happening."

She sighed and tried to find a way to begin. "I love you." That was the best way. "I love you. I don't want this to happen either."

"But you made a promise. You said it wouldn't. Not that you would be sorry if it did, but that you would do what was necessary so it didn't."

"This is something else."

"Jane," he said. "Everything is something else."

"Let me try to explain," she said quietly. "This is going to sound like some kind of legalistic excuse, but it isn't. I said that if somebody came to me and asked for this kind of help, I would tell them I wasn't able to do that anymore. I would have. This is a time when I need you to help me. I want to be honest and tell you everything, so you understand. You heard his voice. His name is . . . used to be Pete Hatcher. He worked for a big casino company in Las Vegas. They weren't honest. He learned too many details. He also made them suspicious. They were busy preparing to kill him when I took him out."

Carey shook his head. "What a shock—something so unprecedented. A gambling outfit that turns out to be dishonest. Boy, I'll bet Pete Hatcher was surprised. Who would have guessed?"

She looked at him apologetically. "That's part of being a guide. Some of the people I've taken out of their troubles weren't innocent, or weren't smart, or caused their own misery. Pete Hatcher is probably one of them. But he hasn't done anything that I consider a capital offense."

"You'd be amazed at how many people like that there are," said Carey. "Billions. Some of them haven't even committed a felony."

Inside, she winced, but she forced herself to say, "If Pete Hatcher came to me out of nowhere tonight, I would tell him no. But he happened before I made that promise. He could be about to die because I didn't do a good enough job. This isn't something I can ignore. It's as though you operated on somebody and left a sponge in his belly."

"It's not exactly an apt analogy," said Carey. "If I had been operating on a patient, I would have been doing it in the legitimate pursuit of my lawful profession, doing what I was educated, trained, and certified to do. I would perform surgery if it were the generally accepted way of correcting a serious and possibly life-threatening condition. I'm part of a system. I'm not just some guy who decided on his own that real doctors aren't doing enough surgery, or doing it well enough, so I try to do a few at home."

She hugged him. "You're right, Carey," she said.

"I am?"

She stood up and went to her closet. "Yep. When you're right, you're right."

"And?"

"And I was right to choose you. Not that there was any choice involved. We're not talking about some profession here, that I had to give up. It's just a trick I learned to do when I was too young and stupid to know any better."

"So you'll stay home—mail him another false ID and forget it?"

She looked at him in surprise. "Oh, I'm sorry, Carey. I didn't mean that." She went back to her packing.

"What did you mean?"

"I meant I'm much sorrier about this than you will ever know. You're my life now. When I get this over with, I'll spend the next few years trying to make it up to you—trying to give you back the confidence and peace of mind I just threw away, so you don't think that any time the phone rings I might go off to do something stupid. Because I won't. I just can't start being smart tonight. I can't pretend I didn't abandon a person out there where I know he'll be killed."

Carey went to her and rocked her gently in his arms. "Is there anything I haven't said that would talk you out of it?"

"No. You've done pretty well."

"You know how I feel about it, right? No point in going into all the stuff about how a man feels letting his beautiful young wife go off to some place where she might get killed."

"I know how you feel," she said. "I can't help this."

He brightened, then looked dispirited. "Threats don't work on you, do they?"

"Not very well," she said. "You could make me very, very sad without trying very hard."

"So whatever I do or say, all I can do is make a bad time worse for both of us." He stared at his feet. "Need a ride to the airport?"

She threw her arms around him and held him as tightly as she could, clutching him and letting the tears run down her cheeks. "Thank you, Carey," she said. She turned and went into the bathroom and closed the door.

Jane lifted the perfume bottle out of the medicine cabinet, opened it, and sniffed. It had a sweet, damp, earthy smell. Periodically, for years, she had collected the roots of water hemlock, mashed them for their juice, then purified and concentrated it. This batch was fresh enough, and maybe stronger than the last. In the old days, when an

Iroquois wanted to commit suicide, he would eat a hemlock root and die within two hours. The perfume worked much faster. She put the bottle into her purse and felt the tears coming again.

She rested her foot on the rim of the bathtub and began to run adhesive tape around her thigh. She wiped her eyes and carefully retrieved the boot knife she had hidden on the underside of the drawer of her vanity. It was thin and weightless and razor-edged, made of zircon-oxide ceramic instead of steel so it wouldn't set off metal detectors. She taped it to her thigh, then put her foot down and let her dress fall to cover it.

She walked into the bedroom and kissed her husband. "How do I look?"

The lights came up to reveal the Miraculous Miranda in a Victorian gown, standing behind tall glass windows in an octagonal set like a gazebo. The back wall of the little room was covered with library shelves. She stood on tiptoes to lift from a shelf a folio volume bound in worn leather, opened it, and turned the old parchment pages as she walked toward a small table. Finally she found a passage and read it with interest. She closed the book, set it on the floor, and snapped her fingers. A bottle of champagne appeared on the table. She snapped them again and a stemmed glass appeared beside it. She stared at the bottle with a scowl of concentration: nothing happened. She took a deep breath, stared harder, and the cork popped fifteen feet into the air. When it came down she caught it happily and held it while it turned into a little bird. She opened the window and let it fly away above the heads of the audience, then closed the window.

Miranda picked up the bottle and poured champagne into the glass, lifting the bottle higher so the stream of clear liquid caught in the spotlights appeared first green, then red, then blue, then the golden color of her hair. She sipped from the glass, then set it back on the small, graceful table, took a step away, and faced the audience to resume her act. But she changed her mind and returned to the table. She poured the liquid into the glass again. The bubbly liquid foamed to the rim, but she kept pouring. The foam frothed over the side of the glass and down the stem, off the table and onto the floor. She seemed to be intrigued by the way the foam kept bubbling and growing. Soon there was a sudsy puddle at her feet that threatened to cover the floor of the little pavilion.

Miranda seemed nonplussed. She righted the bottle and scrutinized the label with curiosity. But while she read it, she noticed that turning the bottle upright had not stopped the liquid from gushing out. It came faster and faster, first like a fountain, then like the eruption of a volcano. She set it on the table and backed uneasily away from it, toward the tall shelves of books.

The audience was enchanted, but Miranda seemed concerned about her long nineteenth-century dress. She held the skirts up with both hands as the sudsy champagne soaked her dancing pumps and rose to her ankles. She looked around toward the wings of the stage, but none of her helpers seemed to be able to see her around the walls of books at the sides of the set. She waved testily above the set at the lighting and music technicians in the glass booth behind the audience, but the fans who turned their heads to follow her gaze saw that the two men were shrugging and shaking their heads in dismay. The lighting man seemed to be the only one with any presence of mind, and he switched on a row of soft lights above Miranda so she could see what she was doing.

As the flood from the bottle rose higher, the audience could see that Miranda was on her own. She turned to the bookshelves, placed one foot on the lowest shelf, pushing the books back with her toe, and began to climb. On the sixth shelf, her foot caught on the hem of the dress and slipped. She lost her footing, dropped with a stomach-gripping jerk, grasped a shelf, and dangled there.

Miranda's toe found a purchase, and that freed one hand. She quickly undid the buttons on the front of the dress and let it fall to her ankles. She stepped out of it with one foot and looked over her shoulder in frustration. With her free hand she gave a hasty gesture, and conjured a wooden hanger floating in the air. She gave the dress a kick and it promptly flew through the air and hung itself on the hanger. She snapped her fingers and it vanished from sight.

Now that Miranda was dressed only in a corset, petticoat, and white stockings, her unnaturally strong and nimble acrobat's body seemed to scale the bookshelves effortlessly. She reached the top shelf at the rim of the structure as the foaming torrent sloshed behind the tall windows, turning the room into an aquarium.

Just as the audience seemed to make the analogy, the resemblance became inescapable. Brightly colored foot-long fish began to flit and glide out of the bookshelves, then swim down into the room to investigate the furniture. The mind struggled to go through the processes it had been trained to do: Are the fish alive, or mechanical, or holograms of live fish projected from offstage into the liquid? But the cogitation stumbled over itself and collapsed, because in Miranda's little pantomimes, guessing the method answered no question at all, and something else was always coming in to change the mixture.

Miranda was visibly fascinated by what she saw in the library below her. She seemed to forget the audience for a moment. She slipped off her stockings and put a toe in. She stood and paced along the top of the bookcase, looking into the pool, and as she did she loosed herself from the corset and stepped out of the petticoat to reveal a bright orange two-piece bathing suit. Then she ran back along the top of the bookcase, sprang into the air, executed a flip, and knifed into the water.

Through the row of tall windows the audience could see her swimming underwater with the bright blue and yellow fish. Suddenly, the unthinkable happened. There was a creaking, tearing sound, the walls collapsed outward, and the water poured onto the stage to be sucked away by invisible drains. Miranda was left lying on the carpet near the table. She stirred, then stood up suddenly, bowed, and blew kisses. Then she bowed very low. Her face assumed that strange, playful, mischievous look as she picked up something from the rubble on the floor and held it up.

It was a big painting from one of the collapsed walls. It was a painting of Lady Godiva riding on her white horse.

Miranda looked down at her bright orange bathing suit, then at the audience. Now her smile was naughty. The audience roared, urging her to do whatever she was contemplating. She propped the painting against the table, picked up the old leather-bound book that still sat beside the bottle. She quickly leafed through the pages, found the right one and read it, and set the book down.

Miranda stepped back a few paces, gestured portentiously at the painting, and then, with a final mischievous glance at the audience, slowly raised her hand and pointed down at her own head.

There was a brilliant flash, a puff of smoke, and Miranda was gone. In her place stood a graceful white Arabian horse. Braided into its mane was a swatch of bright orange cloth that could have been the top of Miranda's bathing suit, and into its long tail, the second piece of orange cloth. The audience was laughing, shrieking, applauding its approval: if Miranda had been a horse, this was the horse she would be.

The horse walked to the table, nosed the old book thoughtfully, as though it were Miranda trying to discover her mistake, then turned to face the audience, extended its foreleg, and lowered its head in a final bow. There was another flash and puff of smoke, and when it cleared, the horse too was gone.

Seaver sat on the folding chair beside Miranda's technician and watched him engage the hydraulic lift, bringing the white horse the rest of the way down under the stage. The gleaming ten-inch cylinder shortened as the hole in the stage floor above snapped shut, the noise of it covered by the deafening music of Miranda's exit. As the black platform moved down to eye level, he saw Miranda was standing on it with the horse. She swung her leg up over the horse's back and mounted it, but she didn't sit up. Instead she clung to it, her hands caressing the horse's face, patting its neck while she spoke into its ear, crooning soft words into its dumb animal brain to keep it from remembering to panic.

When the hydraulic lift reached the level of the concrete floor she swung down from the horse, and now he could hear her words. "Great job, baby. Wonderful show. You made mama have a lot of fun."

A woman who had to be the horse's handler stepped forward with a halter in one hand and a few lumps of sugar in the other. Miranda took the sugar and watched the horse's big prehensile lips nibble them off her palm, then hugged the horse again.

Like a wild animal, Miranda seemed to smell the unfamiliar presence. Her eyes swept the dim concrete enclosure filled with machinery and electronic devices and found him unerringly. Her voice hardened. "Take the horse, Judy." She stepped to Seaver and stopped. The wardrobe mistress expertly slipped the black velvet robe up her arms and onto her shoulders, then receded. Miranda brought the belt around her and cinched it, hard.

She did not speak to him, but her sharp, angry eyes never left him as she called out to her staff, "Who is this?"

Seaver stood up and smiled. "Calvin Seaver. Vice president for security at Pleasure Island." He had known she would be difficult, so he already had in his hand his plastic-coated identification card, along with the backstage visitor's badge he had been issued at the Inside Straight. "Will King and I sometimes get together to check out each other's operations. Professional courtesy."

She studied the badges and looked back up at his face. "Sorry. You could have been a reporter or a trick thief. Real magicians don't do that to each other. Professional courtesy. If you saw anything you didn't know already, please keep it to yourself." She took a step away.

Miranda's stagehands and technicians all seemed to have been held frozen in a spell, not breathing. Now she released them. "Great show, everybody." They relaxed and began working again, moving around each other without pausing.

Miranda took a second step. "Your secrets are safe with me," said Seaver. "For the moment, anyway."

She turned on her heel and faced him. "What do you want?"

"Three minutes," he said. "Five at the most."

"Come on." She walked to the far end of the area below the stage, around two more hydraulic lifts and a console that seemed to have been set up to control the explosive charges wired on stage. She stopped. "What's your pitch?"

"I'm looking for a woman."

"Smile more. They'll like you better."

"A particular woman. Dark hair, pretty, in very good physical condition. Three months ago she helped a gentleman named Pete Hatcher disappear. You might recall the evening, because you slipped him out the back door for her at the start of your midnight show."

Her left eyebrow arched. "Did I?"

"Yes. At first, I thought the dark-haired woman might be you. What you do on stage makes strolling out the door in a dark wig and getting two security men to look the wrong way seem like a small thing."

He reached into his coat pocket, snatched out an envelope, and handed it to her. "So I did a background investigation. All of your legal papers—licenses, birth records, Social Security—say your real name is supposed to be Katie Mullen. Even your union records and personnel file. You're from Ohio. But—funny thing—there's nothing on Katie Mullen that goes back more than eight years."

He watched her look at the credit report, then at the Social Security earnings report, then at the two lists of avenues checked, with "none" or "not found" beside them. She shrugged. "Not much happened to me before then." She folded the papers, tucked them in the envelope, and handed them back to him.

Seaver slipped them into the inner pocket of his coat. "No record of enrollment in a high school class in Ohio."

"You can't get that."

"I use a company that arranges class reunions. They feed all the names into their computer for mailing lists. They ran three years of them for me."

"I lie about my age."

"Your birth certificate says what you say. But I'll bet the paper the original is printed on isn't more than eight years old."

"I'm not the dark-haired woman."

"No, you're not. You're somebody she helped one time. There never was a Katie Mullen. She helped you disappear from someplace, so you helped her."

She leaned against the wall with her arms crossed over her chest. "So who did I used to be?"

He shrugged. "I don't care. All I want to know is who the dark-haired woman is."

"That's it?"

"That's it."

"Then good night." She pushed off the wall and took a step toward the corridor.

Seaver's hand closed on her forearm, and she looked down at it icily until Seaver began to wonder whether he had made a terrible mistake. He loosened his grip until it was too loose, and she snatched it away. "What now?"

"I want you to take one minute to think about what Vincent Bogliarese would feel if he knew what we were talking about."

She looked at Seaver with a sense of wonder. She had underestimated him. She turned to face him. Her impossibly golden hair had dried into a wild mane, the skin of her sculpted face was still covered with a makeup that had little metallic sparkles in it. She didn't look quite human. The big, unblinking blue eyes acquired the mischievous look they wore on stage.

"The back elevator over there goes up to my suite. By now, Vincent is up there waiting for me. Maybe he knows everything you know. Maybe he doesn't. Come with me." She took two steps toward the elevator, then stopped, turned, and looked back at him. Her face was a blank, like a portrait of a woman, but the eyes were burning him.

Seaver tried to decide. If he had been anything but positive, he would never have come here. She had once been in some kind of trouble. She had escaped because she'd had the help of a professional, who had given her false papers and set off whatever changes had transformed her into the Miraculous Miranda. She would not have slipped Pete Hatcher out for any other reason. Who would have the money to pay a performer like her to do anything? It must have been to return a favor, and a big one, at that. Now that he had met her, he was even more certain.

The incarnations he could trace were unbroken for about eight years: first Katie Mullen, the pretty assistant in the brief costume who opened trap doors and distracted the audience for a past-his-prime magician in worn tailcoat named Mister Zenobia; then Magical Miranda, playing kids' birthday parties in the daytime and, at night, doing gigs at supper clubs where part of the deal was waiting on tables. Then, three years ago, the Miraculous Miranda had materialized in Las Vegas.

But Seaver had miscalculated. The eight years should have made him at least suspect it. He had assumed that she had been running from some woman problem—maybe an arrest or two for soliciting, maybe a stint starring in pornographic movies.

Seaver studied her face, and was suddenly lost in amazement at her perfidy. She was trying to look as though she were bluffing, but she wasn't. She had already shown all her cards to Vincent. What she had been hiding was a whole lot worse than Seaver had imagined. She wasn't hiding some embarrassing period of her past from her boyfriend. That wasn't it at all.

She had told Vincent all about it, and that meant it wasn't that there were some videotapes of her going down on one of those pimply-faced druggies that were the foot soldiers of the porn trade. That would have driven a man like Vincent nuts. What she was hiding was a charge that wouldn't get stale after eight years—a class-one felony, like armed robbery or homicide. And of all the men in the world, Vincent Bogliarese would be the last one to write her off for homicide. His own father had a homicide conviction. Whatever Miranda had done in her early twenties, Vincent Senior had done more in his. For that matter, Seaver had always heard that these old families still expected a son to make his bones before he could be trusted with business matters, and Vincent Junior had been running the Inside Straight for at least ten years.

She was trying to get him to think she was bluffing, so he would go up there with her and get himself killed. There was no way in the world he was going to step into that elevator. He had never relished the idea, and now there was no reason to consider it. What he had come for was safe in his coat pocket. When he had handed her the papers, his purpose wasn't to show her he knew nothing. He had just wanted her to touch them. He would have to get one of his old buddies on the L.A.P.D. to run the fingerprints before he knew what it was he had. But he had something. Now it was his turn to let her think he had been bluffing.

"No," he said. "I don't think I'd like to speak with Mr. Bogliarese at this time. You go on without me."

Miranda's smile grew. She winked, spun around with a speed and grace that an ordinary woman would not have imitated, even if she could, because she had no excuse to be bigger than life. Miranda stepped into the elevator and let the doors close on her.

Seaver decided not to take the time to get upstairs and walk out the front door with the customers. Miranda wasn't predictable enough for that. Right now she might be giving her boyfriend some version of what had just happened. Seaver walked straight to the steel door at the back of the stage area and said to a stagehand, "Can you let me out?" There was a sign on it that said, EMERGENCY ONLY. ALARM WILL SOUND, but he knew they must have keys to it, because that was the way Pete Hatcher had slipped out. The stagehand opened it and let him out onto a long narrow asphalt strip beside the building where a few employees' cars were parked.

It took Seaver at least five minutes to walk all the way to the front of the building, then another ten to walk down the covered mall and out the other side to the lot where his car was parked. He patted the envelope in his coat pocket three times during the walk.

He got into his car and started the engine. He had already begun to back out when he realized that patting the envelope was not going to be enough. He stopped the car, pulled forward a little, and slipped it into neutral. He had watched Miranda touch the papers, so he knew exactly where her prints were, and he wouldn't make the mistake of smudging them. She had been hot and sweaty from the show, so the prints would be oily and clear. But thinking of Miranda's show during his walk had prompted a small twinge of uneasiness in him. This was a woman who was world famous for sleight of hand. Could he really be sure that what he had seen was her tucking the papers back into the envelope before she had handed it back to him? The same set of papers?

Seaver reached into the inner pocket of his coat and pulled out the envelope. He held it on his lap where no bystander could see it, placed only the nails of his thumbs in the slot and made sure that they touched only the envelope, then pushed the envelope's sides outward just enough.

There was a blinding flash of light, a sound like an indrawn breath, and a choking smell as though a whole box of matches was burning. A thin, jagged line of orange fire streaked from the bottom of the envelope up both sides until his thumbs held nothing, and a pile of black powder was settling onto his lap. He rolled to the side out of the car, slapping his pants furiously.

In a few seconds, he was sure his clothes had not ignited, and nothing had reached his skin. He stood beside the car for a moment and closed his eyes. He could still see a bright green patch floating behind his eyelids from the flash. He hated that woman. He knew exactly how she had done it. All of the big pyrotechnics in her act had been fired electronically by her technicians, but not the little ones. Somewhere in her costume she must have carried a supply of flash powder, so she could use it when she wanted it. Probably it was in pea-sized, airtight capsules. That way it would be safe and inert, until the mixture was exposed to oxygen and a tiny trace of white phosphorous ignited whatever else was in there. It had to be something like that, anyway, or it would have gone off before he opened the envelope.

He got into the car, opened all the windows, and drove out into the night. He was not going to stick a knife into the Miraculous Miranda. He was not even going to fabricate anything about her to send to Vincent Bogliarese. He was going to forget her. All she had ever been was one avenue to find the dark-haired woman who had made Pete Hatcher disappear. There were others.

Jane flew to Chicago as Karen Roth, then shopped for her next flight by walking along the concourse at O'Hare looking at the television monitors that listed scheduled departures. Hatcher had called her at around ten on Tuesday night, and she had not heard the message until seven the next evening, so he was already in Billings. She diverted her course to a pay telephone, called her answering machine, pressed 56, and listened. "Two messages," said the mechanical voice. The first was Hatcher's voice saying, "It's just me again." She clapped her hand over her free ear to block out the noise around her and waited, but there was a pause, then a click to signify that the call had ended. The second message was just the pause and then another click. Jane put the receiver back on the hook and went to buy her next ticket. Either Hatcher had not settled anywhere yet, or he had decided it was not safe to leave a number, or something had gone wrong with her machine to make it stop recording. Maybe it had failed to disconnect after the first call, and used up all the blank tape recording nothing. Maybe the clock battery had died, or the tape had tangled, or . . . she might as well stop kidding herself. Or when Pete Hatcher had made the first call, standing in a lighted phone booth at a rest stop on Route 25, he had hung up the phone, turned around, and had a .357 Magnum stuck in his face.

She flew to Missoula as Katherine Webster on a smaller plane and arrived at seven in the morning, then went shopping for a car as Wendy Wasserman. The car Wendy Wasserman selected was a two-year-old Nissan Maxima with low mileage and a finish that had been dulled by the first owner's failure to protect it from the winter weather. The owner had left on it a parking sticker that said University of Montana. Jane drove it to the campus and left it in a covered parking structure surrounded by busy dormitories, then walked northwest up Broadway until she found a car-rental agency.

She called her answering machine three times during the day, and each time the machine said, "Two messages." She drove the three hundred and forty miles eastward on Route 90 to Billings as the sun made its way toward the mountains behind her. The eastern side of the Rocky Mountains was high country and forested, but it was dry and hot, the very edge of the Great Plains. As she drove, the forests dwindled and were replaced by huge fields of wheat growing tall in the late summer sunset.

Jane arrived in Billings after dark. She drove the streets for two hours to get a sense of the city, then left her rented car in the parking lot at Deaconess Medical Center and began to walk. She bought a newspaper at a machine on a corner and studied it. There was no mention of a David Keller being found, no Pete Hatcher, and no John Does. If he wasn't alive, the police didn't know it yet.

She tried to imagine his steps. He would have come up on Route 25 until it merged with Route 90 and arrived in the middle of the night. He had probably checked into a hotel at noon. He would have been exhausted by then, and slept until dark. He would have gotten up, dressed, and then realized that he didn't have a good enough reason to go out there in the strange city at night. He would have eaten in the hotel, then returned to his room. He would know that the only place she could hope to find him was in a hotel, so he would stay there. If there was a problem with her answering machine, then he would send her a note in the mail. He would stay put and hope that she could get to him before anybody else did.

If she wanted to get to him and take him out without attracting attention, she would have to look as though she belonged here. Jane went to a shopping mall and studied the women around her. In the twelve years since she had begun doing this, fading in had gotten easier. She had read somewhere that between 1970 and 1990 a mall had opened somewhere in the country every seven hours. One of the changes this had brought was that women in one part of the country dressed pretty much the way they did in all of the others. Her clothes would do for a few days in Billings, but she could still make some purchases to improve her chances.

She found a store that sold T-shirts and bought one with UNIVERSITY OF MONTANA printed on it. She bought a pair of hiking boots like ones she saw on some other women.

She knew a little bit about what Pete Hatcher was going through. At times he would be sure that he had completely, miraculously lost his pursuers. But every time he heard a maid push her cleaning cart down the hotel hallway, he would feel all the muscles in his body go tense. He would try to reassure himself, then realize that he had no external way to tell whether he was perfectly safe or in imminent danger. So he would sit for hours looking out the window of his room for some piece of evidence that had not come from inside his own skull.

As she searched for the store where she would make her last purchases, she reconsidered what she knew about Pete Hatcher. The first time she had heard his name had been in a telephone call from Paula Dennis. Paula was an intensive-care nurse from Kentucky, and it wasn't until the call that Jane had learned she was also a gambler, and she needed help for a man she had met on a junket to Las Vegas. When Jane had asked her what she knew about the man's habits, she had said, "Pete Hatcher is a ladies' man."

To Jane that had sounded like trouble. Men who had that reputation left behind rivals and angry husbands and women who knew too much about them and were bitter enough to tell strangers. But Paula had said, "By that I mean he is a man who could have been invented by and for ladies. He is a perfect gentleman: attentive, thoughtful, kind, considerate at all times and in every situation. You could take him to visit your aged grandma in Charleston. He's also a very naughty fellow, if you know what I mean, but there are no hard feelings afterward. He's at his sweetest when he takes you to the airport. There are no lies, no chances to make false assumptions with Pete Hatcher. You can be sitting in a restaurant with him, and he will not pretend he's not looking at other women below the face. But the way he does it doesn't make you mad. It makes you squirm in your evening gown. One night I saw him doing it and told him so, and we had quite a conversation about a woman two tables over. He made me understand what he saw when he looked at a woman, and honey, it made me like myself better."

Jane had not been moved to enlist in Hatcher's cause just yet, but her curiosity had been piqued. "What, exactly, did he say?"

"He misses nothing—and I mean nothing—and he likes all of it. This is a woman on the downhill side of fifty. I'm thinking, 'A kind face. Nice clothes. Not impersonating a teenager, but not making up the seating list for her wake, either.' He starts telling me about the smile lines at the corners of her eyes, and the calm glow of the cornea that shows wisdom and receptiveness—which from Pete's side of the table seem to be the same thing—and the flecks and color variations. This is just eyes, remember. I'm leaving out the topographical features south of there, which he can talk about well into next week, if you're mature enough to stand it without hyperventilating and falling into a swoon. But he's never exactly wrong, because what he sees is verifiably there if you look for it. He sees what you wish they would all see. You're just this person getting by on whatever you have. You don't think about how you look most of the time. You think about what you're doing, and that's probably just as well, because it keeps us all out of trouble. Pete comes along and looks at you as though you were an object. No question about that, but the object is a flower or a bird or a tropical fish—something that has its own rules and purposes, its own course in life that doesn't have anything to do with his. If you want to come closer, that's okay with him. But if you don't, that's fine too, because he's just glad to be there and see the pretty colors. This is not a deep thinker. But if this is a man who deserves to die, I want the others all killed off first."

Remembering Paula's call made Jane irritable. It wasn't Paula's fault, and it wasn't even Pete Hatcher's. It was her own. She was already feeling a sick twinge in her stomach about Carey, and she was not yet prepared to set aside time to think clearly about it. She had no business leaving a husband of three months. She had no business breaking her promise, so something in some primitive lobe of her brain told her she was going to be punished. What Paula had said had nothing to do with Carey. It should not have made her feel this way.

When Jane had met Pete Hatcher she had understood what Paula had meant. He had been scared and psychologically worn, but while he was standing up politely to shake her hand, his eyes had taken the long route up to meet her eyes. What he was saying at the time was something good-natured and self-deprecating about needing her advice and help. It should have been incongruous and discomforting, but somehow it wasn't.

Carey would never do anything that simpleminded. He was much more . . . what? Highly evolved. Pete Hatcher appealed to women because he was guileless and optimistic. He made it clear that he was having a lot of fun, and that was a form of flattery. His expression said, "You delight me," and delight was contagious and reciprocal. It created a magnetic field around it stronger than gravity.

But women loved Carey because he knew all their secrets, including the ones that weren't any fun—wear and aging and imperfections and scars—and he was always on their side. It wasn't that they seemed glamorous for the moment, or something. His appeal was a quick and sensitive mind but, more than that, an air that conveyed a knowledge that didn't exclude things found in books but was full of things that he knew because of who he was.

Jane felt weak and foolish for letting Carey enter her mind now. She knew it was because she was about to do something that Carey would have had a right to object to. The bathing suit she chose was relatively modest. It was one piece, black, and not cut as high at the hips as the others in her size. She could have worn it at home without feeling uncomfortable. But she was buying it to wear for Pete Hatcher.

She had to be where the hunters weren't looking and Pete Hatcher was. They would be looking at lobbies and parking lots, and he would be looking at women. He would be hiding, he would be scared, but he had a lifelong addiction to studying every woman who passed in front of his eyes. He would look, because runners had a way of falling back into old comfortable habits to calm themselves. She bought a canvas purse and a wraparound skirt, a big pair of polarized sunglasses and a pair of slip-on rubber-soled shoes that she could run in if she needed to.

The next day she allotted two hours to each of the biggest hotels: the Rainbow, the Traveler's Rest, the Mountaineer. It was easy for a woman to get into the part of a hotel where Jane wanted to go. She entered at the end of a residential wing and walked down the corridor of rooms. She left it near the center of the building, before she reached the lobby, and stepped out into the courtyard. She knew that Pete Hatcher would not be in a ground-floor room, because he would not feel safe in a room where an intruder could walk up to the windows. If he had his choice he would be on an upper floor in a room facing the courtyard, so he could not be shot from the street.

At each hotel she walked to the swimming pool, found a big lounge chair, greased herself with sunblock, and lay back to feel the sun. At some point, Pete Hatcher would look out his window, and he would see her. A lot of people would notice that there was somebody out by the pool. Pete Hatcher would not leave it at that. He would stare at her hard, just because she was a woman between eighteen and fifty-five—and he would recognize her.

By noon she was glad that she had found some sunblock that was practically opaque. The sun came down clear and sharp at this altitude. She lay on her stomach at the Mountaineer and stared along the surface of the water in the pool, watching the sunlight break into spots on the surface and ricochet up against the concrete wall of the building.

She saw Pete Hatcher the second he stepped into the bar overlooking the pool. She stood up, put on her shoes, then wrapped the skirt around her and hooked her bag over her left arm while she watched him through the sunglasses. He was talking to a waiter. She walked quickly toward him.

She could see the waiter going to a cappuccino machine behind the bar that looked like the reassembled parts of a steam locomotive. Too late. The waiter was pouring a pitcher of milk into the boiler and flipping levers. She thought about what Paula had said. Pete Hatcher was standing there with a pulse rate that was probably nearing two hundred. He had just seen the arrival of what amounted to his last chance to blow out the candles on his next birthday, and his response was to order coffee for two. She stepped in the door. No, it was iced cappuccino for two, somehow even more absurd and courtly, because it was the right thing to order for a woman who had been lying in the sun.

He carried the glasses to the table, but Jane took his arm and moved him on to another that was out of sight of the door. The waiter was busying himself at the bar, so she leaned close and gave Hatcher a peck on the cheek before she sat down. "Very thoughtful," she said. In a whisper, she added, "Why didn't you call again?"

He looked pained. "I did. Your message ran, but then there was no beep to start the recorder. I said where I was, but I couldn't tell if it picked anything up. I guess it didn't." He leaned close and looked into her eyes, and she thought of Paula again. Those long eyelashes were part of it—he didn't seem to know they belonged to him. "I made a couple of mistakes in Denver," he confided. "I thought I was doing great, but I was absolutely clueless. That scared me. That's why I called in the first place. If you didn't get my messages, how did you find me?"

"Okay," said Jane. "It doesn't matter. You got through. Now, what have you got up in your room that you can't leave there?"

"One suitcase. The one you had me pack the last time. It's got my money in it."

"Give me the key," she said.

He handed her the key, and she looked at it before she slipped it into her purse. He said, "The number's not on it, but it's 605."

"Here's what we do," she said. "You sit here, sip your drink. If it takes too long, drink mine. Stay here with the waiter. If he leaves, don't go to the lobby or follow me to your room or something. If everything unexpectedly goes wrong, don't go to your car."

"How did you know I had a car?"

She smiled sadly. "If they haven't found you yet, all this is practice. If they have, what they've found is the car."

Jane stood up and walked across the deck outside, back into the corridor where she had entered. She followed it until she found a fire door that led up the stairs. At the sixth floor she stood for a moment with her ear to the door. She heard nothing, so she stepped out into the hallway, found 605, and opened it.

The suitcase was neatly stowed in the closet. She tipped it on its side and searched it. There was sixty thousand dollars in hundreds, fifteen little plastic folders full of traveler's checks, seven passbooks for savings accounts in Denver banks. She loaded the money, passbooks, and checks into her canvas bag and looked deeper.

When she found the box at the bottom she stopped. It was gold with a black stripe. It said, ".38 Special. 20 pistol cartridges." She felt almost relieved. He had gone out and bought himself a pistol and a car. There was nothing mysterious about the way they had found him. All they had done was watch lists that anybody could get, until one man's name had turned up on two or three lists. She put the box of cartridges into her bag with the money, then examined the suitcase for anything else Hatcher had neglected to mention.

She went into the bathroom, picked up his bag of toiletries, wiped the faucets and fixtures with a washcloth, then came out and wiped the desk, the television set, the table, the doorknobs. Then she checked all the wastebaskets for receipts or papers that would hold a print. When she was satisfied, she closed the suitcase, put the sign that said MAID SERVICE on the doorknob, and slipped back into the stairwell.

She climbed to the top floor, then onto the roof of the building. She left the suitcase behind a big air-conditioning condenser and went back down the stairs. They would find it in a month or two and have no idea how it had gotten there.

Downstairs she found Pete Hatcher drinking his cold coffee and looking happy. "Time to go," she said.

"Just like that?"

"Just like that."

She led him the way she had come, down the long corridor and out the door at the end of the east wing to avoid the lobby and the front entrance. When they were in her rented car on the next street she started the engine and waited. "Tell me where your car is."

"It's parked down the street near another hotel," he said. "About three, four blocks down."

She was beginning to feel a little more confident. It wasn't a particularly cunning way to hide a car, but at least it showed he wasn't totally unconscious. He was thinking. She turned the corner and drove in the opposite direction. "I hope you're not too attached to it."

"No," he said. "Does that mean we're just leaving it?"

She sighed. "If things were different I think I would be tempted not to. I would find a very good spot so we could watch the car around the clock. Eventually, the people who want you might come along, and I could see who they were. I'm not that curious this time."

"I don't want to imply that I am, but why aren't you?"

"Several reasons. One is the way they found you."

"You know how they found me? Even I don't know."

"I'm not positive, but you did two things that I know of that a person does who's scared and running. You bought a gun and a car. That gave them two things to put together, two lists with the same name on them. So they might already be watching the car."

"How did you know about the gun?"

"Hardly anybody carries ammunition in his suitcase who doesn't have one," she said. "Tell me exactly what happened in Denver." She drove along the same street in the opposite direction and saw no other car turn to follow.

"There was a woman on the street when I was coming home from the grocery store. She looked like she had car trouble, and I walked over and took a look under the hood. She lifted the pistol out of my belt, stuck a big automatic in my face, and said she was a cop. She made me get in the trunk. A real cop came along right after that, and she killed him."

"How did you see that from the trunk?"

"I didn't, but when I got out, there he was."

"How did you get out of the trunk?"

"She opened it, fired four shots at me, and slammed it again. I'm lying there and after a minute, I realize I'm not dead. She actually missed. On most cars there's a latch inside the trunk. You pull it, and the trunk opens. I was alone except for the dead cop. I don't know anything else."

"That's about all we need to know," said Jane. "They managed to find you. I assume you walked to the same store by the same route regularly?"

He nodded.

"They knew that, and they knew you weren't the sort of man who could walk past a woman with car trouble. Not everybody would stop. They knew you were carrying a pistol, because otherwise she wouldn't have grabbed it before she showed you hers. The fact that she didn't pull the trigger means they must have been planning to drive you out of town where they could shoot you without having anybody hear and bury you without having anybody find you."

"Why do you keep saying 'they'?"

"Did this woman look as though she could carry your body by herself?"

"No."

"Then there was someone else who could. There's also the dead policeman. Denver has serious criminals, and a serious police department. Any cop who stops his car is going to be sure he's able to control whoever he sees. So probably he was shot by somebody he didn't see. Not for sure, but probably."

Pete Hatcher looked out the window and watched the display windows of businesses slipping past as the car moved west toward the interstate. "Then the one I didn't see could have shot me the way he shot the cop—while I was alone on the street. Why didn't he?"

"That's one of those bits of good news that's not quite as good if you take a second look at it," Jane said. "Your former friends from Pleasure, Inc., aren't hunting you themselves; they've hired professionals. The problems that raises should be getting obvious by now. Professionals know how to hunt. They know which ways to kill you are smart, and which ways are stupid. Taking you to a quiet, private place where nothing will be seen or heard is smart; blasting away in the middle of a city is not."

"But that's just what they did. They shot the policeman, and then—"

"They didn't plan to, and that's another side to it. When something unexpectedly goes wrong, professionals don't get emotional. Killing you is just a job, and anybody else who happens along is nothing but a little extra work. They know in advance that they might have to get rid of witnesses, so they're primed for it. They react quickly, and don't spend time asking themselves philosophical questions first."

She glanced at Pete Hatcher to see if he was listening. When she saw his face, her breath caught in her throat. His eyes were watering. Could he be crying? She pretended to pay attention to the road behind her for a few seconds. She glanced at him again. His big brown eyes were welling with tears. When he sensed that she was looking, he turned away and wiped his eyes on his sleeve. She waited.

"That policeman," he said. "He lost his life, and I got mine. It was a bad trade. You should have seen him. His head was half gone. I couldn't even tell what he looked like. The world lost him just to get a little more of me."

Jane blew out a breath slowly. "I don't think that's a train of thought you want to follow too far." She stared ahead at the entrance to the interstate, slipped her car into the center of the tight stream of traffic, and found herself silently talking to Paula. *You didn't have a way to say it, did you? In all the talk about his pleasant disposition and nice manners you never told me why you called me.*

In all her years of snatching rabbits out of the fangs of the wolves, she had almost never heard a rabbit so much as wonder out loud what had happened to the other rabbits. They weren't selfish. It always seemed to her to be physical, the body overpowering the mind to save itself. They never thought of looking back until they had run far enough. That was why a sensible nurse who had seen a lot of men would intercede for this one. The fact that he didn't have a fine and complicated intellect was about the same as saying he didn't have a twelve-cylinder Italian sportscar. He was a decent human being who was just trying to drive what he had.

When she looked at him again, she had an urge to give him something. "Okay," she said, "let's think practically. What do we do with what we know? You got a good look at the woman, right?"

"Right."

"And she got a good look at you. Wherever we go, keep looking for her in the distance. She won't be up close again, but she may be in a crowd, or in a window, or in a car that goes by. If you see her again, you go. No hesitation, no wondering if she saw you or not, no decisions. You go that minute. If you're in the middle of a date in a restaurant a year from now, you go to the men's room and never come back." She watched him to see if he understood, and he seemed to. "Only this time, you're going to know in advance where you're going and how to get there."

"Where are we going now?"

"First, we'll drop out of sight completely for a few days, to let the trail get cold. Then we'll start all over again, and do this right. I'll hide you somewhere, but I'll stick around this time until I'm sure we've lost them for good. I'll give you a few lessons I should have given you the first time. I'll help you get used to the next new name, new place, new life. Then I'll leave for good."

"You said the first thing is dropping out of sight. How do you do that?"

"The best way is to do nothing." She smiled. "Missoula looks like a good place to start doing it. We'll buy you a new suitcase, check into a motel, and see if you got lucky and lost them. In fact, that's the good part about what I was saying, and I almost forgot to tell you. They're pros, and from what I can tell, they're near the upper end of the scale of people who could be called that. That means we avoid them or we're dead: there isn't any mystery about the outcome. But the nice thing about pros is that they're in it for the money."

"So?"

"They get paid in two ways. One is that they get all of it when they've killed you. The other is that the client gives them some money up front for expenses, and the rest when they've got you. Either way, your best friend is time. They've just wasted three months for nothing, and spent a lot of money traveling. People like that could have made a lot in three months. Hardly anybody is very difficult to kill. If the client is paying for all this, then by now he's going to be wondering what he's getting for his money."

"I still don't get it. How does this help me?"

"If you wait long enough, pros go away."

"You're kidding."

"No, I'm not. They don't hate you. They're in a business. At the moment when they calculate that the job is a waste of effort, they quit. If they're getting paid for expenses, the time comes when the client makes the same calculation and stops paying."

"Then I'll be safe?"

She cocked her head and pursed her lips, then said reluctantly, "Not exactly. At least not yet."

"Why not?"

"The client in your case can afford to replace them. But the replacement would have to start all over again at Las Vegas. Pros aren't likely to turn over their information to competitors." She shrugged. "I'm not saying you're in the best position possible, but there are worse."

"What's worse than being chased by professional killers?"

She thought for a moment. "I guess the worst is if you've committed some really awful crime and people know it."

"What would you do for a person like that?"

"Nothing," she said.

16

Seaver drove along the desert highway, watching the long, empty gray road ahead wavering near the distant vanishing point as heat waves rose from the pavement. Now and then a dark reflective spot would appear on the road, the eyes would see it as water, but the brain would say "mirage," and it would diminish to nothing as he approached it. He drove quickly, feeling the slight lift of the car's springs as he reached the crest of each little rise, then feeling his body regain a few pounds more than its weight as the car came to the bottom and began the next climb.

Seaver was satisfied that he was going about this in the right way. The three partners had ultimately left the strategy up to him. Earl and Linda were probably getting close to payday by now, so whatever he did, he had to avoid getting in their way. He might have left a message on their answering machine, asking them to get in touch with him. But leaving a message like that on the answering machine of two professional killers required an absolute belief that they could not get caught, recognized, or traced on this job. The world didn't always work that way. Anybody who had worked in Las Vegas for ten years had seen the ball stop on the double zero a few times.

He had considered tracing their movements and trying to catch up with them. But Earl would not look upon his sudden, uninvited appearance as a favor. It was, in the way these people looked at things, a terrible insult and a violation of their agreement.

Seaver suddenly showing up would mean that there were three people for bystanders to notice, instead of just two. And he would have traveled there by a separate route. That doubled the number of trails that later might be traced to Hatcher's body. He was not at all sure that he wanted to place himself in some distant city with those two at the precise moment when he convinced them that he was so unprofessional and unreliable as to be an actual danger to them.

No, what he was doing made more sense. Earl and Linda were looking for Hatcher. He was looking for the woman. After he found her would be the time to think about meeting them. Then he would have something to bring to the party.

He had assigned five men just to talk to people who were in the chase-and-find business—skip tracers, retrievers who worked for bail-bond outfits, freelance bounty hunters—to see if any of them had ever come across a woman like this. A few of them had heard vague stories, but none of them knew anything that could lead to an actual living woman. It was then that he had realized that he was going about solving the problem backward.

The people most likely to know about her would be the ones in the run-and-hide business. He had called an old friend from the police department who had quit at about the same time he had and had gone to work in the California prison system. Seaver had not described his problem but had described the sort of prisoner he wanted to talk to. He needed one who had been in lots of jails in different parts of the country and who had drawn a long sentence the last time out. But most important, it had to be one who had a history of trading information for favors.

Seaver saw the low, drab buildings, the fence, and the watchtowers undulating in the heat waves across a barren field far back from the highway. He turned up the long, narrow drive that led to the small parking lot outside the gate and glanced at his watch. The drive out here had taken longer than he had expected, but he supposed it wouldn't much matter. In order to miss this guy, Seaver would have to be about twenty years late.

As he turned off his car engine, he stopped to glance in the rearview mirror. Then he got out and put on his coat. He had chosen his clothes carefully. He wore a dark-gray summer-weight suit that cost more than his first new car. His white shirt was marine-pressed with the front and collar starched stiff, and the cuffs showed only a glimpse of his Rolex Oyster watch. A naive observer would have interpreted the bow tie as a whimsical touch, but Seaver didn't expect to meet any naive observers. He was going into a maximum-security prison, where it was well known that nobody with a functioning brain wore anything tied around his neck with a slip-knot.

He walked to the gate, handed his driver's license to the guard, watched him compare it to the list on his clipboard, then obeyed the invitation to step inside. He held up his arms and stood with his legs apart as the second guard ran a metal detector up and down his body, then ran a hand through several of his pockets. He submitted to the preliminaries patiently. Security was his business, and he knew that each stage of the process had two purposes. Scanning the human body for chunks of metal or contraband was the easy part. The hard part was studying the visitor to see if he had something hidden in his head. Each of these meaningless little steps was a test. A normal person would gradually get used to following the unfamiliar rules that applied in a place like this. The person hiding some rash and violent scheme would either feel his nerve draining out of him or get frustrated to the point of blind, undirected rage. Security was mainly a question of finding out whom you were letting breach your perimeter.

Seaver was directed into a small anteroom where he could be kept isolated until they were sure that he wasn't carrying anything that would make him a match for more than one man and that the identification he had given them was real. After ten minutes he was admitted to a room with a desk, where he could be observed while he signed in and had time to check off his compliance with each of the regulations listed on a form and acquaint the guards with the purpose of his visit on another form. It was only after his forms had been completed, read, and determined to be satisfactory that the next door was opened and his escort beckoned to him.

When he walked through the doorway, he noted with approval that there were two guards, the first to lead the way and serve as turnkey and the second to follow a half step behind and to his right, either to protect Seaver's weak side or take advantage of it, as events dictated.

They took him on a long trek down hallways broken at intervals by steel grates that had to be opened with a key and an electronic code. They walked under surveillance cameras recessed in wall niches that one prisoner standing on another's shoulders could not reach and covered with plastic plates that would probably stop a bullet. He admired the premeditation of the system and felt a tiny twinge of envy at its blatancy. Here it was an advantage to be obvious—to convince inmates that escape was ludicrous, that movements inside the complex were monitored, and that disturbances could be isolated instantly. Seaver had to work under more difficult circumstances. The few devices and precautions he could use legally had to be subtle and decorative.

The two escorts led him into a windowless room with a bare wooden table and two chairs. He sat down in the chair facing the door and waited. He had sat for twenty minutes before the two guards reappeared with Stillman, Ray Q. He was a little above middle height, but he slouched the way violence-prone convicts often did, the hips forward and the back hunched in a question mark stance that invited an approaching stranger to take the first swing.

When Stillman turned to hold his wrists out for the guards to unlock his manacles, his back looked like the hood of a cobra, spreading wide as it rose from the thin waist, and then rounding inward at the top because of the slouch that kept the hands and knees forward and the gut pulled back.

The guard wordlessly declined to unlock the manacles. He simply glared at Stillman and left. Stillman's predatory eyes focused on Seaver as he sat down, his thin lips coming up at the corners a little to convey his interpretation of the demonstration: I'm too dangerous for you.

Seaver reached into his shirt pocket and produced a pack of cigarettes, pulled the strip to remove the cellophane, tore off the foil, and thumped the pack to raise a cigarette. He lit one with a match, then held it out. Stillman reached across the table with both hands, stuck it in the corner of his mouth, rested his hands in his lap, and waited.

Seaver looked at him for a few seconds, then said, "I'm Seaver. I can't get you out of here. I can't get you a new trial. If you ever get a parole hearing, I won't be there to tell them you cooperated in an investigation. I won't be there at all."

Stillman looked at him expectantly, and Seaver knew he had begun well. They were all experts in the ways that the system could be manipulated, and the ways that it couldn't. After about two convictions they also knew that false hope worked on them like poison, and they hated anyone who tried to force it on them. "Here's what I can do. Captain Michnik is an old friend of mine. If you have the answers to my questions, he will help you right now, starting today. You don't have to wait six months for an official letter that's never going to come."

"What kind of help are you offering?"

"A little slack. You'll get a better job, if what you want won't be so obvious it'll get you killed. If a guard is down on you, he'll be rotated to another block. If you've done anything recently that you need to skate on, he'll give you the benefit of the doubt."

"What does that cost me?"

"I heard something, and I want to know more about it."

"What did you hear?"

"I heard there's a woman who hides people."

Stillman blew out a quick puff of smoke. "A lot of women hide people."

Seaver slowly shook his head. "This one is a professional. If you're in trouble, you hire her to get you out of it. She comes and whisks you away—makes you disappear. I guess she must get you a new name and new papers, maybe a job."

"Which are you?"

"What?" snapped Seaver.

"You thinking of disappearing, or are you looking for somebody?" His head was cocked to the side, and his eyes squinted through the smoke.

Seaver gave a half smile and a snort. "Do I look like somebody who has that kind of problem?" He shot the cuffs of his immaculate white shirt so he could be sure Stillman saw his watch and the perfect fit of his tailored suit.

Stillman shrugged. "You look like somebody who might develop some problems if you got sent to a place like this—or even if somebody in here got out. If you know the captain, maybe you put some of them in."

"Could be," said Seaver.

Stillman nodded with amusement. "That's it, isn't it? Somebody you don't want to turn your back on dropped out of sight?"

"No," Seaver said. "I'm interested in this woman because she made somebody scarce that I want, but the last person he wants to see is me. I'd like to ask her about him."

Stillman shifted in his chair and lifted both hands to pluck the cigarette from his lips. He stepped on it with deliberation. When he raised his face again his blue eyes were opaque, but Seaver could tell he was taking the offer seriously.

"I don't know her." Stillman grinned and held up his chained wrists. "I bet you could have guessed that."

Seaver nodded. "But you've heard of her."

Stillman nodded too. "If you're in here long enough, you probably hear every way that words can be pulled together. I'd like to get a few favors. But there's another side to this. If you can get me goodies, you can also get my ass kicked or worse. What I know is just rumors: third-hand stuff. I send you off, you're probably going to come back and tell the captain I shined you on. I don't know you, but I know him."

Seaver studied him. Something else was on his mind, and the only way to hear it was to get through the easy ones. "Okay, I've been warned. You tell me what you heard, and I won't hold a grudge, as long as you don't add anything of your own." Then he added, as a precaution, "Anyway, I know plenty about her already, so I can figure out which parts you heard wrong." He handed Stillman another cigarette and struck a match, then held it out so Stillman could lean into it and puff until the tip ignited.

Stillman leaned back and said, "Say there really is a woman like this? There would be people in the joint who know about her. Maybe they got helped by her once, then fucked up again and couldn't get to her in time. Maybe they didn't get to her even the first time, but they hope some day they'll make it." He smiled and shook his head. "Even though a germ couldn't get out of here, about one in five of these guys thinks he can."

Seaver's smile mirrored Stillman's. "A lot of sheets get tied together, but you don't see many of them hanging outside the walls of these places." He shrugged. "Anyway, this isn't that kind of situation. I'm not interested in charging her with anything, or even putting her out of business. I want this guy, and I'll pay her for him. She's nothing to me." He caught a hint of skepticism in Stillman's stare, so he said quickly, "Of course, if she draws down on me, I'll have to kill her. But even then, nobody would know you told me about her."

Stillman put his tongue to his lips and spat out a flake of loose tobacco. "Okay, then I know some things."

"Go on."

"It's probably none of it true. People talk about things like that. There's a pair of Siamese twins in Vacaville they have to let out every other week, because one of them didn't get convicted. There's a four-fingered lawyer in San Diego who knows one thing they forget to do in almost every trial, so he can get anybody off who will send him a finger. One of the contractors who built this place was getting kickbacks on the materials, so just in case they caught him, he put a secret tunnel under the infirmary. There's a woman who takes people out of the world and gives them new lives."

"A little bit past her prime with blond hair, right?"

"Not in the version I heard. It was black. She had long black hair, and she was nice looking. I don't vouch for that, because in stories the girl is always that way. It wasn't like you said before, either. I heard the way it works is, you have to come to her. And you have to clean yourself before you do. If you want to bring something you left behind—maybe what you stole, maybe a girlfriend—she'll tell you you're not ready for her. If what you want is another chance to kill the one who set you up, she'll tell you to go do it and not come back. She's in the running business, not the fighting business. You don't just give up your name, you have to give up everything you ever were, ever saw or did. You're a new person, who doesn't know any of that."

"I heard that," Seaver lied. It occurred to him that maybe Hatcher wasn't planning to resurface after all—that maybe this was all a waste of time. But it was way too late for that kind of thinking. It just weakened him, distracted him. The partners had made their decision, and they were waiting. "Where do you go?"

"You mean where does she take you?"

Seaver spoke patiently, almost respectfully. "No. You're on the run. You collect a pile of money for her fee. Where do you take it?"

"I don't know."

"Who did you hear all this from?"

"I heard it a few times, and I can't sort out which part I heard which time. The first one was seven or eight years ago, in Alameda County Jail. It was an old guy, and he was telling a kid. See, the kid was in for the first time. They had a running tab on him. It started out as some kid thing—vandalism or something. He tried to run: resisting arrest. He hot-wired a car to get away: grand theft auto. He drove it fast until a police car crashed into him to run him off the road, so it was attempted vehicular manslaughter. He struggled, so it was assaulting a police officer. On and on. He tried to hang himself, but the old man cut him down with a shank he carried. He said to the kid, 'You got to get yourself in shape so the guards don't know about this. On the day of your arraignment, you're going to get out on bail for a month or so while they dream up more charges. That's your chance. But if they know you did this, they can keep you here and watch you.' He helped the kid get rid of the homemade rope and cover the welts, and then told him about the woman."

"In front of you?"

"No. The old guy never talked to me at all. He didn't like me from the minute he laid eyes on me. The kid came to me later and asked me if the old man was crazy—just jerking him around, or what."

"How did he tell the kid to get in touch with this woman?"

"That was one of the things that made me think it was bullshit. He wouldn't tell the kid the address, because the kid was too green to make it that far. The kid had to wait until he was out and write her a letter, then let her say where to meet her."

"Do you remember where the letter was supposed to go?"

"A post office box in L.A. The next time I heard it, there was a house somewhere."

"Where?"

"I don't know."

"Who mentioned the house?"

"Some counterfeiter. Just what they do is so stupid that you can't believe what they say. They all get caught, then go out and do it again."

Seaver sighed and looked at Stillman. He had seen Stillman's record. The man had been in jails for twelve of his thirty-one years, and there was something he'd done before the adult record had begun that had put him in youth camp. If he ever got out again, he'd be a three-time loser before he even did anything.

Stillman went on. "He wouldn't tell me where the house was. He said the only reason he had the address was because his girlfriend gave it to him just before he got arrested. She didn't get arrested, though. She got away, and never got caught."

"Is that true?"

"I once saw a thing on TV where they said nobody ever saw a U.F.O. until somebody said he saw one in 1947. Once he said it, everybody and his brother started seeing them. Maybe that's the year when the U.F.O.'s got here. Maybe it's just that once somebody makes something up, then it's everybody's. It gets to be another way to seem important, to have something to tell, because nothing that's true about you is worth listening to. Bigfoot, the Loch Ness monster, God, all that."

"Do you think I could get to any of these guys—the old man, for instance?"

"The old man was here for a while, but he's been dead a couple of years. The counterfeiter, name is Bill Ortega, I heard he was in federal prison back east someplace. I don't know his girlfriend's name. If you've got a lot of connections in the correctional system, maybe you can track him down."

"What about the kid?" Seaver's hands moved unseen from his lap to grip the support under the table.

Stillman squinted up into the air and smiled. "Now, him I don't know about. I just don't know. For years I've been wondering. Once in a while, I ask around with the guys who have been in a lot of joints all over. His name was Phil O'Meara. Nobody's seen him, or seen his name on the count, or knows anybody who's met him." He smirked mysteriously. "Maybe he figured out to get the knot behind his ear and hung himself right."

Seaver's feet kicked out under the table and pushed Stillman's chair over backward onto the floor. Seaver sprang up, used one arm to vault over the table, and came down with his knee on Stillman's chest.

He spoke quietly, through clenched teeth. "You're one of them, aren't you? You think maybe, just maybe, they'll forget who you are one day and let you unload the grocery truck so you can strangle the driver. Let me tell you something. It isn't going to happen. And even if it did, and you got to her, she'd take one look at you and shut the door. You're an evolutionary dead end, a throwback. She can smell it on you as well as I can. She can't predict what you're going to do next, because even you can't. You're a bad risk. Don't hold out on me, because it's nothing you're ever going to use."

Stillman seemed to be immune to surprise. His face seemed to slacken, to go blank in the prisoner's stare. He looked past Seaver at the ceiling and said, "Two packs of cigarettes a week. A job in the library."

"Done."

"The box wasn't in Los Angeles, it was in New York City. It's Box 345, 7902 Elizabeth Street, in New York. There's some fake name attached to it—a man's name."

Hours later, Seaver sat staring out through the scratched plastic pane of the window at the baggage carts and fuel trucks slipping past him backward as his airplane was pushed away from the terminal by a tractor with a tow bar. He thought about Earl and Linda again. When he had hired them, he had known a lot about Hatcher, but nothing about the woman. It was just as well, because this way he didn't have to worry about bumping into them on this trip. With nothing to go on, they wouldn't have seen her as the way to find Hatcher.

Now he had a few bits of information, and soon he would have enough. He stared at his watch for a moment, then carefully pulled the stem and set it three hours ahead. When he got to New York, he would still have time for some sleep. The hotel reservation was guaranteed, so the room would be waiting for him. The overnight package from Nevada would probably be there when he awoke. He could assemble the pieces of the gun after breakfast.

The telephone directory said that the 996 exchange meant that the telephone answering machine was in Deganawida. The road atlas said that the population of Deganawida was only 22,000 souls.

Linda Thompson sat at the desk in the little suite she had rented on the south side of Buffalo, her face illuminated by the computer screen. When Earl had initiated her ten years ago, tracking a person still meant going to counters in below-ground floors of old county office buildings and turning the pages of bound books of records while some sour-faced old clerk watched her out of the corner of her eye. Then she would fill out some form with a ballpoint pen with a chain on it, pay a fee in some strange number like three dollars, or six, but never five, and wait weeks for the copy to come in the mail.

Now all she had to do was put herself into a screen-trance, tap in the secret numbers and symbols, and then conjure what she wanted out of the air. She watched the lighted screen as she put in the mixture of upper- and lowercase letters, periods, slashes, pound signs in their correct order. The screen exploded into life with the company's greeting, "Welcome to Probar Commercial Information Systems, Santa Ana, California." There was a graphic of the front of a building with a big closed door like the vault of a bank. "User number?" said the screen.

Linda typed in the Northridge Detectives account number, the door appeared to swing open, and the doorway expanded beyond the borders of the screen as though she were stepping inside. The door was replaced by the menu. It was longer than it had been a month ago. PCIS had been collecting for seven or eight years now, and it had thousands of public records databases. She scrolled down the list quickly.

She moved her cursor to select "Tax Assessor's Rolls." She selected New York State. She selected Erie County. She selected City of Deganawida. The menu disappeared and the screen said, "Access charge five dollars. Do you wish to proceed? (Y/N)."

Linda tapped Y. She was guessing that this Jane woman did not live in an apartment building. The business of making people disappear did not lend itself to renting. It was almost inevitable that from time to time a client might show up in person, and renters on the same floor would wonder about it. Any clandestine business was best conducted from a free-standing building without a landlord who might drop in, and the address had to remain the same.

This Jane had apparently operated in Las Vegas as though she were good at it, and the people who needed to disappear badly enough to hire help doing it probably didn't care what they paid. She could afford a house, especially in a backwater like Deganawida. Linda looked at the list that appeared on the screen. Now that she was in, she could manipulate the list. She asked it how many entries were on the list, and it said 5,864. Linda felt power begin to flow into her. The number was tiny. She ordered her computer to search for the word "Jane."

The computer found sixteen Janes, a Janeway, and fifty-two houses on a Jane Street. She made a copy of each of the Janes. She was feeling more and more excitement as she went along. She had been in western New York for only a day, and already she had the list down to sixteen.

Linda relinquished her hold on the tax assessor's rolls and returned to the main menu. She contemplated Jane. She was twenty-five to thirty-five years old, probably about thirty if Linda could trust Seaver's description. She was tall, thin, dark-haired. She operated a very strange little business from one of these sixteen free-standing buildings in Deganawida. Would she have the office disguised as some kind of business? Linda could not decide. Was Jane one of the seven married women, someone like Ronald and Jane Schwartzkopf, Tenants in Common? Or was she one of the nine sole owners listed—Jane Hanlon, Jane Whitefield, Jane Carmen Rossi? Most of the women listed alone were probably widows or divorcees. Some would be too old.

Jane the woman who made people disappear would have a driver's license. The driver's license carried date of birth, height, weight, hair and eye color. Linda selected the Department of Motor Vehicles records: "Access fee ten dollars. Do you wish to proceed? (Y/N)." She began with the first of the sixteen names and scanned the information that had been printed on the license: Jane Anne Hanlon, DOB 08-09-29. Jane Pildrasky was HT 5-02, WT 160, HAIR BLD, EYES BLU. Jane Rossi's license was RSTR: CORR LENS, DAYLIGHT ONLY. The Jane who had helped Pete Hatcher would never have picked a darkened room and a night escape if she could see only in bright light.

Before she relinquished the Department of Motor Vehicles records, Linda had eliminated all but four of the Janes who owned houses in Deganawida. All were HT 5-06 or better, HAIR BRN, DOB after 1960. She returned to the telephone directory and looked up the four names. She eliminated first Jane Sheridan and then Jane White-field because neither had the right telephone number. But then she discovered that none of the other Janes had it either. Of course. The Jane she wanted had to live a visible life in a small town. She would have a listed number in the book. It was the business phone that would be unlisted. Linda put Sheridan and Whitefield back in contention.

Linda stared at the main menu and let her reverie deepen. She picked up Jane and turned her around and around, looking at her closely, trying to feel her surfaces. Jane was a tall, lean, dark-haired, youngish woman who owned a house in Deganawida but was gone from it for periods of time. She probably operated much the way Linda and Earl did. She would get a telephone call, drop everything, and go to meet a client. Then she would come home and lie around for weeks, getting used to the time zone and letting her aches and pains go away. Linda felt herself coming closer and closer to Jane.

She selected the credit check: "Access fee, thirty-five dollars. Do you wish to proceed? (Y/N)." Y, of course. Now for the federal privacy law. "Please indicate your legitimate legal grounds for requesting the information. You are a Prospective: (a) Lender, (b) Employer, (c) Insurer, (d) Other. Please specify." Linda loved that part of it. They gave you a selection of lies to choose from. She chose insurer. Insurance companies could do virtually any kind of investigation they wanted on anybody, and they often hired detective agencies to help.

When the four credit reports came out of her printer, Linda studied them. Jane Sheridan was employed by the Deganawida School

District. She was a teacher. She couldn't leave town every time the phone rang. Jane Finley was listed as a "homemaker," which was more promising, but her record was full of late payments, credit extended by appliance stores and car dealers, and interest paid to credit-card companies. It didn't make sense for the Jane that Linda was looking for to live that way. She didn't need to, and it made too many people interested in her. Jane Colossi was promising for thirty seconds. She was an attorney. She seemed to spend a lot of money, but the most recent big charges listed for each credit card were for the month of June in France and Italy, when the right Jane was in Las Vegas. Jane Whitefield was the last one in the alphabet. She worked as a "career consultant." She had the right kind of credit rating—excellent. Then Linda found it. Jane Whitefield had two telephone numbers. She probably didn't know the telephone company's computer had spit out the unlisted one when the credit bureau's computer had asked. She was Jane.

Linda looked down the list of debts. There was no mortgage on the house, and none listed as having been paid off. That interested her. Either Jane had paid cash, which would have raised eyebrows, or she had inherited the house.

Linda returned to Probar's menu and asked for probate court filings for the state of New York. She started the computer in Santa Ana on its search for the name and waited. This would take some time.

Linda stared at the glowing screen while she thought about Jane. Linda was beginning to feel her now. She was—how had Seaver said it?—fit. That was it. She did exercises and pushed herself the way Linda did. It wasn't just because she wanted to get the attention that came when your abs were tight and your ass round and firm, but because she might have to run or fight. She had fought a man that night in Las Vegas, Seaver had said—not hit some old night watchman over the head when he wasn't looking, but faced off with a grown man who was trying to hurt her. That meant she was fast and dirty, because there was no other way it could happen. A man could be dumb as a buffalo and lead with his face, and there was still no way a woman, at most two-thirds his weight, could stand there and take turns throwing punches with him. She was probably a lot like Linda.

The computer screen flashed awake again with the probate documents Linda had requested. The former owner of the house was Alice Whitefield. Before that it had been Henry Whitefield and Alice Whitefield. Linda perused Alice Whitefield's bequest. She had died twelve years ago and left everything to her daughter Jane, age twenty-one. Everything had not been much—the house, contents valued at under thirty thousand; a ten-year-old Plymouth; a bank account with nine thousand in it.

Linda left the court files. There was one last piece of information that she needed to conjure tonight. She selected the records of the County Clerk of Erie County. Linda typed in Jane Whitefield's name and address, copied her date of birth from her driver's license. When the Probar computer found the document Linda was startled. She read it twice to make sure. Jane Whitefield had been married on June 21, to Carey Robert McKinnon, 5092 Dodge Road, Amherst, New York.

Linda felt a sense of fulfillment, of completeness. She was beginning to know Jane Whitefield now. Probably this Carey McKinnon had started her out when she was young, the way Earl had started Linda. It had probably been about the time when her mother had died and she found herself alone with an old house and a cheap car and barely enough money for a good vacation. He had told her she was going to learn a lot and see a lot, and make a lot of money. And here she was, ten or twelve years later, out alone, risking her life to make people like Pete Hatcher vanish.

Linda went back to the menu and began to work magic on Carey McKinnon. It took her an hour to find out more about him than she knew about Jane. She glanced at her watch frequently now, because the time was almost certainly coming. She had given Lenny her telephone number as soon as she had moved in, so Earl would have it by now. The telephone rang at midnight.

"Hello, Linda."

"Hi," she said. She wanted to sound unperturbed and self-sufficient. "How's it going?"

"Not so hot," said Earl. "I found his car in Billings, between a couple of hotels. I plugged the gas line so it would turn over but not start, but he hasn't come back for it, and I haven't had any luck at the hotels. Where are you?"

"I'm in a little place south of Buffalo called the Meadowgreen Suites. You get a kitchen and a refrigerator, but you don't have to make the bed."

"What have you got?"

"Her name is Jane Whitefield. She has a house in a little town north of Buffalo along the Niagara River called Deganawida. That's where the answering machine is."

"Is she home, or do I have to watch my back for her too?"

"I don't know yet. My guess is that she's already out there with him."

"When will you know?"

"Tomorrow morning. It's a little more complicated than I thought. She got married in June."

"Know anything about her husband?"

"What I know doesn't make too much sense to me yet. His name is Carey McKinnon, and he's a doctor."

There was a short pause while Earl ruminated. "It could be she dreamed that up as an identity for one of her favorite clients and then got him to marry her—you know, he says he's a doctor that's retired, and he doesn't have to explain why he's got a lot of money and plays golf all day."

"I thought of that," said Linda. "But his credit check says he's actually getting payments from a hospital, and from some surgical group. He's in the A.M.A. directory. They don't let you flash a fake ID and go operate on somebody."

"A double beard, then?" asked Earl. "Maybe he's queer and gets to hide it—nobody wants a surgeon who might have AIDS—and she gets to be that much harder to find. Does he have a separate house?"

"Yeah. But I don't know if one of them is empty. If they don't live together, she wouldn't be much of a beard in a town that size. I just got this stuff an hour ago, and I'm thirty miles from there, but I'll be out early to see if she's at his house or hers, or neither. You know, it occurred to me that he could be some kind of fanatic."

"What kind of fanatic?"

"We know she took Pete Hatcher out. We don't know why, or if he's typical, or one of a kind. There are these groups that take battered women and children out the same way, like the Underground Railroad. The first person to see somebody like that is a doctor. That kind of group might hire a pro like her to do the hard part, and that's how they met. Maybe Pete Hatcher was just the money for their honeymoon."

"Get on them," he said.

"What does it sound like I'm doing, Earl?"

"I mean really get on them," he said. "Hatcher has me out here in Billings, Montana, watching a parked car. I don't think he accomplished that alone. If she's home, I'd like to know it. If she's not, I'd at least like a picture of her so she can't walk up to me on the street and blow my head off. If her husband's gone, I'd like to know that I've got him to expect too, and what he looks like."

"I'll know if they're here in a few hours."

"If he specializes in plastic surgery and he could be busy making Pete Hatcher look like Miss Arkansas, I'd like to know that. I'm dead in the water out here. Whatever you can get me, whatever it takes to get it."

"Whatever?" She let her voice go soft and low. She savored the pause on his end of the line. There was the electrical charge, growing and growing, and the resistance was making the air hotter. There was nothing in the world like hunting, knowing that any click in the dark could be the slide of the pistol locking the first round into the chamber.

He was feeling it too. "I mean do whatever you have to, and then do some more. If you think they're going to pay us a couple hundred thousand and write it off after three months, you're dreaming. One of these days you're going to call home and it won't be Lenny that answers. It'll be Seaver."

"I know," she said. "I'll do my best, I promise."

"If she's there, kill her. I'll call tomorrow night." He hung up.

Linda put the telephone receiver on the hook, lay on the bed, and stared at the ceiling. She toyed with the fear, tested it for titillation. It made her heart beat fast, and a little electric shock clapped her back behind her lungs, then moved down the sides to her haunches like a shiver. Playing for death was better than anything.

But tonight there was something extra, something that made it better and more delicious. It was Jane. She was the attraction. There was an urge to take a risk to beat her. Linda was going to be the one who was smarter, faster, dirtier. She was going to be the one.

J ane left the rented car at the agency in Missoula and picked up the one she had parked on the university campus. Pete Hatcher watched everything she did and listened to her explanations, then nodded his head. He had stopped asking questions, and that set off a tiny alarm in the back of Jane's mind. It would not be out of the question for a man in his position to be contemplating suicide. It was also possible that he was only getting tired and passive. If that lasted long enough, it wasn't much different from suicide.

She drove him northeast on Route 200 away from Missoula, and stopped at a motel in a small town called Potomac. They sat in the car for a moment. She waited for him to ask a question. Finally, she pulled a small leather wallet out of her purse and handed it to him.

"What's this?" he asked.

"We need to sleep now. This is a motel. It isn't part of a national chain, so that makes its records a lot harder to get. If we do everything the way everybody else does, we're invisible. What everybody else does is that the man goes inside and registers. For the moment, we're going to travel as Mr. and Mrs. Michael Phelan of Los Angeles. I have identification that matches. Now go do it."

Too soon, he came out of the office and walked to the car. "They don't have any suites or anything like that," he said. "Should I rent two rooms?"

She closed her eyes and took a deep breath. He seemed to have lost his will to keep his mind working. "Pull yourself together and think. Mr. and Mrs. Phelan don't sleep in separate rooms. Get it over with."

He disappeared inside the office again and came out carrying a key. She watched him open the door, then started the car and pulled it into a parking space a distance from the room and went to join him inside. She surveyed the room. Her eyes rested on the king-size bed in the center of the floor. She forced them to move on. That was an extra problem with hiding a man. Dancing around in cramped quarters to keep the distances proper and the bodies covered became part of the job. She decided not to face that conversation yet. Anything she said now would not get a second bed in here, and would make him more passive and tentative.

She looked out the windows, checked the locks, examined the curtains, and continued her commentary. "When you check in, you take a mental picture of the world outside. The best way out of here is to the left, toward the car. I parked it in front of another door, away from the office. If somebody finds out we're here, he doesn't know which car is ours. If he finds the car, he doesn't know which room is ours. It's late now, so most of the other cars that will be in the lot are already here. Next time you look, what you'll be looking for is newcomers. You lock everything that will lock." She flipped the deadbolt and the safety latch. "If you do all the little things right, you'll sleep better."

She glanced at her watch. "I'm going out for a few minutes. When I come back I'll knock four times, like this." She rapped on the table.

"Where are you going?"

"To make a phone call from the booth at the gas station."

"There's a phone right here."

"There would be a record of the call."

She slipped out and walked toward the car in case the night clerk happened to be watching, then kept going past it and across the weedy margin of the property to the gas station, put a quarter into the telephone slot, and dialed zero, then the number of the house in Amherst. "I'd like to make a collect call. It's Jane."

She heard Carey pick up the telephone. "Operator." The word came out before he had even said hello. "Will you accept a collect call from Jane?"

"Sure," he said. The operator clicked off. "Jane?"

"Hi," she answered.

"You okay?"

"Yes. I found him, and I picked him up, and now I've got him hundreds of miles away. I think we're two hops ahead of them. Maybe only one hop, but it's a good one."

"Where are you?"

The question startled her. She had never talked to anybody at home while she was working—not really talked, because she had always lied. She felt a twinge almost like pain when she said, "I'm in a little town in the Wild West. At least I think I'm in town. There's not much here, so I can't be sure."

"A hotel or something?"

"Sure. It's not the Hilton, but I haven't seen any cockroaches either." She was saying words that were true, but she was lying. He wanted to know everything, and she was giving him breezy nonsense.

"You're staying with . . . him? That can't be safe."

The lie came easily, like breathing, really. "Well, no, not exactly. One of the tricks of the trade. He's in his motel room and I checked into another room across the parking lot. That way I can watch his door, and if anything suspicious happens, all I have to do is dial his room. He goes out the window on the side I can see is clear, and I pick him up on the highway."

She knew it sounded plausible. She had been lying for so long that it was almost a reflex. She had heard the trouble building in his voice, and she had flinched to evade it. She pushed the question and the answer into a corner of her mind and labeled the corner a special exception. She had been trying to save him some anxiety, and the anxiety would have been pointless, because he would have been worrying about a dangerous situation that she had no way to evade. Or maybe, in the back of his mind, he had been worried about . . . something else. That was something she simply was not going to do, so worrying about it would serve no purpose. She loved Carey McKinnon.

Carey was already talking. "I'm sorry," she said. "I missed that."

"I said, Do you know where you're going next, or when you'll be home?"

His kind, patient voice opened a wound in her, and she tried to make up for the small lie. "I'll tell you what I know at the moment," she said. "The attempt these people made was a little worse than I thought. He would be dead now if a cop hadn't happened along in time to take the bullet for him. So he's a mess—I mean psychologically. Guilty, scared, and, consequently, stupid. The hunters are a lot better at it than I had hoped, so I have to be cautious. At the moment the plan is to take him someplace where he'll be almost impossible to find, teach him everything he could possibly need to know, and split. That's what I should have done in the first place, but I couldn't."

Carey's voice was a monotone, as though there was hurt and anger that he was making an effort to keep out of it. "It's starting to sound like it will take a lot of time."

"It shouldn't," she said. Why was she talking to him as though there were lawyers present? "There is nothing in the whole world that I want more than to be with you. Right now. Tonight. But I think this could take a couple of weeks. I've got to be sure I've lost the hunters, and then get him settled. When that's done, I'll rush home and have a lot of fun being Mrs. McKinnon again. Forever. Maybe I'll lock you in the house for a month and see for myself if the bad reputation you have is justified. I'm pretty sure it is, but I'd like to double-check."

She heard him give a small, unvoiced chuckle. "I miss you," he said. She heard a sigh. "Well, I guess there's nothing much I can do except wait and hold you to your word. Do what you have to do, and get home."

She loved him. The lies were a pain in her chest. "I miss you so much I could cry." She wanted to tell him things. A big truck rushed past on the highway and a hot, dusty wind blew off the pavement into her face. "Stupid trucks," she said. "I'm going to try to jump around to a few of these little towns for a couple of days to see if anybody's looking for us, then leave some trails in the wrong direction. After that I'll put him in a place where he can stay for twenty years. But first, the little towns."

"Pick one, and I'll call you there tomorrow."

She felt a chill. "I can't do that," she said quickly. "I'll be using different names, and I don't know which one or where I'll be yet. If I did, I couldn't say it on the phone. I'll call you."

There was silence on the other end. Had he figured out that the name would be Mr. and Mrs. something?

"Carey?"

"Yeah?"

"I'll call you as soon as I can. I know this is hard. I love you." She had never known that "I love you" was what a person said when she had run out of words and couldn't say anything else. It was like reaching out a hand in desperation.

"I love you too. Just be careful, and come home in one piece."

"Don't worry. I've become a very cautious married lady." She took a deep breath. "That reminds me. I guess I ought to get going now."

"I could talk to you all night."

"When we're together," she said. "Then I'll talk until you want to smother me with a pillow. But I'd better go. Some people are born to disappear. This one takes a lot of hand-holding." She drew in her breath, leaned her forehead against the phone booth, and shut her eyes. It was the middle of the night. If Hatcher was waiting for her to come back, the story that they were in different rooms didn't make sense. She said quickly, "I love you," and hung up. She turned and walked to the motel feeling sad and empty.

Jane approached the motel by circling it to study the cars in the lot, the traffic patterns on the two roads that intersected beside it, and the businesses nearby. The town was tiny and clean and presented an unassuming business face. But she could not induce a feeling of safety here. It was not big enough to provide a crowd to hide in, and not remote enough to be hard to find. As soon as Pete seemed rested and presentable, she would get him back on the road.

She thought about her conversation with Carey as she walked. She had been vague and evasive, but she had heard herself say something that she now realized was accurate. She had almost no idea where the chasers were, or what they were thinking. It was possible that Pete, in his novice's panic and ignorance, had managed to leave them behind in Denver. They would certainly trace his car to Billings, but by the time they did, it would be in an impound lot and Pete could be anywhere.

Only if they were spectacularly good or phenomenally lucky—had an unseen person follow his car all the way to Billings—could they know he had gotten even that far. After that she had taken him out in a rented car, changed to still another car, and driven nearly eight hours. It was very unlikely that they could have followed without her seeing them.

If she kept Pete out of airports and big, well-lighted cities for a time, she would at least avoid squandering the lead she had on them. One way to do that was to keep him in suspended animation in the tiny resort towns up here, looking like one of the thousands of summer tourists.

She knew a little bit about the way the shooters must have found him the first time. They had looked at computerized public records and found out that the same man in Denver had registered a car and bought a gun at the same time. Probably they had run a credit check and found that he had also just arrived in town, and then they had flown in to take a look at him.

Now Jane would keep him from doing anything that got him on any lists for a time. Then she could control where and when he did anything else that created public records. She had already bought him a car under the name Wendy Wasserman. She would get him settled in his next apartment, find him a job, and help him fit in with the locals. He had already given in to the urge to buy a gun, and he still had it, so he probably wouldn't make that mistake again.

She allowed herself a small feeling of optimism. Eight hours was not a huge lead, but it was growing. When she knocked on the door of their motel room, she heard him go to the window, saw him move the curtain aside to look out, then heard him step to the door and open it.

She slipped inside, closed the door, and glanced at him. He was in a pair of blue boxer shorts, and he turned away and hastily slipped his pistol into a pile of clothing on a chair. She couldn't help being surprised by the sight of his body, but she fought to keep him from noticing. She had plucked the poor man away from Billings without his suitcase. She had not expected him to sleep fully dressed. She had not expected anything at all, and she reminded herself that she was going to have to anticipate his needs or she was going to wear them both out. She tried to formulate some words that would get them past this moment.

"It looks clear out there." The attempt disappointed her. After all, what he was wearing wasn't different from what men wore on the beach. She was a grown-up married woman. What difference did it make what he wore? Then it occurred to her that she was going to need to wear something to bed too. What she wore did seem to her to make a difference.

She pushed the thought aside and let the space fill itself with a trivial observation that had been prickling the back of her mind. "You did okay a minute ago, but all I've got to do right now is give you lessons, so here's another one. You heard the right knock, so you thought it was me. You looked around the curtain to see if I was alone. Good. But I heard you, and saw you, and that was not so good. If I had been the wrong person giving the right knock, you'd be dead."

"What was I supposed to do?"

"You were right to want to look before you opened the door. The very best time for them would be those few seconds while you and I were standing together with the door open. They could see us both in the light, and if they missed one of us the first time, they wouldn't need to break anything down to get the survivor. But you want to look without letting anybody know you're doing it. Do what the cops do on surveillance: don't move the curtain, just look over the top of the track it's on."

"You can't see anything but the wall," he said. "The track is above the glass."

She moved a chair to the far side of the window, and said, "Trust me."

Pete stepped on the chair and looked down over the top of the metal track. In the two-inch space he could clearly see the step in front of the door, the wall on either side of the door, and some of the sidewalk. "I can see more from here than I could when I opened the curtain."

"Right. It's a view that shows you the likely hiding places around the door. It's above them, which is good, because people seldom look up unless they know what they're looking for. They look to both sides, look behind, look down."

"I never noticed that. Why?"

"I don't know. Maybe it's just the way the skull is connected to the neck. Maybe it's some prehistoric instinct that serious trouble hardly ever comes at an animal our size from above the treetops. Notice anything else while you were up there?"

"It's an odd angle."

"Right. When you were at ground level peeking between the curtains, they could have seen you and shot you through the glass from the left, from the right, or from the parking lot. When you were beside the window and above it, the right side of the window and the parking lot were out. Anybody there couldn't see you. The only danger left was that the person at the door would look up and to his left, pull out a weapon before you saw him do it, and make a world-class shot that hit the thin slice of your body that wasn't protected behind the wall or the woodwork—all of that before you moved. Or, since you had a gun in your hand, before you opened fire on his completely exposed body."

"How did you learn all these tricks?"

Jane sat down on the bed and smiled sadly. "No matter how much you learn, the people who chase fugitives are still better at it. You watch how they work, you pick up what you can, and you keep going."

"Why do you? What made you get into a line of work like this in the first place? Is the money that good?"

She shook her head and let out a little chuckle. "I did it once, I did it again. It never occurred to me to accept pay. Somebody pressed the point, and I said, 'So send me a present.' The jobs got more dangerous, and the presents got bigger."

"But why the first time?"

"Anybody who knows how to swim will jump in and pull out the one who's drowning. I knew how to swim."

"But—"

"Enough," she said. "Things were going to happen, and I made decisions about which ones I could live with, just as anybody does. The choices aren't always limitless. In case you haven't noticed, I was feeling sorry for myself tonight without this conversation."

"I'm sorry," he said. "If you want to be alone for a few hours, I could manage that much."

"Of course not," said Jane. "I didn't mean it that way." She felt ashamed. He was scared to death, and he was volunteering to go out and cower somewhere while she had a fit of the vapors or something. "You're a good guy, Pete. We're going to have to spend a lot of time together for a while. I'll let you know now that I enjoy your company, so you don't have to wonder or apologize for being here. We're going to pull you through this little bumpy stretch and get you started on a new life. Then I'll float off like the good fairy and go to work getting my own life straightened out. Okay?"

"Okay," said Pete. His smile was almost a laugh. He looked strong and comfortable. The muscles in his shoulders and legs elongated as he slouched in his chair. He had that unself-conscious, almost comical look that she had seen on fathers taking little children to the park. "I guess knowing how to shoot people doesn't do much for your social life."

She was surprised at her sudden need to keep him from thinking she wasn't desirable. She drew in a breath to respond, then looked down at her watch. "It's late, and I'd like to get an early start tomorrow morning."

He looked at the bed. "I can sleep on the floor."

"Sorry, that's mine," she said. She took a pillow and the bedspread off the bed. "What I'm worried about is not you, by the way. Tonight I'm going to keep my eyes open for visitors." She busied herself with the bedspread while he got into the bed and turned off the lamp beside it. Then she went into the bathroom, brushed her teeth, and came back out. He was lying in the dim light with his eyes closed. She turned out the other light and lay on the folded quilt in the dark.

"Jane?"

"What?"

"Thanks again."

"Think nothing of it."

She lay in the darkness, staring up at the ceiling and testing the sensation of not being able to detect the difference between having her eyes open or closed. She closed them and thought about Carey. She knew that at this hour he was fast asleep in the big bed at home. She tried to reach out with her thought and place a blessing on him while he slept, but the mere knowledge that he was sleeping cut her off from him. He was dreaming, not thinking about her, like a receiver tuned to a different station. She opened her eyes again and she was back in the motel room in Montana.

As she lay there feeling the floor pressing harder on her spine, she contemplated the absurdity of pretending to stay alert for intruders so she could lie here on the floor when there was plenty of room on a perfectly good bed a few feet away. She knew that she would have the thought again and again, each time she awoke in the darkness waiting for the night to end. It was her penance for lying to Carey about the sleeping arrangements. She couldn't take back the lie, but she could suffer a little discomfort to make the lie almost true.

She dozed off for a few seconds and began to slip into a dream. The vague image of a man appeared and began to resolve and clarify—bare legs, arms, then the features of the face began to establish themselves. She was startled and her body jerked and woke her, pulling her out of it in time to keep the man from being recognizable. But it was too late to keep her from knowing that the sight her mind had been preparing for her had not been Carey.

19

Linda Thompson spent all of her time studying Dr. Carey McKinnon. He was attractive, with a lean body and gangling walk and big hands that made her wonder if he had made his way through college playing basketball. He always looked as though he was late, ducking out of the driver's seat of the BMW, unfolding those long legs, then taking two steps toward the hospital building before the door that he had flicked with his hand slammed shut. Then he would step along toward the entrance without looking to either side or slowing down as visitors did to be sure the automatic door would open in time, and then disappear inside.

When his shift ended, he would come out alone at the same speed, slip into the BMW, and drive off. She watched him travel the same route each time, back to his big old house in Amherst. After a few minutes she would see him moving around in the kitchen. Later there would be the glowing bluish light in a room on the upper floor from a television set. When it went off, he would sleep.

It took Linda two days to grow accustomed to his hours. He was at the hospital for surgery by seven and usually walked across the street to the medical building where he had his office at around one.

Some time in the late afternoon he would walk back to the hospital and stalk the hallways, talking to patients in their rooms until at least seven, and sometimes nine.

After she became used to his movements and had adjusted her internal clock to his, she had long stretches of time when she could let him out of her sight. The mornings were good, because she knew that he wasn't going to leave in the middle of an operation. She spent some mornings with realtors. His neighborhood was wrong for her purposes. The houses were all big and expensive, sitting well back on vast lots. The nearest one that was for sale was two long blocks away, and the view of his house was obscured by a row of old maple trees along the sidewalk. The zoning apparently didn't permit apartment buildings, because there was not one on any of the surrounding streets.

She considered getting a job in the hospital, but only for a moment. Hospitals checked credentials to avoid lawsuits, and she could never create any that would get her a job that placed her in his path frequently enough. At best she would find herself emptying bedpans three floors away from him, with no excuse to leave and follow him.

Linda had an expert eye for bodies and could tell he was in reasonably good condition. He didn't jog or work out at home, so it was possible that he belonged to some local club. She looked up all of the ones in the telephone book, made some calls, and learned nothing.

His entry in the A.M.A. directory told her he had gone to Cornell and then to the University of Chicago Medical School. She opened an account at the bank listed on his credit report and shopped at the supermarkets closest to his house, but never saw him.

She visited the main library in downtown Buffalo and read old issues of the Cornell alumni magazine until she found the right obituary. A woman named Susan Preston had died six years ago in a plane crash. Susan Preston would have been five years younger than McKinnon, so they weren't in school together. She had been survived by various Prestons in San Francisco, so it was unlikely that McKinnon had known her family. Linda took the catalog off the shelf and studied the maps and photographs of the Cornell University campus, then memorized the names of professors and courses. If the university was going to be an entree to anything, she might need to be able to talk about it.

Linda called her house and reached Lenny. She told him to punch the name Susan Preston Haynes onto some blank credit cards, make her a California driver's license, and send them by overnight mail. It was a gamble to use a real name, but it would put her on the right lists, and adding a husband's surname gave her the option of being Haynes any time Preston seemed too risky.

After six days of stalking Carey McKinnon, Linda found an article in the *Buffalo News* about a benefit dinner to be held by the auxiliary of Buffalo Memorial Hospital. She called the number in the article and bought a ticket for a hundred dollars. Carey McKinnon seemed to do nothing but work and sleep, but maybe he would consider a benefit for the hospital a part of his work. She had just taken out the good dress she had brought from California in case she needed it in Las Vegas and begun her preparations when the telephone rang.

"Yes?" she said into it.

"It's me." Earl sounded angry.

"Hi," she said. "Have you got anything yet?"

"Zero," he said. "I've watched his goddamn car for a week. If he's in Billings at all anymore, he doesn't drive anywhere. He's also not visible in any hotel, motel, or park bench in the city. If you don't have anything for me soon, I think we might want to begin considering our alternatives."

"What alternatives?"

"Make some fake ID with Hatcher's picture on it that won't fool even a Montana cop, rent an apartment in that name. We salt the apartment with the ID and the mail we found in Las Vegas, and anything from the car that has Hatcher's prints on it."

"Then what?" She knew he wasn't serious. He was saying it because it sounded desperate and risky, and the thought that he was contemplating such a fraud would affect her.

"Pop some guy Hatcher's size and shape, put him in the car, and torch it. Once the police run the prints we leave in the apartment and identify the photograph on the fake ID, they won't have any reason to strain themselves with a lot of tests, and Seaver won't be able to. If anybody's real curious they might go to the Denver apartment the car's registered to and find more of Hatcher's prints there. We collect the rest of the money from Seaver. End of story."

"What happens if Pete Hatcher shows up later?" She sounded as worried as she would have been if she believed Earl would give up. Earl didn't need safety as much as he needed to win.

"Honey, if I can't find the bastard, you think anybody else is going to?"

"Of course not. Nobody's better than you, Earl. I'm just talking."

"If we wait too long, we might have to do it in reverse."

"What do you mean?" asked Linda.

"Cut and run before Seaver's bosses send somebody for us. Find a man and woman and make it look like this specialist Hatcher hired set a trap and killed us first."

"Please don't do anything yet, Earl," she said. "I won't disappoint you, I promise." Her own voice, sounding breathy and submissive, gave her an erotic shiver. She experimented with making her voice break, not quite a sob. "I've been trying really hard." The effect was good. "I'll have something for you in a few days."

"I sure hope so," he said. "I've got nothing. I've been running computer checks on the two names he used so far, her name, car rentals, everything. None of it leads anywhere in particular. So I'm beginning to think she picked him up and they were long gone before I got here."

"I know it's up to me," she said. "I won't forget it for a second."

Carey McKinnon stood in front of the mirror in the bedroom and studied the man who stared back at him. He had been aware long before tonight that he looked foolish in a tuxedo, but he had consoled himself by renting a tuxedo to look foolish in instead of owning one, and by picking out the plainest model that Benjy's Midnight Tux had to offer, with black cummerbund and white plastic studs and cuff links. Probably the last time this one had been out of Benjy's, it had been taken to a prom. The shoes were his, but only because Benjy's selection of shoes for big feet had the sturdy spit-shined look of military footwear.

With resignation, he brushed his hair into place one last time. The warring cowlicks would reassert themselves in the car. Then he turned off the light, walked downstairs, and stopped. He looked at the telephone before he opened the door. He had been looking at telephones all over the house for two hours, each time remembering that the way they looked had nothing to do with ringing.

It was two hours earlier in Montana, so it was still about five o'clock there. His mind warned him that thinking about time was the first step into treacherous territory. The second was to ask himself what she could possibly be doing that made a telephone call to her husband such a hard thing to accomplish at any hour of the day or night. That brought a hundred contradictory answers into his mind together, elbowing past one another to the front to be acknowledged.

He left the lamp by the door burning and hurried out to his car. As soon as he had started the engine, he noticed the fuel gauge again and cursed himself for forgetting. He hated to stop at the full-serve side of the gas station and wait by the pump helplessly until the attendant happened to glance out the window and notice him, then get so lonely and bored that helping a customer was all he could think of to do. But Carey was determined not to pump gas in a tuxedo. The unwritten laws of physics meant that the pump nozzle would backwash or the hose would leak.

He backed out of the long driveway quickly, drove up the street, and stopped at the light. He hoped the needle of the fuel gauge was still just working its way upward to its correct reading. The light changed, and he turned left to drive the familiar route back to the hospital.

When he reached his reserved parking space he found a big black Mercedes had been backed into it. He paused for a moment with his foot on the brake, then drove on into the visitors' parking lot, took a parking ticket, and found a space. As he walked toward the building, the argument the muscles of his mouth and tongue were rehearsing was that taking a surgeon's space in a hospital parking lot could cost the driver's child the five minutes that might have saved his life some time. He clamped the argument to the roof of his mouth with his tongue. He wasn't going to say it. He wasn't going inside to save anybody's life. He was going in there to kiss that Mercedes owner's rich ass with enthusiasm and sincerity, and hope it bought the hospital a new children's wing.

It was probably somebody he had met before. Around Buffalo, most big money was old money, handed down from the days of the Erie Canal, or at least the days of Civil War profiteering, enhanced by practices like buying up the tax liens on family farms in the surrounding countryside during the Depression and turning them into suburbs.

He walked into the foyer and glanced into the garden. He could see a few fat penguins and their bejeweled consorts loitering out there, flicking cigarette ashes into the shrubbery and sipping drinks where their cardiologists couldn't catch them at it.

He caught a glimpse of Lily Bortoni, the wife of his friend Leo, an orthopedic surgeon. She looked as serene and elegant as she always did at these affairs, every shining chestnut hair in place and with just enough makeup so her skin looked like the smooth surface of a sculpture. She was staring unperturbed through a cloud of cigar smoke at a potential donor as though he were saying something important, so Carey couldn't catch her eye.

As he walked on, a series of conflicting thoughts flashed through his mind. The sight of Lily made him miss Jane and feel annoyed with her at the same time. He felt sorry for himself for having to show up here alone, felt guilty that Leo's wife, Lily, had to work the crowd while Jane escaped it, dreaded having to explain ten times in the next hour why Jane wasn't here. Then he remembered that she could be running for her life right now. He forced the idea out of his mind: she was out finding a new address for some moron. It was unfair to Carey and inconvenient for her, but the danger was over. She was doing what she felt she had to do, and he would just have to cover for her until it was over.

He stepped into the cafeteria, and a hand patted his arm. He turned to look down at Marian Fleming. She had managed to confine herself in a beige evening gown with metallic filigree on the front that looked as though its purpose was to protect her from body blows. Her blond hair was sprayed and sculpted into a spun-sugar helmet, and her ice-blue eyes fixed him with a stare that told him he was not about to be offered any choices. "There's somebody you've got to meet," she said.

Carey understood the words "got to," so he waited.

"Where's Jane?" Her eyes flicked around behind him.

"She's out of town," he answered. "I'm on my own tonight."

He did not miss the tiny twitch above her eye as Marian's mind punched Jane's card. She was already pivoting to push him along toward someone, still talking. "Here's the doctor I told you about."

"You did?" asked Carey.

"Susan Haynes, this is Carey McKinnon. He went to Cornell too." She gave Carey a perfectly benign empty look. "So did his wife, but she's not with us tonight, so he'll have to do."

Carey looked at the woman and smiled. Her blond hair beside Marian's was the difference between polished gold and yellow paint. Her eyes were big, a bright green with flecks in them like malachite, and her lips were full, with a natural upturn at the corners. She gave a reserved smile, as though she were bestowing tiny portions of a powerful spice.

"Hello, Dr. McKinnon," said Linda.

"Pleased to meet you, Miss Haynes. I have a feeling you must have shown up in Ithaca after my time. I would have remembered."

She looked as though she was not surprised by anything men said to her, just mildly disappointed. "I was Sue Preston then."

"It doesn't help," he said. "I've been out about ten years, and you're only twenty . . ." He squinted at her. "Eight."

The big green eyes widened. "How did you know that?"

"I'm a specialist in looking at people as bundles of cells. Yours are twenty-eight."

She looked around her, but nobody was nearby bursting to explain it. "This is some kind of trick."

He shook his head. "Nope. You weigh one hundred and twenty-two pounds, right?"

"I don't know," she said. "I don't weigh myself every day." She lowered her head and conceded from behind her eyelashes, "That's close, though."

He leaned closer, and she turned her ear to listen. "Those guys at carnivals who guess your age and weight?"

"What about them?"

"They're all old doctors."

He could tell she was getting used to him now. She just smiled, showing perfect teeth and spilling a prodigal supply of the precious spice into the room, but it was all for him. "Now I know it's a joke."

"Some do it to save up for their malpractice insurance, some just hate golf. I think some of them do it just to get away from these." He showed her his beeper. "Ever have one of these?"

"I'm not the kind of person anybody needs urgently."

"Good. Don't ever start." He put his beeper away. "Well, I should introduce you to more people. Or you should introduce me. Just because I haven't met you at one of these things doesn't mean I know more people than you do."

"This is my first time," she said.

Marian Fleming drifted up with Harry Rotherberg. "There," she said. "I knew you two would have something to talk about. But I need to take Carey back for a minute. This is Dr. Rotherberg. He's the head of pediatrics, so he can answer any questions you have about the new wing."

Carey flashed a valedictory smile at the young woman and stepped away with Marian. "How am I doing?"

"You're my paladin," she said. "Right now I'm going to jump you over a few pawns and get you to work this bunch over here."

"The captain of industry with the plaid cummerbund?"

"Yep. Know him?"

"I'm pretty sure I've seen his cummerbund at these things before, but his name doesn't leap to mind."

"He's Charlie Fraser. That's his tartan. He comes off as a dope, but he's not. He's given about a hundred thousand so far this year. Be nice to him."

"What a devious plan."

"Oh, and Carey?"

"What?"

"Since Jane isn't here, I've seated you with Susan Haynes. I'm counting on you to romance her a little for me."

"Why?"

"She doesn't know anybody," said Marian. "Harry's a great pediatrician, but ten minutes with him is an evening in Mister Rogers' neighborhood. She's got money and she wants to do good with it."

"I'll get it for you if I have to turn her upside down and shake her."

"I have no doubt. Your reputation precedes you." There was no trace of a smile as she expertly moved him into the space before Charlie Fraser. "Charlie, this is Dr. McKinnon," she said.

Carey shook Fraser's hand and smiled while Marian Fleming said, "And this is Honoria Fraser, his wife."

"I'm glad you could come," said Carey. "I had heard you had given us quite a bit of help in the past, and I wanted to thank you."

Fraser looked shocked. "Who are you, anyway? What do you do?"

"I'm a surgeon."

Fraser leaned over and kissed his wife on the cheek. She laughed, then put her fingers over her mouth as though it were a breach of decorum. Her husband said, "That's another one for you, Honey."

Carey said, "I don't understand."

"I made a bet with Honey two years ago. Every year I get a printed thank-you note with my name written on it so the I.R.S. will be satisfied. But to this day, no actual human being connected with the hospital ever walked straight up like a regular person and said thanks. I said nobody ever would, or if they did, it would be an administrator from fund-raising. You just won her the bet."

Carey looked worried. "Uh-oh."

"What's wrong?"

"If nobody ever did it before, maybe I wasn't supposed to. I guess this means you'll stop giving money now?"

"Do I look like an idiot?" asked Fraser. He looked down at his tuxedo. "Well, I suppose I do. But I'm not. I do lose most of my bets with Honey, but so would you."

Carey looked at Honoria Fraser and smiled. "I can believe it."

"Let me tell you something about fund-raising, since you seem to be sensible," said Fraser. "These dinner-dance things are a mistake. When I want to lure investors into my business, I take them to the plant. I let them meet the good people I've got working for me. They show them the machinery and computers and trucks. They let them see how we make our products, from the quality of the raw materials to the packing and shipping. They show people what Charlie Fraser's going to do with their money. Now, if I was an idiot"—he turned his head to survey the room—"I would put on something like this party."

"Charlie!" said Honoria sharply.

"The doc doesn't care," Fraser assured her. "He can tell I mean well." He turned to Carey. "There's nothing that makes a person who gives money cringe more than a fancy party. It costs money, and if he's reasonably intelligent he knows it's his money. He didn't give it so he could go to a party. He gave it so some poor kid gets his turn on a kidney machine. He'd like to see that. If it comes down to parties, he knows he could do a pretty good party himself for a few thousand, invite whomever he pleased, and serve better food."

Honoria said to Carey, "Charlie's quite the blowhard, isn't he?"

"Yes," Carey agreed. "You are, Charlie. But you're absolutely right. I can't talk Marian out of throwing these parties, but I can do the rest for you." He wrote a telephone number on his ticket and handed it to Fraser. "This is my office. Call any day, and I'll have somebody arrange a tour for you, and for anybody you want to bring. If you see where the money goes, and what it does for this city, I think you'll be proud."

"I am proud," said Charlie. "I'm just telling you how to get more." He glanced at the number on the ticket. "I will do this, you know."

"I expect you to," said Carey. "Bring some friends."

There was a chime, and people began to move beyond the screens dividing the cafeteria in half. "That's dinner," said Charlie. One of the waiters pushed the button to make the opening widen, and Carey could see white linen and gleaming silverware for the only time this year. "If you don't have anybody to sit with, you can come with us."

"Marian's got other plans for me," said Carey.

He drifted across the paths of a few familiar couples moving toward the tables and scanned for Susan Haynes. He found her standing with one arm across her chest and the other holding a glass of champagne, listening to Harry Rotherberg talking about the ultrasound machines the hospital was about to buy. Katie Rotherberg moved in ahead of Carey and separated them.

Carey said, "Dinner time. Don't worry if the meat tastes funny. You're already in the hospital."

" 'Please be seated and the maître d' will call you when your stomach pump is ready'?"

"I can see you've been to benefits before. Why this one?"

She shrugged. "I'm new in town, and I saw it in the paper. Hospitals tend to be everybody's charity. I thought it was a good opportunity to get a look at the local gentry and make it clear I'm one of the good guys."

He looked at her in mock suspicion. "You're some kind of businesswoman, aren't you?"

"Good grief, no." She giggled. "Nobody in my family has 'been' anything in ages. My father used to sit on boards of directors. That way he got mail and was allowed to own a briefcase. But he didn't actually know anything or do anything, or they wouldn't have wanted him around. His epitaph should have been 'He Voted Yes.' "

"Your mother?"

"She voted no. When I was about three. She turned up a few years ago, but we didn't have much to talk about. To complete the whole sordid family tree, I have an older brother. Come to think of it, he's something—a fisherman."

"A commercial fisherman?"

"No, silly. Trout. He spends his summers at his house in Jackson Hole and his winters in rehab places. They don't seem to have any therapeutic value, but it's a quiet place to tie flies, once his hands stop shaking."

"I'm sorry."

She touched his arm, and it felt as though it had been brushed by a bird's wing. "Don't sound so solemn. None of this just happened, you know. It's all old history."

As they reached the newly unscreened section of the cafeteria, Marian Fleming caught Carey's eye and nodded toward the front of the room near the head table. He gave his head a tiny shake, and she picked up two place cards from the front table, ushered Leo Bortoni and his wife from the back to Carey's place, and watched Carey take Susan Haynes's arm and walk her to the rear table. He could see that Lily Bortoni was delighted, having interpreted the move as a sign that her husband was appreciated. He liked them both, and he congratulated himself for having accidentally made them feel good. He pretended he had been looking past them for someone else, gave a little shrug, and continued toward the back of the room.

Carey and Susan Haynes sat at a table for four, but they were alone. He looked at her. "I guess this is where we're supposed to talk about Cornell."

"Do we have to?"

"Briefly. Uris Library."

"Cruel to put it at the top of a hill," she said. "Thought I'd die." One of the photographs in the alumni magazine had shown the view from the library, so its altitude was all she knew about it.

"Goldwin Smith Hall."

"Big, old, and cold." She said it with an air of profound boredom. She hoped that was the long, low one across the quadrangle with the statue in front, but whatever it was, the description seemed to satisfy him.

"Had enough?"

"More than enough." She leaned closer. "So what about your life story?" she asked.

"I was born in this hospital, and sort of never got out," he said. "My education was just a leave of absence. I'm a surgeon."

"Married?" He wasn't sure if she said it so quickly and adroitly because she didn't care, or because she did care.

"Just. Three months ago. She's out of town right now."

"Oh, yes. Marian said something about that. I forgot. What kind of surgeon are you—plastic surgery?"

"If you need anything cosmetic done, Buffalo isn't really the best place. There are hospitals in Los Angeles and Boston that do more of those in a week than we do in a year. What I do is mostly basic medicine. If you have no further use for your gall bladder or your appendix, I'm your man."

Her eyebrow raised in a perfect arch. "Do I look sick?"

"Hardly. But you could be a hypochondriac. The rich ones sometimes give money so they'll have a nice place to stay during their next anxiety attack. I promised Marian I'd explore every avenue."

"You're doing just great," she said. "I feel as though I'd been strip-searched. All my avenues have been thoroughly probed."

"Are you going to cough up the loot?"

She nodded. "Some. I told you before that if I'm going to live here, I have to establish myself up front as one of the good guys. That makes me eligible for unearned invitations and so on."

"What made you pick Buffalo?"

She turned the big green eyes on him and looked at him shrewdly. "I like it. Or maybe it's better to say that I don't dislike it, which is not true of certain other places. And real estate is cheap, so I can sell my house that's teetering on a precipice in San Francisco and buy something nicer here. As you may have guessed, my heart and Mr. Haynes's no longer beat as one. Before that, we spent some time being no longer a fun couple. I used to come through Buffalo when I was in college, and I decided it was the sort of place where I could be happy."

"Because it's not on the circuit you're used to."

"If you're tired of humanity, maybe it's time to meet new specimens. That's the theory, anyway." She brightened. "Did I pass my examination?"

"Sure," he said. "You're healthy as a young Hereford cow and as sane as Monsignor Schumacher." He glanced at the tables around him and nodded. "Evening, Monsignor." He turned back to her. "I think you'll like it here, at least for a time. It's smaller than you'd think, and people are clannish. But you're the sort of person who makes a good impression, and anybody who comes here voluntarily has passed the first test."

"And you've passed yours," she said. The caterers arrived and dealt out plates of food from a cart, leaning down to mutter into each person's ear, "Careful, the plate is very hot."

She tasted the salmon on her plate and said, "You can go unplug the equipment. It's very good."

"That's Marian's fault. She's always destroying cherished traditions. Usually after these things we used to spend half the night admitting people, giving upper GIs and so on. I have no idea what we'll do with ourselves."

She looked at him, her chin resting on her hands. "That brings me to something I'm a bit concerned about myself."

"Oh?" he said.

"Well, it's kind of embarrassing. I leased this big black Mercedes when I got to town, because I figured it would be good on snow and ice. But I'm not very good with it. I managed to steer it to the hospital okay, but about half an hour ago I went out to get my makeup bag from the front seat . . ."

Carey's lips slowly, involuntarily curved upward.

"This is nothing to smile about. I backed into an empty parking space and hurried to get inside, so I wouldn't be late and get stared at by a lot of people who knew each other. There's a color code and a sign, but I guess I didn't see it because I backed in. Anyway, I guess it was for some kind of emergency vehicle, and the police towed my car away. Why are you smiling?"

Carey's smile grew, and he began to chuckle.

"Are you some kind of sadist?"

"No," said Carey. "I'm very sorry. I saw your car when I got here, and I wondered whether I should say something. That's all."

"Then why on earth didn't you?" she asked. "I would have moved it in a second."

He looked down at his hands, then forced his eyes to meet her stare. "I didn't want to seem like a jerk. It was my parking space."

It took two breaths for her face to register confusion, then shock, then understanding. Her eyes sparkled, and her laugh was clear and musical. It seemed to linger on her lips. "You know where I can get a ride to the impound lot after this thing ends?"

"It's the least I can do."

20

Ultimately, it seemed to Seaver, all investigations came down to staring through a pane of glass at some doorway late at night. Sometimes it was sitting in a car that smelled like old cigarettes, and sometimes it was renting a rat's nest of an office like this one, barring the door, and trying to drink enough coffee out of styrofoam cups to stay awake until something happened.

This time the doorway was on a little storefront with a big sign that said OPEN TWENTY-FOUR HOURS, so the surveillance was worse than it had usually been in the old days. And Manhattan presented special problems. You couldn't sit on a street in a parked car for twelve hours without collecting a stack of tickets, and even if you did, there wasn't much chance you could use the car to follow anybody. Suspects in Manhattan scuttled underground to slip into subway trains, or stepped into yellow cabs that barely came to a complete stop before they were off again on a long street that looked like a river of identical yellow cabs, each of them blowing its horn and weaving erratically to keep going ten miles an hour faster than the speed limit. Or the suspect veered into a doorway a hundred feet away and vanished into a building that had fourteen elevators and sixty floors. Cars weren't much use. The quarry had to be stalked on foot and not taken down until he was indoors, away from the hundreds of faces that were always visible on the street.

Seaver had mailed a small package addressed to Valued Cardholder, Box 345, 7902 Elizabeth Street, New York, NY 10003. The outer wrapping was bright orange with iridescent yellow stripes on it, so he would have no trouble spotting it when the mail was picked up. He couldn't sit here waiting for the dark-haired woman to show up in the flesh. There was a better than even chance that the mail would be picked up by some intermediary, and Seaver would have to follow the package.

If the woman had been hiding fugitives for anything like the eight or nine years since Miranda's reincarnation, then the woman must have built some high walls between her and people like Stillman. She couldn't let people like him find her easily. She would know what Seaver had known—that even though some part of a career criminal's stunted brain believed that some day she might be his last chance of surviving, the reason he would need her at all had a lot to do with his inability to choose a future benefit over an extra pack of cigarettes right now.

Seaver was prepared for the intermediary. Inside the package was an expensive sports watch packed with a photocopy of a typed message explaining to Valued Cardholder that it was a reward from Visa for using a credit card. Inside the watch, and running off its battery, was a small radio transmitter with a range of a thousand yards.

If Seaver got lucky, the dark-haired woman might strap the watch to her wrist. Even if she didn't like it that much, she would at least see it was too good to throw away, so she would shove it into a drawer in her apartment. It didn't matter. As soon as she had it, he would have her. When he had her, he would have Hatcher.

Seaver reached over to the desk and pulled the plastic top off the next styrofoam cup of coffee. It was not much warmer than the air around it now, the white powdery substance that symbolized milk already beginning to coagulate in little gooey lumps that floated just under the oily surface. He covered it again and walked to the sink, ran the water until it was steaming hot, stopped the drain, filled the sink a few inches, held the cup in the water, and looked around for something heavy enough to keep the cup from floating up and tipping over.

He could find nothing in the little bathroom to hold it down, so he took the extra ammunition clip out of his pocket and carefully placed it on the lid. Since he had nothing else to do, he used the opportunity to urinate. That was another problem with doing surveillance at this stage of his career. He had not sat around like this drinking quarts of stale coffee in at least ten years, and his kidneys were treating it as a new and unpleasant experience.

He yawned, zipped up his pants, took his coffee cup out of the water, and set it on the edge of the sink while he washed his hands. When he carried the cup back to the window he could still see the bright orange package through the bronze and glass door of the woman's mailbox, so he sat down and took a sip.

He had a perfect view of the small shop from his office window. His elevation placed the rows of mailboxes in his field of vision, and he could see the surface of the counter and part of the workspace behind it where bored employees wrapped, weighed, and stacked packages, sorted letters, and sent faxes. The streetlamp in front of the shop threw a splash of light on the sidewalk outside the door.

He sipped the lukewarm coffee and watched. At this time of night, so few customers came in that his cop's brain wondered whether the purpose of keeping the shop open might be that other customers besides the dark-haired woman were doing something illegal: leave your money in some other mailbox on Tuesday, and come back on Wednesday and pick up your heroin from your own. But he had watched the boxes for a full cycle of shifts now, and he had detected no signs that he could interpret as commerce. Nobody who came in to open a mailbox seemed to take the time to look around him first for cops or thieves. Nobody seemed to bring anything in with him that ended up in one of the other mailboxes.

It was nearly midnight when he recognized the new clerk coming up out of the subway and walking toward the shop for the changing of the guard. The skinny kid with jeans and a black T-shirt came in the door, and the older man collected his belongings—a greenish brown sportcoat that looked as though it had been picked up off a rag pile and a paperback book that he put in the side pocket so the coat hung down and made him look like the scarecrow he was.

But then he did something that made Seaver put his coffee cup on the desk and lean forward. He stepped behind the mailboxes. Seaver saw him reach into Box 345 and start sliding envelopes into a big padded mailer. Seaver watched as the orange and yellow package disappeared with the others.

Seaver snatched up his coat, stepped to the door, and ran for the stairwell. As he hurried down the steps, he switched on his receiver and watched the direction indicator for a base reading. He slipped it into his pocket, stepped out into the darkness at the side of the building, and walked slowly toward the street, his eyes on the lighted window of the little shop. He paused in the shadow until he saw the older man come out the door carrying the mailer under his arm.

Seaver followed the man along the dimly lighted street for three blocks, staying close to the buildings, sometimes keeping his silhouette obscured by the irregular outlines of pilasters and ornamental brickwork on the facades, sometimes pausing in the alcoves at store entrances to be invisible for a time.

The man turned left onto another street and Seaver broke into a run to shorten the man's lead. As he turned the corner, he saw he had misinterpreted the man's intentions. He wasn't on his way to meet the dark-haired woman and hand her the mail. He was walking in a diagonal course along the broad, empty sidewalk toward the curb, where there was a big blue U.S. Postal Service mailbox. When the man had taken the woman's mail with him, Seaver had been sure he wasn't sending it off again. But he was definitely heading for that mailbox. The woman must have given him orders not to leave any packages lying around the store with her forwarding address on them.

Seaver's mind was flooded with disappointment at the unwelcome news. There would be more airline trips, more nights sitting and watching doorways. No, it was worse than that. If that package went into the postal system before Seaver knew the address, he would have no idea whether it was going to an apartment a block away or to Ethiopia. He had to keep that man from reaching the mailbox.

Seaver called, "Excuse me."

The man glanced over his shoulder and straightened. He was surprised to see Seaver suddenly so close. He kept going, a little more quickly.

"Wait!" shouted Seaver. "Sir?"

The man went more quickly, his long legs taking steps that made him strain. Seaver had made a mistake by not letting the man get a clear look at him right away, on a lighted street. In the light, Seaver could easily have passed for a prosperous middle-aged executive coming home from a restaurant. But the man was acting as though he expected to be mugged. Instead of stopping, he went faster. He seemed to want to get rid of the package so he would have both hands free to defend himself. It didn't matter what he thought he was doing, or what Seaver had planned. The man was hurrying toward the mailbox.

Seaver walked faster, screwing the silencer onto the end of the barrel. "Sir?" he called. The man had obviously made his decision. Now he seemed to want to reach the big mailbox and use it as a shield.

Seaver stopped on the sidewalk with his feet apart, bent his knees slightly, extended both arms to steady his right hand, blew the air out of his lungs to keep the carbon dioxide from causing a tremor, and squeezed the trigger. The gun jumped upward and Seaver heard the spitting sound.

The man pitched forward. The mailer fell and slid a few feet, but the man had forgotten it. He was writhing on the sidewalk, bleeding.

As Seaver ran to finish him, he saw that a car had appeared near the far end of the block. He clamped the pistol under his left arm, knelt over the man, and said, "I tried to warn you. There was a guy in a car shooting. Lie still now."

The man seemed to barely hear him. He was squeezing his eyes in an agonized squint and rolling his head from side to side on the pavement. Seaver glanced down at the blood on the shirt. It was bright crimson and bubbly, so the bullet must have passed through a lung.

Seaver saw the car pull up to the curb. It was a yellow cab. "Is he all right?" called the driver. Seaver could see only the dark shape of a torso and an oval head.

"He just tripped and fell," said Seaver. "He'll be okay in a minute." The wounded man struggled to reach out his arm toward the cab, and moaned.

"Does he need to go to the hospital?"

"No," said Seaver. "I'll take care of him." He returned his eyes to the wounded man, shifted his position slightly, and rested his right forearm on his knee. If Seaver heard the click of a car door latch, he would move the hand a few more inches and grasp the gun. He would use the time it took the driver to walk around the rear of the car into the open to pivot and fire.

The driver shook his head doubtfully, then stared anxiously ahead through his windshield for a moment. Just as Seaver acknowledged that he now had the task of killing this one too, the driver pushed a button to roll up the window and accelerated up the street.

Seaver felt an abrupt, wrenching tug, and realized that the wounded man was trying to pry the pistol out of his armpit. Seaver's right hand swatted the man's fingers away, and he straightened his legs so quickly that he nearly toppled backward. He pulled out the pistol, aimed downward, and shot the man through the chest. This time he judged that he had hit the heart. The man gave one spasmodic jerk and went limp. Seaver gave him a kick, but it prompted no reaction. Seaver decided there was no reason to keep wondering, so he fired one more round into the man's head, put the pistol into his inner coat pocket, picked up the padded mailer, stuck it into his belt at the small of his back, and covered it with his coat.

Seaver turned and looked around him. The little discreet surveillance had degenerated into a bloody disaster, a tangle of complications and obstacles and hazards. There was a narrow alley between two buildings to his right, but there was a high iron fence to block it. He could never lift a grown man's body above his head and push it over the fence. He thought he might be able to carry the body a short distance, but how could he do that without attracting attention? As he considered the problem, he saw another set of headlights come around the corner at the far end of the block and head toward him. He saw the lights jump upward as the car accelerated, but then they dipped and stayed low. The car was going to stop.

Seaver stared at it, and saw the color of the paint. It was yellow, and the little marquee on the roof was visible now. It was the same cab. Seaver waved his arm frantically, and the cab pulled to the curb. The driver stepped out, slammed the door, and looked at him over the roof.

"He's hurt worse than I thought," said Seaver. "We need to get him to a hospital after all."

The driver trotted around the rear of the car and opened the back-seat door. Seaver knelt and began to lift the torso of the body. "Give me a hand."

The driver squatted to lift the feet. He backed into the cab and set the legs on the back seat, but that gave him a look at the chest. "This guy's bleeding all over. He's been stabbed or something."

Seaver's hand was already in motion. The gun swung out, he fired into the driver's belly, then raised the barrel higher and fired into the driver's chest, then into his head.

Seaver returned the gun to his coat pocket and walked around the car to get into the driver's seat. He turned on the meter, then drove the cab to the rear of the building he had rented and parked it. He went up the stairs, through his little office, and into the bathroom. He washed his hands and face thoroughly, then examined his suit, shoes, and shirt for blood spatters. He saw none, but wiped his shoes with toilet paper anyway and flushed it down the toilet. He took a big wad of dampened toilet paper and wiped off the gun and wrapped it in toilet paper, then went about the little suite wiping off all of the surfaces he had ever touched. He collected all of his old coffee cups and lids, boxes, and wrappers, and locked the door behind him before he left. He dropped the trash in the Dumpster at the rear of the building.

Seaver started the cab and drove at least twelve blocks south before he found a dark alley between two stores that met a second, longer alley, so he could turn and leave it beside a loading dock. Then he walked a mile, stuffed the still-wrapped gun into the fishy-smelling center of a trash bag inside a garbage can, and replaced the lid. He walked another mile before he came to a theater. People were streaming out onto the street, walking toward parking lots and climbing into taxicabs. He attached himself to the crowd, climbed into a cab, and had it take him to an intersection not far from his hotel.

When he was inside his room, he pulled the mailer out of the back of his belt. He opened it and poured the mail out on the bed. The envelopes were all addressed to Stewart Hoffstedder, C.P.A. That was something that gave him hope, at first, because Stillman had said something about a man's name. But the mail was almost all bills, as though they were for a real C.P.A. The bills were all for credit cards in different names—female, male, even corporate names. Were they all for this woman?

A horrible thought came to him. Stillman's brain was probably not a perfectly developed organ to begin with. Since the age of ten it had probably been shorted out by drugs and jarred by blows. Maybe he had gotten the number wrong. Maybe this was some real C.P.A., a business manager who paid bills for a number of clients. The mail in the pouch seemed to have nothing to do with the dark-haired woman. It was possible that Seaver had scared Stillman so badly that he had cooked up a box number on the spot.

Seaver laid all of the bills out on the bed in a row and began to study them, looking desperately for similarities. On August 8, Wendy Wasserman had rented a car in Missoula, Montana. On August 10, Michael Phelan had rented a hotel room in Potomac, Montana. Katherine Webster had paid for lunch in Condon, Montana, the next morning. Seaver rocked back on his heels and smiled at the ceiling in relief. He had not wasted all this time and energy.

He glanced at the forwarding address on the label stuck to the mailer. It was just another post office box, this one in Chicago. If he needed to, he could go there and watch that one too. But right now, he had something infinitely better. He knew where the dark-haired woman was. She was on the move, driving around Montana with Pete Hatcher.

$\mathcal{C}$arey drove up to the gate of the impound lot and parked. Susan stepped to the gate and rang the bell. Carey could hear the old-fashioned jangling noise a hundred feet away in the little shack in the center of the lot, and that meant trouble. There were no lights on in the windows. He stepped to the gate and stood beside her feeling useless.

Then he walked along the fence and around the corner. There was a small sign that said, LOT HOURS 6:00 A.M. TO 10:00 P.M. He walked back to Susan and frowned apologetically. "It's closed until six in the morning."

"No." She seemed to see herself from outside. She was standing in a dark, desolate part of the city in the middle of the night, wearing three-inch heels and a strapless evening gown. Slowly, the beautiful smile reappeared. She let her arms come out from her sides in a "look at me" gesture.

He said, "Come on. I'll take you home."

They got into his car and he backed out of the drive. "You can't really do that," she said. "It's all the way out in Orchard Park. If you could just drop me off at a hotel near here, you can go home and get some sleep."

"Why would you stay in a hotel?" asked Carey. "It's ridiculous." Why was it that people who didn't want to be any trouble always ended up being plenty?

"It's now after midnight. If you drive me all the way to my apartment, it'll be two before I'm asleep, and probably three before you are. So I'd get three hours' sleep, call a cab, and for eighty dollars or so, he'd drive me to the other end of the county to get my car. That's if I could even get a cab in Orchard Park at five in the morning. But if I stay here, I can be on the spot when the lot opens and drive myself home."

"Here's the problem with that. Look around you—factories, warehouses, and an impound lot. It isn't very scenic in the daytime, so there's a shortage of good hotels around here. By 'good' I don't mean famous, I mean safe."

"Oh," she said.

"On the other hand, I happen to have a perfectly good house about twenty minutes away, with six spare bedrooms, five bathrooms, and clean towels." He held his breath, hoping she would have a better idea.

"I hate to put you to that kind of trouble."

That meant "yes." He had no choice but to push the offer as graciously as he could manage at this hour, and make it sound easy. "I have to be at the hospital by seven, and I can take you to get your car on the way." He glanced at her. "I might even be able to scare up some clothes for you that won't look strange at dawn—like the bedraggled party-goer at the end of an Italian movie. Jane's about your size."

She looked at him with what seemed to be curiosity. "You would do that?"

"Sure." What choice did he have?

"Won't your—won't Jane feel . . . uncomfortable?"

"What for?" he said too quickly. He had been concentrating on his own discomfort, so he had not yet thought about what Jane would feel. He cautiously considered the subject. He had a sudden vision of Jane's eyes resting on Susan, taking an inventory—the long, golden hair, the little wisps on the nape of the long, delicate neck where they had escaped from the place where they had been tied, the impossibly smooth ivory skin—then focusing on Carey. But Jane's look would be completely unjustified.

What he was doing was a simple act of kindness—no, it was even more innocent: an obligatory refusal to be unkind. He imagined Jane hearing his thoughts, and the gaze turned ironic. No, he thought. That wasn't the way Jane would react at all—unless she was just teasing him. He was being irrational and unfair to her. She would never give him that look just because the person he helped happened to be female.

Then he admitted to himself that his deepest motive for taking her home with him had been provided by the needle on his gas gauge. He hadn't insisted on driving her to her place, where she belonged, because he was afraid he wouldn't be able to find an open gas station at this hour on the long, unfamiliar drive to Orchard Park. He might run out of gas, and then they'd both be stranded.

He realized he was taking too much time inside his own head. "If she were here, she would be the one asking you to stay. She's always doing things like this." It sounded true to him, as far as it went. He couldn't quite get himself to feel certain that Jane would invite a woman who looked like Susan to stay in the house while she wasn't there.

She looked at him closely. "I'd feel a lot better about it if I heard her say it. I'd hate to get you in trouble."

He smiled and shook his head. "I'm not going to call her in the middle of the night to wake her up and ask her permission, no. But I'll mention it the next time I talk to her." He drove onto the boulevard and accelerated. "Of course, the first few times you meet her, you'll have to get used to my calling you 'Sister Mary Boniface.' "

She laughed the melodious, liquid laugh again. "Oh, well. I guess I'd rather just be your secret."

Carey was still contemplating those words as he pulled into his driveway. He idled near the front door, where he usually parked in the summer, then found himself touching the gas pedal again to let the car glide the rest of the way up the long driveway before he stopped again at the old carriage house, out of sight of the street. There was no sense piquing the neighbors' curiosity, he thought. The fact that what he was doing was innocent didn't make it a worse story.

He opened Susan's door, led the way to the back entry, unlocked the house, and let her enter first. He reached over her shoulder to flip the light switch just as she stopped to keep from stepping into a dark, unfamiliar room. It would have been much better if they had collided hard, but instead his body met hers softly. "Oops," he said. "Excuse me."

She half-turned to give him an utterly unreadable look, then stepped into the kitchen, looking around her. "Great kitchen," she said. "Do you entertain a lot?"

"No," he said. "At least I don't think we do. Jane might let me know I'm wrong at any time. It's big because that's the way they were in the old days. Everybody hung around the kitchen because it was warm."

She said, "Late eighteenth century?"

"The structure might be that old. Of course, it's been remodeled."

"When?"

"Beats me. If contractors worked the way they do now, they probably started in 1850 and finished in 1950."

He flipped a second light switch up as he went, but when he reached the doorway into the dining room, he paused to let her get a head start. She lingered.

He detected that she was looking toward the cabinets on the wall. He said, "Can I offer you a drink?"

She pretended to decide, then smiled. "Sure. It's a cinch I'm not driving."

"I don't have a lot here, so we'll have to rough it. Let's see. Malt scotch. McCallan. Terrific stuff. Makes you want to strap on your claymore and march against the Duke of Cumberland. Vodka. It's Stolichnaya, but I've run my Geiger counter over it to be sure it was made before the Chernobyl reactor went. Gin, of course. There's also some vermouth if you're good at making martinis. I've seen every James Bond movie, and mine still taste like poison. The usual mixers. Cognac. Wine and champagne in the refrigerator."

"Did you say champagne?"

"I think I did." He opened the refrigerator and found it. He set it on the counter and lingered over removing the foil and the wire. He would have to remember to buy another bottle. Jane would remember putting it in the refrigerator, and the missing champagne was not the best way to lead into telling her there had been a guest. He removed the cork, plucked two tulip glasses from the cupboard, and filled them.

The sound of the telephone was jarring. He snatched the receiver off the hook on the wall. "Hello?"

The operator said, "Will you accept a collect call from Jane?"

"Yes I will," he said.

"Hi, Doc." It was Jane.

"Hi. I was hoping you'd call." He looked at Susan as he said it, and she tactfully strolled off toward the dining room, then suddenly turned around and mouthed the word, "Bathroom?"

He pointed through the living room at the far hallway, and she walked in that direction. He felt relieved. "Where are you?"

Her voice was apologetic. "You know I can't say."

"That isn't what I wanted to know anyway," he said. "I should have said 'How.' How are you?"

"Tired of missing you. Tired of . . . all this."

"That's what I wanted to hear. When are you coming home?"

He heard her sigh. "I just don't know. I wish it were now. But I really don't want to have to do this again. And I really don't want to see this guy's picture in a newspaper."

"Or yours, either."

"You know why I'm doing this," she said. "Just put yourself in my place."

He craned his neck to look out the kitchen doorway and through the dining room. Susan wasn't visible. "Just put yourself in mine."

Her voice sounded worried, pleading almost. "Please, Carey. This is an aberration. It's the last time, a job that I thought was finished, and it wasn't. As soon as I've got him tucked away, I'm done. We'll start over again, from the beginning."

He was silent for a long time. "All right," he said. "One last fling."

"See?" she said. "I knew I could get around you if I batted my eyelashes loud enough."

He knew it had been meant to be funny, an ironic comment on men and women that they were both supposed to laugh at, but he snorted mirthlessly. He tried to think of words that would take his mind off the worry and the emptiness he felt. He stared at the kitchen floor. "Well, I'm exhausted," he said. "Tonight was the benefit for the children's wing."

She gasped, and he began to wish he had not mentioned it. "It was?" Then she said, "At least I missed that. What a relief." He knew he was supposed to laugh at that too, and he was sure he would have, if she were standing here in the kitchen, where he knew she was safe.

"Yep," he said. "You lucked out again."

"Did Marian Fleming ask about me?"

"Of course," he said. "So did a lot of other people. I told them you were in Morocco taking a belly-dancing course."

"Oh, no. I used that excuse last time. Now I'll have to do penance with committee work for the next thirty years."

"Maybe not," he said cheerfully. "But if you don't know how to belly dance, you're going to have to fake a hip injury."

Jane said, "I'll work on it." She said quietly, "I'd better go."

He said, "Do you have to?"

"I'm afraid so."

"Just let me know if you need anything." He knew he had said it that way out of self-pity. She had never needed anything from him, and he was positive that she would never have asked if she had.

"I love you," she said.

"Me too." He hung up the telephone and walked to the counter. He saw the champagne glass and it reminded him that he had a guest. He picked up the champagne and walked toward the living room, but she hadn't reappeared. He set the champagne bottle on the mantel and stared into the fireplace.

In the den off the bathroom, Linda heard the click and dialed the operator. "Can I have the time and charges on that call, please?"

The operator said, "Two minutes and seventeen seconds, billed at three minutes. That's four dollars and eighty-eight cents."

"For three minutes? That can't be right."

"There's a two ninety-five surcharge for an operator-assisted collect call, ma'am."

"Okay, but it wasn't international or something. What are the night rates from Billings?"

"That might be your mistake. The call wasn't from Billings."

"That might be your mistake. She thinks she's in Billings, and I'd bet on her. How could she be wrong about that?"

"It was Salmon Prairie, Montana. It's the same area code, but it's a different calling zone, and the pay phone is owned by another carrier."

"Oh, I see," said Linda. "My mistake after all. Thanks."

"You're welcome." The voice was imperturbable, but chilly.

Linda hung up and hurried down the hallway into the living room. She found Carey sitting on the couch looking at a magazine. He tossed it onto the coffee table. "Sorry. That was my wife."

"You didn't tell her, did you?"

"Tell her what?"

"About me. Sister Mary Boniface."

It caught him by surprise. "Oops. You're right. Forgot. Well, I'll have to tell her tomorrow." He had been wrenched from a sad contemplation of how close Jane had sounded, and how far away she was. Now he felt reluctant to let this stranger see that he was annoyed at himself for forgetting to tell Jane about her. He hated it when Jane called from a pay phone. It was impossible for a person to remember everything he had to say in a couple of minutes.

"You aren't going to tell her," said Susan. The smile was mysterious and amused now.

He was startled, and it irritated him. "Why do you say that?"

"Because this was the time to tell her, and now you won't be able to, because it will look as though you were hiding me." The smile had a trace of sympathy now, the full lips pursed. Then there was mischief in the eyes. "If you try to tell her tomorrow, she'll think that you didn't tell her now because you were hoping to get lucky tonight."

"That's ridiculous," he said. "She's not that way at all."

"That's how women think," she said. "You shouldn't have decided to take one on full-time if you don't know how they work."

He suspected that she would have seemed bright and witty at about eight o'clock, but right now, he was not in the mood to be the butt of any more feminine teasing. "Well, I'd better show you where your room is. It's getting late."

She stood, but she took her glass with her and sipped from it as she headed for the stairs. "Just what I was thinking."

He led the way up the stairs and turned right to take her down the hallway. "This is the best of the guest rooms," he said. He flipped the light on and walked her into the room.

She sat on the bed, bounced a little, looked at the walls, the curtains over the big window. "It's very pretty."

He pointed to the door on the side wall. "Your bathroom is right there. Everything you need should be in the drawers—clean towels, shampoo, soap, even toothbrushes."

Susan glanced in that direction with little interest. She set her champagne glass on the nightstand, stood up, turned her back on him, and bent her neck forward. "Unzip me."

Carey stepped forward. He tried to lift her long hair out of the way without touching her neck, and carefully grasped the zipper without touching her back. He tugged the zipper down eight inches, to where he judged she could reach it, and stepped back. "There. If there's anything you can't find, I'll be in the room at the other end of the hall. Good night."

He began his retreat, but she said, "Not so fast." He stopped and turned. She was holding her hair up off her neck. "What do you think I am—a contortionist? I can't reach that."

"Sorry." He stepped forward, stopped three feet from her, reached out, and pulled the zipper down a few more inches. There was an instant—perhaps two seconds—when several things seemed to happen at once. She was still holding her hair up when she turned a little to say over her shoulder, "That's more like it." But her slight turn inside the dress seemed to spread the two unzipped sides of it apart. There was a tantalizing view of the white skin of the lower part of her back, where it softened and curved inward toward her hips. But worse, the front of the dress had nothing to hold it up. She quickly released her hair and hugged the dress to cover herself, but not before Carey had been presented with a glimpse of her left breast in profile.

"Good night," Carey muttered. As he backed quickly out the door and closed it, the last thing he saw was Susan Haynes facing him, holding the front of her dress up, her big green eyes looking into his with that knowing, amused stare. When he reached his own room at the end of the hall, he closed the door and leaned against it for a moment. The stare was still with him. "Taking her to a hotel wouldn't have been such a bad idea," he muttered. He locked his bedroom door, then undressed and got into bed. He lay in the dark with his eyes closed, but what he had seen came back to him again and again. "That," he thought, "is what the end of a marriage looks like."

At three o'clock, he awoke, lying on the bed on his back. He imagined for a moment that he could feel Jane's soft, silky hair on his arm. He turned to touch her, then remembered. He lay for a moment feeling sad and empty, and then he realized he could hear a voice. Someone was talking.

Carey sat up quickly and looked around him, but he saw nothing. He switched on the lamp beside the bed and squinted against the searing light to see the door. It was still closed, and the room was empty. It must have been a dream. As he reached for the lamp, he heard the voice again. It had to be Susan Haynes. It didn't seem possible that there could be somebody here with her. He got to his feet and walked into the hallway. As he reached the second-floor landing, he followed her voice and looked over the railing. She was facing away, sitting on the couch near the fireplace. The sight of her obliterated the lingering clouds of sleep. She appeared to be wearing only a bedsheet, her legs folded under her and her purse beside her. She turned to look up and the green eyes focused on him, and then she hung up the telephone.

She put a plastic card back into her purse, fastened the white sheet under her arm, and stood up. As he looked at her from a distance like this, the thought that overwhelmed all others was her perfection—the long shiny hair, the smooth, white shoulders and arms, the graceful veiled curve of hip and thigh. When she turned toward him, he saw she was aware that he had been staring at her intently. In order to look up at him she tossed her hair in a gesture that should not have been intriguing because it was self-conscious and calculated, but it was mesmerizing because she was posing for him, trying to look more beautiful. "I was just calling my machine in San Francisco. I didn't want to use the phone upstairs and wake you up. Hope you don't mind."

"Not at all," he said. "I just wondered—"

"Don't worry, though. I used a credit card, so it won't be printed on your phone bill."

He felt a sick chill. It had not occurred to him before that he had somehow become a man who was in the business of hiding evidence from his wife: first the champagne, and now the telephone bill.

Susan seemed to forget about him for a moment. She hitched her shoulder uncomfortably, then did a poor job of retucking the bed-sheet she was using as a sarong. She frowned, unwrapped a little of it, and tried again. It was as though she had unaccountably forgotten she was not alone. But then she abruptly looked up into his eyes, pretended to follow his line of sight and be surprised to find her own eyes looking down at the translucent sheet that covered her body. As she tucked the sheet under her arm she looked up again with the know-ing, amused expression.

"Something else on your mind?" The smile was still on her face as she moved up the stairs toward him. She walked so lightly that her feet seemed not to touch, as though she were floating.

He shook his head, as much to clear it as to communicate with her. "No," he said, already backing away. "No. I was afraid it was a burglar or something. But it was just you. See you in the morning." As he walked back to his room and closed his door, he wondered why it was that virtue had to be so clumsy and inept.

Earl sat up and looked out his hotel window at Pete Hatcher's car. He was through staring at its dusty finish, each day picking out new spots of birdshit on the windshield with his binoculars, never seeing a human being go near it. Now he needed to think ahead. He unfolded his road map and studied it, then picked up the telephone again and dialed.

He heard the sleep in Lenny's voice. "Yeah?"

"It's me," said Earl. "Listen. I want you to close the place up and get on a plane right away. Get a suite at the Rocky Mountain Lodge in Kalispell, Montana. Stay there until I call. It could be two weeks, or the phone could be ringing when you walk in the door."

Earl could hear rustling noises and groaning. Lenny must be sitting up in bed. Lenny coughed to clear his throat. "The place already is closed up. I went to bed an hour ago. What's up?"

"Did you understand what I said? This isn't a dream."

"Rocky Mountain Lodge in Kalispell, Montana. Wait there for you. Right." Earl could almost hear him thinking. "Hey—Rusty and T-Bone. What do I do with the dogs?"

"Bring them."

Earl hung up before Lenny could start protesting about the difficulty of flying dogs around. If people did it with fancy show dogs, then it certainly wouldn't harm two big, muscular beasts like the Rottweilers, and he didn't care what it did to Lenny.

He walked into the bathroom and turned the water on cold, then stepped under the icy stream. He gasped, then slowly let the water warm up. He was fully awake now, confident that he was thinking clearly. It would take ten minutes to dress, pack, and clean his prints off everything he had touched. It might take another ten minutes to check out and get on the road.

It had not escaped Earl that Linda had been talking in a whispery voice over the telephone at one in the morning. That was three A.M. in Buffalo. Linda would have called with Hatcher's location as soon as she could—the first minute when she could reach a telephone. If she was with this Carey McKinnon at three o'clock in the morning, worried that he would overhear her, then there wasn't much question what they were doing. She had been doing it with him for hours, letting him put it to her until he had used himself up and fallen asleep. This was not a simple flirtation where she got a fact out of him that he wouldn't remember saying and probably didn't even know was a secret. This was a full night of it, her hair probably wet with sweat and his sperm still dripping out of her, sticky and warm when she called to tell Earl.

He was enraged. He hated this man, and he felt a mixture of awe and disgust at Linda. She had said she would do anything to find Pete Hatcher. But what she had done was not brave or cunning. It was pathetic, requiring only a fawning sort of guile and a strong stomach. It was like biting the head off a chicken. She was soiled. Unclean. The only way he was ever going to feel right about this was to make it even. He was going to do the same to Jane Whitefield before he killed her. Then he was going to make Linda go back and watch him drop the hammer on Carey McKinnon. Maybe he would make her go back and do it herself.

He stepped out of the shower, quickly dried himself, and dressed, tossing pieces of clothing into his suitcase as he saw them. Then he remembered the way she had cut him off at the end of the call—quickly, abruptly. It was probably because McKinnon was awake again. He nearly reeled with the sudden realization that it was worse, more humiliating than he had thought. McKinnon was awake. She would have put down the telephone and needed to distract him. She was doing him again right now, this second, while Earl was two thousand miles away in a hotel room. He didn't dare close his eyes, because he knew that the sight of it was forming behind his eyelids.

He slammed his suitcase shut, stepped to the door, and hurried out of the room. He took long, purposeful steps down the hallway toward the check-out counter. He was in a perfect mood to kill somebody.

As Jane walked back to the hotel room along the road through Salmon Prairie, she considered whether she had succeeded in leaving the right kind of trail in the wrong direction. She had charged some plane tickets for flights out of Missoula and Helena to credit cards. The accounts were held by male identities that were unripe enough to attract the attention of a hunter who was using a computer network to search. She had made guaranteed reservations for hotels and rental cars in the destination cities so the charges would be recorded and would appear on credit reports.

Her temptation was to use ten identities to build twenty trails in twenty directions. There was no reason to save false faces for fugitives anymore. This was her last trip. But two identities were the right number. If the chasers picked out both of them, they would think that one was an innocent who was not running from anything but didn't have much of a history. But they couldn't pick out one and ignore the other, so they would split up. If she left twenty trails, they would sense that she had made them all and wait.

Everything about the way they had tracked and cornered Pete Hatcher looked like at least two people. A lone woman might play the broken-car game, pop him on the spot, and walk away, but she wouldn't put him in the trunk and expect to drive him away. There must have been at least one man waiting unseen to do the heavy lifting and solve problems. It wasn't easy to kill an armed cop when he was looking at you.

Jane was almost certain that she had made no mistakes since she had found Hatcher in Montana. They had been on the move for a month, traveling as husband and wife. They had spent a lot of time in the car each day, then used different names in each town where they stopped to check into a motel late in the afternoon. Pete was always visible to motel clerks and guests, but always imperfectly and from a distance. Jane would stand at the counter and sign a name, and Pete would be busy with his head under the lid of the trunk pulling out the suitcases, or under the hood checking the oil. Even if the searchers stopped at the same motels later and asked the right questions, the clerks would not have been able to give them a direction. Jane and Pete had gone slowly, taking detours like tourists who had all summer.

She knew that she was just thinking of reasons to turn Pete loose and go home. Carey had sounded as though her call had depressed him, and the knowledge stung her. When she tried to repeat the conversation now, everything that she had said sounded empty and foolish, and she could do nothing to change it.

Jane stared up the road at the hotel and gave herself a reprimand. The quickest way home was to concentrate on preparing Pete Hatcher for his new life. He had already gotten accustomed to using false names, and he had begun to develop a good sense of how to make himself invisible in public places. He had listened carefully while she had explained how the tricks were done and what to do when they didn't work.

Now she had to teach him something more subtle and difficult. The way he would defeat his enemies was to outlast them. While they were staring at computer screens or loitering late at night in airport baggage areas or sitting in cars outside hotels at check-out time studying each male who came out the door, he had to be somewhere living a normal, reasonably contented life. If he could do that for long enough, they would give up. Even the owners of a casino couldn't keep a team of assassins on the payroll forever to search for one man. And the longer he went without showing any intention of doing them harm, the more pointless the search would seem.

Jane had watched the changes in Pete for several days, and she was satisfied with his progress. When she had picked him up in Billings, his personality had already retreated into him like a turtle's head. Now he was slowly emerging, getting his sense of humor back, looking less like a person recovering from some illness. If she could get him to rebuild himself—not to return to the same old Pete Hatcher, but to see the man he now was as normal—then he had a chance. With a few cosmetic changes and a surrounding establishment—a job, a place to live, a car, a couple of promising friendships—he would be better off than the people who were hunting him.

The last danger that she would have to save him from was the biggest. She had to teach him not to throw away the advantages she had built for him, sink into a depression, and stop trying, or grow so paranoid that he jumped at every shadow and attracted attention. That had been her mistake in Denver. She had sent him off to isolation in a small, dark apartment and effectively severed all of his ties to other human beings. To a man like Pete, who seemed able to maintain a sense of himself only by watching the reflections in other people's eyes, the days of solitude had been like continuous, small doses of poison. She was going to have to keep being his buddy, build up his confidence, and make him strong again.

She reached the gift shop of the hotel and found it had closed hours ago. She continued to the room, gave her familiar knock, and used her eyes, her ears, and the soles of her feet to try to sense where he was at each moment. Finally he opened the door. "Very good," she said as she entered and locked the door. "I couldn't have done anything but fire blind through the door, and I would have missed."

Pete walked back to his chair and sat down. She could see he was watching something on the television that featured a lot of men flying upside down in fighter planes and shouting into radios. "Good," he said. "That's one for me."

"I just walked by the pool," said Jane. "There's nobody in it, and the lights are off."

"Then it's probably a septic tank."

"Nope. There's a diving board. I'm going for a swim. Want to come?" She found the bathing suit she had worn in Missoula at the bottom of her suitcase. "We'll have to be quiet."

He glanced up from the television screen for a second, then shrugged. "Can't. No suit."

She reached into his suitcase, held up pairs of pants until she found a pair of jeans with a worn knee. "Are you saving these for the Levi Strauss museum?"

He seemed to consider. "I've heard I could get a good price for those in Tokyo. I don't know how to get there, though, so I guess that's out."

"Good thinking," she said. She put her foot on the bed and pulled her boot knife from her ankle, sliced the legs off the jeans, and tossed what was left in Pete's lap. "I'll change in the bathroom. Knock when you've got those on."

He knocked on the door sooner than she had expected. When she came out, she carried the two big towels from the rack by the tub, holding them in front of her casually to disguise the way the suit rode up at the hip. The suit seemed to her to be less modest than she had remembered it, but maybe it was just the unfamiliar feeling of wearing one at night; there was no sun to warm the places that weren't usually uncovered. She plucked the room key off the table. "Here. You have pockets."

He took the key and she approached him in a way that forced him to go out the door first and start across the lawn to the pool. She dropped the towels, then walked down the steps into the warm water at the shallow end of the pool. She ducked down and swam the length of the pool under water. The pool was so dark that when she reached the end, she nearly crashed into him. Her fingertips brushed flesh, and she came up to find his face a few inches from hers. "Sorry," she whispered, then sank, pushed off the wall and glided away again in the silent darkness of the water.

While her momentum was slowing, she felt a shiver of embarrassment. There was no reason for being so squeamish about touching his belly. She was the best friend he had right now, and she had not done it on purpose. She gave a kick and rose to the surface, looking around for him. He was invisible, under the glassy surface somewhere.

With a sudden start she felt his big arm hook around her waist and lift her in the water. She was held against his big body in a feeling that was at once smothering and too pleasantly familiar. She gave a little cry, and he spun her around to face him.

She could see the white teeth in his smile, and the whites of his eyes, much too close. She leaned away, but that brought her pelvis into contact with his, so she jerked back. The white teeth disappeared and she felt the brush of his shaven upper lip and the touch of the soft lips. "Time out," she said, too loudly. She put her hands on his chest, and she was aware of the hard, hairy torso as she pushed him away.

She could see the silhouette of his head and shoulders, but his face was in shadow. "I made a mistake," she said quietly. "I never told you I was married."

She could see him tilt to sink backward into the water like a man blown over by a sudden wind. He rose to the surface floating on his back, took a couple of shallow breaths, and bobbed to his feet again. "I'm the one who made a mistake," he said. "I apologize. Please, forget it ever happened. I didn't know, and . . . I guess that's just me. I meant no harm."

Jane found herself in a depth where her toes brushed the bottom, so she stood on them. "Look, don't overdo it," she said. "It's reassuring to an old bat like me. It's just that—well, you know—I'm taken."

She swam the rest of the way to the shallow end and sat on the bottom step with the water up to her neck. From here the light of a fixture on the wall of the hotel reflected on the surface and she could see him swimming. He was not very graceful, but he was strong, each armstroke pulling him a few feet. She knew he was trying to work out a way to face her after making a pass and being turned down flat. It occurred to her that it was probably a new experience for him.

Jane wished she had never thought of swimming at this hour. The night was unseasonably warm, and she had wanted to get him involved in something that was careless and fun. Now she was afraid he was going to withdraw again. But there was something worse going on, and it was something that she had not prepared herself to defeat. She had almost let it slip out while she was saying no, detected it crowding up behind the other words and put her face into the water to keep it from coming out. It was, "I'm not offended. I don't have anything against sex."

If she weren't married, if this had all happened years ago, she might very well have let Pete Hatcher's hand stay around her waist, might have stayed in the water and waited with great interest for it to move where it pleased. And even worse, if she had not considered the marriage vow unconditional and permanent, Pete was exactly the sort of man she might have chosen to disregard it with, and this was exactly the sort of time and place when it could have happened. The incredibly clear, warm night air with the strange brightness of the stars, the feeling of floating weightless in the dark water might have made it seem to be an exception.

Pete disappeared again and surfaced at her feet. He was smiling tentatively, the water gleaming on his smooth, hard shoulders. "I think we'd better clear the air," he said.

She nodded. "Good idea."

"I'll never put you in a position where you have to feel uncomfortable again."

"Thanks," she said. "I won't do that either. What you did wasn't exactly assault, you know. It was a question. The answer is no, that's all."

"You don't wear a ring, you never mentioned a husband. Maybe because we spent so much time alone, I've been holding you under a magnifying glass. I interpreted a lot of things wrong—movements, words, everything. I like you. You're not like anybody I've ever met, and—"

"Relax," said Jane. "I like you too. I've said that before, and maybe I shouldn't have, or I said it wrong. We'll still be just as close. Maybe closer, because of this. But I'm your sister, not . . . not anybody else. Have we said enough?"

"Hi." The quiet female voice came from the shadow beside the hotel doorway. Jane spun her head and saw the shape of a woman. Jane's muscles tensed, and she let herself slip lower into the water, but the balls of her feet found traction on the rough surface of the pool steps.

"Hi," said Pete. Jane's jaw tightened. If this was the woman who had tried to kill him in Denver, he had just helped her locate him in the dark water.

"Hello," said Jane. Maybe two voices would complicate her directional fix on Pete. She studied the silhouette as it took its first step toward her. The towel was wrapped around the waist like a skirt, but there could easily be a gun tucked in back. Then she saw a second silhouette step from the entrance, and for a half second she was sure. She took in a breath to prepare to move, but the two shapes stepped into the dim swatch of light from the lamp at the same time.

She could tell from their bodies that neither was a young girl— not seventeen or eighteen. The curve of hip and thigh and breast were too pronounced. She could see their faces now, and they were both mildly attractive, but to determine age she needed to see them in bright light, where the texture of the skin would show mileage. The thinner one with red hair stuck her toe in the water near Jane's face. "Oh, good. It's really warm," she said. She whisked the towel off and tossed it on the deck. Jane was satisfied that this one was not armed. The green two-piece bathing suit would not have hidden a razor blade.

The second one took off her towel and knelt to touch the water with her fingers. "You're right. It's perfect. Just like a bath." She was wearing a suit that Jane guessed had probably come from the same store, but on this one it looked even more obvious, almost indecent. She was shorter and blond, with big white breasts that seemed painfully confined by the top, and when she stood to dive in, Jane saw the lower part of the suit as a blue line bisecting a heart-shaped flash of white buttocks.

The blond one surfaced near Pete. "I hope you don't mind our coming in with you. We saw you from our room, and it just looked so good . . ."

"Not at all," said Pete. "We're glad to have you. This way we don't have to wonder if we're crazy, because you are too."

"I'm Pam," she said. Jane could hear something in the woman's voice. Then she decided it just sounded tense because she was treading water and in the effort her throat muscles had tightened. "And this is Carol."

Jane tried to analyze her unpleasant feeling. It was the way body-guards must feel when their charges decided to go into a crowd. The bodyguard's adrenaline flowed, her muscles contracted for action, and then the threat turned into a mere distraction.

Pete said, "I'm Jim Holstra. This is . . . Mary. She's my sister." Jane's distracted thoughts suddenly crystalized. He was using her own words.

"Oh, really?" said Carol. She half-turned toward Jane and smiled faintly. "You two must get along pretty well, to travel together."

Jane had no direction of escape from this conversation. Was he doing what she thought he was doing? The distraction had blossomed into an annoyance. "Yes," she said.

Her mind was prickling with irritation. They were gently closing doors on her. She reminded herself that whoever they were, they weren't killers. They were making it obvious that they were intrigued by Pete. If anyone asked later if they'd seen him, they could hardly forget, but what could they say? She couldn't take them seriously as a threat to Pete's safety. She could not think of a reason why they seemed so threatening to her.

The one with the red hair glided out into the deep water and bent at the hips. Her bottom broke the surface and then her feet, and she disappeared in the direction of Pete and the blonde. Jane had to fight some inner resistance to bring the names back. The blonde was Pam; the redhead Carol. In a few seconds Carol emerged again, beside Pete. For a minute the three held on to the tile in the deep, shadowy end of the pool. She couldn't hear what they said. Then Pete floated out into the center.

Jane saw the copper head slip very close to the yellow head, cup a hand, and whisper something. The blonde gave a little squeal, and they started whispering again, then giggled like two unappealing children in a conspiracy. Then they began to swim slowly on either side of Pete. She stared at the two of them, and found herself thinking, Wait until he gets them under the light.

She was horrified at her thought. She was acting as though she were jealous. For the first time she was glad he had offered himself so she had gotten the opportunity to turn him down and acquit herself of that charge. Why was she suddenly feeling angry? The anger didn't seem entirely real. It occurred to her that it might be her mind's way of protecting her from something else, and she could even identify what that something was. It was regret at the loss of something that never could have been, something that would have been beautiful, but was now being transformed into something tawdry. Why did she call it tawdry?

She moved to the top of the steps and she realized that she had been unconsciously moving away, to escape the place where this was happening. She shivered when the air touched her skin. She stopped.

If she left, went back to the room, these two almost certainly weren't going to try to kill Pete Hatcher. But if she weren't present to control the situation, they might ask him questions he was not prepared to answer, or even attract attention that would get him killed.

She felt the urge to hear what they were saying. She slipped back into the water and drifted toward them. Suddenly there was splashing. Pete was out of the pool walking toward the hotel room. He opened the door and disappeared. Jane looked after him in confusion.

The two women suddenly appeared on both sides of her, heading for the steps. "Your brother is really something." Pam laughed. Jane altered it: little turned-up nose, pink all over—Spam.

"Yes," said Jane. "He's a lot of fun." She loathed them.

"Aren't you coming?" asked the other one, turning to the side to wring out the long copper hair. She seemed hopeful.

"Coming where?"

"To our place, for a drink."

"Your place?" asked Jane. She let her feet touch and began to walk along between them.

"Yeah," said Spam. "We've got a little suite, and we've got supplies."

Jane's head began to ache, but she hid her distaste at the idea. It was after one in the morning. If these two got tipsy and festive, they could be loud enough to get Pete arrested. Then there would be fingerprints, public records for the killers to find. "Sure," said Jane. "We'll stop by for one drink."

She saw the look that passed between Carol and Pam. They were not pleased.

Jane was still twenty feet from the door of the hotel room when it opened and Pete stepped out wearing a dry pair of jeans and a T-shirt, carrying some glasses. He walked to a room two doors from theirs and waited while Carol unlocked it. She considered calling to him, but it would have to be loud if she wanted him to hear it. She tried to catch his eye, but he was looking down, as though he were staring at the lock.

The two women were busy pretending they didn't know he was looking at them, and they seemed to enjoy the task, giving little shimmy-shivers they could blame on the cold, then tiptoeing into the room ahead of him.

Jane stepped into her room. She stripped off the wet suit quickly in the bathroom and hung it in the shower. She glanced at her own naked body in the mirror and caught herself making the comparison that seemed inevitable at this strange instant in her life. It made her feel a little better: she was not the hag she was feeling like. She was pretty.

She stepped into a pair of jeans and pulled a sweatshirt over her head. At the door she stopped, stood absolutely still, and took a breath. Why am I doing this? Because if I sit in this room alone, I could wake up alone and wish I had kept him from getting himself killed.

She blew out the breath, closed the door behind her, and walked to the women's room. The light was on, so she was sure it was the right one. She knocked. The door opened a crack, and she pushed it cautiously to come inside. The connecting door to the next room was open, and a dim light was on in there too. Carol, the copper-haired one, emerged from the next room still in her bathing suit, set two glasses of brown liquor and bubbles on the table, and headed into the bathroom. She stopped in front of the mirror and began to blow-dry her hair with a loud dryer. She yelled over it, "Where are you two from?"

Jane picked up the drink that was closest to her and walked to the doorway of the bathroom. "More important, where are Jim and Pam now?"

Carol clicked off the dryer and began brushing her hair, an amused little smile on her face. "Didn't they come in there?" Then she stopped brushing. "Why, that little . . ."

Jane turned toward the open connecting door and Carol stepped to her side. "If you can't see them, do you really want to go next door looking for them?"

"Probably not." She took an experimental sip of her drink. It was warm and sweet, like bug repellent.

"Are you really his sister?"

"Sure."

"You don't look like him."

"Different fathers. Our mother was a magnet for bums." Jane wasn't sure why she had chosen to make up this kind of story, but it fit her mood. It occurred to her that Pete could easily be telling a different story. "Jimmy might not tell you that, because it's not nice. And I think men make up nice stories because they need a father they can admire. But we're all grown-up women here. Are you and Pam related?"

"Just friends," said Carol. She pulled down the top of her bathing suit and Jane looked away involuntarily to see if Pete was behind her seeing this. But the door to the next room was now closed. Carol slipped the tight suit down from her hips, and Jane looked at her objectively. She had been given to understand that men liked red hair, and hers was at least real.

Carol caught her eye and smiled. "We're on vacation together from the car agency." She cocked her head. "You wish we'd drop dead, don't you?"

"No," Jane lied. "Why would you think that?"

Carol found a small perfume bottle in the shoulder bag on the counter and dabbed a bit on her neck, then another on her belly, close to the patch of red hair. The little smile was conspiratorial. Jane's stomach felt hollow. Carol leaned close to the mirror and began to make up her eyes. "I don't know. That's what I was wondering."

"That's not the way I feel," said Jane. "But he's my little brother, and maybe I'm protective." She walked into the outer room and sat at the table.

In a few seconds Carol walked out to join her. Only then did she carelessly slip on a terrycloth robe and tie it. She sat on the bed and switched on the television with no sound. "I guess you should be protective," she said. "He's such a hunk. Of course, if you're his sister, he probably doesn't strike you that way."

"I can see," said Jane. She needed to add something malicious. "He seems to attract one after another."

It didn't seem to touch Carol. She shrugged. "Life is short. He might as well have some fun."

Slowly, against all of Jane's hopes, she began to hear faint noises coming from the next room. The walls were so thin that they muffled none of the sounds. There was a soft, female moan, and then the springs of the bed. She needed to talk. "You said you and Pam work together?"

Carol stared at the silent screen of the television set, but Jane could see she was listening to the sounds behind the door. "Uh-huh."

"And this is your vacation. Have you been up in the mountains?"

Carol looked at her, the blue eyes focused on something behind Jane's head. "A couple of hikes." The voice in the next room was up an octave now, and louder, sounding almost distressed. "Oh," it said. "Oh, oooh, yes. Please."

Jane considered that this was one possible way that hell could be. It was torment, and it was designed to make her know, and to feel, that she was bad and weak. She could do nothing but talk to this idiot on the bed, and talking to her was like looking in a mirror and seeing a grotesque parody of herself. Carol was lying there and the robe barely covered her anymore, but she didn't think to close it, and her face showed that she wasn't just hearing, she was listening, and wishing more fervently each second that it were she instead of her friend. "Are there any good hikes that we shouldn't miss?" asked Jane. "We've been sticking to the road a lot."

"No," said Carol absently. "I don't really think it's much fun." She turned to glance at Jane, then said to the television set, "You get hot, and sweaty, and out of breath." She lifted her glass to her lips, tasted it, and made a face.

"What's wrong?" asked Jane. Talk, damn you.

"These taste awful without ice. We need ice."

Jane almost sprang to her feet. "I'll get some," she said. "Do you know where the ice machine is?"

Carol shook her head. "I'll get it. It's around a couple of corners." She stood and walked to the door. Jane noticed that she put no shoes on her feet. She paused and studied the two room keys on the table, then seemed unable to remember which one fit this room and slipped both into the pocket of her robe.

For the first few seconds, Jane was relieved to be out of Carol's company. But as minutes passed, the sounds from the next room seemed to grow louder and more frequent. Jane tried not to hear them, then knew that there was no way not to hear them and let them induce clear, detailed visual images in the mind. She was ashamed, and she resented having to feel that way. Her mouth was dry and she detested the drink in her hand, and she needed to clear her throat, but if she did, then Pete and the blonde would hear her, and it would show them that it was impossible for her to be in this room without eavesdropping. She could not even deny to herself that she was listening now, feeling each minute that this was some low ebb in her life and that it was sinking lower, and she with it.

Then Jane heard a new sound. For a few seconds, she wondered why it had surprised her. It was the voice of Carol, coming to her through the connecting door like the other one. "Oh, Jim," it said. "Oh, Jim." Jane carried her drink to the bathroom sink and poured it out. Then she walked out of the room. When she reached her own room, she remembered that Pete still had the key in his pocket.

She was not going back. She picked a credit card out of her wallet without looking at it, curved it a little so it would fit between the door and the jamb to depress the plunger, then slipped inside and stood alone in the darkness.

She was amazed. She had left her husband and rushed all the way out here, maybe to walk in front of a gun muzzle, because that man had called for help. Then she had carefully piled up day after day of invisible, anonymous travel to let his trail get cold. Now he was busy burning up all of her efforts, making himself as memorable as any human being could be to two women who probably couldn't wait to meet the next strange man in the next hotel. She hated Pete Hatcher. He had done this to punish her for rejecting him—wanted to make her imagine, know what she had thrown away, and learn to want it. No, that was too simpleminded. It had been for both of them, to prove that he was still attractive, still manly, still Pete. He had done that better than she would ever let him know. The word *ever* struck her ear as accurate, so she said it aloud: "Ever."

23

She heard him before he put the key in the lock. She let him sneak in without acknowledging his presence, or the bright sunlight that shone in the door when he opened it. She had gone out twice during the night to walk the perimeter of the hotel grounds, studying the cars in the parking lot and the windows of rooms that were on the court, but had seen nothing that worried her, and then she had slept.

She waited until ten to get out of bed. While she was in the shower he got up too, and she found him packing his suitcase. "Good morning," she said, carefully modulating her voice to sound as cheerful and unconcerned as she could.

"Good morning," he answered. He stepped past her into the bathroom without meeting her eyes, and then she heard the shower for a long time.

She finished packing, latched her suitcase, and spent a few minutes selecting identities for the day. Today they would be Tony and Marie Spellagio, who had not yet made an appearance in Montana. She laid their credit cards and driver's licenses on the bed in a row, so that Pete could examine hers too.

Then she made her preliminary inspection of the grounds through the windows. It was another perfect late-summer day in the

Rockies, with the sun glaring from what seemed to be just over their heads, and no sign that anyone was near enough to be watching.

Pete came out fully dressed and with hair wet from the shower, picked up his cards and both suitcases, and followed the usual routines. He set the suitcases down beside the car, dropped something so he could look beneath it, peered under the hood, and then loaded the trunk while Jane checked out. She came back and said, "You want to eat breakfast before we move on?"

"No," he said. "If you don't mind, I'd like to get down the road a bit before we stop."

Jane nodded and got into the passenger seat. She was not sure whether he was feeling queasy from the syrupy drinks or wanted to be gone before his little playmates woke up. As he drove off the lot onto the highway, he answered her question. "I don't want to run into Pam and Carol."

"Why not?" she asked.

"Because they want to travel with us for a few days. It came up last night. I can't think of a good way to refuse without hurting their feelings. Everything I tried last night had an answer. This way I'm a jerk, and that will burn off the attraction. Because I left them both, neither one will take it personally. In a day or two they won't mention me, even to each other."

Jane did not speak, because he was probably right. His famous understanding of women seemed to have come back to him. It shouldn't have been a surprise: he had given himself a giant dose of femininity in the past twelve hours. She studied her road map.

They stopped outside a big restaurant in Swan Lake. There was no evidence on the signs on nearby businesses that the name referred to anything but a lake that had once had swans in it. They walked inside and the head waitress noticed them. "Would you like to sit inside, or outside on the terrace?"

Pete glanced at Jane, who said, "Inside" and moved into the interior of the restaurant. "Is that booth over there taken?"

"No," said the waitress, "but I could seat you by the window if you like."

"No, thanks," said Jane.

When the woman had left the menus and returned to her post by the door, Pete said, "What's wrong? Are you hungover?"

Jane leaned forward, her forearms on the table, so she could talk quietly. "It's a beautiful spot, so most people want to sit where they can see it. This time you don't want what everybody else wants."

"I don't?"

"Sitting here is a precaution that costs you nothing, loses you nothing. It makes you invisible to anybody but the people to the side of this booth."

His eyes moved to the side. "There aren't any people to the side of this booth."

She smiled. "That's why I picked this one instead of another. Almost all precautions are simple and effortless. After a time you'll take them without thinking each one through. The important thing is that you look at each situation and modify it to make yourself comfortable. If there's a choice between a tiny bit of vulnerability and none at all, you pick none."

"I thought the best place to hide was in a crowd."

"It can be. If a crowd is immobile and on display, then it can't hide you. If what you want it for is to hold off shooters by surrounding yourself with witnesses, then twenty is better than a thousand, because they can't shoot even twenty, and all of them will see. So you don't stand in long lines to go to movies or plays or games. You do your waiting at home. When the movie has been out a month, you can walk right in."

"What if it's a game? You can't wait a month for that."

"Watch it on television. If it's so important to you that you still want to go, then it's important enough to pay for the safest seats in the stadium."

"Which are those?"

"Down near the field. The only ones who can see your face in a stadium are the ones below you. A hunter scanning for you would look up toward the seats in the back—not only because the back seats feel like a hiding place to an amateur, but because they're all the hunter can see. So you pick the front seats. Everything is a choice." She smiled. "You're getting a feel for this. All you have to do is keep trying it out in different situations until they're all automatic."

Another waitress arrived and took their orders, then bustled off to the kitchen window to clip it to a stainless-steel wheel for the cooks to read.

Pete stared at the table. " 'Different situations.' You're trying to be tactful about the mistakes I made last night, aren't you?"

Jane looked away for a moment, then back to him. "What was wrong last night? You tell me."

"We met two strangers. I let them get too close before I was sure they were okay."

"Go on."

"I went to their room. Somebody could have been waiting."

She waited, but that was all he was willing to say. "Or been called in by one of them while the other one . . . kept you busy. Prostitutes have been robbing clients for thousands of years, so the routines are pretty slick by now. You couldn't know all of them."

"For starters, they weren't prostitutes."

"I'm teaching you how to live by your wits, not by luck. Neither of us knew anything about them when they showed up. What about my mistakes?"

"Yours?"

"Sure. You can learn from those too."

He seemed shocked. After a moment, he said, "I guess you let them get too close."

"Good. I never saw them coming until they were by the corner of the building. I should have kept scanning the entrances to the court- yard while I was swimming."

"Like those Secret Service guys," he said sadly. "What a way to live."

"It would have been easier than that. All I had to do was keep my mind on the possibility, and looking would have been unavoidable. As it happened, it didn't matter. As soon as I saw them, I was certain they weren't dangerous."

"How?"

"They showed up in the skimpiest suits imaginable." She saw Pete wince, but she went on. "In certain situations that would be omi- nous. Maybe they had been sent to distract you, keep you from look- ing in another direction. But it also let us see that they couldn't be armed. And their presence wouldn't make it any easier for someone else to kill you: they might get hit in the dark, and they could hardly expect me to be stupefied by the sight of a girl in a bikini."

"Stupefied?"

"I'm sorry," said Jane. "Distracted."

"I'm the one who's sorry. Once again."

Jane's eyes flicked to his face and then around the dining room. He was miserable, and she wasn't being fair. "I guess we have to clear the air some more, don't we?"

Pete shrugged. His face was apologetic and appealing, like a lit- tle boy who wanted to be forgiven.

Jane took a deep breath and saw the waitress striding toward them on rubber soles, carrying a tray. Jane waited until the waitress had served them, said, "Enjoy your meal," and hurried away.

"Back to that air," she said. "I'm a guide. I lead people who are about to be killed to places where nobody wants to kill them. I give them pieces of paper that say they're somebody else. To the extent that I can, I train them to be the new person—how to look, act, think. If they're being actively hunted, I give them a few tricks that can fool hunters."

"And?"

"And then I turn them loose and go home." Jane stared into his eyes and watched him to see if he understood everything she was saying. There was light behind his eyes, but it seemed only to be the life force, the glow of the eyes of a big, healthy animal.

"What is he like?"

Jane stiffened. "That wasn't . . . I wasn't talking about him."

"No," he said. "You know everything about other people, but they're not supposed to know anything about you."

It wasn't a statement Jane could ignore. "It's true, and it's not an accident. It protects him, and it protects me, and it protects you. When I take on a person like you, we both have to be aware that some day I might very well be caught. Years from now I might be asked where you are and what name I gave you. There are things that could be done to make me want very much to tell. My promise to you is simply that I won't tell. If there's no other way, I'll commit suicide to avoid it."

"Really?"

"Really." She let the knowledge settle on him for a moment. He seemed unable to take the next step. "If I tell you about my family and friends, are you willing to do the same before you'll tell anyone?"

He thought about it for a long time. "I would want to. I don't think I could."

"And you don't have to, because you don't know about them. But I can't help knowing about you, so I'm stuck. I gave my word."

Pete nodded thoughtfully. "We're back to last night, aren't we?"

"If you want to be," she said.

"Why you said no."

She sighed. "Marriages are fragile. When you boil off all the nonsense, what they amount to is a promise."

She could tell he had no trouble understanding her. If she could break that promise to her own husband, then strangers like Pete Hatcher wouldn't stand a chance. "Okay. I won't grill you anymore."

"Keep asking questions. It's what we're doing together," said Jane. "I want you to learn everything you can. I want you to get as good at this as I am, because in one more day I'm going to take you somewhere, get you settled, and go home. You're my last trip."

He stared at her. "In a way, I'm glad," he said. "I'm a little scared. One more day isn't much time. But I'm glad for you. This is a crazy way to live."

"It took me a long time to reach that conclusion. I guess I had to find another way to live before I could admit it. But I'm taken care of. Let's get rid of what's still bothering you."

"I don't know," he said. "I seem to be having trouble imagining a future. That makes it hard to ask questions about it."

"I know some of it," Jane said. "You'll live in a place that's pleasant, but maybe has a few security features most people wouldn't pay extra for. This morning I was thinking that one of those small, gated developments might suit you. The identity I'm going to give you is terrific, so you could survive the checks they do on new residents. The rent-a-cops wouldn't present much of an obstacle to the people who are after you, but the entry gates make it difficult for them to drive through and browse. They're pros, so their main concern is getting out afterward."

"It sounds logical."

"We'll find you a job. You were a manager in Las Vegas, so we'll get you something at about the same level in the new town. It will have to be something where you have less contact with outsiders, so we'll pick a company that limits it, somehow—maybe one that sells equipment only to doctors, or physicists, or—"

"How?"

"How what?"

"How do I get a job at that level in a business I've never been in?"

She smiled. "That's something I'll help you with. I'm a representative from an executive head-hunting agency. I've got a promising prospect. I sell you to them. I've already checked all your references, et cetera, so the company doesn't have to."

"You can pull that off?"

"Sure. I do it by not cheating too much. Your résumé won't list your real college, but it will have equivalent courses from another one. Your references won't come from Pleasure, Inc., but they'll come from a company that has a similar corporate structure, and I won't lie about your place in the hierarchy. And I'll be very clear about my fee."

"You actually collect a fee?"

"Of course. It will be the same fee other companies like mine charge. Otherwise your employers would know I'm a fraud."

"So now I have a condo and a job. Good start."

"A condo in the center of the development, that can't be watched from outside the gate. A job you like and are qualified to do, that keeps you busy. All you have to do is keep from making mistakes."

"Mistakes—you mean the ball games and movies and all that."

"I said that I train you to be the new person, to the extent that I can. What I can't do is give you an identity that doesn't fit." She paused. "That's why I'm glad last night happened."

"You're working up to writing me off."

Jane smiled, but her brows knitted. "I thought we were past that game. You pretend to be shocked at your own behavior and deeply humiliated that I know about it. This forces me to choose between two roles—the scandalized schoolmistress who talks to you with pinch-faced distaste, or the conspiratorial madam who tells you it's cute. Either way, we evade the real issue."

"What is the real issue? My sex life?"

"Your life, period. Suppose I tell you that having sex with strangers is dangerous. Is that news? Does it change anything?"

He looked down, silent.

"How about that it's even more dangerous for you, because the people who are chasing you know that you do it?"

He watched her, but still said nothing.

"You could improve your chances a lot just by being slightly more selective. Women who go to church social groups are less likely to be decoys than ones who step out of dark doorways after midnight wearing two ounces of nylon. And church groups are notorious for being exactly what you need. Join a group for singles. Every woman there is looking for a man, and they outnumber the men two to one. Someone like you would be very welcome."

"Are you trying to help me, or get back at me for embarrassing you last night?"

"I'm being realistic. Even if I were trying to embarrass you, who cares? Will anything I think about your personal life matter when you're on your own? No, and it shouldn't."

"So where does that leave us?"

"When I sent you to Denver I hadn't had time to get to know you. I expected you to live like a monk. Maybe you did too. This time, let's get it right. Those security-minded condo places are that way because they're full of young, career-minded women. You'll find them hanging around the pools and the exercise rooms. Some of the owners' associations even have parties where the eligible women will push themselves in front of your nose. Take them. Enjoy yourself. But stick to your story. Never reveal anything that doesn't fit."

Hatcher looked at her sadly. "I thought you were just being the pinch-faced schoolmarm. It's way past that, isn't it? You sound like a scientist talking about rats."

She reached out and touched his hand, then regretted it and pulled back. "I'm sorry. I'm just being professional. If you're happy, you'll be able to stay in one quiet, safe place for a long time. If you're not, you'll take risks to get happy. So I need to make you happy for as long as I can."

"But you don't feel anything."

"I don't feel what you feel. You see any woman on the youngish side with round breasts and the right ratio of hips to waist, and you want her. I can know that, but knowing is all I can do. It's all any of us can do. And what you did last night wasn't shocking or particularly newsworthy. It was just something I needed to be reminded of."

"You're taking one incident and weaving it into a rope to tie around my neck."

"No," she said. "This is hard for me to talk about, so let me get it all out of the way. Last night I watched a young woman strip off a wet bathing suit to put on makeup at two A.M. so she could lure you away from her best friend. Ignoring the power, the need that makes people do that would be stupid. Will you personally take the chance of getting killed for sex? Sure. Scratch the topsoil anywhere on the planet and you'll find the bones of people who maybe didn't all know it, but who died over the instinct to mate. It's not an opinion, it's a fact. What I think about it, or feel about it, or what the implications are for romantic love or babies or families or anything else is irrelevant. All I can do is get out of the way. In this case it means putting you in the right location, so you'll survive."

"Why?"

"Why?" He had surprised her again.

"Yes. You don't think much of me today. When I ask you why you save people's lives, you say it's because you're a woman who saves people's lives. I want to know if you care about me. I know I have no right to ask you to care. I just want to know if you do."

Jane patted his hand and gave him a smile that was achingly false. "Of course I do. You're the best brother I ever had."

She turned her attention to the plate of food in front of her. He had been eating while she had been talking, and her scrambled eggs had turned cold and rubbery. She put some into her mouth. She could feel tears beginning to gather behind her eyes. Something was very wrong this morning, and she could not find a way to fix it. Maybe she had placed too much weight on her young, tender marriage. She had somehow gotten the impression that it was going to be a shield that protected her, kept her at a distance from certain kinds of hurt, certain ugly facts of other people's lives. If nothing else, it should have made her immune to feelings about men like Pete Hatcher.

Jane swallowed her eggs and turned her attention to the people filling up the dining room for lunch. There were the usual number of older people with gray hair, the women in shoes like nurses wore and the men in socks that matched their shirts, and lots of stuff in their pockets. There were two families with children who had sat in cars all morning and now fidgeted and thought of excuses to get up and wander in the dining room. She let herself wonder if some day she and Carey would be like this, threatening their kids in low voices to make them behave, or later, growing old together and wandering around like the couple in the next booth.

Then she saw two people who intrigued her. The woman was tall and thin with long black hair, dark almond eyes, and high cheekbones. Around here the blood was probably Blackfoot or Kootenai or Flathead. The man was big, blond, and broad-shouldered—not muscular, but fit in the way that tennis players were.

The head waitress moved them from an inner table and seated them at a table beside the window. They watched her set their plates in front of them and talked quietly. Jane wished she had not seen them. The woman looked a little like her, and so she had wanted the man to resemble Carey. It was a childish and primitive impulse to make the world bend into congruence with what she wanted, to have the universe send her an omen that everything was all right. She did not want to notice at first, and then she did not want to acknowledge the truth. If the man looked like anybody, it was Pete.

She looked away. But before her head had finished its turn, she sensed that she had seen something strange. Her eyes shot back to the couple, focused on the high hillside through the window beside them. She gazed at it for several seconds, but the sight did not come again. She had imagined a small, bright flash of sun on metal. She stared down at her plate, not aware that her brow was furrowed.

Pete noticed her expression and said, "What's—" just as Jane had put the pieces together. She stood up quickly and took a step toward the couple, and time ran out.

She saw the windowpane shatter and the man by the window stop, his mouth open to receive the fork with a piece of pancake on it.

His head seemed to bob toward Jane, his ear striking his shoulder, then bouncing back a little. Jane saw the splatter of blood, bone, and dark tissue that had to be brain in the air all mixed with glittering, sparkling fragments of glass.

The dark woman's eyes grew white-wide, her fingers curled like claws, and she shrieked as the rest of the people in the crowded dining room took in a single gasp and let it out in a shuddering moan. People began to scramble. Chairs fell, plates broke.

Jane dashed over the shards of glass, yanked the woman out of her chair, and pushed her into the crowd that was backing toward the doorway just as the second shot shattered another pane of the window. She turned to search for Pete and he bumped into her, then held her to keep her from falling. The details flooded her mind now: there had been no report of the weapon, so it must have a silencer; no crack of a bullet breaking the sound barrier, so the ammunition must be subsonic. It probably didn't have the velocity to pierce any walls. She said, "Hold on to me," and set off, with Pete's hands on her waist.

They threaded their way into the crowd cowering in the restaurant foyer. The cashier was shouting into the telephone and the dark woman was off to the right screaming while two elderly women held her. Jane's mind raced. If the shooter had finished firing and was already slipping away, then she should get Pete out of here before he discovered his mistake. But what if he wasn't running away? His rifle scope had enough magnification to let him put a bullet through the wrong man's temple from the mountainside. If he was using this time to creep down the mountain, then in a few minutes he would be close enough to see faces clearly.

Jane knew she had to do something that was not going to make her proud, and she had to do it now. She began to push toward the door and yelled, "I'm not going to stay here and get killed!"

The people who had been standing paralyzed, waiting for some voice to suggest a remedy for their terror, shifted in a single wave. The double door ahead of them opened, then began to wag back and forth as each person nudged it aside to get out.

Jane tugged Pete out in the middle of the throng. As she had expected, once they were out in the sunlight and fresh air, sanity seemed to descend upon the crowd. They saw how open and unprotected they were in the parking lot, so they began to spin like dancers, looking in every direction to see where the danger was coming from as they retreated toward the overhanging roof and brick wall of the restaurant.

Jane sprinted to the car and crouched until Pete had joined her. As she had expected, her run—a definite, unhesitating move—seemed to some in the crowd to be shrewdly based on information they did not have. They ran to their cars, started them, and wheeled out of the lot to the highway.

"Drive," said Jane.

Pete ducked into the driver's seat and they joined the line of cars streaming out onto the road. Pete gripped the steering wheel hard, holding it steady with effort as though its natural inclination were to veer off into the woods. "I saw it," he said. "I couldn't think fast enough."

"Saw what?" said Jane.

"I was thinking they looked a little bit like us. Like you and me."

"Drive," said Jane. "Don't worry about the speed. Out here what they do when they want somebody is put up a roadblock. When they do, we'd better be on the other side of it."

Jane studied the road map while Pete drove. She traced the red and blue lines meandering through the mountains, searching for turnouts and alternative routes. It was the wrong part of the country to evade someone in a car. The Rocky Mountains didn't offer many vulnerabilities to road builders.

"Where do I go?" asked Pete.

"No choice but to keep going up 83 for a while," she said. "There's no place to switch until Bigfork."

"What then?"

"I'll tell you when I know. Right now, if you do that much, we're not dead. When there's a straight stretch, try to look behind you and make a list of all the cars you can see. Get to know them."

"How do I know if he's in one of them?"

"You don't. Most of them will drop out at Bigfork to look for a police station or a telephone. The one we need to worry about won't."

He drove for fifteen minutes, and Jane noticed no cars coming toward them in the left lane. Finally, three police cars flashed past, driving hard toward Swan Lake. She turned to look after them, then switched on the car radio. After some static and blurts of music she found, "The police have asked us to report that Route 83 is closed south at Bigfork and north at Salmon Prairie. It will remain closed until further notice." She switched it off and muttered, "Of course."

"What?" said Pete.

"I hadn't thought of that. They think they've got a sniper back there still taking shots across a highway at a restaurant. They don't want to block the road out until they get people evacuated. What they're blocking is the way in, so nobody gets shot."

She went back to her road map. "All right. At Bigfork, turn right onto 35, to Creston, and keep heading north when it changes to 206."

She set the map aside and stared out the back window. Maybe the shooter had not made it to his car in time to follow. He had been up above on the hillside, at least three hundred yards away. As soon as she had thought of it, she knew she was being foolish. It wasn't likely that a pro would strand himself that far from his car and open fire. His car had been up there too, probably parked beside one of the firebreaks or timber roads cut into the forested hillside.

The reflection had not come from his equipment. All he had needed was a rifle and a scope, and the good ones were designed with that problem in mind. It was cars that were covered with chrome and mirrors. He was probably right behind them now, if not among the first few cars, then in the next pack.

"We have to talk," she said.

"You start."

"We have a problem here. I don't have any idea how they knew where we were."

"Obviously I don't either." He turned to her, eyes wide. "You don't suppose Pam and Carol—"

"No," she said. "If they had put two girls in your path to get you alone, that was when they would have killed you. And we left this morning before those two were up. They couldn't have told anybody where we were going, because they didn't know."

"Then what could we have done to tell that guy where we were?"

"Maybe they have some spectacular new way of instantly picking out charges on the credit cards we've been using. Maybe they somehow found out about this car the day I bought it, and hid a transmitter in it. Whatever they're using to trace us, it might as well be magic."

"You're making me more nervous than I am already, and I can hardly hold the wheel steady as it is."

They passed a sign that said BIGFORK 5. She said, "We have five miles to make a choice. What I'm saying is that they shouldn't be here. When I play this game, if my side wins a round, we get to play another round. If the other side wins one, the game is over."

"A nice, sporting way of saying I'm dead."

"We'll both be dead. I'm trying to tell you we haven't won any rounds. They had you in Denver, until the policeman got in the way. They had us twenty minutes ago, and that poor man took the bullet. They haven't got you, but they haven't exactly missed yet, either. It's important to remember that. In a few minutes we'll be in Bigfork. There are cops on the road there now, and more on the way. We could stop, tell them our story, and they would take over."

"You mean give myself up?"

"You haven't committed any crimes. They would protect you, beginning in four minutes. In a day or less, you could be a thousand miles away, telling the Justice Department what you know about Pleasure, Inc. They would keep you safe, at least until you testified in court."

"Yeah, but what then?"

Jane threw up her hands and let them rest on her lap. "I can't be sure. Probably they would do what I did: give you fake papers and a plane ticket. You'd be a protected witness. I'll be honest with you. They're very, very good at protecting you until you testify. After that you're a drain on the budget and not much use. At that point you come back to me and I'll try again."

"I can't go to the police," said Pete.

"You said that when I met you. Now is the time to be sure."

"There are three men who own Pleasure, Incorporated. I know enough about all of them to get the cops a warrant to investigate, and a few tips on specific places to look, and I'm done. I didn't see things happen. I put two and two together. I heard them tell Calvin Seaver, the security guy, someone was a problem, and then read an obituary. I saw a rough count of the day's take on a piece of paper, and then a lower number on the ledger in the computer. The paper's gone. I'm not an eyewitness, I'm a rumormonger."

Jane heard an edge in his voice. "You're not telling everything. You did something."

"The reason I was getting ready to leave was that I was expected to do things that could get me in trouble. I signed receipts when I knew the count was wrong. I deposited money that came in from side businesses I never saw, and sent it to investors without reporting it to the I.R.S. I never sat down and listed all the things like that, I just got out. I think the cops could find evidence against the owners, but I know they could find some against me. I'll let you out of the car in Bigfork, or anything you want, but I can't go to the police."

"The people you worked for think you can." Ahead, she could see the police cars parked at angles in the other lane.

"I've been over this in my mind a million times. They must think I saw more than I did, or took evidence with me, or God knows what. But I didn't. I won't end up in some protected place. I'll be in a Nevada State Prison, and they'll hire some lifer to kill me." He drove past the roadblock, and Jane felt a little twinge in her chest.

Jane watched him take the turn just before the buildings began to cluster at Bigfork. He swung onto the smaller road and accelerated. She said, "Creston is eight miles. Bear right again there." She turned around in her seat to stare out the back window. She saw a few cars go the other way, toward Kalispell and Whitefish, and wondered if that would have been the way to safety. The road always seemed to have forks in it, and all she could do was pick. Maybe what she was watching recede into the distance was her chance to ever go home again.

They were at the Creston intersection in ten minutes, then onto 206 and climbing again, higher into the gray mountains. At Columbia Heights they switched onto U.S. 2. The road curved around big stony outcroppings, always climbing. Ahead were towns too small to hide in—Hungry Horse, Martin City, Coram. Always Jane studied the map. The idea of moving around in these mountains, where there were places to stay and everyone was a tourist, had seemed to be a good one. But now the roads reminded her of the chutes in a stock pen. Each opening looked at first like a way out, but each was an irrevocable choice. The walls were too high to jump and the animal couldn't turn around. The animal had no way to go but forward, pushed by the ones behind it. Somewhere, waiting at the end of the chutes, was a man with a hammer.

The hunters could see what the map told Jane as well as she could. She could leave this road only by two routes—along the east side of Glacier National Park and then north on Chief Mountain Highway to the Canadian border, or north along the west side of the park by the Flathead River on 486.

She looked more closely at the map. Route 486 stopped at the Canadian border. There were no little flags there to indicate a point of entry, as there were on the Chief Mountain Highway. She couldn't risk choosing a road that might lead to a dead end with a fence across it. She turned the map over and studied the little detailed map of the area on the back.

The map showed Route 486 ending at the border. It showed the customs checkpoint on Chief Mountain Highway. But the checkpoint had a note under it in small black print. "Closed September 15–May 15." After September 15 there was only one way to Canada by car.

Jane looked at Pete, driving the car along the highway.

He seemed to feel her gaze. He turned. "What?"

"Take the entrance to Glacier National Park at West Glacier. If there's a store in any of the towns before then, stop there."

"Do you have it figured out?"

"I think I know a way out of this, if that's what you mean."

"Whatever it is, I like it better than your last idea about the cops."

"Wait and see."

By five in the morning, Linda had searched the house as thoroughly as she dared with Carey sleeping behind the closed door at the end of the upstairs hallway. There seemed to be nothing lying around downstairs that could tell her more than she already knew about where Jane was or what she was likely to try next. The pads by the phones had no useful jottings on them, and darkening the top sheet with a pencil revealed no impressions that Linda could read. There seemed to be no weapons hidden where she could find them, no papers that would give her the false names Jane and Hatcher were using. When she began to fear that Carey would wake up, she retreated into her guest room.

She told herself not to worry. She had not failed completely. She had given Earl the name of the town, and if Earl caught up with them at Salmon Prairie, it didn't matter what they had been calling themselves: they were going to be John and Jane Doe. But she had not come all this way and worked this hard to get into Jane's house only to have Jane's husband push her out again.

The thought made Linda's throat contract in an angry gulp. Somehow Carey had become the worst part of this job for Linda. The thought of him made her sick with humiliation and regret. She had used every opportunity to show him that she was available. Could he be so stupid that he had not understood? No, that was just a way of salvaging her pride. She had even given him an eyeful of what was being offered.

She looked in the mirror above the dresser. It was so unfair. That body was absolutely perfect. Her face was captivating. How could he go scuttling down the hall and lock himself in his room like that? Jane could not possibly be prettier than Linda was.

She walked to the telephone by the bed and forced herself to concentrate. First she looked in the telephone book and tried dialing a few numbers. She settled on one that belonged to a restaurant that sounded too fancy to serve breakfast. It rang twenty times before she hung up. She copied the number and began to dress.

At six thirty, Carey knocked quietly on the door. Linda stopped at the mirror, checked her hair and makeup, and then opened the door.

"Good morning," he said. "I hope I'm not bothering you."

She gave her best smile. "You're not. I don't sleep in an evening gown." She made her eyes twinkle. "As you know."

Carey glanced at his watch. "It's six thirty . . ."

Linda's brows knitted in apologetic distress. "I'm afraid I've got another problem, Carey."

"What's wrong?"

"I've been calling the impound lot since quarter to six, and they're not answering. Didn't the sign say they opened at six?"

"I'm pretty sure that's what it said." She could tell he was trying to look as though he were hiding his worry, but what he was hiding was irritation. "When did you call last?"

"A minute ago. I know you have to be at the hospital by seven . . ."

"Let's try it again. The only place for a phone is in that little building, and they could be out on the lot." He stepped into the guest room with her and picked up the telephone. "What's the number?"

She handed him the little pad from the telephone where she had written down the number, and he dialed. He let the phone ring longer than she had, and finally hung up. "It doesn't really mean they're not open. I'll drive you there, and if nobody's around, you can always get a cab at the hospital."

"Can I make another suggestion?"

"Sure."

"They're sure to be open by nine or so, right?"

"I would think so."

"Then it would make me happiest if you would just go to work. I'll call a cab to pick me up here at eight. If we're both wrong and the place is deserted, the cab can keep going and take me home. That way you don't leave some patient waiting on a gurney. Better still, I'm not left on the street in an evening gown in an unfamiliar city. And I'm not seen driving back to the hospital wearing last night's clothes with a married man whose wife is out of town."

She could see that the suggestion had the desired effect. It contained reasoning he could follow, and it also gently reminded him of what could have happened. He seemed flustered as he shrugged. "I'm sorry. Everything seems to have gotten complicated." He was fiddling with his keys. He handed her one of them. "Would you mind locking up when you go? You can just pop the key into the mail slot in the front door."

She took the key. "No problem." She touched his arm. "And I'm the one who's sorry. I didn't mean to be this much trouble."

"No trouble at all," he lied.

"I'm very grateful," she said. "More grateful than you know."

He backed away from her gratitude toward the stairs. "It's getting late."

"Oh, Carey?"

He stopped. "Yes?"

"I promise this is the last thing I ask. But do you think you could lend me something of Jane's—an old pair of jeans and a sweater or something? Just to get me home."

He seemed surprised, then reluctant, but as she had expected, he did not know how to refuse. "Of course," he said. "I offered last night and then forgot. I'm sorry. Her closet is in the master bedroom. Take what you need." He hurried down the stairs and out the front door.

At two thirty, Linda Thompson dialed the telephone and heard the machine in her suite come on. She pressed the two-digit code and listened while the machine rewound. She could tell there was something on the tape. There was a click, and Earl's voice came over the line.

"I picked them up at Salmon Prairie and followed them as far as Swan Lake. I drilled a man through a restaurant window from five hundred yards. Felt pretty good about it until I saw their car pull out of the lot with them in it. They took off to the north. They could be heading to Canada. Lenny's with me, and we're going after them. When you find out where they are, leave a message on the machine at home. As soon as I've heard it, I'll erase it from here." There was a loud hang-up sound, and then a beep. Linda put the receiver back on the cradle. Earl had not said "If you find out." He had said "When."

Linda felt a shiver of fear that started in her shoulders, crept down her spine, and shot back up again. She could tell from the chill in his voice that he thought he had figured out exactly what Linda had needed to do to find out about Salmon Prairie.

That made Linda feel afraid again. His voice had sounded cold and detached on the answering machine, and that was very bad. He was resenting her for it, and Earl's resentment was always acted out.

She was in trouble. She had not done what he thought she had done, but he was going to punish her for it. And here he was, sending her back for more, knowing deep inside that he was going to hate what she did this time even more than the last, and he was saving it all up.

The telephone had not rung since Jane had called from Salmon Prairie. Carey knew nothing more recent than that, so no matter how devious Linda was about asking him where his wife was now, he couldn't tell her. She would have to buy time.

The best way would be to stay very close to him—move in with him, so she would hear the telephone ring and he would tell her, not because she had asked but because he wanted to. And the only reason he would want to tell her was to convince her that his wife was still very far away, that she was not about to burst in the door and find Linda with him. If Linda hoped to accomplish that, then she would have to make Carey want very much to keep her near him. Last night she had been sure she had him. He had not been as adventurous as she had anticipated, but there was no question he had been tempted.

Linda lay back on the bed and tried to coax from her imagination ways to make Carey interested in her. There was a special kind of titillation in the images she conjured, because even as she planned, she could feel Earl thinking about her on the bed with Carey and getting that strange combination of jealousy and arousal that was most exciting to her. Linda knew what her punishment was going to be, because she was going to submit herself for it.

She was going to make the big, wet tears come, and make her voice go small and helpless, and say, "Then he did this, and this, and this." And Earl, because he was Earl, would make her do again everything she described for him. She could already hear his voice, through clenched teeth, whispering, "Like this? Was it like this?" And she would be beside herself with excitement, because with Earl it wasn't like being with a man. It was like being possessed by a demon—part guilty, shameful sensation, but mostly fearing and sharing all of that power. A necessary part of her fantasy was that Earl would begin her punishment only after he had killed Carey. She liked to imagine that he would do it with a knife.

As the sign for Hungry Horse drifted past her window, Jane said, "Keep your eyes open for a sporting goods store. If we don't find what we need here, go on to Coram. If you see a military surplus store or one of those places for survival psychos, don't pass it by."

They both saw the store at the same time, and it seemed to be a little of each. The sign was big and crude, but the merchandise in the window included skis and toboggans. "Park off the street," she said. Pete found a space behind the building between two delivery trucks and they entered.

Jane picked out two of everything—compasses, canteens, sleeping bags, waterproof matches, flashlights. Pete hovered beside her to take the merchandise she selected, a worried look on his face. She whispered, "You wanted another option. Without this stuff we don't have one."

She carefully picked out their clothes: rainproof ponchos, olive-drab woolen pants with belted ankles, pullover sweaters, hiking boots, wool socks, long underwear, M-65 field jackets, gloves, and watch caps. Next she found a pair of ten-power binoculars, polarized sunglasses and Swiss Army knives for each of them, packets of dried food, a cook pot, and, finally, two backpacks to carry it all in.

Then Jane joined Pete at the counter, where he stood beside the pile of purchases he had built. As an afterthought, Jane picked up a small foam fire extinguisher, added it to the pile, and paid the clerk in cash.

When they had loaded all of the bags into the car, Jane began to sort out her purchases and pack the two backpacks while Pete drove. "There will be some kind of ranger station or visitor center at West Glacier. Stop there too, but put the car between two tour buses or behind a building or somewhere."

"Pretty authentic disguises," said Pete. Behind the thin sound of hope in his voice there was dread.

"I'm afraid they're not disguises," she said.

"They're not?"

She looked at him unapologetically. "Not exactly. It's something I stumbled on by looking at the map. We're brought up to see the world as a lot of roads. It's like a grid, with dots for the towns at the intersections and nothing between the roads at all. These people will keep chasing us if we stay on the lines. We have to stop now and then at one of those dots at the intersections, and they'll catch up. So we'll see the map differently for a couple of days."

"We're going camping? What does that get us?"

"I'm not sure yet, so I'm not making promises. I think they're using commercial computer databases to track us; the lists of people who buy handguns, cars, or rent hotel rooms. I've never used the same names or credit cards two days in a row, and that's always worked before. But it's not working now. I made some phone calls, but they were from pay phones. They don't transmit the numbers of pay phones for caller ID to pick up, so nobody can be intercepting the signal and finding us that way. Even if they managed to find out where I live and tapped my home phone, I never said where I was calling from. Our phone bill comes at the end of the month, so they're not reading it. I don't have any idea what these people are doing, or how. And that scares me."

"Isn't it possible that they just followed us?"

"Maybe. Maybe they out-thought me—figured what I would do, then drove along the right road and showed your picture to hotel desk clerks and waitresses. But it's not a great method if what you plan to do after you find the person is kill him. It's also possible that they're tracking this car electronically."

"How do we find out—search it?"

"Dump it."

"Where do we get another car out here?"

She gave her sad little smile again. "We don't. I'd love to get a new one and drive until the tread is off the tires. But we tried that, and a shooter turned up. I'd love to put on a blond wig and step onto an airplane to anywhere. But unless we know for sure how they're tracking us, we can't do anything that puts us in a predetermined airport at a prearranged time. The safest tactic I can think of is to do the opposite: go where there are no people to see us, no schedules, and no records for anybody to break into. It's not a great idea, but it's an idea. We've got to keep moving."

"Keep moving where?"

She sighed. "I think we have no choice but to dump everything we had when we walked into that restaurant this morning, and cross the border."

"Canada?"

"If they're using computer data files, it's possible crossing a national border will make it harder. A lot of businesses are national— not international. If their car gets searched at the border, there will be guns in it. There might be other advantages, but there are no disadvantages that I know of."

As the road wound up into the mountains, Pete seemed to be concentrating on his driving. "Shouldn't we leave this car someplace to mislead them?"

"I don't want to confuse them," she said. "I want them stuck."

"How do we manage that?"

"It's September thirteenth. In two days they'll close this road for the winter. If the chasers don't get this far by then, they'll have to go back. If, after that, they find out we left the car inside the park, they have the same choices we had: go on to the Chief Mountain Highway, drive to the border, and get stopped, because the customs station closes on the fifteenth too; go east to the next road that crosses at the Piegan-Conway crossing; or go all the way back along this road to Whitefish and drive up Route 93. Either way, we'll be in the space in-between, at least thirty miles from them with no road to get to us."

"And then?"

"And then we walk out of the woods in Canada and pay somebody to drive us far enough away to catch a bus. I'm not getting on any more planes until I know they haven't tapped the reservation system."

They drove into the park at West Glacier, bought a trail map at the ranger station, then joined the long single-file line of cars on Going-to-the-Sun Road. The progress was slow because the road was a Depression-era two-lane pavement with high, rocky cliffs on the right and Lake McDonald on the left. Drivers ahead of them pulled over whenever there was a turnout to take pictures and stare at the icy, glass-clear lake and the surrounding forests.

Pete said happily, "It looks as though we won't be needing that winter gear we bought. The weather's beautiful."

She turned in her seat to look at him. "I guess I should have asked you this before. Have you ever spent time in the woods?"

He pursed his lips. "Let's see. By woods you don't mean a bunch of trees next to the fairway, do you? I mean, this is a park, right?"

"I'm glad I didn't ask. Here it's seventy and sunny. The altitude is three thousand feet and it's three o'clock in the afternoon. In an hour or so, we'll be at seven thousand feet. The temperature drops about five degrees for each thousand feet. It could be fifty up there now. Sunset tonight is about six twenty. That's when it sinks majestically below the horizon if you're on the ocean, not if you have a mountain or two to the west of you to cast a shadow. It's also windy on mountains. So that fifty could already feel like thirty."

He frowned. "Thirty degrees? And you're sure today's the day the teddy bears have their picnic?"

She stared at him for a second, then laughed. "You've lost your mind."

"You know what?"

"What?"

"No matter what happens to me after this, it won't be anywhere near as interesting."

"I wouldn't give up yet."

"I know that sounds idiotic," he admitted. "I've been thinking about it for a couple of days now, and I kept wondering if I'd bumped my head. Then I was thinking that if I told you, I would just convince you that I was too stupid to be scared. But I'm scared all the time, and it still feels true. If they find me and kill me, it will just be a sharp pain, and then nothing. If they don't, I'll try my best to live a quiet life. But right now, every second is full of possibilities, full of things I never thought about or looked at before. I've never wanted to stay alive so much in my life."

Jane had not sensed that trouble was coming, and here it was again. It was not that she would be tempted to have a fling with Pete Hatcher. This was the fling, and she was having it. She felt the same exhilaration he did. This time the hunters were the best she had ever faced, and Pete Hatcher was her last client, and after this great flaming burst of clarity she was either going to die or let her life settle down to a steady unchanging glow like a pilot light. From then on, when evil came, it would come in some equivocal form—spite or pride or jealousy—sidling up to her and leaving her nothing clear and direct that she could do to fight it. This was the guide's last trip.

Jane studied the road ahead and saw the Loop coming. It was the only hairpin turn on the highway, eight miles out of the way to follow the course of the McDonald River and eight miles back under Mount Cannon. "Pretty soon we'll be there," she said. "If you're not willing to do this, tell me now."

"I already told you," he said. "I want to live."

He drove the long curve, then climbed again, higher into the mountains. When he pulled into the big parking lot at the Logan Pass visitor center and stopped, Jane said, "Pull over by the garbage Dumpsters and wait for me."

She opened the trunk and went through the suitcases one last time. She put Pete's pistol in his pack and the ammunition in hers to even the weight, then split his money between the two packs, closed them tight, and dropped the two suitcases into the Dumpster and covered them with garbage.

Jane used her Swiss Army knife to unscrew the Montana license plates and replace them with Colorado plates from a nearby car. She got into the car again and parked it as far from the road as possible, then handed Pete his pack, bedroll, and canteen. Finally she sprayed the inside of the car with the fire extinguisher and tossed it on the floor in the back seat, left the keys in the ignition, and walked away.

"What was that for?" asked Pete.

"The spray is just carbon dioxide. It'll be gone in a little while, but so will the fingerprints. If somebody traces the plates, they'll have a problem because the car's not registered in Colorado. It might buy us some time to make them trace it in other states."

"Why did you leave the keys?"

"Out of a million visitors, we can hope for one car thief. They must take vacations too." She handed him her canteen. "I'm entitled to one last phone call. Go fill these up with water from the tap over there while I make it."

She went to the telephone at the far end of the row, put in a quarter, dialed the private line on Carey's desk in his office, waited for the operator to tell her how many more she needed, and put those in too. Change made noise in pockets, and there would be no more collect calls for her. She couldn't be entirely sure that the shooters weren't using the telephone company's billing system to trace her.

"Hello."

"I love you," she said.

"What?"

She laughed. "I said, I love you. At least I hope it's you, or I just made a fool of myself for a perfect stranger."

"No," he said. "Not perfect. Do you have time to talk?"

She looked around to see if anyone was near. "Not much, but probably more than you do."

"Good for you," he said. "Having fun?"

"Not much," she began. Then she stopped herself. Could she tell him that a few hours ago she had watched a rifle bullet churn its way through a man's head because he looked like Pete Hatcher? Not if she wasn't also going to tell him it was over. "We're not out of the woods yet. Literally. I won't be able to call for a few days. We're traveling on foot, and there won't be any phones."

She could hear him breathing on the other end, then: "Why on foot?"

"It's safer. I'll tell you all about it in excruciating detail when I get home."

"That's what I was wondering," he said. "Can you tell me when you're coming home?"

"We've got to go about twenty miles, but that's measuring it straight. I figure two or three days to get up there, and then two weeks more to finish this for good. Then I'll be home."

"Why do you need two weeks?"

She sighed. "Because I never, ever want to do this again. If I do it right, it's over."

She waited a long time for his answer. Finally, he said, "I understand," as though he didn't. "Just promise me one thing."

"What's that?"

"Before you get on the plane, give me a call. I want to pick you up at the airport."

"I can probably find a phone before then."

"I know, but that's something else. Promise?"

"Sure," she said. She had spent her adult life inventing lies, and she could tell when somebody was hiding something. If Carey wanted to arrange a surprise for her, it was worth playing dumb to keep from ruining it. "I promise."

"Good. Do you need anything? Money or something?"

"No, thanks," she said. "I'd better get going. I love you."

"Me too."

"Bye."

They both hung up. As she walked away from the telephone, she fervently sent a wish across the mountains. Let the surprise be flowers and champagne. Don't surprise me by having the upstairs bathroom remodeled. Then she felt guilty and unworthy. The man she loved and wanted to spend her life with was planning a surprise. Whatever it was, she resolved to smile and throw her arms around his neck and kiss him as though all future happiness depended on it. She was not foolish enough to think that it didn't.

Jane walked out of the park building and found Pete Hatcher on the steps with their two full canteens. She cinched hers onto her pack and did the same for Hatcher.

"I thought you were supposed to wear them on your belt."

"Soldiers have to put up with two quarts of water whacking their butts, but I don't," she said. "Unlike them, we can stop and take off our packs when we want without getting shot."

"I hope," he said.

She walked across the lot and waited at the edge of the road. "Did you feel the change yet?"

"What change?"

"We just stepped across the Continental Divide. If you spill your canteen now, it goes into the Mississippi instead of the Pacific."

"I'll try to be careful to preserve the levees."

There was a break in the traffic and they hurried across the road. Pete stopped beside a wooden sign that had nothing on it but HIGH-LINE TRAIL and an arrow pointing north. "Just how long is this trail?"

She began to walk on the soft, irregular ground, under hemlocks and cedars. It forced Pete to take the first step off the pavement, then hurry to catch up with her, and then they were walking along and the decision was over. "How long?"

"Long."

"What does 'long' mean to a woman like you in miles?"

"On the map it looks like twenty as the crow flies, and maybe thirty if you take it in sections, point to point. The map isn't big enough to take into account all the meandering, which is what trails through wilderness do. And it's two-dimensional, so I can't tell just how hard the climbing will be. It could be fifty miles and seem like three times that."

"Do you mind if I keep asking questions?"

"Nobody can hear us, and the trail is shorter if you talk."

"What if they find the car?"

"Then they have to make a guess. If they think we changed cars, then they'll drive fast away from here to try to catch up and see the new one. If they think we abandoned it and walked off into the mountains, they have to guess which trail we took. If we went north toward Canada, there are a dozen branches ahead that come out pretty far from each other. But most likely they'll think we left the car so it would look as though we headed north for Canada, but turned south or east or west instead. Those trails all reach roads at some point."

"What if they don't fool themselves, know we headed for Canada, and pick the right trail?"

"Then they have other choices. They have to guess where we'll surface when we get to Canada, drive up there, and wait, or come up the trail after us."

"That's the one I don't like: some guy with a gun coming out here after us."

"Even if they do, they still have choices. We're carrying about what a cautious person would take on a day trip. A smart person would know there was the possibility of not making it back by dark and having to spend one night out there. Anybody who follows could choose to travel lighter than that for speed, or they could carry tents and heavy clothes and a week's food and water. If they travel lighter than we are, they could easily have to turn around and give up. If they load themselves down with lots of gear, they'll have a very hard time catching up with us."

"Especially with all those guns."

She laughed. "I wasn't going to mention those." She looked at him for a moment as they walked along. He seemed calm. "But you're right. Good sniper rifles are heavy—ten to fifteen pounds with the scope. The ammo isn't light, and this guy isn't likely to scrimp on that. It's usually made for the military, so it's 7.62 millimeters wide and 50 millimeters long. He'll also carry a sidearm of some kind, and ammo for that. I'd say he'll be carrying an extra twenty pounds of metal that we're not."

"Maybe we'll wish we were."

"I doubt it, because if he's carrying the weight, he probably won't catch us. What you do when you're running is put lots and lots of forks in the road behind you. Each time the hunter comes to one, your chance of losing him is fifty percent. Next fork, fifty percent. We've put a lot of forks behind us already. If we stay ahead of him, then even making all the right choices won't help him."

She looked up at him as they walked. He was tall and strong, and he was in acceptable physical condition, because all the women who got off airplanes in Nevada would have found that attractive. "How do you feel?"

"Scared."

"Me too. Are you dizzy or light-headed, sick to your stomach?"

"No more than I have been for months. Why?"

"Then you don't have mountain sickness. I didn't think you would, after three months in Denver. Are your muscles warm and loose?"

"Don't tell me," he said.

"I'm sorry," said Jane. "But we've only got about two hours of light left. I'd really like to get the first of those forks in the trail behind us." She began with a slow trot, the pack shifting at each step and making clanking noises. Pete trotted along, making even more noise. When Jane felt the sweat beginning to come, she lengthened her steps a little, watching the trail for rocks and roots and trenches.

He said, "We sound like a pair of skeletons on a tin roof."

"The noise is good," she said.

"It is?"

"Bears don't like surprises."

As Carey made his evening hospital rounds, he kept thinking about Jane. Here it was late summer, but in the Rocky Mountains it must be getting cold already. She had sounded well and confident that she knew what she was doing, but he suspected that she would never have called if she had any doubt that she could convey that impression. She had been perfectly capable of lying to him about what she was doing for over a decade, and he had never suspected her. That was a train of thought he decided not to follow. She would get her client to wherever he was going, and she would come back to him. She would be very surprised at how welcome she was going to be.

He left the room of Mr. Cadwallader and walked down the hallway toward the nurses' station to make his notes. He was pleased. Cadwallader would be moving around nicely by noon tomorrow, and home by the next day. As he pulled Cadwallader's chart from the holder, Nancy Prelsky tapped him on the shoulder. "Telephone, Doctor."

"Huh?" He looked up. "Oh, thanks."

As he took the receiver, he assumed it would be Joy at his office. "Dr. McKinnon."

"Hello, Carey." The voice shocked him. How could Susan Haynes have known where to call him? Of course. The main switchboard had tracked him down and connected her. He hoped they had done it because it was a slow evening, and not because she had implied it was an emergency.

"Hello," said Carey. "Look, I don't want to be rude, but didn't they tell you I'm on duty right now? And this phone is at a nurses' station on a floor with some very sick people."

"I apologize for calling you at work, but I'll make it brief. After last night's fiasco I'd like to start over again, and invite you and your wife to a dinner party with a few friends. There will be about twelve, and that takes a little advance notice."

He winced. He hated dinner parties, and he was appalled that this woman would call a surgeon in the middle of his rounds to arrange some social event. "I think that's the sort of problem we ought to talk about at another time. If you'll leave your number with my answering service, I'll try to call you tomorrow."

"Please. You have to give me a way to thank you, and this is the way it's done. Can you tell me when Jane will be home?"

"I'm afraid I don't know."

"You don't know? Why in the world not?"

"I just don't."

"I'm sorry to be pushy, but this kind of dinner party takes a certain amount of thought and arranging. Would you please call her and ask?"

He found himself looking around to see if Nancy was still within hearing range. He glanced at the call board and saw that there was a trouble light flashing on the board to signal that an IV had come loose in Room 469. "I can't call her. She'll call me when she can—probably in two or three days."

"Two or three days? Where is she—in jail?"

He tried to be patient, but he could feel the anger growing. "She's hiking in the mountains, and the place she's going is about twenty miles away, by air. Since she doesn't have wings, it'll take that long to get to a phone, and then she'll call. I'll try to remember to ask her then, and let you know. That's the best I can do."

"Fair enough," said Susan. "I'll let you go now. I'm sorry to be such a pain, but I want to make it up to you for last night, and I'm warning you I won't take no for an answer. Good-bye."

As soon as she heard a fresh dial tone, Linda quickly punched new numbers into the telephone. She had wanted to goad him into making just one telephone call to Jane, instead of always waiting for her to check in. If he had agreed to call Jane, she could be sure he would have done it from his home telephone: he was too self-important about his work to do it from the hospital. Then Linda could have tape-recorded the tones of the number he dialed, just as she had done in Hatcher's apartment in Denver. The tactic had not worked this time. Jane had not brought Hatcher to a long-term hiding place yet, so she hadn't given Carey a number he could call. But what Carey had given Linda was better. It was fresher, harder to get, and so it proved that she was better.

As she listened to the telephone ringing, she began to tease herself with thoughts about what she could say to make Earl feel the way she wanted him to. By the time the hotel operator answered, Linda was already beginning to feel choked with the emotions she had induced. When she gave the room number, her voice came out in a brave, sad little sigh.

Earl sat waiting in Lenny's hotel room in Kalispell. He lifted the new British Arctic Warfare sniper rifle out of its fitted transit case and began to break it down so he could clean and oil it. He lovingly ran his fingertips along the smooth nylon foregrip, then loosened the Allen screws. He took out the trigger assembly and adjusted the pull and travel once again.

He had fired from a crook in a tree on the hill at five hundred yards through a window and drilled that guy's temple. If he could have propped him up again and taken more shots, he could have grouped them within an inch of the first. He had supposed that watching her client's head suddenly spout blood across breakfast would be sufficient for Jane for the moment, so he had not searched for her in the crowd and tried to hold her in the crosshairs. He wanted something more complicated and meaningful to happen to her.

The rifle had a simple, unambiguous integrity. The rifle was perfect. Earl was not. He had let himself be seduced by the beauty of it, the smooth, skinlike touch of the nylon stock against his cheek, the dull gleam of the barrel and the clear, soundless image in the scope. He had found the car in the parking lot, he had seen a man with light wavy hair sit down in the window with a dark-haired woman, and he had reached out and harvested him.

Earl had not needed to force himself to wait to make the shot true, because the rifle was perfect. He could exert three pounds of pressure with his finger and the man would certainly be dead. It was only after he had felt the recoil against his shoulder and the scope had settled on the window again that he had perceived that something had gone wrong. He had expected that the restaurant would be abruptly churned into turmoil, with people standing to bump into each other and spilling things, because he had seen it happen before. Seeing the second dark-haired woman pass across the field of the scope had not convinced him. It was driving down from the mountain and seeing that the car he had followed from Salmon Prairie was already heading up the road.

He pushed the knurled lever on the left side of the receiver, slid the bolt out of the rifle, and set it down on the table beside the Allen screws. Every piece of the A.W. reminded him by its weighty, elegant, and indestructable steel, machined to an exacting tolerance, that he was not its equal. This time it had not been a cop stumbling blind into the middle of the hit. This time it had been Earl getting so confident of his invincibility with the new rifle, and so eager to exert it, that he had reacted like a kid, popping the cap because his overheated mind had assumed that any creature that came along a deer run had to be a deer. People were a sorry commodity compared to precision rifles.

When the telephone rang, he glanced at his watch and noted that it was four o'clock. That made it six in Buffalo. He respectfully set the rifle on the bed and picked up the telephone. "Yeah."

"Honey?" She had called him that maybe twice. Her voice was wet and gulpy as though she had been crying.

"Yeah," he said.

"They're hiking in the mountains. They're going twenty miles if it were a straight line, but it isn't, so it will take two or three days. During that time they won't be near a phone."

"Hold on," he said. He stared at the map on the table. He tore off a sheet of paper from the pad with the hotel's name on it, measured twenty miles on the scale, then ran it in a circle from Swan Lake. "It can't be twenty miles from where I last saw them. There's nothing they couldn't have driven to in about a half hour."

"Is there any place that would look safe to them? A private airfield or something?"

"Nothing I can see. Maybe Canada." He ran his finger along the road they had traveled: Missoula, Salmon Prairie, Swan Lake, always north. What if, instead of going left at Bigfork toward Kalispell, as he had, they had gone right? He took the sheet of paper with the twenty-mile mark and ran it slowly along the top of Montana at the Canadian Border. "Glacier," he said.

"What?"

"They could have turned up into Glacier National Park by now. There's only one big road through the middle of it, and it takes a loop

up about halfway across that would put them about twenty miles
from the border." He held the map close to his face. "Logan Pass."
He pushed his thumbnail into the map and left a crescent-shaped
mark so he could find it again.

"I should go," she said. Her voice was low and whispery and
quiet, like a child's.

"You mean he's there now?"

"He just fell asleep."

"Good." It was as close as Earl could come to a friendly statement. His relief was for himself, because now he wouldn't have to
spend the rest of the night thinking about Linda spread out on the bed
with that faceless stranger going into her, over and over.

He heard Linda give a little sob, then sniff it back. She said, "He
wore himself out . . . on me." The sob came out again.

Earl found himself standing, and the telephone crashed to the
floor, but he could still hear Linda's voice, crying quietly. Earl could
feel surges of blood pounding behind his eyes.

"He's a doctor, Earl. He knows things about a woman's body—
the nerves and things. He brings me up, all the way up so I can't control myself, and then keeps me there, won't let me stop."

Earl squeezed his eyes closed. He wanted her to shut up. "It's
okay," he said. "It'll be over soon."

"Ten minutes ago I begged him—"

"Enough." Earl's voice was harsh and dry. He wanted to tell her
to drive a tenpenny nail through the man's chest while he was sleeping, and then walk out. He wanted to, but he couldn't. Not yet. "Just
do the best you can. The minute I've got them, I'll call you there." He
found a pen on the nightstand with the little questionnaire about the
maid service. "What's the number?"

She read it to him off the telephone dial. "But if you call me here,
he'll get spooked. Leave a message on the machine at home or at the
apartment I rented."

"Right," he said, but he wrote the number on the questionnaire.
"I'll call you." His writing was a scrawl, so even he could barely read
it. He was in a horrible confusion of jealousy of this McKinnon that
somehow merged into his rage at Pete Hatcher for putting him into
this spot. He felt disgust at Linda for being a woman—a creature that
had no other way of getting what she needed from a man, but who
could do it whenever she felt like it, because any man would accept
the offer. He felt shame and humiliation because he had been able to
invent no better way to find Pete Hatcher than to let his own woman
turn herself out as a whore.

He thought back on the shot he had taken at Swan Lake and wanted to bite his finger off. She had already given away everything she had just to buy him that shot, and he had squandered it. Then he had the shadow pass across his vision that maybe Linda, deep down, wasn't as miserable about this as she had to make him think she was. He brushed all of these thoughts into the back of his mind. "You just think about what happens to him the minute I've got Hatcher. You'll get to do the cutting. Keep your mind on that."

"You can bet I will," said Linda. Her voice was hardening now into cold, clean anger, and that made Earl feel better. But then her voice changed again, and he could tell her mouth was away from the receiver. "In the bathroom," she called. Her voice was soft and thick. "All right." To Earl she whispered, "I've got to go," and hung up.

Earl placed the telephone receiver into its cradle and put the telephone back on the nightstand, then stepped to the door to the next room and looked at Lenny.

He was lying on the bed staring at the television. The two black dogs lifted their heads and looked at Earl, but Lenny kept his eyes on the screen, where one man was chasing another one along a catwalk in a dark factory.

"Load up the car," said Earl. "Keep the camping gear on top."

"We going someplace tonight?" He said it as though the idiocy of loading the car at night would be self-evident.

"Yeah, tonight. And get the dogs into their carriers. They're going too."

Linda pushed her chair away from the kitchen table and stood to hang up the wall telephone. She smiled to herself contentedly. Linda looked around at the bright, clean surfaces. She loved the careful, economical use of the space. The pots and pans were all heavy and old; only French gourmet companies still made them that way, and they charged hundreds of dollars for them.

She padded around the kitchen in her bare feet, collecting the ingredients and implements she would need for this recipe. As she bent down to pull a big pot out of the cupboard, she acknowledged that Jane's blue jeans felt a little tight in the thigh and the ass, but she wasn't sorry. When Carey got home from the late shift at the hospital, that wouldn't be something that he minded. Even men who thought that wearing tight clothes made you stupid would look hard at whatever you let them see.

She filled the pot with water and set it on one of the back burners to boil, then opened the door of the big old-fashioned pantry.

There, hanging on a brass hook, was Jane's apron. She slipped the loop over her head and tied the strings behind her back in a bow. She looked down at the apron and smiled. It was dark blue with a red ribbon border and little blue cornflowers and yellow buttercups embroidered on it. It was almost too pretty to use.

She began to open the drawers under the counter, looking for ladles. In the second one she opened, she found an old boning knife that had been sharpened like a razor. She recognized instantly that this was the perfect tool. It was simple to hide and felt good in her hand, too secure to slip, too sharp to be brushed away. She set it sideways just inside the drawer, where she could find it quickly without cutting herself, and opened the next drawer. "Now," she whispered. "Where do I keep my ladles?"

An hour later Earl drove the car past the sign that said GOING-TO-THE-SUN ROAD OPEN MAY 15–SEPTEMBER 15. Jane was about a day too early. Earl was simply too much for her. He forced himself not to acknowledge the way he had come by the information, because that would make him think about what Linda was doing right now. Earl was the one who was too much for all of them. When you won the pot it didn't much matter who put what chips into it.

He could drive quickly now that it was dark, gliding into the turns and accelerating out of them to keep his traction. Lenny gripped the door handle but kept silent. Earl reached the Logan Pass visitor center, pulled into the parking lot, and studied the cars that had been left there overnight. When he didn't find the one he had followed in the morning, he drove past the building and found it parked at the edge of the woods not far from a garbage Dumpster. "That's it."

Lenny said, "We going to do something to the car?"

"Yeah. We're going to look at it."

He parked beside the car and looked inside. The keys were in the ignition. He opened the door, took out the keys, unlocked the trunk, and found it empty. He could see that they had cleaned the car out thoroughly. He said to Lenny, "Don't touch anything. Just let the dogs out, but keep them behind the car. They don't let dogs in the park."

Lenny let the two big black dogs out of their traveling cages. They panted and huffed for a few seconds, wagging their tails and trotting in circles. Earl opened the doors of the abandoned car. "Get in," he said. *"Einsteigen in."*

The dogs leapt through the doors, sniffing the car, the upholstery, the steering wheel. Earl turned to Lenny. "Give them a few minutes to get the scent." He took a flashlight from Lenny's car, walked to the Dumpster, and opened it. He found the two suitcases covered with garbage. They would be of no use.

Earl gingerly reached down, pushed the garbage aside with his light, and opened the first suitcase. Clothes . . . they had left clothes inside. His heart beat faster as he took out his pocket knife.

In a moment he was back at the car. He said quietly, *"Herauskommen."* The dogs jumped out of the car and waited for his command. He held the two shoes up so the dogs could take their time sniffing them. *"Fund!"* he said.

The two big black dogs circled the cars for a few seconds, looking puzzled. They sniffed the ground and came back, then turned their wide heads to stare in various directions. Lenny looked at Earl nervously, but Earl said, "Give them as long as it takes."

The dogs finally agreed that the visitor center building was the right direction. They trotted to the door and sniffed the steps and nosed the glass. Earl said, "They probably walked over there, but they didn't come back."

Earl picked up his backpack, then eased his arms into the straps and walked to the visitor center. *"Auf den fersen folgen."* The dogs fell into place at his side. He crossed the road with them and watched their faces. They seemed not to smell the scent, but maybe to dimly suspect it.

Lenny joined him beside the sign that said HIGHLINE TRAIL. He gazed at the dogs. "Doesn't look like they picked up anything here."

"No," said Earl. "The two of them bought new shoes. The first time they wore them was probably when they got out of the car and walked over here."

"Then why did you get them to sniff the car and the old shoes?" The man's head might as well be a helmet. His was a mind that never failed to disappoint.

"Because in a day or so, when we need help, the new shoes are going to smell exactly like the old ones."

Earl stood and stared into the darkness where the trail led off under the trees. His mind formed the words, "I'm coming. You'll wish you had put a gun in your mouth while you could." He wasn't sure precisely whom he was talking to. The distinction didn't mean enough for him to try to sort it out. He would have all of them in their turns and in the ways that they deserved.

It seemed to Calvin Seaver that he had called Earl and Linda a hundred times—first from Kennedy Airport, then from his stopover in

Chicago, then Denver, and finally from Billings. He had never gotten anything but the answering machine, and he could hardly leave a message telling two killers that Pete Hatcher was in Salmon Prairie, Montana.

It was in the Billings airport that he saw the story on the television news, and he was glad that he had been cautious. There was film of a lot of people milling around outside a restaurant in Swan Lake, just a few miles up the road from Salmon Prairie. The newsman, who looked enough like the one Seaver usually watched in Las Vegas to be his brother, said a sniper had fired through the window and killed a man. What caught Seaver's attention had not been the body bag being wheeled out on a collapsible stretcher. It was the woman with long black hair who was being helped into a police car beside the ambulance.

He checked into a hotel in Billings and watched the report over and over on every local channel. For the first couple of hours he could feel that although his mind was still unsure, his body was already celebrating, pumping blood through the arteries in hard, dizzying surges, his breaths tasting sweet and full.

Seaver had been in the trouble business for over twenty years, and he had developed a clear idea of the odds. Swan Lake was a tiny town in the middle of the mountains. The population of the whole state was just a bit over eight hundred thousand. There probably hadn't been a shooting in Swan Lake since the Indian Wars. How could it not be Earl who had done it? How could that dark-haired woman not be *the* dark-haired woman? But Seaver needed to be positive. He sat on the edge of the hotel bed, the remote control in his hand, switching from channel to channel for three hours.

At ten o'clock, when the local news came on again, there was a photograph of the shooting victim. It was a portrait of a man wearing a suit and tie, his expression in a forced smile. It looked a little bit like Pete Hatcher, but it wasn't. The newswoman was telling Seaver that it was just some guy who had gotten himself shot—some unsuspecting dope who had been eating breakfast in front of the wrong window. Seaver couldn't believe it.

His mind shuffled quickly through the possibilities, looking for hope. The picture was a fraud. Earl had hit Hatcher, but Hatcher wasn't dead. The dark-haired woman had slipped the newsmen a fake picture to keep Earl from trying again while Hatcher was in the hospital. Or Earl had shot Hatcher, and Hatcher was dead. The picture was taken off some stolen ID the police had found in his wallet, and that was why it was a picture of somebody else. The more Seaver thought about it, the more he liked that theory. It made a lot of sense, especially if Hatcher had been shot in the head. Most people could barely look in the direction of a fatal head wound without fainting, and even if they did, there was so much blood on the face and so much distortion of the muscles—a slackening at first and then a tightening into a rictus—that any resemblance the corpse bore to a photograph of anything alive would have been accepted as a match.

Seaver clung to this theory for another half hour, waiting impatiently for the newswoman to come back from a commercial and announce that the initial identification had been wrong. His hope ended when the newswoman came back from a commercial with, instead, footage of the victim's parents leaving the coroner's office after identifying the body.

He wearily leafed through the pile of tourist magazines the hotel maids had left on the coffee table. They contained very little except ads for stores and restaurants in the area, but finally he found one with three pages of maps in it and spent a few minutes studying them.

Tomorrow morning, after he had caught up on his sleep, he would drive up to Kalispell. It looked like the only town up there that was big enough to hide a stranger comfortably. He would check into a hotel there and spend some time trying to pick up signs of Earl and Linda.

27

Jane led Pete along the trail in the waning light. She kept them at a double-time pace, along the long high cliff the map called the Garden Wall and on to Haystack Butte. When she judged that they had traveled two miles, she slowed to a walk. She waited for her wind to come back and then listened while Hatcher's deep, labored breathing slowly became quiet. She said, "How do you feel?"

"Lousy."

"Does your head ache?"

"Yes."

"Dizzy?"

"Yes."

"Green spots on your hands?"

"Yes."

"Liar."

"Yes." He walked along at her shoulder, taking deep breaths and blowing them out. She listened to them attentively without speaking. There were no whistles, no bubbly liquid sounds that would mean he was in trouble. There were people who simply could not tolerate high altitudes. Unless they were brought down, their lungs filled up with fluid until they drowned. Starting Pete off with a two-mile jog probably had not been the safest way to find out that he wasn't one of them, but she had needed to know before they had gone too far to turn back.

She had not lied to him about needing to use the last precious hour or two of light efficiently, to put distance between them and the road. It was already getting too dark to run. A twisted ankle would make the next thirty miles into a nightmare.

As she walked, she subtly increased the pace again. She tried to keep her steps regular enough on the uneven, winding path to hold her speed. The end of the long summer had come, so the trail was as beaten down by other boots as it would ever be, and it had been laid out at about seven thousand feet, along the ridges just below the tree-line, where soil was thin and poor and the constant winds stunted the fir trees.

After another mile they had passed Haystack Butte, and in the dusky light she saw the change she was looking for in the slopes to her left. There was a low, lush dark carpet of bushes and evergreens—lodgepole pine, spruce, fir—all young and thick. Among them loomed tall, ghostly gray trunks like the masts of sunken ships.

"Look at that," said Pete. "I wonder why it looks like that."

"A fire," said Jane. "In 1967 this patch burned."

He craned his neck to look at her with ironic amusement. "You from around here?"

She shook her head and smiled. "Of course not. I spent half the day in the car looking at maps. This is one of the places I picked out to get my bearings. If we get lost up here we're not going to enjoy the experience."

"What do we look for next?"

"After another mile or two, we should be able to look up on our right and see glaciers. First a little one. That's Gem Glacier. Then a really big one, called Grinnell Glacier. Then Swiftcurrent Glacier, all in a stretch of a couple of miles."

"And after that?"

"If we get that far before it's too dark to travel, I'll be very surprised."

He walked along for a time, then said, "I guess I should be delighted at the news that I don't have to keep trudging along all night. To tell you the truth, though, the farther we get from that guy with the rifle, the better I feel. And there's even something about it getting dark that's comforting. I've been having a prickly feeling in the back of my neck, like he's back there looking down the barrel at me."

Jane turned and looked up at him with an enigmatic smile. "He wouldn't be looking down the barrel. Nobody puts a round through somebody's temple from that far out without a scope."

"You're a very strange woman. You know that?"

"Of course I do." She smiled. "It's something I've cultivated over the years. But I'll bet you want to keep going even more than you did a minute ago, don't you?"

He seemed to be consulting an inner voice as he walked. "You're right. It worked. I feel bad enough to walk for hours."

"Bad isn't exactly the feeling I was looking for, but that's the price. As long as you never let your brain stop working, thinking about what's behind you, you'll be very hard to kill."

"So the prickly feeling in the back of the neck doesn't go away."

"That's right. I have it right now."

Pete half-turned his head to look as he walked. There was nothing behind them but the empty trail as far as the last bend. "You think they're back there?"

"If I did, I'd be running for my life," she said. "I think they're good. They'll find out the car was left in that lot in about three days, when it's towed out of the park. By then the only road here will be closed to visitors, the nearby car crossings into Canada will be closed too, and the long detours that go up there don't go to where we'll be. What I think they'll do next is give up."

The sky was darkening quickly now, and she saw the glow of his teeth that had to be a smile. "Really?"

"They've been following you for about a hundred days. They've committed two murders they won't get paid for. They've exhausted the computer searches, because from here on we aren't going to use credit cards or even names, if we can help it. That means the hunting is going to get much harder. Following you into a foreign country adds a level of extra risk. I think for a professional, the point of diminishing returns has come. They're in it for the money, and if this goes on much longer, the money's not good enough. They could have made more of it more easily doing bitter divorce cases and premature life-insurance payouts."

"Won't Pleasure, Inc., hire somebody else?"

"There are several possibilities. One is that these killers will tell Pleasure, Inc., where they lost you. Pleasure, Inc., will decide that if you're in Canada, then you're not planning on talking to American police. A second possibility is that the people who are after us now will keep Pleasure, Inc., on the hook—tell them to be patient, they're on your trail—but not waste any time actually hunting. Once a month they'll use the computer to see if your aliases turned up again."

"So I should feel good, right? I'm not being stupid."

"No. Because in a week or so they'll probably be off stalking somebody else, and if they're replaced, the new ones will be starting at zero. This morning you were talking about a different feeling you had—that you were glad to be alive. It's not gone, is it?"

"No."

"The quiver in the back of your neck doesn't go away, but the good feeling doesn't either. Now that you've had it, every day is going to feel as though you won it in a world championship."

He laughed. "It already does."

"You'll notice other things later."

"What things?"

"Good things. The kind of ambition that's stupid, the kind that makes you want a fancy car and a big house and flashy clothes, goes away."

"Why?"

"Because having them makes you feel as though people are looking at you, and that's uncomfortable. Being average, normal, makes you feel comfortable, and it isn't very different unless you read labels very closely. That was always true, of course, but now you'll be able to feel it, because you know that being a regular guy is a million miles from being dead."

The trail led them up between thickets of berry bushes, across meadows of wildflowers now dry and well past blooming. As the light died for the night, Jane could see the higher peaks on her right, but the blue-white glacial ice was lost in the black silhouettes of the mountains. They walked on, sticking to the center of the path in the dark. Jane took her flashlight out of her pack and let it play on the ground in front of her. Finally, as the trail led them up into a stand of stunted pine trees, she stopped, knelt on the ground, and studied the map.

"Are we lost yet?" asked Pete. She felt his shoulder beside hers as he knelt down to look at the little circle of light.

She put her finger on the map. "We're here." It was a spot where twisting dotted lines seemed to radiate in all directions, like the strands of an unraveling rope. "The trail on the left goes back to the road, then up Flattop Creek. The one on the right goes through Swiftcurrent Pass and connects with this whole network of trails up here. This one in the middle is the one we want." She aimed her flashlight up the path, and in the glow around it, Pete caught a glimpse of a wooden sign.

"So what's the problem?"

She frowned. "Never give up a chance to deceive. This chance is a beauty. I'm just trying to figure out how to use it."

He said, "Switch the sign?"

"They wouldn't be looking for one trail or another. They'd be looking for us, probably our footprints. We've already put about seven miles of them on the path, and if they were following, by now they wouldn't have much trouble recognizing them."

Pete sat and waited while Jane stared at the map, then stood up, opened his pack, and handed him his flashlight. "This is probably a waste of time," she said. "But if they do follow us, it isn't. You go down the left path as far as you can until it gets so narrow you can't step off it. A quarter mile would be great, but at least a couple of hundred yards. When you get to that point step off, and come back parallel with the trail, never stepping back onto it. Meet me here."

Jane walked down the trail to the right alone. She stopped once to listen for Pete's footsteps, and when she heard them they sounded as though he was doing what she had asked. One of the qualities that made Pete Hatcher worth saving was that he never resisted. He wanted to live, so if she was willing to help him, he would do what she asked. Simple.

As she walked, she imagined herself taking Carey out of the world. Everything he said would be a question too, but the questions he asked would come from a more complicated intelligence, one that would be sifting and evaluating and testing alternative logical paths. The problem with classically intelligent people was that they seemed to be able to discern too many alternatives to pick any of them during the brief periods when what they did still mattered. She wondered what she had meant by that, and was back to the night ten months ago when Carey had asked her to marry him. She had said she would not marry him right then. She would tell him about her last trip—about who she really was—and then give him a year to think before he asked again.

He had not listened and then said instantly, "I don't care about any of this. Marry me now." He had listened judiciously and then let the waiting period begin. When he had thought about it for a month, instead of sticking to the terms and letting her spend the year cutting her ties, he had realized that he didn't want to wait—not shouldn't, but didn't want to. He had been unfair. He had focused his intellect on convincing her to marry him while she still had no business marrying anyone.

Her mind abruptly collided with something and jumped to another track. That story was fictitious. Jane Whitefield walked through the world with her eyes wide open. She could not pretend she had not known what might happen, or what she would do if it did. She had always felt contempt for women who accepted the theorem that if they were unhappy it could only be because their husbands had not made them happy. This must be how it started: constructing convoluted proofs that their mistakes were not actually their mistakes but their husbands' failure to prevent them or cure them. Not me, she thought. I did this, because I wanted his love more than I wanted to be careful. Now I'm going to get through it and go home to my husband, who is impatient because he adores me.

She watched the path narrowing, the rock slope on her right rising into a wall, and the little margin of weeds on her left thinning into a ledge that bordered a steep chasm. She put the flashlight into her back pocket, leaned both hands on the wall, placed her toes on the weeds, and began to sidestep back the way she had come. She had inched along for fifty feet before she was able to stand upright again. Then she carefully took a diagonal course down a gentler slope and headed for the crossroads.

When she approached the rocky knoll, she saw Pete Hatcher waiting patiently for her. She switched on her flashlight so he would see her coming and not be startled. "Been waiting long?"

"No," he said. "Just got here. I went as far as a streambed, where it started to get wet. I came back through the woods."

"Very good," she said. She sat beside him. "Now we change our socks." He watched her untying her boots for a second, then did as she said. When they had their boots on again, she said, "Now put the old socks on over your boots."

"It's a tight fit," he said as he tugged and stretched.

"It's okay," said Jane. "Now stuff some of these dry weeds under the soles of your boots, inside the sock, for padding. Don't use leaves, because they'll squish and get juicy. No pine needles, because they're slippery."

When they had finished, she led him off beside the center trail. They did not step onto the trail again for fifteen minutes, at the start of a stretch of bare rock that extended beyond the flashlight's beam. Pete stopped and shone his flashlight back the way they had come. "No trail at all," he said. "You're amazing."

"It cost us a half hour, but it always makes you feel better to do what you can. And if we are being followed, it will do more than make us feel better. You have to remember this isn't the F.B.I. that's after us. It's probably just some guy who discovered early on that it was easier to pull a trigger than learn algebra."

As Jane set off across the rocky plateau, she discovered that what she had told Pete was a lie. Stopping to disguise their trail had not made her feel safer. She tried to measure the prickly sensation in the back of her neck, and her body gave a convulsive shiver. She pivoted suddenly in her tracks and stared back into the forest. The sight gave her no comfort: the individual silhouettes of the trees had merged together into a shadowy mass of twisted limbs ready to assume any shape her imagination gave them.

"What's wrong?" said Pete.

"Nothing," she said. "Just checking to see if you were keeping up." She turned and began to walk quickly, and as she walked she searched for a way to exorcise her uneasiness.

She caught herself wishing she could have spotted the shooter on the mountainside this morning—if only a running human form, a solid shape in the windshield of a speeding car. As it was, the restaurant window had suddenly imploded in a shower of glass, and a bloody hole had appeared in a man's head. There was nothing mysterious about the way that had been accomplished, but to some part of her subconscious mind, knowing the mechanical workings of rifles and silencers was information too meager to lay to rest the sensations she had felt.

Since she had left home it had not felt to her as though professional killers had been logically tracing Pete Hatcher's movements. It felt as though they had given up physical form entirely, and rode the wind, waiting to materialize wherever it suited them.

Earl readjusted Lenny's load. When he cinched the straps to make everything secure, he nearly tugged Lenny off his feet. "Think you can keep your balance?"

Lenny slipped the tumpline over his forehead and took a few steps. "Sure," he said. "In the army we used to pack ninety pounds of gear and add the extra ammo on top of it. This can't be much worse."

Earl's jaw worked impatiently. Whenever Lenny was feeling resentful, he would just happen to mention that he had once been declared worthy to sign up to get his head shaved and hang around Fort Leonard Wood in case they needed extra cannon fodder. Earl was never quite sure whether Lenny was implying that cleaning latrines had made him Earl's moral superior, or excusing his inadequacy by saying that those wasted years had set him too far back to ever recover. It didn't much matter. Whatever they had done for him in the army, it hadn't given him big enough balls to challenge Earl directly, so Earl tolerated the talk.

He said, "Just use your map and compass, like they taught you, and don't lose your own ass out here." He turned to T-Bone and Rusty. *"Raus!"*

The two dogs galloped down the trail to the first bend, then waited and stared back at him. Earl adjusted his own pack as he set off. Lenny's military career had brought Earl one benefit, anyway. It had made him think of moving through these mountains the way armies did. He had loaded Lenny's strong back with all the camping gear and supplies, so Earl could carry little and forge ahead with the dogs. If he wanted anything Lenny was carrying, he could meet him on the main trail.

Earl walked along the path after T-Bone and Rusty for a few hundred yards to let his pupils open to the dark and his muscles get warm. Then he stopped and did a few stretching exercises against a tall cedar. When he was ready, he began to run.

As he ran, Earl considered his circumstances, and he found them to his liking. Jane Whitefield and Pete Hatcher had graciously gone to a great deal of exertion and inconvenience to put themselves into a place where he was strong and they were weak. Hatcher had been saved twice by the simple fact that it was hard to kill a man in a public place without committing suicide. Now it was only one day before the whole national park closed, and there would be no more tourists setting out into the high country to get in the way.

Earl moved through the woods with a hunter's practiced lope. He had always been a sportsman who loved to take the long, difficult shot, so he had spent many cold mornings running patiently through rough country, trailing wounded deer until they began to choke and cough too much blood to go on. Tonight he used his dogs to find his way and keep him on the path. He could hear the difference when their panting came from higher or lower, left or right, and the thuds of their big paws told him the nature of the surface they were running on. Turning on a flashlight in these woods would have given his presence away to anyone looking back from the ridges above, and the glare would have made his pupils contract, leaving him half-blind for several minutes.

Earl habitually held his head a little to the side as he ran, because the best night vision was at the edges of the eyes, and none of the wind from his running distorted the sounds. He knew his long legs carried him farther at each stride than his prey could step, and his stamina would keep him going longer than any man who had spent his days lounging around in Las Vegas.

He knew that the two of them must have started hiking at least four or five hours ago, but that did not bother him. They would walk for a few hours, until the moon was high and the wind up here started to howl, and then they would take their own exhaustion as an assurance that Earl would be too tired to follow. They would camp, make a shelter and a fire, and curl up. Maybe they would be cautious enough to tramp a distance off the main trail first, but they wouldn't risk going too far.

They didn't know what was after them. Earl could just discern the black barrel torsos of Rusty and T-Bone ahead of him in the dark—beasts with as much mass and muscle as small men, that could hear a twig the size of a toothpick snap under a boot, smell a fire in the woods for miles, and see with a predator's vision that didn't bother much with subtle gradations of tone and color but had evolved to pick out unerringly whatever was alive so they could sink their teeth into it.

As Earl ran, he could feel the strange, triangular field between him and Rusty and T-Bone, the dogs' attentiveness to his sound and scent holding them in position. They were as alert to any change in his will as to the sights and sounds ahead of them. The dogs were part of him now. He was a creature with three heads and sharp teeth and a rifle and a man's brain, galloping through the forest sniffing the wind for the smell of live meat.

Carey had finished his hospital rounds at seven, but he had found over the past ten days that each night he went home a little later. The old, comfortable house where he had grown up now seemed cavernous and empty because Jane wasn't there waiting for him. Tonight he had gone back to his office and spent two hours making notations in the files of his patients, signing forms and letters that Joy had typed and left on his desk, then looking over the latest pile of medical journals for articles that he needed to study. At nine he walked back to the hospital lot, climbed into the BMW, and remembered that he still had not stopped to fill up the tank. In the midst of that Susan Haynes business last night, he had forgotten, and then in the morning she had managed to delay him long enough so that he had not had time.

He turned the key carefully with dread in his heart and listened intently. The engine turned over, and the car violated Carey's sense of the laws of physics by starting, then taking him to the gas station without running dry.

As Carey drove up to the big old house in Amherst he was thinking about food. It was nearly ten o'clock, and he had not had dinner yet. Maybe he would just make himself a sandwich and go to bed. He saw that there were lights on in a couple of the downstairs windows. Susan Haynes had obviously forgotten to turn off any switches before she had locked the door this morning . . . if she had remembered to do that much. He pulled into the long driveway toward the garage. As he reached the place where the drive turned the corner of the house, his headlights lit up the bright-red tail reflectors of the car parked by the back door. It was the big black Mercedes that Susan Haynes had leased.

Carey stopped his car, pulled it forward around the big Mercedes to keep from blocking it in, and killed the engine. He glanced at his watch again. It was nine fifty-six. This woman was in his house at nine fifty-six waiting for him to come home. He closed his eyes and felt a constriction in the muscles of his throat.

His mind surveyed his mistakes leading backward in time like stepping stones. He should never have given her his key. He should never have invited an unattached woman to stay the night, never have given her a ride, never even have let on that her car had been towed to clear his parking space. He batted away the excuses that his mind automatically fabricated and spit out for him, like a machine that had short-circuited: no, he had not done it because she had really needed his help. He had done it because she was beautiful and he had not wanted to stop looking at her; because she was smart and distracting and he was tired of being alone. He had liked her. The nervously clinical words of an old study of physiological responses came back to him. Affection—even the most innocent kind—was found to prompt a "slight tumescence of the genitals." And that, in turn, would probably prompt a rationalization.

He knew that he could not start his engine again, back out of the driveway, and abandon his house until this woman got tired of waiting and went away. The only other option he had was to go inside and find out what she thought she was doing. It took him a moment to identify the source of his reluctance to face her. It was the instinctive alarm that made animals shy away from one of their kind that was behaving strangely. It had probably kept a lot of epidemics from spreading to healthy animals and wiping out entire species. This time the instinct was serving no purpose. Neuroses weren't contagious.

He walked around to the front door, found it unlocked, and stepped inside. The smell of food cooking overwhelmed him and reminded him how hungry he was. Susan had sneaked into his house and cooked something for him. He was relieved. It was unwelcome, but at least it was comprehensible, possibly even within the boundaries of normal behavior. He tried to analyze his lingering irritation at her. What had she actually done? He supposed that what had annoyed him most was that she had playfully set off a sexual longing that he was not entitled to feel. As soon as he had admitted it, he felt ridiculous for resenting her for it: blaming women for stimulating impure thoughts had gone out with witch trials. Or it should have.

He detected that he was also straining against some primitive territorial reaction she had triggered by coming into his lair without permission. The hostility was misplaced—just another legacy from earlier primates that had begun to get in the way. She wasn't trying to harm him. She was trying to be kind, after all. A lot of people believed that the rules should be abrogated for surprises. Carey was not one of those people, but he had to live in the world. "Hello?" he called. "Anybody here?"

When he heard no answer, he ventured into the living room. He moved into the dining room, and saw her. She was facing away from him, wearing a pair of jeans and a sweatshirt that he recognized as Jane's. If it had not been for the long, golden hair he might almost have convinced himself that she was Jane. She was pouring champagne into two glasses. The table was elaborately set with the best silver, and the candles were lit. She turned and held out a glass. "Hi," she said. The reserved, distant smile was on her lips. "Have you eaten dinner?"

"No," he admitted. "To what do I owe all this?" He realized that his jaw was tight, the muscles working. He smiled to cover the tension.

She shrugged, and he wished that it had not made him aware of the movement of her breasts under the fabric. "I'm showing you my gratitude. You've been very nice to me."

"I thought you had your heart set on a big dinner party." He looked around the corner toward the living room. "Should I expect the Rotherbergs and Bortonis to leap out from behind the curtains?"

She grinned and shook her head. "No, it's not a surprise party. It's just a surprise." She sipped her champagne and looked into his eyes. "For you."

"Why?" He tried to seem casual. "I mean, I guess I should just say, 'Thanks.'" Unexpectedly, the rest of it came out. "But, to be honest with you, coming in and finding someone inside my house is not my favorite experience. I suppose that for a lot of people, it must be an accepted custom: it seems to turn up in television plots almost as often as the Evil Twin or the Long-Lost Father, and nobody else seems shocked. But I am. If I want somebody to come, I invite them."

The suddenness of her smile staggered him. It seemed to come from absolutely nowhere, and to be immune to anything he had said. She shrugged. "I gave you every opportunity, but you don't seem to let yourself think about anything personal until after work, and that would have been too late, wouldn't it? If I'd known it would bother you, I would have done it another way." She turned away and began fiddling with the objects on the table again.

He was positive that he was right, but he began to regret having said the words. When she spun around to face him, she seemed to have forgotten he had spoken at all: the smile seemed more radiant. "This doesn't get you out of my party, by the way. When your wife comes home, I'm still going to have a bunch of the local gentry over for dinner. That pays you back officially for helping me last night."

He waved his hand at the table. "Isn't this enough?"

She cocked her head at him. "This isn't the official thanks, which will be completely insincere and self-serving, and which Jane and I will like more than you do. This is something I thought of after I called you today. You're all alone and you don't know when your wife is coming back, and you sounded unhappy. Now is the time when a woman can offer something that will actually do you some good. So I decided to cook you a meal. Big deal."

She pointedly set her champagne glass beside the nearest plate and pulled out the chair at the head of the table. "I've done enough explaining and I'm hungry. So sit while I serve you."

Carey sat in the chair and she reached over his shoulder, then ceremoniously placed the linen napkin on his lap. "This is really something," he conceded. He turned his head as he said it, and found her still leaning over him, her face much closer than he had anticipated. He could smell the subtle scent of her hair, see the big liquid green eyes glinting in the candlelight.

"It's meant to be," she said. "No empty promises."

He was relieved when she brought out the big pot and began to serve the food. She had made bouillabaisse, and it had certainly not gotten worse during the hours after she had expected him to arrive. He tasted it.

"A small, neatly inscribed thank-you note would have been more than sufficient, but the food is wonderful," he said.

She tasted it too. "It turned out okay. I gave myself a tour of the house while you were out. When I got a good look at the kitchen, I figured I'd have to take this seriously if I was going to give you what you were used to."

"Well, thank you. You really know how to cook. You must like to."

She shook her head. "I hate it. I learned because men like to eat, and I like men."

He hurried to change the subject. "I just remembered that I saw your car in the driveway. Did everything go all right?"

She shrugged. "It was pretty much what you said in the morning. They were there all the time. The man I paid the ransom for my car said they don't always hear the phone ringing from outside."

"How much was it?"

"Three hundred. Isn't that outrageous? A hundred for towing the car down there, and two hundred for the fine. And they don't take credit cards."

Carey said, "I feel terrible. It was partly my fault. I'd like to pay for it." He had a strong impulse to make all accounts even, so the give-and-take would stop.

Her amused look returned. "That's very chivalrous. But it's not the money, it's the effrontery." She seemed to realize something that hadn't occurred to her before. "And anyway, the whole point of the evening was to get out and meet people, and I guess it served its purpose. I met a lot of people, and made one friend."

He gave a noncommittal smile and a little nod. He tried to decide why the idea made him so uncomfortable. Maybe living in a small city all his life had made him conservative and timid about meeting new people, but he had known Susan Haynes little more than twenty-four hours. The word "friend" sounded premature, almost presumptuous.

There was also an element of danger in it that he did not find appealing. She was enormously attractive, and her conversation always had a sexual edge to it that seemed uncalculated but that his common sense told him could not be. It wasn't entirely clear whether she was overtly tempting him or treating him as though he were asexual. Maybe she was just behaving with a kind of adult openness that he had become entitled to as a married man, and he wasn't used to it yet. Maybe when you were happily married, women simply accepted you as safely ineligible for sexual relationships and became less guarded. But it was difficult to imagine a friendship with Susan Haynes extending into the future. Conversations would be full of tension and ambiguity. He suspected that Jane would take one look at her, listen to about three sentences, and announce that she hated her.

Carey realized that the silence had gone on for too long. "Did you make more progress in getting settled today, or just slave over a hot stove?"

"Not much progress. I spent most of the day thinking about you."

"Oh?" Trouble.

"Oh?" she mocked. "As if you weren't thinking about me."

He decided he had better not evade that one. "To be honest with you, over the years I've gotten to be pretty good at keeping my mind focused on my work during the day. I find I lose fewer patients that way."

"I'm sorry," she said. She shook her head and stared down at her lap. "I'm doing it again. It's like a reflex. I guess that's why I couldn't get you out of my mind—you're the witness to my gaffe. I made such a mess of things last night. It was completely unfair."

He noticed that Susan had stopped eating some time ago, and he had eaten as much as he wanted. "What was unfair?"

She smiled apologetically and shrugged, then looked at him from behind a strand of blond hair. "Sometimes when you meet somebody— even though you like them, or maybe because you like them—you start off wrong, and just keep going that way. You know it isn't the way you want to be with them, but somehow you can't figure out how to stop and start all over again. What I should have done last night was have a pleasant dinner with you, then call a cab and go home."

He silently agreed with her. He fervently wished he had made some excuse and called her a cab. "I really didn't mind giving you a ride," Carey lied. "None of this was any trouble at all."

"Of course you minded," said Susan. "I was being childish last night. Teasing you, instead of being honest and direct. So now I'm trying to start all over again."

"I don't even know what you mean," said Carey.

Her smile was beautiful, a little embarrassed. "Let's just say that I didn't really need your help undressing last night."

Carey felt his collar tighten as the blood rushed up to his head. He nodded. "I see." He had to find a way to end this. "Forget it," he said. "I admire your sensitivity very much. And I'm in awe of your honesty. Now we're more than even. And I really appreciate the wonderful dinner. I had almost forgotten how hungry I was until I was here. Thanks a lot."

Susan stood up and stepped toward the door of the dining room, carrying her glass. She stopped and looked back at him. "Is it time for a new start?"

"Absolutely," he answered. Anything to get past this. He picked up his glass and followed her into the living room.

She sat down on the couch by the fireplace. He hesitated, then chose the easy chair on the opposite side, ten feet from her. He took a sip of his drink and glanced back at the dining room.

"Don't worry about the dishes," she said. She stood up and slipped the sweatshirt over her head and off. "I'll do them in the morning." She was wearing a black lace bra that made her white skin look somehow more bare than it should have.

He suddenly realized that he was gaping. He shook his head. "No," he said. "That isn't what I meant."

"We're being honest now, Carey," she said. "You wanted me last night. If you hadn't, then nothing I did would have made the slightest difference."

"I think you misunderstood," he said. "Or maybe I did."

She unbuttoned the jeans, slipped them down, and stepped out of them. More black lace, more smooth, milky skin. "I'm making up for teasing you last night. I'm not teasing now."

"Hold it," he said. "Could you please stop taking your clothes off for a minute and let me talk?" He took a deep breath. "I'm married."

"So am I." The full lips formed themselves into the reserved smile he had seen when he met her. "You're looking, though, aren't you?"

"It's hard not to."

She seemed to take this as permission to continue. She unhooked the black bra and slipped it off. Her breasts were round and full, whiter even than the rest of her, and the nipples were like rosebuds. She saw the alarm in his eyes and her voice went lower, almost a whisper. "It's okay. It's perfectly okay."

"No," said Carey. "It isn't okay." He resolutely kept his eyes on hers, but her eyes were teasing him now. "This isn't what I want. This could wreck my life."

She smirked, confidently aware that her nudity was power, and words were only a way of keeping him faced in her direction. "No, it couldn't. I'm married too, and that's what makes it perfect. You don't have to remember my birthday, and I don't have to entertain your poker buddies. My husband and your wife are thousands of miles away. Tonight, we can do anything, and it's free. There are no possible consequences."

"Your marriage may be ending, but mine's just beginning. I love my wife."

She smiled at him again. Her hands had moved to the waistband of the panties, and as she spoke, her thumbs hooked over it and began to slide slowly along the inner side of the elastic, toward her hips. "Good for you," she said. "I'm sure she'll be panting for you when she's here—just as I am—but tonight she's not. So this doesn't take away anything of hers. This is just for fun. To be alone together in this house and not do it would be unnatural." Her smile disappeared. Her eyes lowered, she bent toward him slightly to slip the panties down past her hips, then stepped out of them, naked.

Carey was gripped with self-loathing. He did not belong here, listening to this nonsense and watching this woman strip. He stood up abruptly, then moved to the couch. He saw her smile return and the lids of her eyes go down like the eyes of a purring cat. "You're one of the most beautiful women I've ever seen in my life," he said. "You're funny, clever, and very persuasive. If I were ever going to cheat on my wife, this would have been the time." He snatched the pile of clothes off the cushion of the couch and tossed them to her. "Now get dressed and go home."

He walked to the dining room and began to carry dishes out to the kitchen and set them on the counter. On his third trip into the dining room, he heard some rustling sounds, then the front door closing. He closed his eyes, took five deep breaths, poured another glass of champagne, and drank it down. Then he went to the living room and looked: yes, she had left his key on the end table.

J ane found a shelf above the trail that was sheltered by big rocks on the north and west, where the cold mountain wind was coming from. "This is a good place," she said. "Does it look homey to you?"

Pete stopped and looked up at it doubtfully. "I could keep going for a while," he offered.

"We've come at least eight or nine miles in the dark," she said. "We might run out of steam in the middle of an ice field or on a mountaintop, and then be worth nothing by the time we find another safe spot. That's how you get hurt."

"Sold," he said. "Should I build a fire?"

"The rocks will protect us well enough from the wind." She reached into his pack and handed him his knife. "Go collect boughs from the fir trees down there. Not branches, just the soft parts near the tips. I'll get us unpacked."

Pete carefully made his way down onto the trail, then disappeared into the trees. In a moment she heard the whispery sound of pine boughs tossed onto a pile.

She had wanted Pete to be gone while she used her flashlight and a forked stick to search the cracks and crannies along the rock shelf. It was the sort of place where a rattlesnake would curl up to get out of the cold, then sun itself in the daytime. When she was satisfied that they would be alone, she searched the packs for the items they would need and laid them out.

Pete labored up the little path carrying a pile of boughs the size of a hay bale, dropped them on the rock, and saw her sitting cross-legged in front of a group of small packages. "What's that?"

"Canned beef, biscuits, dried fruit, and nuts," she said. "The bad news is that it's dinner. The good news is that if we eat it, we don't have to carry it."

"You should have been in marketing." He sat down across from her and imitated her as she opened cans with her Swiss Army knife. He took a bite of meat and a bite of biscuit. "It's kind of frightening. That stuff they've been saying about fresh air and exercise all these years could be true. This actually tastes good."

When they had finished, Jane stood up, sealed the empty cans and packages into a plastic bag, and put it in her knapsack. "More bad news: the garbage truck isn't due until a road is built—figure a thousand years or so. We have to pack the trash out with us." She looked at the pile of pine boughs. "Time to go to bed. Watch carefully."

She spread the boughs like a mat on the rocky shelf, then laid one of the waterproof ponchos on top of it and set the other one aside. "Unless it rains, most of the cold and damp comes from below."

Jane took off her jacket and boots and propped the boots under the rock shelf. "Your boots need to dry out while you sleep or you'll get blisters. You put them in a place where you can reach them and rain can't. You wear as little as possible while you're in your sleeping bag, and an insulated jacket makes a great pillow." She pulled her watch cap on. "This helps. You lose most of your heat through your head, so it'll keep you warm."

She fiddled with the zippers of the sleeping bags for a moment, then zipped the two bags together and slipped inside. "You sleep on that side, where you're farther out of the wind. Your blood is probably still thin from living in the desert."

Pete sat at the foot of the sleeping bags and looked up at her while he arranged his boots and jacket and put on his hat.

She could feel him staring at her in the darkness, trying to read her mind. She sighed, then said in the kindest voice she could summon, "No, I haven't."

"Haven't what?"

"Changed my mind about . . . anything. All I want is your body heat. This is the way to sleep if you want to be warm without a fire."

"Sure," he said. "I've heard that somewhere."

He carefully slipped in beside her, holding himself in a straight, rigid position so far from her that a cold breeze blew under the taut surface of the sleeping bag and chilled her toes. She laughed. "I'll tell you what. If this is too weird, we'll each go it on our own. I don't think we'll freeze tonight."

"No, no," he said. "It just takes a certain mental . . . what's the word? Insensitivity." He nodded sagely. "I can manage that."

"Good," she said. After a long silence she said, "But if I wake up with a hand on my ass, I'm going to pinch it. The one who says 'ouch' had better be me."

It worked. She heard him shifting on the bed of boughs and then felt the sleeping bag regain some of its slack and warm her back. She closed her eyes and listened to the wind blowing past above her head and the sounds of trees moving back and forth, whispering like the sea. In a moment she was asleep.

She was not cold anymore. She felt the hot, mild breeze where her skin was exposed to the air, then sank lazily beneath the surface. The warm water supported her, made her feel as though she were flying. She slowly, effortlessly glided above the bottom of the pool, the light resistance of the black water running along her body like a warm touch.

She looked up at the silvery underside of the surface, saw the bright moon wavering above it, and let herself rise up to meet it.

She came to the surface and took in the first dry, sweet breath, then let her muscles relax and floated. She was in suspension now, drifting passively, waiting. She reveled in the knowledge that he was sure to be here, and fretted, teasing herself with the lie that he would not.

She heard the water sloshing somewhere behind her head and looked up at the moon, her body going tense with anticipation and longing. When his big arm slipped around her waist, she let out a gasp that was certitude and joy and laughter at the same time. She let him pull her close. She could feel his chest against her back, his lips softly kissing the back of her neck. She leaned her head back on his shoulder. He was strong and gentle, and warmer than the water. She could feel his hands moving, never leaving her body, instead touching her lovingly everywhere from her scalp to the tips of her toes, the hands returning, lingering on each of the places she would never have let him touch.

He slowly turned her around and she looked into his eyes. There was no question in them, no uncertainty that would force her to speak. They did not have to talk, because they had been through this before, and he had somehow sensed this time that her answer had changed. She had just misspoken, forgotten on that other night that this was all right. The first kiss was slow, their lips drawn together and barely meeting at first, then staying together. She let it go on as long as she could bear it, feeling so safe, being cradled in his arms and cherished.

She slipped the straps of her bathing suit off her shoulders, then took his hand and made him peel it down and off. Pete's bathing suit came off too, or maybe it was already off. They embraced again in the warm, dark water, and this time it was so much better, with the water tickling the exposed skin to remind her it was bare. She felt so free that she was surprised at how constricted and uncomfortable she must have been before. She and Pete floated weightlessly, and something about the motion of the water seemed to make them drift together.

She let herself savor the moment, the world so dark and quiet around her, but her feelings so bright and hot and clear. She was so glad she had found out that this was allowed. But then she sensed that off in the dark beyond the pool, there was some kind of disturbance. Maybe someone was coming. "No, not yet," she pleaded. "Just a little longer." But Pete seemed to lose his solidity, to slip away from her. She reached for him.

Jane felt cold. Why had the water turned cold? She slowly rose toward consciousness to investigate her surroundings and opened her eyes to a terrible sense of loss. Then she was suddenly, abruptly, wide awake. She was shocked—frightened—not by the dream but by the realization that she was the dreamer. It was an enormous relief that it had not happened. She had not committed adultery, thrown her marriage away. She had not betrayed Carey. She had not done anything at all.

She sat up, as careful not to touch Pete as though he were a rattlesnake that had slithered in beside her for warmth, and extricated herself from the sleeping bag. She felt deeply depressed as she slipped her jacket on and walked across the cold stone shelf to retrieve her boots.

The Old People had studied dreams the way they studied every other event that passed before their eyes. When somebody awoke from a dream, he would immediately do his best to interpret it and fulfill whatever command it had brought him. Something was bothering the dreamer, something he had not given sufficient attention to while he was awake. Now that he was conscious again, he had to correct the oversight—overcome the inertia, the fear, or the inhibition that had prevented him from seeing clearly before. If Jane had lived in the Old Time, she would have been required to wake Pete up and demand that he act out the dream with her to set her mind at rest.

As she tied her boots, she looked over at Pete Hatcher. He was lying on his side facing her, his eyes closed and his jaw slack in sleep. He would be one of the seventeen men on the planet who looked good when he was asleep. She fought off the urge to resent him. None of this was his fault. She was just lonely for her husband, and she had been alone with Pete so much that her misguided subconscious mind had somehow drafted him to stand for Man. No, she thought. The dream had been too convincing and too specific for anything so abstract. Pete was an attractive guy who had the morals of a stallion and had made it disconcertingly clear that she was the one he wanted. Some part of her mind obviously had not taken her refusal as final but had been mulling the offer over.

She found her watch in her jacket pocket and consulted it as she strapped it to her wrist. It was only four o'clock, but she wasn't going to crawl back into that sleeping bag with him right now.

She heard the distant screeching of birds. She cocked her head to listen, but she could not identify their kind. She did sense that they weren't singing, they were frightened. Something must have come too close to their nesting place. She heard the wings of a flock of them passing overhead in the dark. It was too early for the birds she knew to fly.

"Pete!" she said. "Get up. It's time to move."

It was dark and still and cold, and as Jane and Pete rolled their sleeping bags and ponchos and put on their jackets, she could see thick clouds of steam puffing into the air from their nostrils.

Hatcher whispered, "Why are we in such a hurry?"

"Some birds woke me up," she whispered back. "I think something scared them."

As Jane gathered the pine boughs and carried them below the trail to hide them, she knew that she was not being foolish. This was unfamiliar country, but she had begun to get used to the sights and sounds, and the birds were behaving strangely. When she had removed every sign of the campsite, she used the last pine bough as a broom to sweep the rock shelf, then all of the footprints that led to it from the trail.

Jane set a brisk pace as they moved up the trail in the frigid predawn stillness. She led Pete northward, past thickets of berry bushes in alpine meadows, up rocky inclines that skirted the treeline. When the sky began to take on a blue-gray luminescence and she could see objects in depth, she began to hear other birds. She listened to them as she walked, trying to detect any sudden calls from behind that might be warnings. When the sun had turned the peaks to her left a dull orange, she said, "Are you up to a little run?"

Pete said, "Ready if you are."

They jogged until the sun was high, going single file on the narrow footpath. Jane listened harder for sounds that came from behind but heard nothing. When she saw a mountain that might be Iceberg Peak on her right, she stopped running and walked while she studied the map.

"Where are we?" asked Pete.

She pointed to the spot. "What we want to look for next are more glaciers: Ahern Glacier, Ipasha Glacier, and then Chaney Glacier, all middle-sized, close together on the right. Then we take a fork in the path. It looks like a good five miles from here."

"It's rough country," said Pete. "Are you planning to run all the way to Canada?"

"I wish we could," she said. "I'll probably feel better when we've passed that fork in the trail—one more chance to send a tracker in the wrong direction."

"Do you seriously think somebody could have followed us this far?"

"I honestly know some people could do it. I don't think it's likely that these people made all the right decisions and did it, but I've decided that it's stupid not to minimize the risks."

"How do we do that?"

"Move faster, stop less often, and keep traveling as long as the light lasts."

Pete walked along beside her, ducking now and then to shrug a branch past his shoulder. After a moment she realized he was trying to get a close look at her face, so she turned it to him. "Something wrong?"

"I was just having a fantasy."

"Pete . . ."

"It was about dancing. Honest."

"Pretty tame, for you. It must be the lack of oxygen up here."

His hands came up to gesture as he described it. "See, we're at this ballroom. It's got one of those old-fashioned spinning balls in the center made out of mirrors. The light is dim, except for that. I've got a tuxedo on. You're wearing—"

"A blue business suit."

"A black velvet dress: straps, just low enough to hint that the endowment is adequate."

" 'Endowment is adequate'?"

"Nice tits."

"Sorry I asked. Are we done yet?"

"No. I walk up to your table. You smile. You stand, you hold out your right hand—"

"And wave good-bye."

"No. I take your hand. The music begins." He hummed a waltz as he walked, his eyes closed. Jane waited, but he kept humming, the waltz going on and on.

She looked at his face. "Is that smile supposed to make me uncomfortable? Pete?"

"Sssh. Don't interrupt my fantasy. I finally got to lead."

She stared at him for a moment, then the laugh fought its way out and she slapped his arm. He opened his eyes and shrugged happily. "A guy can dream."

"I'm sorry," she said. "I apologize. I'll let you make the decision. Do you want to get to Canada quickly, or do you want to stroll along like this for a few hours, sleep on a frozen rock in a forty-knot wind, and maybe get killed?"

"Lead on," he said.

She pulled ahead of him again. For the rest of the morning she tried a new routine. When they were in thick cover among the evergreen trees she walked, striding along with a purposeful gait, trading the time lost for the chance to catch her breath. But when the trail led them up into grassy fields or onto bare, rocky ridges, she broke into a run, taking them across the open ground as quickly as she could. She never let herself forget the rifle.

Earl sat under the set of trail markers and rested while his dogs sorted out the conflicting sets of footprints. T-Bone raced off up the right-hand trail and Rusty took the left, sniffing the ground methodically. It was good to see that Jane had tried to throw him off like this. It had certainly taken her longer to do it than it would take him to find the right path. Almost as soon as he had formed the thought, he saw both dogs coming back, sniffing the grass beside the trail.

The dogs converged again beside the third path, the one that didn't have a sign anymore, and Earl stood up to watch the dogs work. They were staying beside the trail instead of on it, and in places

Earl could look ahead of them and see spots where the weeds had been pushed aside by feet.

Earl found the first footprints a hundred yards farther on. The first ones were hard to see, so he wasn't positive yet, but his heart beat a little faster and he hurried on. He found the next set in a muddy depression, and they were much clearer. They had wrapped something around their boots to disguise the zigzag treads. He took in a breath that tasted thick with tantalizing possibilities. *"Auf den fersen folgen!"*

Rusty and T-Bone scrambled to his side, and he knelt by the prints while the dogs sniffed. He saw their eyes brighten, as though the smell were some kind of drug that actually conjured an image in their brains. They looked at Earl, ran ahead a few steps, then came back, panting and pleading with him. He was sure now. Hatcher and the woman had done the worst thing they could. Maybe it was a piece of a shirt, maybe even a sock. But it wasn't something they had picked up along the way. They had tied something around their boots that had touched their skin, something they had worn and sweated on. Now the dogs had their scent.

Earl adjusted the straps on his pack, tightened his belt, and said, *"Jagen!* Hunt!"

It took the dogs fifteen minutes to reach the place where the prey had spent the night. At first Earl was not sure, because there was no sign of charred wood or scorching, but the dogs showed him the pine boughs, and then he knew.

He headed down toward the trail, and the dogs hurried to beat him there. They galloped off along the trail, no longer set in motion by his command or the pleasure of running along a smooth dirt path in the woods with him. They had picked up the scent, verified it, and found it again. They were eager now, because at each leap they were closer, the scent was fresher.

Earl worked himself back up to a jog. He held his head up, staring into the middle distance and breathing deep, easy breaths. He gauged his speed to keep the dogs in sight and let them work without inhibition. He had no apprehension that they might forget their training. When it was time, they would let him come in and join them in the kill.

Jane kept Pete moving through the afternoon, running across the open spaces and walking quickly among the thickets and the stands of gnarled, stunted trees. In midafternoon the air turned cold. She found Chaney Glacier and then the fork in the path appeared as though in answer to a wish.

Jane stopped and turned to Pete. "This is the last place we can hope to fool them if they're on the right trail. Want to do a good job?"

"Of course," he said.

She sent him down the slope to uproot small bushes while she began to dig with her knife. She took the trail markers down the path that branched off to the right, then transplanted small shrubs in the middle of the trail that went north. She worked quickly, planting them in random patterns wherever the ground was bare, then spreading dead leaves and pine needles from the adjacent grove to cover the fresh dirt at their roots.

When Pete came back, trying to peer around the thick bushes in his arms to see where to place his feet, she sent him off again to gather rocks.

Jane stuck clumps of weeds into the ground in a second random pattern among the shrubs, then told Pete, "Don't just set the rocks into the mix. Bury some of them enough so they look like they've always been here."

When she was able to step back along the trail and look at the camouflaged spot without distinguishing it from the surrounding brush, she and Pete went back into the forest and collected more leaves and debris to spread among the bushes.

They stopped to look at their work. "I should take you home with me to landscape the yard," she said.

"If you get me through this I'll remodel your whole house."

"Let's go. Take the trail signs."

They set off below the trail into the undisturbed woods, then made a turn to angle back and rejoin the trail a few hundred yards farther north. They moved quickly now to make up for the time they had spent. Jane found a deer run along the trail a half mile on and stuck the trail markers into the ground there.

They moved on faster, and finally Pete said, "We seem to be going down."

"That's right," she answered. "This stretch goes almost due north for ten miles along the Waterton River."

He gave a tired snort. "Then it goes straight up, right?"

"Wrong. It flows into Waterton Lake. The lake is long, like the Finger Lakes in New York. Ready for even better news?"

"More than ready."

"It straddles the border. About two-thirds of it is in Canada."

"Let's do some more running."

They jogged along the trail, feeling the lower altitude and hearing it. Somewhere among the big cedars and hemlocks, a woodpecker rapped on bark. In places they had to slow their momentum to keep from losing their footing.

They reached the river bank as the light was fading. "Are you hungry?" Jane asked.

"Starving."

"Don't you want to stop for dinner?"

"I want to do what you said this morning, before dawn. I want to use the light, wring every last bit of distance out of this day. Then I'll stop and eat a moose or something."

She grinned as she moved along the trail.

"What are you smiling at? Don't tell me it's your turn for a fantasy."

"Don't you wish. No, I was worried about you, but now I'm not. You're doing great."

"I told you a couple of days ago that I don't feel like giving up. I like living too much."

"That wasn't a couple of days ago. It was yesterday."

"See? I'm getting more out of time now. I feel as though I've lived a year since then."

Jane said nothing. Exercise was one of the therapies that doctors prescribed for depression, because it increased the flow of oxygen and released some chemical into the blood that fooled the brain into an unfounded sense of well-being. Whatever had happened to Pete Hatcher, she hoped it would last.

It was deep darkness when they reached a deserted campground. Jane pulled out her flashlight and played it around the big clearing until she found the sign.

Pete read it aloud. "Goat Haunt?"

"Beautiful, isn't it?" she said. "We made it. The tip of the lake should be right up there."

Pete waited, but she didn't move. "Are we going on, or are we going to sleep here?"

She looked around her with the flashlight. "There's a lot to be said for official campgrounds. The rangers generally put them in the best places they can find, so this is probably the most sheltered spot around here. It's a lot colder tonight than last night. There are hearths for fires, so if we build one, our ashes won't be a sign of anything to anybody once they're cool. People have built fires here all summer."

"You don't sound sure."

"I'm not."

"Why not?"

"I don't know," she admitted. "Maybe because I'm so exhausted from walking and running. Maybe because in order to get through that I had to get scared." She swept the area on all sides with her flashlight again. "I guess it's just nerves. I guess we're not going to accomplish much by tromping on in the dark. Let's eat and get some sleep and try to cross the border when we can see it."

This time Pete set off to find soft boughs without her saying anything, while she rummaged in the packs and unrolled the ponchos and sleeping bags. They ate the rest of their canned food with some powdered soup Jane heated over the small fire she had built.

They joined their sleeping bags and slipped into them after Jane had carefully cleaned the pot and put all of the cans into the plastic bag.

Jane lay on her back, closed her eyes, and felt the warm, living mass of Pete's body beside her, breathing deeply, then almost immediately falling asleep. In another few days she would be out of this life forever, lying safely every night beside Carey in the big bed with the maple tree outside the window.

The night breeze blew cold, and she could feel it caressing her face. She tugged the watch cap lower, pulled the sleeping bag to her chin, and let the wind soothe her to sleep. Tonight part of her was waiting for the dreams to come, but sleep was a jumble of images that never seemed to coalesce.

Sometime during the night the constant mountain wind disappeared and the air turned cold and still. It was three in the morning when Jane heard the howl.

She opened her eyes and lay still, then began to take inventory of her surroundings. The fire was out, and the dew had frozen on the ground. Her cheeks were tingling, so she rubbed them to get the circulation back. She decided it must have been a dream and rolled over, pushing her face deeper into the sleeping bag for warmth. Then she heard it again. It was a high, long yowl, and then it broke off into a series of yelps. She sat up quickly and listened.

There were supposed to be a couple of packs of wolves that had come back into the wild country above the border in the past few years, but the call hadn't sounded like a wolf, exactly. There was no shortage of coyotes anywhere in the country, but as soon as she had thought of them, she knew it was wrong. She heard another bark, but this one was closer, off to the left. It sounded like an answer to the first. She pounded Pete's shoulder, then kicked her way out of the sleeping bag. He sat up quickly and looked around.

Jane tossed his boots into his chest. "Dogs!" she said. "They've tracked us with dogs!"

She pulled on her boots, snatched up their packs, and used her flashlight to find the sign she had seen when they had reached the campground: "Boulder Pass Trail."

Pete had his boots on now, and he began to roll up the sleeping bags.

"Leave them," she said, and handed him his pack.

Jane began to run. She heard Pete fall into step behind her. When she had passed the sign and taken a few steps onto the forest trail she turned off the light and slipped it into her pack. She tried to wake herself and consider the implications as she ran.

All of her ruses and misleading trails had meant nothing. A man would have been fooled and walked on past the shrubs and plants and rocks she and Pete had carefully placed to cover the path. A dog would not even pause, just plunge on through them, following the scent. The spot had probably served the dogs as a beacon, because the sweat from the hard work must have been all over the rocks and shrubs they had moved. She had a sudden vision of herself moving trail signs along the way. All the effort and all the delay would have been worth it if only dogs could read.

"Couldn't it be somebody else?" The low, raspy whisper from behind reminded her that she had to keep him from being confused.

"No," she said. "Dogs aren't allowed in the park." She heard a bark and tried to gauge the distance. It sounded as though the dog was far behind them, but when she tried to decipher what that meant, she found that she couldn't. The dog had a deep-register voice, but that didn't mean it was loud; there was no way to know if the dog was even facing in their direction when he barked.

She ran harder, ducking and weaving to avoid low branches but making no attempt to keep her footprints off the trail. She searched her mind for strategies she could use to fool the hunter. The only one that offered any hope was to outrun him. She and Pete had traveled half of one night and a full day, from before sunrise until late evening. They had wasted only enough time to try to disguise their trail and eat and pee. That thought made her feel worse. That was how dogs marked their territories. The occasional smell of human urine in the bushes along the trail had probably been overwhelming to a dog.

Running was the only answer. If she and Pete had traveled quickly for thirty-six hours, then this hunter and his dogs had traveled faster. In order to be anywhere near the campsite at Goat Haunt by now, they must have kept going through the cold and darkness for five or six hours while she and Pete had eaten and slept. The hunter must be an intimidating physical specimen, but she and Pete were warm and rested now, and ready to run. He would be worn out and hungry.

She ran on as quickly as she dared in the darkness. The trail wound upward through the trees against the path of a small creek she could hear to her left. Sometimes she could see a brief glimpse of moonlight on water.

She ran until the sun began to throw her shadow on the trail ahead of her, then she walked for a few minutes, listening to the harsh huffing sound of her breathing. Pete's breath was louder and deeper, and she could tell by his heavy footsteps that he was tired enough to stumble now and then. She pulled the pack off her back and onto her belly, found the map, and studied it.

"If we stay on Boulder Pass Trail, we'll reach a fork in the path, then go west to Kintla Lake or swing south to Bowman Lake."

Pete looked over her shoulder at the map. "They both look like a long way."

"Maybe twenty-five miles. Neither one leads to what I would call civilization, but I would be very glad to see a few park rangers with guns about now."

She studied the map more closely. There was a thin, jagged line like a crack in a teacup that crossed Boulder Pass Trail and zigzagged north to the border. "There is a closer way, if we wanted to take a big chance. See this line?"

"What is it? Another path?"

"No such luck. It's the border between Glacier County and Flathead County." Her finger followed it northward. "In Canada it separates the Kootenay District and the Lethbridge District."

"What are we looking at an imaginary line for?"

"Because it's not straight and regular and even. See the Canadian border? It's the forty-ninth parallel, because some politicians drew a neat line on a map in a comfortable building thousands of miles from here. But this line is all sawteeth and wiggles. That means it wasn't done that way. Surveyors actually went there. Somebody walked that line. Even if it was a hundred years ago, somebody was up there."

"Sure. It was probably one of those old-time mountain men that looked like Bigfoot and smelled the same, and his faithful Indian guide."

Jane shrugged. "They've got nothing on us."

"What do you mean?"

She answered the question she wanted to. "We've done pretty well so far. We just had food and a little sleep. The guy behind us didn't."

"How can you know that?"

"He was still up and chasing at three A.M. He was trying to make time and kill us in our sleep. If we want to outrun him, then the rougher the country, the better."

"I'm not so sure."

"Did you ever watch a dog climb a ladder?"

"I don't think so."

"They're lousy at it. If we have to do any heavy climbing, they'll hold him back, and maybe stop him."

"So this is where he's going to give up?"

"No," said Jane. "That's what I used to think. I don't believe that anymore."

Earl followed T-Bone and Rusty into the deserted campsite at Goat Haunt. The dogs streaked across the clearing and nosed the two sleeping bags that lay in a pile on the ground. Earl hurried to the stone hearth beside them and held his hand over it. He felt no warmth. He picked up a pine bough from the nest they had made and stirred the ashes. Sparks rose from glowing embers and ignited the pine sap on the bough. He set it in the hearth to burn and watched his dogs.

The scent was fresh, probably no more than an hour old, so the dogs were wide-eyed and impatient. He sat down to rest and gave them a chance to investigate all of the smells and sort out the trail. T-Bone kept dashing to the edge of the forest and stopping to look back. Rusty went back and forth across the campground methodically sniffing the ground, then trotted over to join his brother under the trail sign.

Earl read the trail marker and took out his map. They must have heard the baying of the dogs, got up, and run. The question was, Why had they chosen the Boulder Pass Trail? He traced the long, meandering line with his finger. There was a fork in the trail at Brown Pass.

The south trail swung down along Bowman Lake, then Bowman Creek, to a patrol cabin and a road. The north fork went at least twenty-five miles, then to Kintla Lake, another patrol cabin, and a road.

They knew he was coming now, and they had chosen to try out-running him. He sighed. It wasn't a bad strategy. He had been on the trail all night while they had been resting up. If they had not both been in reasonably good condition, they would not have gotten this far.

Lenny was a problem. By now he was hours behind, walking up the Highline Trail loaded like a pack animal. Earl considered resting the dogs and curling up on these sleeping bags while he waited for Lenny. But that way he would risk losing his two targets. He studied his map. Even if he waited for Lenny and set him on Boulder Pass Trail, Earl could be fairly sure that Lenny and his supplies would be of no use now that they were running.

Earl opened the two cans of dog food that he had left, dumped them out on two flat stones, and whistled. Rusty and T-Bone trotted over and ate. Earl found an old-fashioned pump and pumped some water into the trough underneath it for them. Then he filled his canteen, dropped in a water-purification tablet, and sat down to eat jerky and trail mix. Rusty and T-Bone licked the last of the meat from the stones, leaving wet swaths from their tongues, then walked over to lap water and lay down at Earl's feet.

"Decisions, decisions," he said to them. That was it. Jane was presenting him with choices. If she presented enough of them, one time he would make the wrong choice and go tromping off in the wrong direction. He was not going to do that. He hurried to the sleeping bags, gathered them up, walked with them into the bushes, and tossed them there to keep the sight of them from distracting Lenny. He covered them with the pine boughs.

Lenny would come up the Highline Trail, see no sign that anyone had been here, and keep going north beside Waterton Lake into Canada. When Earl wanted him, he would be able to find him at the Waterton Township campground.

Earl emptied his pack. He quickly assembled the A.W. rifle and attached the sling to it. He clicked one box-style ten-round magazine into it and put one more into the left side pocket of his jacket. He put the .45 pistol into the right pocket and slipped his knife into his belt at the small of his back. He put his map and compass into one breast pocket and then filled the remaining spaces with jerky and biscuits. He slung his canteen over his shoulder to counterbalance his rifle, then hid the pack with the sleeping bags.

Earl tested the weight of his load. He was twenty pounds lighter, with nothing rattling or slowing him down. It was a gamble to set off on another unfamiliar mountain trail with no more than this, but people always carried enough to get them there and back, so he didn't need to. After he had killed them, he and T-Bone and Rusty could have a feast on whatever was left in their packs.

He walked toward the trailhead, then called over his shoulder, "*Jagen!* Hunt!" The two big dogs bounded past him up the trail. Earl gave them a chance to get a good head start before he, too, began to run. After a time, he knew, the man and the woman would wear themselves out and see that all the running was doing them no good. Then they would go to ground and prepare to make a stand. He smiled. Nobody had ever ambushed a dog.

It was ten o'clock before Jane and Hatcher reached the fork in the path at Brown Pass. "This is it," said Jane.

Pete looked at the two paths leading west and northwest. "Which is it?"

"Neither." She pointed up to her right at the high rocky promontory above them. "That snow up there is on Chapman Peak. We climb from here. We'll have to go up about a thousand feet in a mile, moving almost in a straight line until we get to the lower edge of the glacier."

She watched his eyes move upward. Then he turned his head to take a longer look back up the trail. "After you," he said. It confirmed her suspicion. He was trying to keep his back between her and the bullet. She set off along the hard, rocky ground that began to rise in front of her immediately. Let him be noble. She would be quick.

They climbed through the zone of deciduous forest, up into the belt of pines and subalpine meadows, each of them stopping now and then to look out over the green treetops without appearing to be looking for anything specific.

By the time the sun was at its midpoint they stood at the foot of the glacier. Pete looked up at the field of ice above him as Jane studied the map. "You know what I'd like right now?"

"An ice-cream cone?"

"A big box of dynamite. I'd wait until this guy was standing right about here and roll an avalanche down on top of him."

Jane surveyed the bright, frozen expanse. "It's a dumb idea, but keep thinking. If he gets close, we'll have to do something." She folded the map. "We move west from here along the ridge."

"What sort of landmark are we looking for? I'd hate to miss it."

"We won't. It's called Hudson Glacier."

They moved rapidly along the jagged, rocky area below the crest of the mountain, their eyes down to watch where they planted their feet. It was another hour before Jane heard the bark of a dog, then a second dog answering. Pete turned to look behind them, but Jane grasped his arm and pulled him ahead.

"If you do see him, he'll already have seen you. The best hope is to keep moving." This time her voice was tense, tight in her throat. She had been wrong again. The way up the mountain had not been hard enough. There had been no stretch where a dog couldn't scamper up, so the man had not been held back at all.

She tried not to think about the man, but it was impossible to keep him out of her mind. He must have been up all night, and most of the day before. He didn't seem to need sleep, food, or shelter. He never gave up, he never guessed wrong. He killed anyone who might be Pete Hatcher, and anyone who might get in the way, and still kept coming.

A chill suddenly made the hairs on the back of her neck stand. She had never actually seen the dogs. She had heard howling in the forest as something followed their scent. The rangers didn't even allow anybody to bring dogs through the gate into the park. She shook her head to get rid of the feeling.

She knew she had climbed to about nine thousand feet now, and the air must be making her giddy. There were crazy, malevolent people, but their craziness didn't buy them the power to turn into dogs. They took shots at strangers with high-powered rifles. That was what she had to worry about, not old superstitions.

When they rounded the slope at the foot of Hudson Glacier she began to feel stronger. If she was maintaining their lead, then for a while the slope of the mountain would be between them and the rifle.

They turned northward, moving along the ridges, staying high, where there were plateaus with dead grass and stunted trees. The north wind picked up as the sun moved westward, blowing hard into their faces and making their progress slower.

At two o'clock, she heard the dogs again, and they seemed to be closer. She turned, but she could not see them. She said, "Ready to run again?"

As she ran into the wind, her steps were shorter, as though the air were catching her in midstride and pushing her back. She and Pete leaned into it, trying to stay low, but before long they were just scrambling over rocks and climbing up steep grades, buying each yard with too much of their strength.

At four fifteen, when Jane had Mount Custer on her left and Herbst Glacier on her right, she looked back and saw the man. He was little more than a small vertical line of darkness against the horizon. She could see two more spots of darkness ranging ahead of him, low to the ground. Jane took out her binoculars and found him.

She watched as he stopped, then sat on the ground with his knees bent, fiddling with something. At this distance she could not resolve any of the details of his face. Very deliberately he raised both arms in front of him at once. The gesture seemed oddly familiar. When his head cocked to his right, she shouted, "Get down!"

They both dropped to their bellies, then heard the whip-crack sound as the bullet broke the sound barrier above their heads. Jane counted seconds, listening for the report of the rifle, but it never came. He still had the silencer. She lifted her head a little and saw the man running.

"Let's go," she said, and pulled herself to her feet.

She and Pete ran together, side by side. She heard the whip-crack again, and this time she saw chips fly off a boulder ahead of her as the bullet ricocheted into the sky. There seemed to be no hope. Each time they ran, he would shoot. Each time they stopped to hide, he would run closer.

"We've got to get out of the open," she said.

"Agreed."

They ran to the west, moving diagonally down the slope of the mountain. As soon as they reached the first stand of scraggly pine trees, the shooting stopped. Twice Pete let his momentum build up, tripped, and rolled, then stood and ran again. They ran until the sun was beyond the western mountains and the dim afterlight threw no shadows. They stumbled into a long, narrow valley meadow with thickets of berry bushes as the light began to fail.

The bear was a hundred feet away, busily rooting on the ground, snuffling and grumbling to itself. Jane stopped. Her mind seemed to explode into fragments that scurried in several directions at once, looking for a way out. She knew immediately that the enormous tan animal was not a black bear. Its back had a big hump on it, and the profile of its face was flatter, with the snout turned slightly upward. Jane remembered the warnings on the little flyer she had picked up at the park entrance.

Grizzlies stayed in the high altitudes in the remotest areas of the park, and if any place was more remote than this little trough between two mountains, then it couldn't be reached by a human being. There wasn't even enough animal traffic to make a path in the weeds. She could see the thicket was full of berry bushes. The bear seemed to be finishing off a low branch, and now it raised a paw and swatted the next one to shake the berries loose. That reminded her of another problem. This was the time of year when they were voracious, trying desperately to fatten themselves for the winter. Never hike at dusk. That was the part that had been printed in bold letters.

In her peripheral vision she could see Pete slowly reaching into his pack for the pistol. She touched him and shook her head. Then they began to walk toward the far end of the narrow valley. It seemed hopeless. A bear could outrun a man. This bear was hungry. The gun Pete was still searching for would be about as much protection as a fly swatter if a bear like this one decided to come for them. Nobody even knew what made a bear decide to amble away one time and attack another time, but there were theories. Suddenly she remembered the rest of the warning. This was the reason no dogs were allowed in the park.

She whispered, "Keep going. Don't run, don't stop."

He looked alarmed. "What are—"

She pushed him forward, and he kept walking. She was aware of each pace he took as he moved farther away from her. Jane slowly turned her head to look back at the way she had come, then across the field to the far end. She carefully chose the spot where she would make her stand.

The bear stopped eating the berries, shook its wide, shaggy body, and raised its head to stare directly into her eyes. She did not know if she was held in the huge animal's gaze for a few seconds or a minute. The bear's undistracted intensity brought back to her phrases from stories her grandfather had told. Bears could read minds. Probably in the Old Time, the listeners would all have known what it was like to stumble on a bear in the forest. They would have nodded their heads, maybe chuckled nervously at the memory of this stare. It was said that if he knew your real name, you couldn't escape him, and to her it felt as though he were probing her mind for it now. The stories were proof that what was happening was unchanged since the beginning of time. There was only one bear, and one small woman walking through the wild country.

The bear sniffed the air and smelled her fear. It took one step toward her, then another, tasting the breeze. She could see its ears move back and its face elongate, and she knew what was about to happen. There would be no chance to run, no way to fight. Her only chance was the one that had existed since the first Nundawaono woman and the first bear. Nothing had changed. Those who lived, lived by their wits.

Jane knelt in the grass, slipped off her pack, and watched the bear erupt into its charge. It surged forward with growing speed. As she fumbled in her pack, she watched the progress of his huge, powerful body across the field of dry grass, and said aloud, "Is it the truth, Nyakwai? Are the old stories true?" She whispered, "They had better be."

Her hands shook as she tore open the packets of honey and peanut butter, raisins and dried meat, then dropped them into the plastic bag with the garbage.

The bear was almost on her when she sprang to her feet. As Nyakwai always did in the stories, this one reared back on its hind legs. It seemed to Jane to be eight or nine feet tall as it towered over her, its thick, powerful forelegs opened wide to grasp her in its claws and hold her while it gnawed through her neck.

Jane flung the plastic bag of food and garbage hard at the bear's chest. As they always did, Nyakwai's lightning-quick animal reflexes clapped his big paws together and caught the bag between them, his long claws digging through it into the pungent mess it held.

Jane pivoted and sprinted for the far end of the field. She judged it was a hundred yards of open grass before the ground again rose into rocky outcroppings and sheltering trees. By the time she had finished making her estimate it was eighty. . . . Now it was sixty. She clenched her teeth and pumped her arms, making her toes dig in and tear at the ground with each stride. Forty. . . . Thirty. Just before the trees began, she glanced over her shoulder, then kept running.

In the stories, the trick was to get the bear to catch a small log, and then quickly swing a war club down on the top of its skull. But this bear was still in the spot where she had left it, peacefully rooting deep in the plastic sack, lapping out the fatty meat and peanut butter, the sweet, sticky honey and the crumbs of biscuits.

Jane took one last look at the bear. "Stay right where you are, Nyakwai," she whispered. "Something is coming—something evil."

Earl trotted down the steep hillside after the dogs. Everything seemed to come hard to him this trip, like the stiff north wind smacking into his face all afternoon. He had run until he had thought he would have to stop, and then he had at last spotted them on the bare ridge ahead. He had kept his head and run on, trying to gradually shorten the distance and buy himself the best shot. But he had seen the woman stop and turn around, so he had gone low and used the telescopic sight of the rifle to see what she was doing.

When he saw that she was holding a pair of binoculars, he'd had no choice. The range must have been a thousand yards. He had known that even though he was holding the best sniper rifle that money could buy, he was aiming it into the sunset at a receding target bobbing up and down over uneven ground with a forty-mile-an-hour wind blowing at him. He had tried to hold the man's back in the crosshairs long enough, but it was a ridiculous shot, and the round had gone high. When the gun had settled from the recoil and he had found them again in the scope, he discovered they had dropped to their bellies.

He had sprung to his feet and run toward them, using the time to shorten the distance and get into reasonable range. When they got up to run again, he had taken a second shot to make them go down again, but the tactic had not worked. Jane had obviously figured out that hiding while he moved closer could only end one way.

She had dodged to the left, moving across his field of vision to make his shot even harder, and then scrambled down here into the gulch. The sparse smattering of scraggly pines on the slope would not have provided cover from fifty yards, but from eight hundred, the tree trunks had multiplied in the scope's optics into an impenetrable wall.

Jane was a clever bitch. She had taken Hatcher from a mountaintop, where he'd stood out against the sky, down into a narrow mountain pass the sun had not reached for an hour and where enough soil had been deposited over the eons to let thick, leafy vegetation grow.

This was the moment he had known for days would come. Some runners would just keep running until they dropped, and then lie there to get their throats cut. But Hatcher had already shown that he wasn't one of those. Linda had taken a gun off him in Denver, and that meant he was the sort that would probably make some lame attempt at fighting. Jane was a pro, so it went without saying that when running got to be pointless, she would still not concede that she had used up her options.

Earl took long, leaping steps, almost flying a few feet and landing on both heels to stop himself, then taking a running start and doing it again. When he reached the bottom he moved out of the trees into a long, narrow meadow. The light was fading quickly, and the sky above him had already dimmed into that gray opaque surface that would turn deep later when the stars began to show.

A shiver of anticipation began in his spine and moved up to the back of his neck. He could feel that they were straight ahead, waiting for him. He cocked the slide on his pistol to chamber a round, then lifted the precious rifle across his chest like a skeet shooter and held it ready. Then he turned his face to the dogs.

"T-Bone," he whispered, and swept his hand to his right. "Rusty," he whispered, and swung his hand to the left. The two big black dogs began to advance through the meadow on either side of him. He could see they smelled something ahead in the meadow.

They stalked with their ears pricked forward, their necks extended, and their bodies held low to the ground. This was it, all right. He saw that there were bushes growing in big clumps, like haystacks here and there in the open field. Most likely the man and woman were crouched behind one of them, or even in the middle. Hatcher would be clutching the one little pistol he had bought that Linda hadn't gotten, probably sweating so much he could barely keep the grip in his hand.

Manhunting was all strategy, and Earl had them this time. If they stayed put, the dogs would sniff them out and Earl could lie prone out of pistol range and keep piercing the bushes until he had bagged them. If the dogs flushed them, they would have to run the whole length of this narrow valley to get out of the open. Earl could fix them one at a time in his flashlight beam and pop them at his leisure. It occurred to him that he didn't even have to do that. He could let the dogs run them down and tear them up first, then shoot them on the ground.

T-Bone and Rusty both stopped, stood stiff-legged, and began to growl. At first it was low, a sound like anger building. But then they began to move forward again, still low but faster now. He could see their muzzles contort to bare their long, glowing teeth—not just the biting fangs this time, but the big jagged grinders in the back for gnawing through bone.

Earl rasped, "*Abschuss!* Kill!" The word was more a cheer than a command, because they seemed already to be in motion when it began, streaking forward toward the big thicket ahead of him.

Earl chose a standing position so he could sidestep quickly to either side. He held the flashlight in his left hand under the foregrip of the rifle so that it would throw its beam wherever he aimed. He pushed off the safety and waited. The dogs tore into the thicket from both sides.

In the dim remnants of light from the sky he saw T-Bone take a hard run forward, his teeth bared to emit a sound that was half growl and half cry of joy. As T-Bone left the ground, Earl knew he was leaping for a throat. At almost the same time he saw Rusty dash in low from the other side of the thicket, and he knew they were attacking the way he had seen them go after the bloodhound—one for the throat and the other for the hamstrings. Earl danced to the right, trying to create a better angle in case the dogs had left one of the runners unoccupied.

Earl heard a sound that made him drop the flashlight in his haste to push the switch. The air seemed to turn thick with it, a noise that had a groan in it like the roar of an enraged man, but a noise that had fangs and hair, far too loud and deep to have come from a human throat.

Earl saw T-Bone fly through the air, spinning a little to land in the tall weeds. Then Earl saw the bear. It charged out of the thicket after Rusty, its maw wide open in a crocodile gape as it tried to corner the dog.

Earl found his flashlight and caught the bear in it. The head, a foot wide with a wrinkled snout and tiny black eyes, turned to him in a snarl. The flashlight seemed to have enraged the bear, but it had blinded Rusty. The bear's thick paw shot out, the black claws gleaming in the light like the teeth of a rake, and swatted Rusty's side. Then the bear, with astonishing speed, disappeared behind the thicket again.

Earl thought he saw the bushes move. He raised the rifle, fired, cycled the bolt, and fired again, but the bear had somehow gotten ahead of him in the dark. The bear found the dazed T-Bone and, in a second, reared up with his jaws clamped on T-Bone's throat, gave the dying body a neck-breaking shake, then dropped the carcass and headed back toward Rusty on four feet.

Rusty crouched, barking and snarling as the bear trotted toward him, then seemed to realize that he had finally met something he could not even injure, let alone kill. Rusty wheeled and began to run.

Earl turned on the flashlight again. In the rifle scope he could see the bright reflection in the dog's eyes. He could see its long tongue hanging out, and bright, honey-thick slaver dripping from it. Behind Rusty, the bear was methodically building speed, bounding along now, first both forefeet, then both hind feet, its close-set black pig-eyes gleaming. Rusty was running for his life now, to the only place where he would be safe. His idea of sanctuary was leading an eight-hundred-pound bear right back to Earl.

Earl steadied the rifle and held the running animal's head in the scope. He placed the crosshairs between the two rust-brown spots above the eyes and fired.

Rusty's forelegs crumpled and he collapsed, dead before his muzzle hit the ground. The bear stopped, gave a quick swat with his claws, and made sure the dog was dead.

Earl quickly switched off the flashlight and crouched, holding the scope on the big black shape. The wind was blowing from the bear's direction. Earl made no noise. As he watched the shape of the bear he tried to remember. He had fired once at Pete Hatcher, then once more. He had fired at the bushes twice: four. Then one for Rusty: five. But was he really sure he had started with ten rounds? Old hunting stories came back to him. People had shot grizzly bears ten or twelve times in places that were supposed to be fatal and they had not even slowed down. Earl kept his eye in the scope, slowly and quietly released the box magazine from the rifle, found the full magazine in his pocket, and clicked it in place.

He knew that if the bear charged, there was no way he could outrun it. He had to kill it before it reached him. He went to a prone position with his flashlight against the foregrip again, and waited.

As he waited, the third possibility, the one he had almost forgotten, occurred. The enormous dark shadow seemed to rise and grow as it lifted its snout from Rusty's carcass and turned its head toward Earl. It had finished feeding on the dog. It sniffed the air, turned, and slowly walked away.

Earl lay curled up on the top of the ridge, sheltered from the wind by a rock outcropping. It was cold enough to snow now, and he was almost sure the flakes would begin to fall before sunrise. A man could easily freeze to death up here with no sleeping bag, no tent, no tarp, no . . . He decided not to make a list. All of the gear was on Lenny's back right now, somewhere behind him on the other trail. If the dogs had been alive, he could have lain between them and used their body heat.

The slaughter of his dogs was the very last offense that Earl was going to suffer. He knew who had done that. Jane had fed the bear something to keep it in Earl's path. She had known that the bear would kill the dogs and probably Earl too. Great upwellings of rage came out of his chest with each breath like convulsions, making his head pound with anger.

About now she would be certain Earl was either being eaten or clinging to a tree limb someplace down in that valley waiting for the bear to go away. A woman like her would be too smart to try to make her way north down there in the dark, through a forest that had never been cut. She would have to travel up here where the vegetation was almost nonexistent and she could take a step with some confidence about what was going to be under her foot when she put her weight on it. She would have felt the change in the wind and the drop in the temperature too, and she would want to be out of the mountains before the snow hit.

Earl lay still and kept his eyes focused on the long expanse of bare ridge ahead. When he heard the first sounds below the heights, he held his head up a few inches and listened, trying hard to pick out the noises he had sensed were different. Their footsteps were slow coming up, as though they were picking their way with difficulty. No, it was caution. Jane was that smart. She knew that if Earl was alive it was because he had backed away from the bear, staying downwind and heading for the heights, where there was nothing for bears to eat, so he wouldn't repeat the encounter.

She seemed to satisfy herself after a minute. He heard her footsteps begin to quicken, and then the bigger, heavier steps came faster too.

Earl took his hands out of his pockets, where he had been warming them, then slowly rolled onto his belly and pushed the A.W. against his shoulder. This was the sort of shot he had waited for. They would be moving away from him with their backs fully exposed.

He listened and strained his eyes to see, but he could not quite tell where they were. He picked up the flashlight and clamped it against the foregrip with his left hand, then turned it on.

For an instant he saw them: the man on the left, the woman on the right. But the flashlight had an unforeseen effect. The woman seemed to pitch forward onto her face, and the man crouched beside her and fired. Earl saw the first bright flashes as the man fired the pistol at his flashlight.

Earl ducked low and switched off his flashlight. He heard the ricochets as the next two bullets pounded off the rocks behind him. Then, after one more shot, there was silence.

Earl thought hard. Hatcher had fired. Jane had not. It had been a reasonable shot—certainly the best they could hope to get. Why had she held her fire? Earl crawled a few feet away to a new hiding place and peered over the rocks. He could see nothing.

He steadied himself, aimed the rifle, and switched on the light. Hatcher leapt up from his crouch and ran, but Jane stayed on the ground. Hatcher dashed to the left, back toward the woods. Earl followed him in the scope, but suddenly sensed something was wrong: Jane could have sent Hatcher off to draw Earl's attention while she rushed him in the dark. Earl held his fire and quickly swept the light toward the woman. She wasn't dashing toward Earl. She was still lying there. When the light hit her, she rolled to her side and screamed. "Pete! Don't leave me here!" There was no answer, and her voice came again, lower and with less hope. "Please!"

Earl swept the light along the slope of the mountain, but Pete Hatcher was gone. Then he turned the light back on the woman. She still didn't fire, and she still didn't get up. She began to drag her body along on the rocks, using her left leg and her hands to try to slither out of the beam that pinned her there. She couldn't be faking it. She knew as well as he did that if the bright white beam could reach her, the bullet could too.

Earl's heart beat faster. He knew exactly what had happened, because for two days he had been afraid it would happen to him. She had been startled when the light went on, turned her head to look at it, taken a blind step, and twisted her ankle in the rocks.

Hatcher had certainly emptied his pistol firing at the light. That could not be faked. When he had no bullets left and Jane was not about to do any running, there wasn't much he could do but take off and hope Earl took his time killing her. No, Hatcher probably didn't even have that much calculation in him. He had panicked, as they always did at the end. Now he would run until he was exhausted and lost before he remembered there was such a person as Jane.

Earl began to walk toward her. He could probably have bagged her from this distance, even in the dim light of the flashlight and with her lying down, but doing it that way made no sense. He had only ten rounds left, and after that the beautiful precision rifle would be seventeen pounds of useless metal. He began to relish the chance to look into her eyes before he killed her. He could afford to do that. Pete Hatcher was going nowhere. He would never have gotten this far without professional help, and now he was alone with an empty pistol in mountain wilderness with a snowstorm coming. There was a good chance he didn't even have the map and compass. Jane never would have let an amateur do the navigating. Earl would search her body and find out.

When Earl was fifty feet away from her, he turned on his flashlight again. Her eyes squinted against the glare and she struggled to rise to her knees, but she didn't seem to be eager to put weight on the ankle. Earl moved closer.

"Don't bother to get up on my account, Jane," he said.

"How do you know my name?" She could not keep the fear and shock out of her voice. How could he possibly know her real name?

Earl kept walking. "I know everything about you. You've been mine for months. Since June, I think."

As he approached, he watched her. She fidgeted in the beam as though it were intense heat instead of ordinary light.

"What are you waiting for?" asked Jane.

"I was just trying to decide. One part of me says you ought to go just the way my dogs did—gutted and left to lie there for a while before you die."

He could see that Jane had to force her mouth into that unconvincing skeptical smile. "We're both professionals. You won, I lost. You can afford one bullet to the head and be on your way. Those are the stakes, not torture."

He set his rifle on the rocks, took his pistol out of his jacket pocket, and came closer. He was within fifteen feet of her now. "Is that so? What you've been putting me through—is that just business? You've been slowly sawing my balls off."

He began to pace on the rocks. The flashlight's beam whipped across her face, then bobbed up and down on her body.

She tried to make her voice sound calm, almost cheerful. "I'm sorry," she said. "It wasn't personal. I don't know you." She could see that his agitation was growing.

He stepped quickly toward her. "Well, you're going to, because I'm going to do just what he did to Linda."

She tried to decipher the words, but her mind stumbled, and gave her nothing but the terror. "Who? Who's Linda?" The grimace on his face and the abrupt, jerky movements of his body told her that whether Linda was a real person or "what he did to Linda" was just a slang way of saying something awful, what this man was planning was not a mere execution. She watched, mesmerized, as he bent his knees to set his lighted flashlight and pistol on the ground a few yards from her feet, where she could never hope to reach them.

As he stepped away from them toward her, his big silhouette caught in the dim aura of the flashlight, Jane brought Pete Hatcher's pistol around her body and fired it four times into his chest.

Earl's eyes squeezed tight with pain, then opened wide with knowledge. He knew why Hatcher had still been kneeling beside her in the dark after he had emptied the pistol, when he should have been running. It was to hand it to her, so she could reload it and lie there with her body hiding it.

He toppled forward across her legs.

The weight was smothering, confining. She used all her strength to lift his torso an inch and pull her legs out, then dropped him. It was not until she had stood up and taken a step backward that she was sure he was dead.

She took two deep breaths and heard Pete's running footsteps, coming along the ridge. He had completed his circle to come up behind the hunter, and now he was carrying the sniper rifle. He side-stepped around the body, keeping his eyes on it, horrified at the body and still frightened that the man might be alive.

She bent and picked up the hunter's flashlight and his pistol. She said, "I'm going to ask you two questions. No matter what the answers are, I'll show you how to get out of here and leave you safe. But I have to know."

He looked at her, uncomprehending. "Anything. Ask."

She knelt beside the body, clutched the belt and the shoulder and rolled him over, then shone the flashlight on the face. "Have you ever seen this man before?"

Pete Hatcher stepped close and stared down at the blood that had soaked the front of the shirt. "Uh," he grunted. Then he kept walking around to the man's feet to see the face right side up. "No," he said. "Never." He seemed to shiver once to get the sight out of his mind.

Jane moved the light to Pete Hatcher's face. "Do you know somebody named Linda?"

Pete's shoulders came up in a shrug and stayed there. He seemed to search the night sky for a moment. "A few. Linda Horn. I dated her in college. Linda Becker. She used to do my taxes, but she married a lawyer and they moved to New York. I don't know. . . . Give me a hint."

Jane didn't move the light. "We're miles from anywhere, where nobody can hear. Obviously I'm not going to tell anybody about any of this, ever. Is there a reason somebody named Linda might wish she'd never met you?"

She could see he was genuinely confused, searching his memory over and over without finding an answer. "No. I don't think so."

Jane switched off the flashlight. She looked up. The moon and stars had never come out, and the cold wind was pushing low, dark clouds in an endless stream across the sky. "You'd better go find a soft place and start digging a hole for him." She looked back down at the body and began searching the pockets.

"What are you looking for?"

"Hurry. Snow is coming."

Jane searched the man's pockets, pulled up his shirt and his pant legs to search for anything that might be strapped to his body, took off his jacket. She found a map like hers and a good compass, a magazine for the rifle with six rounds in it. There was a knife stuck in the belt at the small of his back. The coat was stuffed with jerky and crumbled biscuits. When she had taken them out, she felt a stiff spot in the lining, so she sliced it open with his knife and found a thick plastic packet full of money and identification cards.

Jane picked up her flashlight and searched the plateau carefully and methodically, beginning with the spot where she had first seen the man, then the hiding place where he had opened fire, then backtracking until she found the tracks where he had come up out of the valley, then simply walking back and forth to sweep the rocky, windblown expanse with her light.

When she returned, she found Pete waiting for her. They each took an ankle of the corpse and dragged it to the hillside. Pete had rolled some big stones aside and dug in the soft earth beneath them, filling his jacket with dirt, then dumping it out and filling it again. He had managed to dig about three feet down before he had hit bedrock. Jane helped Pete drag the body into the hole and push all of the dirt over it, then roll the big stones into place.

They walked back to the spot where they had left their packs, and Jane began to redistribute the gear. She put all of the money and most of the food in Pete's pack with his pistol and his ammunition. Then she handed him the dead man's map and compass. He said, "Why are you giving these to me?"

She turned on her flashlight and held it on the small pile of belongings the dead man had been carrying. "Besides the map and compass, he had identification, money, biscuits and jerky, bullets."

"So?"

"Think about what he didn't have. No tent, no bedroll, no pack, not even a change of socks. No car keys. There's somebody else, coming along the trail carrying the heavy stuff."

"Then let's get moving," he said. "If they're carrying all that stuff, it should be easy to keep ahead of them."

She handed him his pack. She pointed north along the ridge. "Go as straight as you can, to the north. In an hour, maybe three at the most, you'll be able to see a lake below you on the right. That's Cameron Lake. It's in Canada, and at the end of it is a big, modern road."

"But I can't leave you out here alone, waiting for some killer."

"You can't do anything else," she said. She put on her pack, stuck the killer's .45 pistol in her jacket pocket. "I don't work for you anymore. I quit. If you walk in that direction until dawn, you can be in Lethbridge by noon, and on a plane by dinner time. Head for Dallas. Rent a place like the one I told you about. If you use the papers in your pack, you'll be safe."

He held her shoulders. "Come with me," he pleaded. The next words came out as though he thought they would be a surprise. "I love you."

She bobbed up on her toes and kissed his cheek. "I love you, too. You're my brother." She slung the big sniper rifle over her shoulder, turned away, and began to walk.

Pete Hatcher stood and stared after her as long as he could, a tiny human form diminishing along the dark, rocky plateau. Twice he watched her drop onto a lower shelf where he could not see her, then reappear, climbing the next one. The third time, he did not see her again.

Lenny made his way along the trail with difficulty. It had been hard enough to walk ten miles a day carrying a hundred and fifty pounds of gear along a rough trail, but during the night a steady snow had begun to fall. The rocks and tree roots had acquired a thin glaze of ice and a covering of feathery snow that could turn an ordinary step into a broken leg. The path was getting harder to see, and in a few hours it would look just like the sparse pine forest around it. He stopped frequently to consult his compass and look for identifiable landmarks, but the snow whitened the air and hid the crests of the mountains like a fog. He was beginning to feel more and more uneasy.

At six in the morning he had calculated that if he kept to the trail, he would make it to the campsite at Goat Haunt by eight. Now it was after ten, and he was not sure he was even on the trail. The scraggly evergreen trees were beginning to look ghostly and unclear. A packing of white along one side of each trunk had made them begin to fade into the stillness of the landscape.

The fact that he had allowed himself to be put into this predicament was a source of amazement to him. He tried to follow the logic of events backward, but his mistake—his share in the blame for this disaster—could not be found in the recent past. It wasn't anything he had done. It had only been his vulnerability to people like Earl.

A month after he had gotten out of the army, he had begun his long search for something to do that didn't involve some guy who was no better than he was giving him orders. He had driven a cab for a while, but then a cop had pulled him over one night at the Burbank airport. The cop had said he didn't have the right kind of driver's license and then asked to see his cab permit, and then started writing tickets. There was the fine for the license, the fine for the business permit, and a ticket that said he couldn't even ask for permission to get into the cab business unless he spent twelve hundred bucks repairing the cab. Lenny had not argued with him, because he was afraid the cop would search the cab and find the gun. Driving a cab at night in a big city was dangerous, and he had already needed to flash the little SIG Sauer P 239 to save the cash box on two occasions, but the cop wouldn't have cared.

Lenny had used the cab to deliver pizzas for a while, until the expenses had outpaced the tips so dramatically that he'd had to sleep in it. Then he had traded the cab for an old pickup truck, a skimmer, and sixty feet of hose and become a pool man. That was how he had met Earl and Linda. At first Earl, at least, had seemed almost normal. When Lenny had come to clean and backwash the pool, Earl had generally been out working or training the dogs or something. But soon he had noticed that Linda never seemed to have anything at all to do. He would see her behind the curtains in her room, just standing there for twenty minutes, brushing her hair and watching him.

At first, the pool business had seemed to be right for Lenny. Just about every house in the San Fernando Valley had a pool behind it. If he could build up a list of forty clients, allot an hour a week for each one, and charge seventy bucks a month, he would clear twenty-eight hundred a month. With tips at Christmas and a markup on chemicals, he could stretch it to maybe thirty-five hundred. The best part was that it didn't take Lenny anything like an hour to clean a pool. It took twenty minutes, tops.

After a few months Lenny had become convinced that it was virtually impossible to work the pools; keep replacing customers who moved away, got pissed off, or never paid at all; buy the chemicals; keep the books; and still live a decent life. If he drank too much one night, he couldn't call in sick. He still had to spend the next morning squinting against the glare of the sun that flashed off the shimmering surface of some swimming pool.

He was just at the point of admitting to himself that the business was not as practical as it had looked, when Earl had begun to toss him tidbits to keep him solvent. Earl did it with the same manner that he used when he tossed a chunk of meat to his dogs: "I got something for you, if you want it." At first it had just been watching the house and feeding the dogs while Earl and Linda were away.

For a long time he had not even known what business they were in. He could tell they made money at it, but sometimes it seemed to Lenny that everybody in the world was making money except him. It was like a joke that they had all heard and he hadn't. Linda had been the one to tell him they were detectives.

Earl had asked him to watch some guy's apartment. He had sat for three days listening to people on the radio bitching about the government, told Earl when the guy came home, and collected a thousand in cash. Another time, Earl had asked him to go pick up a package in Chicago. Lenny had received another thousand for taking a plane ride. The ease of it had suggested to him the plan of transforming himself from pool man to detective. The only way to get a license was to serve an apprenticeship consisting of two thousand hours of work for a detective agency, but he was, in a manner of speaking, already working for one.

It was only after Earl had agreed to put him on a time sheet but just pay him when he needed him that he began to see that the detective business was not what it seemed any more than the pool business was. He had logged barely a thousand hours on Earl's fabricated time sheets before the day came when he called Earl to say he had found a suspect, and then watched Earl walk to the window, poke a shotgun through the screen, and blow the guy's head off. That had been five years ago.

All of his history up to then—as soldier, businessman, entrepreneur—and all of the experiences he had endured since then that he didn't especially want to enumerate at the moment had led him to this. He was loaded up and slogging through snowy mountains like a damned Sherpa, and he was becoming more and more suspicious that he might be lost. The world around him seemed inconceivably enormous—much bigger than it seemed in the city—and yet he felt hemmed in by it, because moving across it was a matter of inches and heartbeats. Going in any direction in this snowstorm was like making a colossal bet. If he was wrong, there would be no recovery. But already, when he picked out his spot on the map, he could not be positive that he was pointing to where he was, or where he wished he were.

He devoted the next mile to hating Earl. It was Earl who had done this to him, left him here laboring through the snow, probably toward his death. Earl's method had not been much different from the alternation of fear and gratification that he used on his dogs. It was mortifying. For a second he hoped that Earl was lost somewhere out in the deepest wilderness, freezing to death.

Without warning, Lenny experienced a moment of clarity. That was what Lenny's personal story was about: Earl was going to get killed—maybe not on this job, but some time—and Lenny was going to inherit Linda. He would also take possession of all of Earl's stuff, as a matter of course. There was money, the house, the detective agency, and so on. None of that was important in itself. Its only purpose was to allow the man who had Linda to keep her comfortably.

As soon as he had discerned his destiny, Lenny began to feel better. He marched along with a dreamy certainty, thinking ahead in time rather than space. As long as he kept his face pointed toward the north, he would survive. He began to develop a notion. It was too new, too vague and unformed to call a plan. He would meet Earl somewhere on this trail. He would learn that Earl had caught up with the man and woman he was chasing and bagged them. Earl would start off along the trail toward home. Maybe Lenny would let him get five or even ten miles before he pulled the P 239 out of his pocket and fired it into the back of his head. Lenny would hurry back to California and console Linda.

When he reached a hundred-yard straight stretch between parallel rows of trees, he set off more quickly. He must have been on the trail all along. With the unbroken snow ahead, the path looked like a sidewalk. He had taken ten steps before the woman separated herself from the trees. She stood absolutely still and erect, and at first he wondered whether he had imagined her.

He kept walking, and he was sure. She was gazing at him, but her eyes never moved. For a few seconds he squinted at her, and his mind insistently offered him interpretations so frightening that he forgot to stop walking. Maybe she was dead, frozen to death leaning against a tree. Maybe Earl had killed her, and this was her ghost, lingering on the spot. Maybe she had always been something not quite human, and she had lured Earl away from the trail to get lost and die and was waiting to do the same to Lenny.

For the next few seconds he calmed himself. She was not a spook. She was a woman. He could see the long black hair streaming down from a navy watch cap, and there was a strap across the front of her chest that had to be her pack. Spooks didn't need to wear packs. She must have circled back and come out on the trail behind Earl, and now Lenny had her.

She must have seen him by now, but still she didn't turn to run. Maybe she didn't know Lenny had seen her. He had seen rabbits behave the same way in the first snowfall of the year when he was a kid in Michigan. They seemed to think the snow had made them invisible, so you could walk right up and knock them on the head. He kept his eyes fixed on her and kept walking, narrowing the space between them.

At seventy yards, with less snow falling between them, he could see her more clearly. She was definitely staring straight into his eyes. Then he recognized the strap across her chest. The dark line above her shoulder that his eyes had interpreted as a branch of a tree was the barrel of Earl's new rifle.

Lenny shrugged off his heavy pack and heard it hit the ground. He pulled his pistol out of his jacket and charged her. He paid no attention to what was under his feet, just dashed toward her. He fired at her as he ran, a loud, echoing blast. He saw the snow kick up five feet from her. He fired again as she stepped to the side, and a small gash of white opened on the pine tree behind her. She stopped a pace away, beyond the snow-plastered trunk of a dead tree.

He saw her swing the rifle sling over her head and grasp the big sniper rifle in her left hand. He saw her put the fingers of her right hand between her teeth and pull the glove off to bare her trigger finger. She raised the rifle to her shoulder, brought up the bolt, slid it back, forward, down. He had to keep her pinned behind that tree, afraid to stick her head out.

Lenny fired twice more, quickly. He was so close now that he saw her push off the safety. He heard her yell, "Stop! I want to talk!" and then, "Stop or I'll shoot!" She was staring at him through the scope, but her small, female voice reminded him that he could do this. If he could make her flinch, duck for better cover—anything—he would be on her before she could recycle the bolt and take aim again.

Lenny raised his pistol again and tried to hold it on her as he ran. He fired again and again, his shots going wide, high, low, hitting bark and snow and rocks. She stood as still as the trees. He saw her finger start to tighten, and then he stopped seeing.

When Jane reached the trailhead at Logan Pass, it was night and the snow was a foot deep. The visitor center was dark, and the windows had been boarded over for the winter. She found the car that she and Pete Hatcher had left, and she could see that the keys were still in the ignition. She decided that it was best not to leave it here, where the search for lost campers it prompted might lead to shallow graves, so she drove to the next trail at Siyeh Bend, drove it into a snowbank, and walked back to Logan Pass.

She used the key she had taken off the body of the second man to open the rented four-wheel-drive Toyota and start the engine. She sat for a minute enjoying the sensation of being out of the cold wind, then drove out onto Going-to-the-Sun Road. At two in the morning, she reached the row of yellow steel stanchions set into the pavement to block the road for the winter. She had hoped the barrier would be fragile enough to crash through, but this one had been made with people like her in mind. She found her way out by backing up a quarter mile, driving through a small wooded grove and an open field, then coming out on the highway beyond the gate.

Jane drove ten miles from the park before she found a level, paved turnout on an exposed plateau, where the wind had swept away enough of the powdery snow to bare some of the blacktop. She stopped and left the motor running while she completed a cursory search of the vehicle. Under the seat was a key to a room at the Rocky Mountain Lodge in Kalispell, and in the glove compartment was a rental receipt for the Toyota.

She arrived in Kalispell before dawn, carried everything that had been left in the vehicle into the motel room, and began to study it. The men had left nothing in the room, but Jane had not expected them to. People in professions like theirs—or hers—didn't leave things where other people were likely to find them. She opened the two men's suitcases and sliced the linings enough so she could fit her hand inside to feel for hidden papers. She slashed the insoles of the shoes to see if they had been opened and glued back. She took apart their flashlights, the carrying case for the sniper rifle, then held up each piece of clothing and shone a flashlight through it to be sure nothing had been sewn into it.

When she had finished, she walked back out to the Toyota. She knew that there had to be a hiding place. After ten minutes of studying the engine compartment, removing door panels and carpets, taking out the spare tire and the gas-tank cover, she realized that she had looked at it and missed it. These killers wouldn't simply have hidden their secrets: they would have wanted them guarded.

Jane hurried inside and began to dismantle the dogs' travel cages. By the time she had pried out the false floor of the second one, she had confirmed her assumption that the licenses and credit cards the men had been carrying were counterfeit. The ones she found in the dogs' cages were older and bore scrapes and dull finishes from being carried in men's wallets.

She read the name on the cards in the first packet: Leonard Tilden. Leonard Tilden's California driver's license said he lived at an address in North Hollywood with an apartment number tacked onto it. He had only one credit card, and it carried the name of a bank that Jane recognized. The bank advertised credit cards for people with bad credit ratings who deposited enough to pay the limit. Tilden's picture on his license identified him as the man who had been following along behind to carry the gear. He wasn't a serious professional killer, he was a caddy. It was possible that she could use him to find out if the cards were real.

She stepped to the nightstand by the bed, picked up the telephone book, found the area code for the northern part of Los Angeles, and dialed Information.

A young man's voice came on. "What city, please?"

"North Hollywood."

"Go ahead."

"Do you have a number for Leonard Tilden, T-I-L-D-E-N?"

The young man was gone, and in his place was the familiar female voice of the information computer. "The . . . number . . . is—" Jane hung up.

The man she was interested in was the other one, the man who had carried the fancy sniper rifle. The little packet that contained his license, three gold credit cards, and one platinum card also contained fifty hundred-dollar bills. She dialed the Information operator again and asked for the number of Earl Bliss in Northridge. The computer came on and said, "We're sorry. That number is unlisted."

She slipped the two men's identification cards into one pocket and the money into the other. Then she repacked the suitcases, making sure that everything the men had left here was inside. As she was about to go and load all of the luggage into their vehicle, she heard a sharp rapping on the door. She dropped quietly to the floor, held her breath, and listened.

Calvin Seaver waited on the doorstep and knocked again. He had stopped in Missoula to buy a down jacket, but his feet were wet and cold after the short walk from his room to Earl's. He listened at the door but heard nothing. He thought about the size and configuration of his own room, tried to imagine not hearing a knock on the door, and found that he couldn't. He rapped on the door a third time, harder, but he had already admitted to himself that his wait was not over yet. He had thought that maybe the new vehicle he had noticed in the parking lot had meant that Earl and Linda had returned, but apparently it hadn't. He stepped back along the snow-covered walk, placing his feet in his own footprints, opened the door of his room, and went inside.

He stepped to the corner of his room, where his suitcase sat on a folding stand, opened it, and took out his other pair of shoes and a dry pair of socks. He looked at them, then put them back. The snow had not gone away. He had heard that once it began to fall in the Rockies, it often never went away until spring. A dry pair of shoes wouldn't stay that way long enough to get him to his car. He was going to have to drive down the street to one of those upscale sporting goods stores and buy himself a pair of warm waterproof boots and some wool socks. If he got going right away, there would probably be some places open.

He sat at the desk and tried to anticipate the mistakes he might be making. After a moment of thought, he quickly wrote a note on a sheet of paper from the phone pad in front of him and looked at it. "Come see me in Room 3165." He fretted for a long time about the signature. He had been very careful so far. He had not left a message on Earl's answering machine or put anything in writing that could connect him to Earl if anything went wrong. He had paid the up-front money in cash that had come in across the tables in the casino. He had found Earl here without speaking to outsiders.

He had been able to do it because of a combination of luck and curiosity. When he had met with Earl and Linda in Los Angeles, they had made the deal in the car and had eaten lunch in a restaurant without saying anything that could be overheard. When the waitress had brought the check, Seaver had pulled out a credit card to pay it. But Earl had shaken his head and said gruffly, "I'd better pay that." Seaver had hesitated, but Earl's eyes had told him that he considered this a part of their business relationship, so he had put away his wallet. He had expected Earl to pay in cash so no record of the meeting would be created, but Earl had used a credit card, added a big tip, and signed with a flourish. It had caught Seaver's attention that the name he had signed seemed to be much longer than Earl Bliss. As Earl and Linda had stood up to leave, Seaver had surreptitiously opened the leather folder, glanced at the receipt, and seen that the name was Donald R. Brookings. As soon as Seaver had arrived in Kalispell he had called Pleasure, Inc., and asked that the credit department add to today's long list of names for credit checks the name Donald R. Brookings. When he called again, he learned that Donald R. Brookings had charged meals and rooms in Lake Havasu, Denver, and various places in Montana. The last ones were for this motel in Kalispell.

Now Seaver was in a delicate situation. If Earl Bliss got a note that was not signed, he might think just about anything. He might imagine it was a note from Hatcher and the dark-haired woman, inviting him to talk about a buyout of his contract. That could not be anything but an ambush. Earl would know that, and he would respond by arranging to have something ugly happen in this room suddenly and without warning. And Earl had been in this business for a long time. There might be any number of loose ends and potential paybacks swimming around in that fevered brain of his that Seaver didn't know about. Earl might kill Seaver tonight in the dark just because he was about the size of one of Earl's loose ends. What was already happening was risky enough. Seaver was showing up and surprising Earl Bliss either just before or just after Earl had killed somebody.

Seaver tried to look at the issue of the signature from a positive point of view. Would leaving an unsigned note in the room down the walk protect Seaver from suspicion if the ones who found it were the police? No. It had his room number on it. He wrote "Seaver" clearly at the bottom of the page. Seaver looked at it for a moment, crumpled it up, and threw it into the wastebasket. What had he been thinking of? This was not the time to get impatient and do something foolish.

Seaver walked back past Earl's room and slogged off through the snow toward his car. When he got to it, he had to clean the snow off the windshield and the rear window with his bare hands. He started the engine and then sat in the car holding his cold fingers over the defroster for a minute or two until the numbness went away and he felt ready to drive. While he was at it, he would buy some gloves, too, and a hat.

Jane crouched behind the door and listened. When the knocking on the door had stopped, she had watched the man walk off and disappear into Room 3165. She had waited a few minutes, then returned to the work of packing up the men's belongings. She'd had a half-formed plan to take all of them out the back window of the room and bring the Toyota around the building and out of sight before she began loading.

But then she had been startled by the heavy crunching sound of footsteps outside the door. She crouched beside it and clutched the pistol she had taken off the second man. She stayed where she was, barely breathing, until she heard the footsteps again, this time getting fainter as the man moved off across the lot.

She recovered a little of her composure as she watched the man ineptly sweep the thick layer of new-fallen snow off his windshield and rear window onto his own feet, then drive off and have the pile of snow he had left on the roof slide down to cover his rear window again. The snow meant that the car had been here for hours, and the dress shoes and suit pants the man was wearing meant that he had probably come here from somewhere else and been caught unprepared by the early snowfall.

Jane's eyes rested on the elaborate carrying case for the fancy sniper rifle. She put on her gloves, knelt on the floor beside it, opened it, and began to take out the rifle parts that she had hidden in her pack and place them, one by one, in the precisely shaped indentations of the travel case. Magazine here, suppressor here, foregrip here, bolt here, buttstock here. There was a peculiar satisfaction to the task. It was like feeling the pieces of a puzzle slip perfectly into the spaces where they belonged.

When she had finished, she loaded all of the items she had found in the room into the Toyota. Then she carefully walked down the snowy pavement, stepping in the man's footprints to Room 3165. She used a credit card to open the door and looked around her: a single suitcase, a suit hanging in the closet. She searched the suitcase, but there was nothing in it but men's clothing with brand names that could be bought anywhere. She went to the closet and looked at the label sewn inside the coat of the suit: Callicott Haberdashery, Las Vegas. It could hardly be a coincidence that a man who bought his clothes in Las Vegas had knocked on the door of the two shooters she had met in the Montana mountains. He must be one of the team.

She went into the bathroom and looked at the items he had left on the counter: razor, toothpaste, comb, hairbrush, deodorant—just the usual stuff. She stepped back into the other room and noticed the wastebasket. She reached inside, unfolded the single piece of crumpled paper, and read it: "Come see me in Room 3165. Seaver."

She had heard that name. Seaver was one of the names that Pete had mentioned when he was talking about the casino. Seaver was the one who had been told somebody was a problem just before Pete had read an obituary. But he hadn't been some hit man. He was the chief of security for the whole company.

Jane put the crumpled paper back into the wastebasket. Seaver was the customer, the one who had hired the killers. He was the one who had been sitting in Las Vegas all this time, comfortable and immune, while they had gone out to hunt Pete Hatcher for him. They had murdered a young policeman in Denver and some unsuspecting tourist in Swan Lake, but nothing they had done could ever reflect on Seaver. He had kept his distance until now. What was he doing up here? Was he checking up on his employees? No. What could he say that would have made them try harder, and what sanctions could he apply if they failed? Probably he had considered it safer to hand them their final payment as soon as they came out of the mountains so they wouldn't knock on his door in Las Vegas. It didn't matter. He was here.

Jane hurried out to the Toyota, took one piece of luggage out of the cargo bay, went back into Seaver's room, and knelt to slide it under the bed.

Jane drove to a supermarket in Whitefish, unloaded the rest of the men's belongings into the big Dumpster behind the building, then drove back to Kalispell. It was the middle of the night when she parked the Toyota outside the gate of the rental agency. She threw the key over the fence so it hit the door of the office and dropped to the top step, where they couldn't help finding it. Then she walked to the small airport at the edge of town and paid in hundred-dollar bills for a seat on the first flight to Los Angeles.

It was not until she was sure the weather had cleared enough and her flight was boarding that she went to a pay telephone and made her call to the police. She said quickly, "There's a man in Room 3165 at the Rocky Mountain Lodge. He told me last night he killed that guy over in Swan Lake." The woman on the other end was talking over her insistently, saying, "Your name, please. Give me your name." But Jane said, "He showed me the gun," and hung up. Probably the woman had not picked up everything she was saying, but it didn't matter. They recorded all the calls, and in a minute she would be playing it back for some superior.

Seaver was in a daze. None of this felt real to him. The cell was like something out of the movies: old, with things written on the walls that had come from a succession of madmen stretching back at least a generation, thoughts that no functioning brain could contain scrawled in letters like shrieks, with every fifth word misspelled, and anatomical pictures that made him queasy.

Seaver couldn't be here, not in his waking life. When the door had burst inward onto the floor he had been lying in bed, so maybe he had been asleep and what he saw now just proved that his subconscious was getting better at constructing nightmares. The guns had all been pointed at him as the intruders sidestepped to spread out around the bed. Some of the men had looked at him with cold contempt, but the faces of others were empty, just concentrating on lining up the sights with his chest, his head, his belly, waiting to fire.

He had known enough to lie motionless on his back, both arms stretched out from his sides as though he were being crucified. He had known that speaking was a bad strategy, not only because he might say something that would come back to haunt him but also because it was in his best interest to keep the ones with the empty faces calm.

They would do the job they had been sent to do, and then they would realize they had the wrong man and leave.

Then one of them had dropped to his belly, slithered under the bed, and dragged out a long, narrow case, opened it, and nodded to the leader before he closed it. "He's got it," he said. Rough hands had rolled Seaver onto his belly, applied the handcuffs, dragged him to a car, and driven him to the local police station.

While he had been fingerprinted and photographed and searched and pushed into the cell, he had been thinking frantically, trying to catch up with time. They had to be after Earl. Somehow Earl had done this to him—read the note, slipped the gun under the bed, and left. Then Linda had called the police on the way out of town. He wanted to shout, "But why?" loudly enough so they could hear it. Was it just because he had violated the unspoken terms of their agreement and come to Montana? Or could Earl have thought that Seaver had grown so impatient that he had come here to get his advance money back?

Seaver kept reminding himself that it didn't matter. He was in trouble, and he had to concentrate on what was going on now. The police had found his false driver's license and credit cards. They had performed a trace metal detection test on his hands by swabbing them with hydroxyquinoline and holding them under ultraviolet light. He was fairly sure he was in the clear on that one, because the glowing purplish specks that indicated steel and brass were small enough to be ambiguous.

But they had also done an atomic-absorption test on his clothes. That was bad. He knew they must have found antimony, barium, and lead. The only defense he could think of was that he had worn the same clothes for legal target practice at home in Las Vegas and not gotten them cleaned. He could hardly say he hadn't fired a gun in them. He had, but it had not been a rifle. It had been the pistol he had fired into the two men in New York City. The shorter barrel, close range, and downward angle probably accounted for why so much powder residue had stuck to his clothes.

Seaver might be able to account for most of the evidence in a trial if he got the right lawyer, but the rifle was like a mathematical problem that he couldn't figure out how to approach. When the ballistics tests were completed, he knew they would show a match between a test-fired bullet and the bullet that had killed the man in Swan Lake. Otherwise there would have been no reason for Earl to plant it in his room. As Seaver reflected on it, the whole issue of the rifle was perhaps his biggest problem. The lieutenant who had first interrogated him had mentioned, almost casually, that it had come with a silencer. If it had a factory-made suppressor on it, then it had to be a military or police-only model. The prosecutor would drag out Seaver's record and reduce his years of honorable service as a policeman into a set of connections that would make it possible for him to get his hands on a rifle like that—something not a lot of people could do.

He reviewed his own record from the point of view of a prosecutor. They could drag out his expert marksman ratings. Those would be far from enough to prove he could put a round through some guy's temple at five hundred yards, but there wouldn't be any other suspect around who could have done it on the best day of his life. The prosecutors would be sure to dig up his four shootings in the line of duty. The fact that four boards of inquiry had cleared him would mean nothing. Juries looked at internal investigations as what they were: routine, obligatory checks just to be sure there was nothing so obviously wrong with a shooting that the public was sure to recognize it instantly. The shootings would establish that Seaver had dropped the hammer on other men at least four times and not been turned into a shaking wreck by the experience.

The longer Seaver thought about his prospects, the worse they seemed. He had enlisted in the service, done fifteen years as a police officer, then eleven years in a responsible, respectable executive position in an American company with a recognized name. But to the twelve Fundamentalist farmers, old women in pearl necklaces, and fish-bait salesmen who would make up a jury around here, being vice president for security at a Las Vegas casino would sound like he was a gangster.

And what the hell was Seaver doing up here in the first place? The only thing strangers did up here was nothing—go on vacation. What was there to choose from? Hunting, fishing, skiing, horses. Could he salvage the whole rifle issue by saying he'd lied about it at first because he had planned to use an illegal weapon on a hunting trip? No. If rounds from the gun matched the bullet in a murdered man's head, it wouldn't matter why he said he had brought it. He had to stick to the story that the gun wasn't his. He had no fishing tackle or skis, no clothes he could wear to ride a horse even if he had known which end of one to climb onto. He had to say he had been here on business. But what sort of business didn't involve meeting with anyone?

He pondered what he knew about the way Pleasure, Inc., was run, but his mind kept getting mired in the depressing details of the one-of-a-kind project in upstate New York that had gotten him into this mess. Then it occurred to him that this wasn't such a bad project to think about. He could be here in Montana scouting for a place that Pleasure, Inc., could develop as a resort. Companies like Pleasure, Inc., really did keep that kind of scouting a secret. If word leaked out too early, the price of land would triple overnight, competitors would start nosing around, and the local lunatics who always turned up when anybody built anything would begin to organize. A scouting trip accounted for all of his aimless driving, and for his not being dressed or equipped to do any goofing off. A scouting trip would account for his using a false name: it kept competitors and speculators from suspecting anything.

Suddenly, the angle Seaver had been sifting for appeared to him. The sleazy reputation that clung to Las Vegas casinos could be used not to hang him but to make him a victim. It was not Seaver but unscrupulous competitors who had used the rifle to whack that guy in Swan Lake. They had done it so they could plant the rifle in Seaver's room and discredit Pleasure, Inc., seriously enough so the company could never build in Montana.

Seaver knew he would have to retrace all of his movements since he had arrived in Montana to find anything that supported his story and lose anything that didn't. He had arrived in Montana when? Two days before they had arrested him. He had gone right to his hotel in Billings. Could he verify that? Yes. He had flown under a false name, but the police had found identification in the name he had used. If necessary, his lawyers could find somebody in the airline or even on the flight who remembered his face, so that proved it wasn't a lie. The hotel would have his check-in time. Then what had he done? He had gone to his room and watched the television . . . and seen the report of the killing! It was already on TV. The guy had gotten himself killed before Seaver got here! How could Seaver have forgotten the most basic step in proving a murder charge? He had an alibi!

Seaver was free. He was as good as out the door. He rehearsed his story again and again, adding tiny bits to it that he could be sure came from his memory and could be cross-checked by the police later. As he did, he discovered that the rifle had been magically transformed from a damning piece of evidence to a complete exoneration. If Seaver had not been here, he could not have fired the rifle. But the ballistics would show that somebody had fired it through that guy's head in Swan Lake. If the person who had fired it decided the best thing he could do with it was put it under Seaver's bed, then Seaver certainly was no friend of his. Presto! No murder charge, no conspiracy to commit murder, no accessory to murder, not even a felony charge for possessing a silencer.

It wasn't until many hours later, after Seaver had told the police the whole story and walked out of the police station, that his euphoria began to wane. He had only gotten himself out of one small scrape. He had been sent out by the three partners to handle a problem, and he had not handled it yet. He had gotten himself arrested instead. While he had been in jail, it was possible that things might even have gotten worse. There had been photographers on the jailhouse lawn, and men with video cameras that had the call letters of television stations on them.

If Earl Bliss had seen those reports, he would also see the reports that Seaver was free. He might decide that failing to frame Seaver meant he had to kill him. If Pete Hatcher was alive, even he could figure out that the reason Seaver was in Montana was to find him. It might be enough to drive him into the arms of the F.B.I. And if the Italians in New York had seen the reports, they might start asking questions too. He might have to think of a whole new story just for them. He was going to have to check with Foley, Buckley, and Salateri as soon as possible to find out where he stood.

As soon as he was out of Kalispell and down the road to Missoula, he checked into another hotel and walked down the street to a convenience store where there was a pay telephone. He called the private number of the partners' offices in the Pleasure Island casino, but nobody answered. He tried calling their houses but got nothing except the voices of servants who told him politely they were writing down his name. Then he tried the operator at the hotel.

"This is Calvin Seaver," he said. "I need to have you reach Mr. Foley, Mr. Salateri, or Mr. Buckley for me. Any one of them."

"I'm sorry, sir. The resort owners can only be reached through their assistants during normal business hours."

"I know better than that. They can be reached any time of any day of the year. If you don't know me, call up the emergency notification list. I'm at the top."

"Your name, sir?"

"I just told you. Calvin Seaver."

"I'm sorry, sir. I've been instructed to inform any callers that there is no Calvin Seaver connected with the hotel. All inquiries regarding a Calvin Seaver are to be immediately referred to Mr. Bennis in hotel security."

"So refer me. Get him on the line."

There was a silence, and Seaver could tell from the duration that the operator was talking to Bennis's office. No, damn it, that was Seaver's office. Bennis was a flunky, a man Seaver had picked out of the ranks because of his canine loyalty and his ability to keep his mouth shut.

"Bennis," said the voice.

"This is Seaver. I'm at a pay phone, so there's no tap at this end. You might want to check your bug detector."

"I already did," said Bennis. "It's clear."

"I'm in Missoula, Montana. The police got convinced they had the wrong man and let me out. I wanted the big guys to know. I'm coming home."

"Cal—" There was an unpleasant sound to Bennis's voice that Seaver had not noticed before, almost a whine.

"What?"

"You've been good to me, so I'm paying off the favor. Don't come here."

Seaver felt as though he'd had the wind knocked out of him. "What does that mean?"

"They hired some people."

"They were going to kill me in jail? Without even hearing what happened or giving me a chance to fix it?"

"Look, I don't know any more."

Seaver's field of vision had a red aura at the edges, and his heart beat so hard he could feel it. "They didn't hire them. They don't know who to hire, and they wouldn't let themselves get within a mile of anybody like that. You hired them. They called you into the office and told me I was a problem, a serious liability. Did you even tell them I wasn't? That I would never talk?"

Bennis's voice was calm. He sounded as though he were on the other side of a huge chasm, watching a disaster that had nothing to do with him. "You know them, Cal. They make a decision, and that's their decision. You don't talk them out of something like that."

"You're right," said Seaver. "I'm glad you told me. And you know what else? I'm glad you're the one they picked to replace me. You deserve it."

Seaver hung up and took two steps back toward his hotel. He was tired, and had to sleep. No, there was no way he could go back up there and sit around all night. He had told Bennis he was in Missoula. He had to get on a plane.

He looked at his watch. It was three in the morning. What was the date? September 16—no, 17. It was a date that he would always remember. As he walked toward the hotel, he shook his head, and was surprised that the violent movement traveled to his shoulders and spine. He probably looked like an old dog shaking water off his back.

Seaver gave a quiet snort of a laugh at the thought. That was about right. For eleven years, since the day he had gone to work for Pleasure, Inc., he had been moving a third of his salary into accounts in the Caribbean under the name Luther Olmstead. How could men as smart as Buckley, Salateri, and Foley not have guessed that? When they had met him, he had just finished fifteen years as a cop, where there had been no opportunity to put away a dime. Then he had landed a job that paid over two hundred thousand a year with virtually no expenses. The taxes alone would have been more than his old salary.

He would stop in Los Angeles just long enough to pick up traveling money and his passport. That was the main thing—getting out. After that, he would consider what else he wanted to do. The three big guys probably thought that, given his history, his impulse would be to call the police. They would be busy in a few hours getting rid of evidence. But his experience as a policeman had not given him an interest in calling the police. And that was not his only option. He might not know the names of the old men in New York that the three partners were afraid of, but he did know the names of some similar men in Los Angeles, and he just might decide to give them a call. They would appreciate the opportunity to give their friends in New York a timely warning. He had always heard that the Mafia worked on reciprocity and favors, and this was a time of his life when it would not hurt to have them think of him with gratitude.

34

Jane found Earl Bliss's address in the early afternoon. She drove past it slowly, looking for signs of danger, then continued up the road to study the next few houses. Out here on the northern rim of the San Fernando Valley, the stretches of pavement could hardly be called neighborhoods, because the houses were set at the ends of long winding gravel driveways on weedy parcels that seemed to her to be five acres or more. Some of the places consisted of old, rundown frame houses surrounded by the bodies of half-assembled cars, while others were like Earl Bliss's, little fenced-in compounds with sprawling suburban houses in the middle. Two miles down the road she turned around and came past the house in the opposite direction. The house remained as she had first seen it: no curtains had moved, no cars had suddenly appeared in the driveway.

She had no evidence of how many people had been engaged in the hunt for Pete Hatcher. Committing murder for money was not a business that lent itself to large teams. But she did know that at least one person was not accounted for: the one who had trapped Hatcher in Denver had been a woman.

Jane did not return until after midnight. She turned off the lights of her rented car, pulled far enough up the drive to keep a passing cop from getting curious, and walked toward the house. The chain-link fence was topped with barbed wire, but there were no insulators for electricity, so she pried off ten feet of it with the tire iron from her rented car, climbed it, and dropped to the lawn.

There was a kennel in the back yard with a pen and a long exercise run, but she knew that the dogs were far past barking, so she skirted close to it and studied the house. It was a five- or six-bedroom one-story ranch structure coated with white stucco. She walked around it, looking for motion sensors, automatic lights, indications of the sort of alarm system it had. There were no security company's signs anywhere on the property, no stickers on any of the windows. Most of the windows were dark, but she could see two with dim lights glowing behind them. She cautiously approached the first and peered inside. Through the curtain, she could just see a lamp on a desk. She moved to the other side of the window and looked at the place where the cord led to the electrical outlet. She could see the little plastic box and the circular dial. The light was on a timer.

She walked to the other lighted window and saw another lamp on a timer. She considered. The timers meant that nobody was home. There were no signs of an alarm system. It made sense that a professional killer would not want to have his house wired with devices whose sole purpose was to summon the police. And most of the time, the dogs would have warned him long before any intruder came close enough to enter the building where he slept.

She decided to take the chance. Earl and the second man were dead, but there was a strong likelihood that they had left some notes, some information about Pete Hatcher that could give a new set of killers a start. And there was still the woman who had trapped Pete in Denver. The woman might not be the sort who would come after Pete alone, but unless Jane found out who she was, there would be no way to predict anything about her.

Jane walked to the kitchen door, swung her tire iron to shatter the upper pane of glass, reached inside, unlocked the door, and entered. There was no noise, and there was no electrical contact in the frame that could have set off a silent alarm when the door opened.

She felt for the light switch and turned it on. The kitchen was modern and very expensive—a professional-size Wolf stove, Sub-Zero refrigerator, vast surfaces of green marble, the dull gleam of stainless steel—but when she looked in the drawers and cupboards there were few containers or implements to indicate that much cooking went on here.

She walked into the living room. There was electronic equipment, all small modular boxes piled up into towers and banks along one wall. Some of it she recognized—television monitors, VCRs, speakers, compact disc players, cable TV descrambler, tape recorders of various kinds—but among them were other boxes and monitors that seemed to belong to computers. To her it appeared that the man who lived here simply bought things. It occurred to her that each item in this house probably represented some person's life. People had been changed into leather couches and marble counters and electronic gadgets.

She moved up the hallway and found Earl's bedroom. Her nostrils picked up the faint scent she remembered smelling when his body had fallen on her, a mixture of sweat and gun oil and some kind of hair tonic. She waited for the wave of nausea it induced to pass, then began her search by the telephone, but she found no paper in the room for writing down numbers or messages.

She opened the sliding door beside her and found a custom-built closet with drawers and racks and hanging clothes. It was the hat rack that caught her eye first. There were a dozen baseball caps with the logos of teams and manufacturers of trucks and farm machinery, but others that said FBI, POLICE, or SWAT TEAM. In a bottom drawer she found two black ski masks with eye and mouth holes and a wide selection of gloves. He didn't wear those in southern California to keep warm.

She stepped to the rack of hanging clothes and confirmed the impression that had been building in her mind. There were clothes of all kinds—conservative suits and moth-eaten wool hunting shirts, a tuxedo beside an army field jacket that was in a plastic bag because it was covered with dirt. Earl had uniforms. There were the midnight-blue shirt and pants of the Los Angeles Police Department beside the hot-weather version with short sleeves, a khaki Highway Patrol uniform, a blue windbreaker with the word POLICE in bold reflective letters like the ones plainclothes cops slipped on for raids. There were work clothes for the Department of Water and Power, Southern California Gas, Pacific Bell. Earl had been able to impersonate virtually anyone.

She left the bedroom and went up the hall to see what Earl had kept in the other rooms. She reached the door on the end, turned on the light, and drew in a breath.

It was a woman's bedroom. Earl had not lived in the house alone. It was inconceivable that a man like Earl would have one woman who lived in a house with his collection of police uniforms but asked no questions and a second who went out with him to kill people. This was almost certainly the woman who had ambushed Pete Hatcher in Denver. Jane opened the nearest closet. The clothes on the hangers were like everything else in the house: they bore very expensive labels without being especially appealing or tasteful choices, and all of them seemed too recent. There was such a profusion of new clothes that Jane wondered how anybody could spend so much time shopping. She tried to focus her mind on the immediate need to use her time efficiently. If the woman lived here, then there was a strong possibility that she could show up without warning. She had been in Denver, but Jane had seen no sign of a woman in Montana.

Jane spent ten minutes searching for framed photographs, albums, anything that might tell her what the woman looked like, but she found nothing. She looked more closely at the clothes in the hope that they would help her form an image of the woman's size and shape, but it was a pointless exercise. It seemed to Jane that every woman she had seen in California was a size eight, between five feet six and five feet eight.

She kept searching. The woman was vain and a bit self-indulgent. The room beside this one was a dressing room with a huge lighted mirror. The cosmetics, creams, perfumes, and oils in tiny jars and bottles were all brands so expensive that most women would not have recognized them.

She went into the bathroom connected with the bedroom and found it to be the same. There was a glass shower with marble walls that would have held five people and complicated fixtures for spraying water at different intensities and different angles. There was a sunken bathtub with Jacuzzi jets, a steam machine for facials, and here, too, the same profusion of unguents and lotions and oils, enough to last several lifetimes.

The door on the far side of the bathroom opened into the exercise room. There was a stationary bike, a treadmill, a Nautilus machine, weights, padded benches, step-stairs, pulley contraptions. The whole inner wall was one immense mirror with a ballet barre. Jane tried to understand this woman. The size of her clothes indicated that she took care of herself, but the equipment in this room was not of the quality or variety that most people put in their homes. It was all the industrial-grade gear that gyms bought. She lifted the bar of the exer-

cise machine. If the setting was for the woman, then she was a specimen, Jane thought. Maybe Earl had used the equipment too. Through
the French door on the outer wall, Jane could see a thin strip of
moonlight on water—a pool, too, right at the woman's doorstep. But
it wasn't the pretty kind, or the sort where people had fun swimming
together. It was a single-lane lap pool. It reminded Jane of the dogs'
exercise run by the kennel.

Jane moved back into the woman's bedroom. The whole house
made her uncomfortable, vaguely afraid. She was fascinated and re-
pelled by the mundane details, the fixtures of the man and woman's
daily life here. She could not get herself to set aside the thought that
each extravagance looked like a single spree, as though one day they
must have come home from killing someone and used the money to
buy a room full of exercise equipment. Another day they would come
home and hire a contractor to remodel the woman's bedroom. She
wondered if they thought about the people afterward: this room was
cutting John Smith's throat, and this one was shooting Bob and Betty
Johnson through their heads in their sleep.

She looked around her at the place where the woman slept. The
woman dressed as other women did, and liked the amenities that
other women liked, but there was too much of everything, and it all
seemed a little bit off. It seemed to Jane that it was like the room of a
man impersonating a woman: transvestites never seemed to wear an
oversized sweatshirt and blue jeans. She remembered the weights in
the exercise room: maybe she had stumbled on the truth. She took a
pair of slacks out of the closet and measured the ratio of the hips to
the waist. No, the clothes would not have fit on a body that had not
been born female.

But everything in the house was wrong. The kitchen was not a
place where anything was cooked. It was a hoard of appliances and
glossy surfaces. The living room looked as though no one ever sat in
it. The furniture was all too well matched to have been bought any
way but at once, and it was spatially arranged to be neither attractive
nor comfortable, just placed so that there would be room for a lot of
it. She looked at the bed. It was king-sized, too big for one person, but
she could not imagine the people who had lived here doing anything
so human and comprehensible as sleeping on it together.

Jane opened the second closet and found the boxes of wigs. The
woman had good ones, all genuine human hair. There were short
ones, falls to take on and off, curly ones and straight ones. Jane took
a quick inventory. The woman had light brown, dark brown, red,
black, auburn, even gray. The only kind missing was blond.

Jane pushed aside some clothes and saw the door of a gun cabinet. It was built like a safe, with a five-digit combination lock. There was no hope of looking inside, but Jane decided that she had seen enough of Earl's arsenal already: what she wanted would be on paper. But the gun cabinet struck her as part of the impersonation. The room was so aggressively, insistently feminine, so exclusively the domain of a woman, that it was a perfect place for a cache of weapons.

She still had rooms to account for. She closed the closet and left the bedroom, then walked down the hall into an office. It had two desks, two telephones, two computers. There were no photographs here, either.

The filing cabinets were full of records of payments—some made by Earl Bliss, some made by Northridge Detectives—but no records of receipts, no notations relating to income, no lists of clients. Whatever useful information existed, it was probably in the computers. She searched the desk drawers. At first she found only office supplies, but the deep one on the right side of the second desk was full of electronic gear. There was a box of tiny short-range audio transmitters for hiding inside household objects, more powerful ones with prongs for plugging into wall sockets, even one that had been disguised as a night-light for a child's room. There were receivers and long-range microphones. She closed the drawer.

The place had once been a bedroom, so there was a closet here, too. She opened it, and the sight made her shiver. There was a handyman's pegboard. On it hung handcuffs like the police used, thumbcuffs with jagged inner edges that could do terrible damage if a prisoner struggled, a two-foot coil of piano wire with handles on both ends, a couple of long spikes like skewers. She lifted a small box from the shelf and took off the top. There were hypodermic needles and bottles. She read the labels and she could see they had been stolen from a hospital: anectine for stopping the heart, insulin for inducing shock, heroin for an overdose the L.A. coroner would find familiar and explicable. She put the box back and found the little press.

She looked at it without understanding until she opened the box beside it. Inside was a stack of blank gold plastic cards, all bearing the symbols of Visa and MasterCard. The machine was a die for pressing names and numbers into fake credit cards. Her breath caught in her throat. Maybe some of the blanks had the woman's picture on them. She shuffled through them eagerly, but found no picture. Her eyes passed across the little press. There was still type clamped in the die. She read it backward: Susan Preston Haynes. Of course it was a false name, or the woman wouldn't have needed to make the credit card at home. Knowing a false name was not going to get Jane any closer to the woman.

She looked around her at the room. The malevolence of the house was strongest here. The perverse eagerness to hurt, to render human beings into money made her sick. She glanced at the computers. Without codes and passwords, they were locked as tightly as the gun cabinet.

Jane sat at the nearest desk and tried to defeat the sick, nervous feeling in her stomach. Her mind had been calmly, logically working its way toward the conclusion that she had to wait as long as it took for this woman to come in the door, and then kill her. It was simple, practical, rational, and utterly wrong. She had just shot two men. But there was an immense difference between shooting back at a killer and crouching in this horrible place with the lights out, waiting for the door to open so she could bring a knife across a person's throat. She was not going to do it.

She looked around her, and her eyes rested on a small sheet of paper that said Federal Express. It was a receipt, the carbon copy of the mailing label on an overnight package. The date on it was two weeks ago. She picked it up and looked at it closely. The address box said, "Susan Haynes, Meadowgreen Suites, Orchard Park, New York 14127." Orchard Park was seven or eight miles from Buffalo, no more than fifteen from Amherst.

Jane found herself standing. She had to stop herself from dashing outside and running for the car. She looked around her at the walls that enclosed her. This house seemed as much of a threat as though it were alive. The computers were probably full of information about Hatcher and about Jane, but there were undoubtedly backup disks hidden somewhere else in the building. The building was full of hiding places, locks, and secrets that she could never hope to break. There were probably photographs of Hatcher, and maybe of her too. There might even be electronic equipment that was running right now, taking videotapes of Jane's visit.

She stepped to the kitchen, where she remembered seeing books of matches with the names of restaurants on them. Then she went outside, sliced off five feet of the garden hose attached to the house, went into the garage and syphoned gasoline out of the tank of the Mercedes into a bucket.

Jane poured the gasoline liberally around the office and on the computers, in the two bedrooms, in the closets. She filled the bucket again, then poured gasoline along the inner walls of the living room, the exercise room, the bathrooms. She poured another bucketful along the baseboards and carpets at the outer walls of each room.

She dribbled a trail of gasoline down the hallway, across the living room rug, and through the kitchen to the back door. She poured gasoline on the kennel and along the walls of the garage. Finally, she poured a stream of gasoline from the kitchen steps to the garage, to the kennel.

Jane climbed back over the chain-link fence, lit a match, and tossed it on the back lawn. The vapor ignited with a *poof!* and a flash before the match could land, and bright yellow and blue flames raced in three directions. Jane hurried to her car. She saw the bright flare-up when the fire reached the kitchen floor, the flames licking up the kitchen walls.

As she started her car and backed out of the driveway, she saw the quick, purifying flames lighting up one window after another. When she reached the first turn in the road, she glanced in the rearview mirror and saw flames billowing out of the front windows, illuminating the clouds of black smoke that rose into the night sky.

35

J ane stepped into the airline terminal, stopped near the door, and scanned the monitors for the schedule of departures. There seemed to be no flight for hours that stopped in Buffalo, so she chose a nonstop flight to New York City that was leaving in ten minutes. She bought a ticket under the name Julie Sternheim and ran for the gate.

As soon as the plane was in the air and the seatbelt sign above her head went out, she used the Marie Spellagio credit card to activate the telephone built into the seat in front of her and dialed the number of the house in Amherst. She heard the phone ring ten times, and she let it ring five more before she gave up. She glanced at her watch. It was already four A.M. here, so it would be seven in Buffalo. By now, Carey had probably scrubbed and entered the operating room.

If the woman had been in Buffalo for two weeks, she must have gone there straight from Denver—been sent there from Denver. Earl Bliss had been the designated shooter, and he seemed to have had all the money, so probably he had been the one who made the decisions. He must have been smart enough to know that from the moment Pete Hatcher had seen the woman's face, she had become a liability. So he had sent her to western New York.

As Jane followed the path of logic, she felt her stomach tightening. The woman had not simply been excused from the hunt and sent home: she lived in Los Angeles. She had not been bundled off into hiding in a place that just happened to be near Jane's hometown. They had sent her something there by overnight mail. People in hiding didn't need anything urgently enough to require that it be sent in a way that left a record.

Jane tried to invent coincidences that would confute her logic. Had she given Pete any false identities that could have tied him to the western part of New York State? That was impossible. She never sent chasers across her own trail. Did Pete have any close friends or relatives there? When she had asked him about friends and relatives, there had been none east of Nebraska.

The address in Orchard Park might mean something. Orchard Park wasn't a big, bustling city where people came and went by the thousand without attracting attention. It was a suburb, a small upper-middle-class bedroom community. It wasn't a place to remain anonymous. It was a place to establish an identity.

This woman could not have been sent to spot Pete Hatcher. She was the only member of the team whose face he had seen. There was only one reason Jane knew of for this woman to be in western New York. That night on the mountaintop, when Earl had been deciding how to kill her, he had called her Jane. The woman must have known much more.

Jane began to sweat. The woman had been there for two weeks. She'd had enough time to find out—what? Where Jane lived, certainly. And that meant she knew who Jane was married to. Jane snatched up the telephone again and inserted her credit card. When she had punched in the area code, she stopped.

Every time Jane had taken Hatcher in a different direction, Earl had turned up with the rifle. Jane's throat was dry, and her head was throbbing. She had made some terrible mistakes. The woman had probably found her address in a day, and on the next day had broken into the house and bugged the telephones. Jane had obligingly called every few days, and that had somehow given her a location. Now this woman was waiting in Buffalo, probably watching Carey, and Jane could not even call to warn him, because the woman would be listening.

Jane forced herself to be calm and tried to think of another way. She could call Carey's office. No, that was foolish. If the woman had been listening for a call from Jane, she could not have assumed it would come to the house. The woman would also have tapped the lines in Carey's office.

Carey was at the hospital right now. There were hundreds of phone lines at the hospital. Tapping into all of them would be a job for a team of electrical engineers, not one person who knew how to plant a bug. Jane searched for a way to use the complexity of the place. Carey would be in surgery for the next couple of hours, where an outside telephone call could not reach him. After that, he would be all over the building, walking the halls to examine and discharge patients, read charts and scribble in files, look at X rays and test results. There was no way to predict precisely where he would be. If the operator didn't have a pretty clear fix on him, what would she do? She would page him.

Jane could not let that happen. The person this woman wanted to find was Jane. The woman could not assume that Jane would not show up in person instead of calling. The woman could monitor her telephone taps with a tape recorder, but she would have to watch Carey with her own eyes.

Suppose Jane didn't call Carey directly. She could call the nurses' station in the recovery room. Carey would certainly show up there immediately after surgery, and then again later to clear the patient to be transported to his own room upstairs. But what could Jane say to a nurse? She could hardly ask some stranger to tell Dr. McKinnon he might be in mortal danger because his wife hid fugitives.

For the moment, Carey was as safe as he could be. Nobody could get into an operating room. The big metal doors wouldn't open unless someone inside hit a switch on the wall. After that, he would be surrounded by people, going about his business as he had been doing for two weeks while this woman had been watching him.

The woman had not come to Buffalo to harm Carey McKinnon. There was no extra pay for that. She had come to watch him and use him to find out where Jane was. Carey was only valuable to this woman if he was alive and unsuspecting. He would be safe until . . . when? The moment when the woman saw Jane.

She sat strapped in her seat, rigid. Maybe she should not be going home. Maybe the best favor she could do for Carey McKinnon was to stay as far away from him as possible. If she stayed away for long enough, the woman would have to give up and go away. But then Jane realized that she was wrong. If this woman had been keeping Carey in sight for two weeks, then the woman could not be sure that Carey had never caught a glimpse of her, never seen her face. If the woman got tired of waiting, she would not just go away. Before she did, she would put a bullet in Carey's head.

Linda stared at the red zero on her answering machine. If Earl had done it and gotten back to civilization by now, he should have left a message for her. But maybe he had called home. There was no question that he would call as soon as he could reach a telephone. He would be thinking about what she might be doing to keep Carey McKinnon occupied, and he would want that to end as soon as possible.

She dialed the number of her house. The telephone rang once, twice, and then there was an unfamiliar high-pitched tone. A recorded voice that sounded like a middle-aged woman came on and stated authoritatively, "The number you have reached is not in service. If you think you have reached this number in error, please hang up and dial again." Linda took her advice.

After the third try, Linda began to feel panicky and worried. Was it possible that in all this traveling she had forgotten to pay a phone bill? Her mind searched for a way to reassure itself, but it came back with nothing. She weighed the danger of calling the long-distance operator in Los Angeles and explaining the problem. She could think of no reason not to, so she did. After a few seconds she was connected with the billing department. The woman on the other end consulted a computer and said, "You're right. I'm seeing it as out of service. It's not a billing problem. I've already checked your records, and you're up to date on your payments. But the phone is out of service."

"Doesn't whatever you're looking at say why?" asked Linda. "I'm expecting a very important call, and if they can't get through I'm going to be a very unhappy customer."

"I'm sorry," said the woman. "They don't tell us what the problem is. It could be a lot of things—a malfunction in the equipment in your home, for instance. Or with the line that goes to your house. If a tree on your property fell and pulled it down, I would have no way of knowing from here."

"Well, I certainly have no way of knowing from here, do I?" asked Linda.

"I understand that," said the woman.

"Can't you send somebody to check?"

"Is there anyone there now to let the repair technician onto the premises?" Linda could tell it was an official question, the sort that brought some rule into play.

"No."

"Then we wouldn't be able to send anyone, no."

Linda closed her eyes and let her voice carry some of the frustration and defeat that she was feeling. "If you were me, what would you do about this?"

Now that the woman had her victory, she issued a reprisal. "When you go out of town it's a good idea to leave a key with a friend or relative. You might call a neighbor and ask her to look across the street to see if there's anything obviously the matter."

The defeat was complete. "Yes, thanks," she said. "Maybe I'll try that. Good-bye." She hung up. Something was very wrong. She goaded her imagination to think of a way to find out what it was from the other end of the continent. She couldn't call the police and have them check the house, because what they might find would send her and Earl to jail. She and Earl had always been so careful to remain unapproachable and anonymous that she not only had no acquaintances among the people who lived nearby, but she could not now recall any of their names.

She used her laptop computer to call up the Los Angeles telephone directory Northwest section and scanned it. Finally she called the number of a florist a half mile from her house, ordered a dozen roses to be delivered to Linda Thompson from Earl Bliss, and charged it to the Northridge Detectives credit card number she retrieved from the memory of her computer. She made it sound like an afterthought when she asked to talk to the delivery driver. She heard the man turn his head away from the receiver and shout, "Enrique! Phone!"

She explained to Enrique, "These flowers are supposed to be a surprise, so it has to be done in a certain way. It's a house with a high gate. Drive up to the gate. Ring the bell. If anyone is home, give them the flowers. If nobody is home, there's a great big mailbox right by the gate. Put the flowers inside, so she finds them when she looks for her mail. Can you do that?"

"Sure," said Enrique. "Anything else?"

"Yes," said Linda. "When will you be back from your deliveries?"

"About an hour from now."

"Fine. I'll call you, because I need to know where you put the flowers. Okay?"

"Okay."

A little over an hour later, Linda called again and asked for Enrique. If a line was down, he could hardly have avoided noticing it. If—God forbid—there was a bigger problem, he would have seen something she could interpret. If the time for killing Pete Hatcher had run out and the one waiting in the house was Seaver, or if the house was under police surveillance, somebody would have appeared at the gate to talk to the delivery man. She waited for a minute and a half before Enrique picked up the phone and said, "I'm sorry, but I couldn't deliver the flowers. The boss says he'll cancel the order and credit your card for the money."

"What do you mean, you couldn't deliver them?"

"There's nothing there. The lady's house burned down. You want to find where she's living now, we'll be happy to deliver them there." He paused. "Lady?"

Linda stared at the wall of her apartment, but no words came to her, because her mind was moving too quickly. "No thanks," she said at last. "Just cancel the order."

She tested each of the possibilities. Had it been a simple accident—a short-circuit or something? But why would it happen now? The odds against that were astronomical, with nobody in the house to leave anything turned on. Maybe Earl had failed again, and decided it was time to burn the house with two bodies in it that matched his description and hers. No. That had not been a plan, it had just been talk. Earl never panicked. More likely, he should have done it but hadn't, and this was Seaver sending them a message.

What would Earl want her to do now? The answer came to her slowly, in simple, incontestable statements. Earl never gave up. If the house had simply burned by itself, she and Earl would need the money for killing Pete Hatcher more than ever. If Seaver had burned the house, then Earl would want to kill Pete Hatcher so he could add the cost of rebuilding to the fee and make Seaver pay for it. No matter what had happened in California, when Earl came for her, he would want to see some evidence that Linda had been doing what he had told her to do in New York.

She stood up and began to pack her belongings. When she had finished, she locked her suitcase in the trunk of her car and came back to put the items she would need into her purse. She walked to the door and looked back before she turned off the light. The only thing left in the room that she had brought with her was the telephone answering machine. With the house gone, it could be Earl's last way to reach her.

36

Jane was already standing when the hatch of the plane opened.
She lockstepped up the aisle with the others, then broke free and hurried along the accordion tunnel and into Kennedy Airport. She rushed along the concourse, took the escalator two steps at a time, stepped to the ticket counter, and found that there was not a flight to Buffalo until 3:30. She bought the ticket, then walked to the bank of telephones along the opposite wall.

Jane called the toll-free reservation number of every airline that flew from Kennedy, then worked her way through the ones that left from La Guardia and Newark. Only two airlines had flights that were scheduled to take off earlier than hers, and both were already full. Jane was not surprised. Buffalo was not the sort of place people visited on impulse, so the flights tended to be booked in advance. She would have to wait three hours—no, only two hours, now.

She used the rest of her time to work the airport shops. She found some leather bomber jackets and selected one a size too big for her. It had big map pockets that started at the belly and ran up her ribs. The jacket would pass as cute if a woman wore it, but the look was decidedly male. The big shoulders and the roomy fit would disguise her shape; the thick, stiff leather would provide a distinct advantage against a knife. Anything metallic she put in the map pockets would serve as body armor. She found a smaller shop that sold monogrammed clothes, picked out a black wool baseball cap, and declined to have it monogrammed. She found a pair of soft black leather gloves. It was often a woman's hands that gave her away at a distance. She decided the blue jeans she was wearing were sufficiently nondescript, as were the boots she had worn in the mountains.

The flight to Buffalo took less than an hour, but to Jane it was endless. Carey was out of surgery now, and probably in his office down the street from the hospital. If she wanted to warn him, this was the time. She could avoid his telephones entirely, by calling Jake Reinert. There was absolutely no chance that the woman had tapped Jake's telephone. She could speak freely to Jake and ask him to go to Carey's office and tell him in person. The problem was that she still was not sure what to tell Carey to do.

The woman was a professional, so she would be watching for particular signs, and she would know what she would do if she saw them. What would she do if Carey received a visitor, then abruptly closed his office and left for the day? She would follow him. The answer always seemed to come out the same.

The plane began its descent just west of Rochester, and in ten minutes it was gliding up the runway at Buffalo International. Jane hurried past the car rental desks and went outside to flag a cab. The woman had been here for two weeks, and it was likely that she had rented a car at the airport. If she had, then she would have come out and seen the three or four fleets of nearly identical cars lined up behind the terminal. When she saw one of those four models in the right color, it was possible she would know the person in it had just come from the airport, and begin to wonder.

Jane had the taxi driver take her to an agency close to the center of the city, where she rented a Dodge minivan with tinted side and rear windows. If she was going to use it to watch for the woman, then she had to be able to look without having her head visible in the driver's seat.

Jane drove up the street toward Carey's office, her gloved hands clutching the wheel, the collar of her new jacket up, her hair tucked under her hat and a pair of sunglasses over her eyes. She circled the block, trying to take in all of the sights at once. There was nothing out of place. The cars behind the building belonged to Carey's receptionist and three nurses. As she came up the next street, she noticed that the lights were off in the examining rooms and in the little office where Carey talked to patients. He was gone.

Jane glanced at her watch. It was five forty-five, and Carey had undoubtedly gone back to the hospital. As she drove past the big white building she admitted to herself that it was getting dark. She would have to take off the sunglasses before she went inside. She had hoped not to need to go inside at all. She didn't know most of the people who worked in the hospital, so the woman would have a fair chance of picking Jane out of the crowd before Jane noticed her. The few people Jane did know were all old buddies of Carey's. If she walked in and one of them called, "Jane!" ugly things could start to happen.

Jane parked her van. She was on the same side of the street as the hospital's front entrance, so she wouldn't have to hustle Carey across the open, empty pavement, but the distance was greater than she would have liked. She glanced at her watch again and tried to steady her nerves. This was just like taking a runner out of the world. She had done this before. It should be easy. The doctors always went in and out of the rear entrance, where their reserved parking spaces were. If the woman was watching the car, she would be in the back. Jane would find Carey, push him into an elevator, and lead him to the front door. She would do it about ten minutes before he usually left, get him into the van, and whisk him off to a place where he would be safe.

Jane walked to the doors with a group who seemed to be relatives of someone who'd had a baby. There were a white-haired couple wearing the benevolent grandparent expression and a young dark-haired man who carried a bouquet of roses in a florist's vase so that water dripped on his coat. He seemed to be looking through objects rather than at them, while his mind made a rare visit to the realm of philosophy.

Jane judged that they would make a good camouflage. She opened the door for the parents before the man could transfer the roses to his other hand. He grinned apologetically and she grinned back at him in understanding. She said softly, "Are you a new daddy?" and he nodded proudly. "Congratulations," she said. She pushed the roses up. "Carry them this way, so the water doesn't leak out."

The little family group kept Jane surrounded all the way to the elevator, while Jane scanned the lobby for anyone who could possibly be the woman—blond hair, five foot six to five foot eight, size eight. But the lobby was only beginning to fill up with the early evening visitors now, and none of the women were the right age or size. She slipped away from the family and into the stairwell.

Jane hurried up the steps to the second floor, then the third. Carey's recovering patients were always on the third floor or the fourth. She stepped out of the stairwell and walked purposefully along the third-floor corridor. She turned the corner and stared down the next hallway at the nurses' station to be sure Carey wasn't there, reading charts or talking to someone. She went back the way she had come, then turned the other three corners, looking in each open door until she could see the nurses' station from the other side. She caught a glimpse of Nancy Prelsky hurrying across the hallway and into a patient's room. Jane waited a few seconds to be sure Nancy was occupied in there, then stepped across the hallway and into the other stairwell.

Jane repeated her tour on the fourth floor, but she saw no sign of Carey. There were three orderlies pushing head-high carts loaded with trays full of covered plates along the corridor, then stopping at each room to make a delivery. She looked at her watch: six twenty. Carey wouldn't come in to examine anybody during dinner.

She waited until the orderlies had moved around the corner to the rooms on the other side of the nurses' station, then stepped to a door. There was a chart with notes on it, and she recognized Carey's scrawl. She hesitated, then decided. If the person in here was eating dinner alone, then he wasn't too sick and he wasn't asleep. She knocked and heard a muffled response. She took off her hat and opened the door just enough to stick her head in.

The man was in his thirties, and his leg had a cast on it that went from a metal stirrup at the ankle nearly to his hip. He had a fork in his right hand and a television remote control in his left. When he looked down from the television at her, he seemed pleased.

"Excuse me," said Jane.

"Sure," he said.

"I'm just checking to see if Dr. McKinnon has been in to see you yet."

The man nodded and let his eyes be drawn back up toward the television screen above the bed. "Yeah. About . . . a half hour ago."

"Thanks," said Jane. But this time she did not smile. She was looking past the man on the bed. The windows on this side of the building looked out on the parking lot. Through his, she could see Carey's empty parking space. She closed the door, slipped into the stairwell, and began to run down the stairs.

At the bottom of the stairwell, she paused, put her cap on her head, then stepped out and stared at the floor as she hurried across the lobby and out the front door. She trotted to the van, climbed in, and started it. She spent five seconds checking the mirrors before she threw the van into gear and drove off.

It took twenty minutes to get to Amherst, and while she was driving the last glow of the sunset disappeared and late afternoon turned into evening. As she made the turn onto the street where she and Carey lived, she studied the parked cars, noted the houses that had lights on and the ones that didn't, searching for anything that seemed wrong or out of place.

Jane parked a few doors away from the house and moved to the back of the van to look at it. Carey's car was not visible in the driveway, and there were no lights turned on. Then she saw Carey's BMW make the turn at the corner and come along the street. She moved back from the tinted window and watched it glide past her.

Jane forced her attention away from him. Her eyes devoured the sights of the neighborhood, scrutinizing them for the tiniest change. Had a shadow passed behind the set of blinds in the window across the street? Had a curtain moved? She pivoted to stare up the street, then down it to see if a new car had come around the corner after his. His arrival had not prompted any visible response.

The sky was black now—as dark as it would get tonight—and it was still early enough so that the normal activity in the neighborhood would keep her from standing out. It was time to move. She switched off the dome light in the van, slipped to the passenger side and out the door. She kept her body in the deep shadow of the van and studied the street again. When she was sure that there were no headlights approaching, she drifted quickly across the open pavement and up the driveway along the tall hedge that hid even her silhouette.

As she approached the rear corner of the house, she saw a square carpet of light suddenly splash onto the grass in the back yard. He had turned on the kitchen light. She would step in the back entrance, let him see her, but cover his mouth before he could say her name. She would tug him outside, out of the house before she spoke, in case that woman had planted a microphone like the ones she had found in the house in California.

Jane turned the corner of the house and looked at the big maple tree in the back yard. The glow of the red and yellow leaves above her made her stop and step back into the shadows along the house. She looked up. The light had come on in the bedroom.

Carey had come in the front door, walked through the living room, the dining room, and into the kitchen. He had not had time to climb the stairs and turn on the light in the bedroom. Jane quickly moved to the kitchen door, unlocked it, and stepped inside. The room was empty.

She hurried to the dining room, but he had already passed. She heard his footsteps above her on the upstairs landing. She ran across the living room to the stairway and climbed, taking the steps three at a time. As she reached the top, she saw him—the long legs, the familiar shape of his back, the unruly light-brown hair that stood up from his head, glowing in the light from the bedroom doorway.

Jane quickly moved along the second-floor hall as he stepped into the room. She heard him say, "What's going on?" It was too late to prepare, too late to think. She slipped into the room and stepped in front of him.

The woman's pretty face contorted into a mask of fright as she snatched the bedsheet to cover herself. Her green eyes shot to Carey's. "Who is she?"

Jane's mind fought to sort out what she saw: blond hair, size eight, the right age. But this wasn't the way she had expected to find her—in bed, with her clothes in a pile on the chair. This had to be some kind of deception, and Jane sensed instinctively that she had to make the woman believe it was succeeding. Maybe she would not think she had to kill them if she thought they were fooled. Jane could only play the role that the woman had invented for her, and pretend to be the wronged wife. Jane said, "I'm just the woman who lives here—his wife." After a pause she added, "You seem to have us mixed up."

But Carey was gulping and staring, his face longer and emptier than she had ever seen it. "Jane. I just got here myself. I didn't—"

Jane kept her eyes on the woman, but she patted Carey's arm. "Stop," she said. "I know you didn't arrange this."

"I'm glad."

"You might come home late for dinner, but you wouldn't have been late for this." She struggled to figure out what was going on. The woman had been in here with the lights off until Carey had come in the house. The woman had come into the house to do something or other, and Carey had interrupted her.

Jane's heart beat faster. If the woman had been interrupted—surprised—then pretending she had come to seduce Carey would be a good tactic. All she had to do to be convincing was take off her clothes. But she had seen Jane now, and she wasn't doing anything. Jane stared at her. It was just possible that she wasn't armed, and that she was afraid Jane might be.

Maybe she just couldn't reach the gun. Jane kept her eyes on the woman and walked to the chair by the wall where the woman had left her clothes. There were suede leather pants, a silk blouse, underwear, a black leather purse. Jane reached down and tossed the clothes onto the bed where the woman could reach them. She squeezed the purse and tested its weight, then tossed it on the bed too. She felt her muscles go slack with relief. She had been right. The woman had not brought a gun. Jane could still get Carey out alive.

Jane took Carey's arm and began to lead him out of the room. "She's going to want to get dressed."

The woman's voice startled her. It was soft and low, teasing and seductive. "Aren't you going to say anything, Carey?"

Carey and Jane both stopped and turned as the woman swung her legs out of the bed. She stood up, casually naked. Jane felt shock, a flash of rage. Just what did this woman think she was doing? The woman seemed to read her mind. She shrugged. "He's not seeing anything he hasn't seen before." She reached into the pocket of the suede pants and held up a key. "I guess I won't be needing this anymore. Did you find the one I left the other night?"

"Yes," said Carey irritably. He walked toward her, but kept the bed between them and reached across it for the key. The woman's eyes were on Jane, and the big red lips began to turn up at the corners.

The sights in the room seemed to burn themselves into Jane's brain. The familiar shapes—the chair, the picture of Carey's parents on the bureau, Carey's golf bag full of gleaming silver clubs in the open closet beside her—all were distractions now. The key. What did the woman gain by the business with the key? Forget the key. Jane lifted her eyes toward the bed.

The woman was standing beside it now. She had pulled on the suede pants, and she was buttoning the white blouse. She stopped and tilted her head in a pantomime of false sympathy. "I know how this must make you feel. But it really wasn't anything serious. I just saw a chance to have some fun, so I thought I'd borrow him. We never thought that this could happen."

Jane stared at her, mystified. Why was she trying to make it look as though they'd already had an affair? What did it buy her? She should want to get out of here. Jane's heart beat faster. Something was wrong.

Carey moved to his dresser and opened the box on top where he kept small things he didn't want to think about—single cuff links, loose screws, keys that fit nothing. As he reached into his pocket to find the key, he said coldly, "Please don't imply that something went on between you and me. It's bad enough that you're here in the first place, but you're not going to—"

Jane raised her hand and shook her head. "Please. Stop." She tried to sound annoyed, but she was feeling a growing fear. "There's no point in discussing this. Let's leave this woman alone so she can get dressed and go."

The woman glared at her. "Not 'this woman,' " she said. "Susan Haynes."

Jane's body grew tense as she stared at the woman. She couldn't know that it was the name Jane had seen on the machine for making false credit cards. But she shouldn't be saying it. She should not want Jane to hear any name.

Jane saw the woman's hand slip under the bedsheet and grasp something hidden underneath, and she drew in a breath as she recognized the shape of it. As the hand began to come up off the bed, Jane was aware of Carey, still turned away to put the key in the small wooden box on his dresser.

Jane's right hand shot out beside her and plucked a golf club out of Carey's bag. The three-iron flew up inside her grasp until the handle reached her hand. She tightened her grip and swung it downward, hard.

Jane's eyes caught everything during the instant when the shining club swung down. She saw the woman's eyes read the trajectory, fix on Jane's eyes, and convey the terrible message: Not you . . . him! The gun had already begun its move to the left toward Carey, so Jane's swing sliced through empty air and onto the wooden footboard of the bed.

The club struck on the metal shaft, and the heavy head broke off, bounced once on the bed, and fell to the floor. Jane saw the woman's thick lips curl upward as the gun continued its rise toward the back of Carey's head.

Jane screamed, "No!" as she hurled herself toward the woman. She jabbed out at her with the only object she had. She felt the long, thin metal shaft stab into the woman's body below the rib cage. The woman shrieked and shrank backward, but the pistol swung around toward Jane's face.

Jane had committed herself. She could only push the shaft of the broken golf club harder, up under the rib cage and into the heart. The woman clawed at it, tried to push it out, then fell backward.

Jane watched Carey hurtle across the bed, kneel beside the fallen woman, touch her carotid artery, put his ear on her chest. He turned to stare at Jane, and his face was a mixture of horror and incomprehension.

"She's dead," he said. "I can't . . . Why would she—"

"She was staying near you because she thought I would call and tell you where I was," said Jane. She looked away so she did not have to see the expression of shocked understanding forming on Carey's face. As she surveyed the room, she tried to sound calm. "Since the easy way wasn't working, I'll bet she planted something in here . . ." Her voice sounded as though it belonged to someone she didn't know.

Carey stood up, his big hands held toward her, the fingers open in an unconscious gesture as though he wanted to stroke her and soothe away her hurt. "Oh, my God, Jane . . . I let her in. Days ago, before I knew—or thought I knew—that she was out of her mind." He seemed to have an afterthought, and it startled him. "I didn't sleep with her, I just didn't think—"

She came to him, put her arms around him, and rested her head on his shoulder. "I know," she whispered. "I got fooled, and you got fooled." It felt wonderful to be in his arms, familiar and new at the same time and, most of all, safe. She wanted to close her eyes and stay like this, but she could not. She released him and frowned thoughtfully at the dead woman on the floor as she walked around the bed.

Carey stood stiff and still, staring at the body. "This is what it is, isn't it? It's not just helping somebody run away." He paused. "That was what you were trying to tell me that night before you would marry me. That some day I might have to watch my wife stab somebody to death in our bedroom."

She stared at him, her face expressionless, waiting.

His eyes flicked away from her toward the body on the floor, and Jane could tell he was seeing its last moments again and that what he had seen was different from what she had seen. Jane had seen the cruel eyes narrowing, and quick hands in motion and then a gun muzzle that looked cavernous, and Carey had seen the beautiful, smooth, living white skin being pierced, running with fresh, bright blood, and then turned into this cold, waxy effigy of a woman.

Jane said, "Say what you're thinking. In a few minutes it will be too late."

Carey held up his hands, his eyes full of pain, but he was not able to find the words he wanted. He seemed to know he had to try. "I love you." So he had discovered it too, she thought. That was what you said when you couldn't say anything else. He tried again. "You're the best person I ever met . . . and this was the worst thing I've ever seen anyone do. And you did it for me, and that makes me feel awful, and grateful, and sick. And if we somehow get through this, I'll do everything I can to make sure you never do anything like it again. No more fugitives."

She turned her face for a second. Then she picked up the telephone, unscrewed the earpiece, removed a small electronic transmitter, set it on the floor, and stepped on it. "So much for that mystery. We'll probably be finding these for months." Then she sat on the edge of the bed and screwed the earpiece back on.

Carey came closer. "Maybe I should be the one to talk to them," he said. "I'm the one who knew her." He held his hand out for the telephone.

Jane set the receiver back on its cradle, then looked at Carey sadly. "I'm not calling the police."

"Why not? It was self-defense."

She took a deep breath and let it out. "This is a time when we don't have the right kinds of answers for the questions they would ask. This woman was a professional killer. If the gun has ever been registered, it wasn't to her. And if we get our names and pictures in the newspaper, there will be other people coming—ones who knew her, maybe others who have been looking for me."

"Then who are you calling?"

"Nobody." She watched his eyes. They looked as though they were gazing into the emptiness for the first time: there was nobody to call, no agency or institution that could do anything now but hurt them, no friend they could burden with this knowledge, because the risk it carried was too great. Jane said, "Here's what you do. Go right back to the hospital. Check on your patients again, haunt the nurses' stations, read charts, write notes. Act as though you had never left. Don't come back until after ten."

He shook his head in amazement. "You think I can leave you here alone?"

Jane stood and walked toward him. "Neither of us wanted this, but here we are. We're in trouble. I know the way out, and you don't." She pushed him toward the doorway, hard. "So go. We have to use every second."

He stopped, took a last look at her, then turned and walked down the hallway toward the stairs.

At ten thirty, Carey McKinnon unlocked his front door and stepped into his house. He called, "Jane?" but there was no answer. He discovered that he did not want to raise his voice and try again. It took an extreme act of will to ascend the stairs and enter the bedroom. For a moment it seemed as though he had lost his senses. There was no corpse, no blood. The bed had been made with crisp new sheets and blankets. The floor had been scrubbed. It was as though nothing had happened.

Gradually, he began to sense that he was not alone. He whirled and saw Jane standing in the doorway. She was wearing a blue dress with a flower print that he had always liked, but which she hardly ever wore. At her feet was a small leather overnight bag. She said, "Come on. We're not sleeping in that room tonight. You're going to take me to a hotel."

He waited. "That's all you're going to say about it?"

She shrugged, picked up the overnight bag, and handed it to him. "I'll just say it's the last thing you'll hear from me tonight that includes an order, or the word 'no.' " She turned and walked down the hallway of the old house toward the stairs.

"What about tomorrow?"

He could hear the smile returning to her voice as she said over her shoulder, "Ask me tomorrow."

The radiance of the sun just rising behind the horizon outside the east windows made entering the big conference room at dawn feel like walking into a dream. The light was beautiful, golden. In a few minutes it would shine through the broad, moist leaves of the jungle plants outside the glass with such intensity that the droplets left over from the three-thirty watering would evaporate in minutes. But the sky to the west was still that deep purple-blue of the desert night that made the colors of the Las Vegas lights glow brighter, like millions of flares burning at once.

Max Foley looked around the room and verified with mild satisfaction that he was the first to arrive. He supposed it wasn't surprising. The complexity of Buckley's mind seemed to Foley to have been built up like a muscle by a lifetime of worrying about eighty things at once. He had probably spent much of the night getting up over and over to see if any news had come in. Salateri had probably spent most of his night screaming into his telephone to find out why it hadn't. All three partners had been living in their suites upstairs for two months, and it was starting to feel like a siege.

Foley walked to the private bathroom at the far end of the room and knocked, then opened the door with his key. He glanced at the key, as he often did, before he put it back in his pocket. There were only three copies of that key. He had seen them listed once on the roster for the hotel complex: Universal Grand Masters. They were the keys to the kingdom. They would open any lock that any other key in the hotel would open, and a few more besides. "We three kings of Orient-Tar," as his kids used to say. That was—what? Two marriages back, before he had become rich enough to make giving away half his visible assets too steep a price for getting laid now and then. Foley stared in the mirror at his shave, combed his hair, and went back out into the conference room, then looked at his watch. It was after five o'clock, and he was getting impatient.

Foley walked to the end of the vast conference table and sat down in his chair. He glanced at the three identical piles of newspapers that had been left here for the partners and picked up the paper on the top of this morning's pile. It was the *Idaho Statesman*. He thumbed down the pile, reading the mastheads: *Salt Lake Tribune, Denver Post,* Spokane *Spokesman-Review*. It looked as though the staff had just bought every paper within a thousand miles of Kalispell. He returned to the top and spotted the words in the lead article that had been circled.

"Montana State Police confirmed that Calvin Seaver, the Nevada man held for questioning in the shooting, has been ruled out as a suspect and released."

The muscles in Foley's shoulders and elbows locked. He let the newspaper drop from his hands as he tried to reconcile what he had read with what he knew. Foley and his partners had sent Seaver out to find Hatcher and kill him. A man had been shot. Seaver had been caught a few miles away with the murder weapon in his motel room, powder residue on him, and false identity papers. Foley had always acknowledged that there was some remote possibility that Seaver might not be convicted of the murder—there could be warrant problems or something—but the notion that he would be released had never entered Foley's mind.

Foley's eyes fell on the pile of newspapers in front of Buckley's seat. He leaned forward and lowered his head to be certain. Yes, if he looked at it from the side, he could see an indentation in the shape of a circle. Buckley had set his coffee cup on the newspaper. Buckley had been here and gone.

Foley studied Salateri's pile of newspapers, but they seemed to be untouched. He swung his chair around, picked up the telephone, dialed Salateri's suite, and let the phone ring fifteen times.

He walked out of the room to the partners' private elevator and used his Universal Grand Master key to activate it, then rode it back up to the thirtieth floor. He rapped on Salateri's door, then kept knocking until his knuckles were sore and the knocks grew fainter. He took out his key and unlocked the door.

Foley pushed the door open, stepped into the big living room, and surveyed the rest of the suite through doors left ajar. Drawers had been yanked out of the built-in dressers to be dumped into suitcases, then thrown on the floor. Salateri had not even bothered to close the floor safe and push the antique Persian rug over it after it was empty.

Foley went out, locked the door, and walked along the hallway and up the fire stairs to Buckley's suite. He unlocked Buckley's door and took in a sharp breath. The place looked untouched. Maybe Buckley was asleep in one of the bedrooms. Foley stepped in, closed the door behind him, and took two steps toward the master bedroom before he noticed the painting over the sideboard. The Matisse on the wall had been replaced by a reproduction of a Watteau. Foley spun around to look at the lighted glass display case on the wall behind him. The spot that Buckley had designed as a shrine for his Fabergé egg was now occupied by a small black-and-orange urn that had curly-headed Greek wrestlers squaring off along the sides. To Foley it looked about as real as the ones in museums, but he knew better. It was a cheap fake, and Buckley was gone.

Foley stepped from room to room in the suite and savored Buckley's premeditation. He had left nothing here that was likely to be of value, but a casual observer would not have noticed that anything was gone. Buckley must have spent several nights packing up treasures, slipping them out of the hotel, and replacing them with junk. No, Foley decided. This was all too elaborate. Buckley had probably been preparing for something like this for years, the way people in flood zones kept a bag packed.

Foley closed this door behind him too and locked it, then walked down two flights to his own suite. As he packed his suitcases he tried to estimate the dimensions of his problem.

Seaver had been hired because he was a cold-blooded, competent watchdog. Now he was a watchdog with rabies. He was already locked inside the house with the family, and he was certain to be getting the urge to bite somebody. He must have used his cop experience and credentials and connections to cut himself a spectacular deal. But a spectacular deal was something like a short sentence, or even a reduced charge, not a free ticket on a murder. What did Seaver have to offer that the cops wanted more than they wanted the man who had shot some hapless schmuck through a restaurant window? There was only one possibility. He must have given them a sniff of the project in upstate New York.

Foley tested the opposite point of view. Suppose Seaver had not turned informant? If Seaver had an alibi, the cops would have had to let him go. God knew, if anybody could set up a solid alibi and go kill somebody, it was Seaver. But the thought only gave Foley a sick feeling. Hiring a couple of killers to go after a nice, gentle kid like Pete Hatcher was one thing. Sending a team of thugs to stab a man like Calvin Seaver in jail and having them arrive after he was loose was another. Seaver was an old pro, and the ones looking for him were a pick-up team of second-stringers hastily assembled and sent into the game without a plan. Even if he didn't know yet that his bosses had sent killers to silence him, by now he knew that they had cut him loose when he got arrested. He had been made into an enemy.

If Seaver now had an impulse to come here and get past the security to pay his respects to his bosses, it was hard to imagine a way to stop him. He had designed the whole system personally, supervised the installation of the hardware, hired the men and told them where to stand. Making Seaver into an enemy had been the wrong decision.

Foley stopped himself. He had to fight this new, neurotic tendency to construct ways to blame himself for everything. This problem was not Foley's fault. It wasn't. He and Buckley and Salateri had been absolutely right to assume that Pete Hatcher was a threat. After waiting three months for the threat to be removed, they had been right to send Seaver out to handle it. That was his job, and they paid him more than enough to be entitled to assume he would do it. When Seaver bungled it and got arrested, they had been right in acting immediately to disassociate themselves from him and act to cut their losses. The only way Seaver could have gotten out of that mess was to talk.

Now Foley had to assume that Seaver was sitting in some secret, safe location—didn't they usually put people like him on some military base?—giving investigators from Washington everything. In a day or less, there would be the F.B.I., the Justice Department, and the police agencies of several states. They would make travel impossible and staying here unthinkable.

A couple of days after that, there would be raids at the offices of politicians in Albany, New York. A few powerful old men in New York City would start to notice that there were a lot more parked delivery vans, and city crews digging up the streets near their favorite haunts. Those old bastards wouldn't wait around for some grand jury to vote an indictment. They would do exactly as Foley would do in their position: act to cut their losses.

Foley packed very efficiently and methodically. He had never seen the attraction of sinking enormous amounts of money in paintings and bric-a-brac like Buckley, and he didn't have fifty pounds of gold jewelry hidden under a Persian rug like Salateri, so he didn't have to think very hard. He nearly filled his two suitcases with cash, threw on top an accordion envelope that contained a few passbooks for offshore banks, last month's stock and bond statements, and his passport. He slipped a few personal papers in with them, put on his favorite sportcoat, stuck his prescription sunglasses into the pocket, and walked out the door.

As he stood in the private elevator and felt it descend thirty floors, he marveled at how simple and inevitable it suddenly had become to walk away from a two-billion-dollar company. There really was no decision to make. If Seaver had not talked, he would probably be on his way here to kill whoever was left. If he had talked, the police were on the way, and so were people a hell of a lot scarier than police. And if Seaver hadn't talked, and wasn't mad, then Pete Hatcher had probably heard of Seaver being caught running around the country with a gun, and that would convince Hatcher that *he* had to talk. And as of this morning, even if none of this happened, Foley would have the problem of explaining to the world the disappearance of his two partners. Foley's position had become untenable. This was like walking away from a burning building.

The elevator opened and he dragged his two suitcases out on the garage level. Then he thought about selecting the right car to take to the airport. His Saab was probably the best one for this, because it didn't look like something a man like Foley would drive.

He took the keys off the board and carried his suitcases over to the dark-green, stubby Saab. It was the name of the car that suggested his first destination. He would go to Sabi Sand Game Reserve in South Africa. He would stay at the Singita Lodge and begin making calls to find his next stop while he was there. For the moment he had a strong interest in places where he could see people coming from a long way off.

Foley opened the trunk. As he lifted the first suitcase in, he had a sudden, uncontrollable urge to look over his shoulder. It was like a chill at the back of his neck. He whirled quickly. There was nobody in the dark behind him, no visible shape at all on this level except his four other cars. But there could have been. It could have been the first F.B.I. agent, or Calvin Seaver waiting to get even, or some nightmare guy that the Mafia had sent to get rid of a bad memory. It could even be nothing more than a thief, somebody who knew that Foley had a lot of money. In a day or so, when the word got around that the three partners had bailed out, there would be a lot of people like that. He would have to watch for them, too.

It occurred to him that he was never going to be able to stop looking over his shoulder, even if he lived for a year or more. As he started the car, a familiar thought entered his mind, but it was for a new reason. He wished he knew a way to find that woman who made people disappear.

About the Author

THOMAS PERRY was born in Tonawanda, N.Y., in 1947. He received a B.A. from Cornell University in 1969 and a Ph.D. in English literature from the University of Rochester in 1974. He has been a laborer, maintenance man, commercial fisherman, weapons mechanic, university administrator and teacher, and television writer and producer. His other novels include *The Butcher's Boy* (awarded an Edgar from the Mystery Writers of America), *Metzger's Dog, Big Fish, Island, Sleeping Dogs, Vanishing Act,* and *Dance for the Dead.* He lives in southern California with his wife and two daughters.

About the Type

This book was set in Sabon, a typeface designed by the well-known German typographer Jan Tschichold (1902–74). Sabon's design is based upon the original letter forms of Claude Garamond and was created specifically to be used for three sources: foundry type for hand composition, Linotype, and Monotype. Tschichold named his typeface for the famous Frankfurt typefounder Jacques Sabon, who died in 1580.